MW00618689

*OF NEW ORLEANS TO
THE MOST ELEGANT
HOUSEHOLD OF THEM ALL...*

KATIE RASPANTI—Driven from home by an unspeakable act of betrayal, she entered a world of wealth and privilege dominated by the Eagans. But her beauty, courage, and inner fire made her a threat to the dynasty she was hired to serve . . .

STEPHEN EAGAN—The oldest son in the house that brilliance built and defiance destroyed; the man who dared to reject all his family held holy to win the woman he loved . . .

WARREN EAGAN—The golden boy. So handsome, so spoiled. The world was his oyster, but his one desire was for the pearl beyond his grasp.

**THEY WERE DRIVEN BY DREAMS
AND A PASSION TO MAKE THEIR
DREAMS COME TRUE!**

NIGHT JASMINE

Mary Lou Widmer

A DELL BOOK

Published by
Dell Publishing Co., Inc.
1 Dag Hammarskjold Plaza
New York, New York 10017

Copyright © 1980 by Mary Lou Widmer

All rights reserved. No part of this book may be
reproduced or transmitted in any form or by any
means, electronic or mechanical, including photocopying,
recording or by any information storage and retrieval
system, without the written permission of the
Publisher, except where permitted by law.

Dell ® TM 681510, Dell Publishing Co., Inc.

ISBN: 0-440-16558-X

Printed in the United States of America

First printing—November 1980

for my father,
whose incomparable memory and fond recollections
helped me to capture the ambience of 1906

and for the first Katie,
my mother-in-law, on whose life this story is
partly based

NIGHT
JASMINE

Chapter
ONE

Katie turned back the covers and got out of bed. It was not yet dawn. Shivering, she tucked the thin cotton blankets around her two little sisters who shared her bed. They were nested together in the valley of the mattress, their long black hair fanned out across the pillows.

Standing barefoot on the linoleum, Katie reached for her shawl on the bedpost and wrapped it around her shoulders. Teeth chattering, she groped for her shoes beneath her bed and then fished inside them for her woolen stockings. She pulled them on, rolling the garters just above the knee. They felt warm and comfortable. She crisscrossed her shoestrings, looping them around the hooks that ran from toe to ankle.

Throughout this familiar routine she was aware of her mother moving about in the next room, changing from nightclothes to day dress, putting on shoes and stockings and the long apron that covered her generous bosom as well as her skirt. Now she was wielding a hairbrush, grooming the long black mane into a bun at the nape of her neck.

It was Frances Raspanti's movements, quiet though they were, that had awakened Katie. They were her signal that her own day had begun, for Katie was the eldest, and it was she who must help her mother light the heaters, get water from the cistern, and bring in wood for the stove before daylight found the family up and ready for breakfast.

Hurriedly Katie took her brown cotton dress and apron from the nail on the wall and fumbled in her highboy for warm bloomers. Once dressed, she combed her hair and braided it into two ropes that fell over her shoulders.

Squatting on the floor before the kerosene heater, Katie carefully unhooked the metal top and turned it back on its hinges, turned the wheel to raise the wick, and lit the kitchen match from the box on top of the highboy.

Katie trembled inwardly as she remembered the morning she had nearly caused a fire. The cylinder had tilted on its flimsy three-legged base, spilling kerosene across the floor of the room where her brothers and sisters were sleeping. That day a match was already aflame in her hand. Thank God she had not panicked and dropped it on the floor. The whole room would have gone up in flames, and the kitchen, too. Maybe the whole three-story building. She thought of the Macalusos on the second floor and the Campos on the third, and she shuddered.

As ever she recalled her father's rage, his booming voice filling the two-room apartment. He had come charging into the room, his fist raised to strike her, till her mother's voice stopped his hand in midair.

"Joseph!" she had called out. Katie could still hear the ring of authority in that voice. The big man had stopped and walked back slowly to the kitchen sink where he had been shaving. "Don't you ever hit Katie!" Frances commanded. "*Prepotente!*" she spat out the invective. "She's your own child. Not some working woman off the street. It was an accident."

"An accident that coulda killed us all!" Joseph grumbled into his shaving mug.

"She cooks. She cleans. She scrubs the clothes. She takes the little ones to school and never complains she not go there herself."

Listening in the bedroom, Katie had buried her face

in her apron, trying to hold back the tears. Whenever they spoke of school, her throat constricted. It was something she yearned for with all her heart and would never have. Her mother needed her at home, and that was the long and the short of it.

She remembered hearing the sound of her father's shaving brush clinking against the inside of his mug, fighting to make lather from hard, dry soap and cold water.

"What she need with school?" he asked. "She grow up, she marry, she have babies."

"She's a good girl. She never complain."

"What she got to complain?"

"Go tell her you sorry you raised the fist."

Katie listened, but she heard nothing. She could picture her mother tilting her head in the direction of the bedroom, pleading with her large, dark eyes. By this time her brothers and sisters were awake, but when her father appeared in the doorway, they feigned sleep and turned their backs to him. A huge man, he stood before her for a long time, trying to make himself say the words. Katie did not look at him but riveted her eyes to the floor. She was in an anguish of distress, for him, for herself.

At last her father said awkwardly: "You good girl, Katie." It was as close as he could come to an apology. Then he left the room.

Shaking off the memory, Katie lit the wick and closed the lid of the heater. Wordlessly she passed through the kitchen, pecked her mother on the cheek, and picked up a bucket beside the back door. Then, wrapping her shawl around her shoulders, she slipped out of the kitchen and crossed the flagstone yard to the cistern. Later she made oatmeal while her mother poured boiling water through the coffee in the agate pot.

Little Joe and Davey came tumbling into the kitchen,

in knickers and stockings and lŏng-sleeved shirts, pulling suspenders up over their shoulders. Jenny and Lala followed, turning their backs to Katie to have their dresses buttoned and their sashes tied. The children took turns at the sink, washing their faces and brushing their teeth. Their father allowed no talking at meals, so breakfast was a hurried affair, followed by much shuffling back and forth to the bedroom for shawls and coats, caps and school books.

At last, lunch cans in hand, the four younger Raspantis departed for school, with Katie in the lead. At the school gate she kissed the little girls good-bye, taking a moment to pull up their stockings, and watched the flock disappear behind the mysterious wooden doors. She strolled along the iron fence of the play yard, letting her fingers trail lazily along the bars. Sighing a deep and audible sigh, she headed home.

"Kids get to school okay?" Frances asked from the kitchen sink.

"Okay."

It was a daily question, and a daily answer.

Katie hung up her shawl, pushed up her sleeves, and went to the bedroom to straighten up. Suddenly a deep, melodious voice sounded from the street.

"Ah got ba-na-na, lay-dee."

"Katie," Frances called out, drying her hands on her apron. "The vegetable man. Get the basket."

The call had announced the arrival of a grizzled old Negro and his wagonload of fruits and vegetables. To accommodate the ladies who lived in the "service wings," the vendors passed behind their houses in the service alley that cut across the middle of the block.

The "service wings" were book-shaped, three-story buildings, with roofs slanted like carpenters' chisels and balconies on the second and third floors. They stood like volumes on a shelf, each separated from the next by a courtyard. Every service wing and its courtyard was situated behind the row house on Julia Street to which it had once belonged. In the 1830s, when Julia Row had been built, the service wings had been constructed to house the slave quarters, the kitchens, and the privies of the main houses on Julia Street.

Julia Row, in its heyday, had been the pride of the American colony in New Orleans, with its fanlight transoms and ornate cornices. Now, at the turn of the century, it was in a state of deterioration, its facades defaced with ugly fire escapes, street-level shops, and boardinghouses that offered beds "by day, by week, by month." When Julia Row had gone commercial, the service wings to the rear had been bought up by speculators and converted into the meanest kinds of hovels, in each of which three families could be housed.

A few of the houses facing Julia Street still retained fragments of their original finery: mahogany balusters, carved newel posts, and intricately designed moldings; but these were of little interest to the whiskered old men who knew the buildings only as flophouses, where they could rent a cot for two bits a night. They spent their days sitting on the front steps, playing checkers, weaving crab nets, and spitting tobacco juice on the sidewalks.

Frances had given her children strict orders never to walk on Julia Street, but to come and go by way of the service alley.

Now Katie and Frances were approaching the vegetable wagon just as Mrs. Macaluso and Mrs. Campo came down the steps.

"*Buon giorno*, Mrs. Campo," said Frances. "How's you husband's arm?"

"Pretty good," the woman answered. Mrs. Campo was a tall, heavy woman with a trace of a mustache. "He go to work today."

Frances reached the wagon and leaned over the back of it to feel the bell peppers. "I think you peppers kinda soft today," she said to the vendor.

The old Negro straightened his battered top hat and

reached a gnarled hand to touch the peppers. "Dey feels nice an' firm to me." he said.

"I don't think I buy them," Frances said, shaking her head. "You got no fresh corn?"

"Sho' do," said the Negro, hopping down from his seat. He walked around the back of the wagon and pushed aside some potatoes, revealing huge green ears of corn with their brown silk tassels. He pulled back a strip of husk for Frances's inspection.

"How much?" she asked, her eyebrows pinched.

"Ten cents a dozen," the black man answered, tilting his head deprecatingly.

"Okay," Frances said, turning the knobs of her change purse. She paid the vendor, and one by one each ear was stripped and scrutinized before it was dropped into the basket Katie was holding.

Back in the house Katie and Frances finished the dishes and the bed making and sat at the kitchen table to shuck the corn. With a secret smile Frances walked over to the pantry and returned with a small bag of lemon drops which she offered to Katie. Katie popped one in her mouth, closed her eyes, and sat back to savor the tart candy. Her mother did the same. It was their midmorning treat, something Frances reserved for just the two of them, their reward for having been up before dawn to make the house warm and to fix breakfast for the others.

Frances had a sweet tooth, and her children shared her weakness. Katie watched her mother enjoying her candy, her eyes shining happily.

Frances Raspanti was a striking woman with creamy skin and dark eyes and hair. She was short and plump, with small dainty hands and a slender throat above her high-necked blouses. She was a dynamo of energy, and despite a life of drudgery, she never lost the gift of laughter, the constant renewal of love for her children and her gruff, fearsome husband, and the ability to find pleasure in little things. She had an effervescence that seemed to spring from an inner source, and it colored everything about her. No house she kept could be poor or bare. She strode through the apartment as if it were a palace, her head high, her cheeks flushed in anticipation of her next task.

Katie looked around the huge, high-ceilinged kitchen with its one long window and a transom over the door leading to the yard. She and her mother were sitting at the round oak table where the family ate, did homework, played cards, prepared food, and chatted with neighbors. It was the focal point of all their lives. Surrounding it were rough wooden chairs. In one corner of the room was a wooden sink with a dishdrainer, her father's shaving mug, and a small round mirror at eye level. Beside it an old icebox dripped incessantly into a pan. Flour-sack curtains, like those in the window, concealed a floor-to-ceiling pantry, a catchall in the closetless apartment. Most of the heat in the apartment was provided by a wood stove set against the kitchen wall that adjoined the bedroom. Ropes of garlic hung in braids beside the door to the yard.

At night the kitchen became a bedroom. Joe and Frances slept on a mattress on the kitchen floor, which allowed them some measure of privacy. Early each morning Joe stood the mattress on end behind the kitchen door, securing it there by means of a latch that hooked the door to the wall.

Frances finished cleaning the corn and put it in a pot to soak. She walked over to her husband's shaving mirror to smooth her hair. Katie brightened and grabbed her shawl and basket. They were going to market.

"Good thing we get out of here before Mrs. Macaluso come down," Frances said, giggling like a schoolgirl. "She wastes my time with her Sears Roebuck catalog, tellin' me she's gonna buy this, I'm gonna buy that. If I buy everything she says, I never have a copper cent."

Katie and Frances laughed together. Mrs. Macaluso

seemed to have a lot of time to kill, Katie thought, and she loved to spend it with Frances. Of course she was not the housekeeper Frances Raspanti was. Her sink was always piled with dishes, her linoleum was streaked, and her boys were not only dirty, but badly raised. They used to pinch Katie on the behind whenever they passed by her. Once Katie had swung around and punched Salvatore in the nose. Since then she had had no trouble with the Macaluso boys.

Whenever Mrs. Macaluso visited, she made eye signals to Frances that she could not talk in front of Katie, and Katie discreetly disappeared. She never came without her catalog, and Katie surmised that the things Mrs. Macaluso wanted to show her mother were remedies for "women's complaints" or underwear or other mysterious curatives or cosmetics. Mrs. Macaluso should have realized, Katie thought, that she was growing up. She had started her periods a year ago, and her mother had explained all about it. Frances had promised to tell her more about life, later on, when she could understand it better. Katie was fifteen years old, but she was small and quiet and unobtrusive, and although her body was developing rapidly, the ladies on the block thought her no more mature than their own much younger children.

Katie and Frances walked along St. Charles Avenue to Poydras Street. The streetcar clanged as it passed them by. "The "cala woman," fat and black, her head wrapped in a tignon, waddled by them with a basket as big as a washtub on her head. Her cries of "Bels calas, tout chauds," floated down the street on a musical note. Frances had bought Katie rice fritters once, and her mouth watered at the memory. Frances checked her purse and shook her head. No *calas* today. There was barely enough money for meat.

"Bla-a-ack berries, berries very fine," another vendor sang out in a strange falsetto harmony with the cala woman. Mules pulling wagons clop-clopped by, and sleek horses hitched to fine carriages.

The smell of roasting coffee saturated the neighborhood. Six blocks away, near the riverfront where coffee was unloaded, several processing plants had been established.

The morning was brisk and the five-block walk exhilarating. The Poydras Market was an arcaded structure, two blocks long, set right in the middle of Poydras Street, with enough room left over on each side for wagon traffic. Two buildings, one for meat, the other for produce, were supported by pillars, through which damp breezes and flies passed unchallenged.

The market was a scene of feverish activity. Choctaw Indians from Bayou Lacombe sat cross-legged on the ground outside the buildings, selling roots and herbs and filé, the powder Creoles used to make their gumbo. They sold baskets and leather goods which they made by hand while waiting for customers.

Fruit and vegetable stalls lined the inside of one arcade, relegating customer traffic to a narrow center aisle. Humidity hastened the ripening process, and produce gave off a cloying aroma. The other building housed a series of butcher blocks, where aproned surgeons in derby hats and starched collars took orders for meat throughout the day. Bone saws, meat cleavers, and sides of beef hung from the rafters, and flies were everywhere.

Frances stopped at her regular butcher's stand, inspected the meat, and ordered veal rounds.

"Thank you very much, Mr. LeGrand, an' I be seein' you soon again, okay?" she said.

The man touched his derby and attempted to smile.

Passing back between the two buildings, Katie saw the colored women and the few poor whites who had come to the market to get "day's work." Early in the morning there were always many more, but as it was almost eleven o'clock, those who were still there had little chance of getting hired. Yet they hawked their services as loudly as the vendors did their wares.

Out on the sidewalk a crowd had gathered around four or five small Negro boys dancing a kind of slap-foot dance, hoping for a shower of pennies. They were called "spasm bands" because of their loose-jointed gyrations.

The old black mammy was sitting at her regular place, at the entrance to the market, selling her coconut pralines in their sweet-sugar colors of pink and white and brown. They were a penny apiece. Now that her shopping was done and there were still pennies in her purse, Frances bought two.

The rest of the day sped by. By the time Katie went to pick up the children after school, veal stew was bubbling on the kitchen stove and the linoleum smelled of pungent Octagon soap. Later, for a quiet hour, Katie and Frances sat in an old garden swing and worked on a quilt that they had been stitching for as long as Katie could remember. It was Frances's hobby, that and the herb garden she had raised in a corner of the yard.

At dusk Big Joe came home, and the dinner hour passed in silence. Then he lit the gas fixture in the kitchen with a long waxed taper, and the children gathered around, books in hand, to do their homework.

"I think I take a walk and stretch my legs," Joseph told Frances. He reached for his derby hanging near the door.

"Okay," she said, not looking up from the kitchen sink.

Katie noticed her mother's tight expression. Where did he go every night? Katie wondered. Mr. Macaluso and Mr. Campo sat on the balcony smoking their pipes and talking. But not her father.

Frances put an end to the homework at eight o'clock. She lined up her children for their nightly scrubbing, after which they brushed their teeth at the kitchen sink and filed out to the privy with a kerosene lamp. The day was ending.

Back in the house bedsprings squeaked. The heater was turned off. Giggles and arguments rose and subsided.

Some nights Katie heard her father come home. She heard the mattress being dragged from behind the kitchen door, and then the flap of sheets and blankets. But not tonight. Tonight she didn't hear him come home at all, and it was not the first time. It wrung her heart that her mother could not even go to bed until he was there to take down the heavy mattress.

By the light of the kitchen lamp she could see her mother, now in her nightgown, braiding her long hair over her shoulder. She heard the gentle trickle of water at the kitchen sink as her mother washed her face. Katie fell asleep then, thinking it no more than an ordinary day, not knowing that in the morning she was to see a side of her father that was to change her feeling for him for the rest of her life.

Chapter TWO

Katie was on her way back from bringing the children to school when she saw Theresa Campo running into the front door of one of the row houses. Katie stopped short and frowned quizzically. It was against their parents' orders, and she wondered what was happening.

Theresa lived on the third floor in the same service wing as Katie. The house she had entered was the main house to which their service wing had once belonged. It was vacant now, but no one who lived in the service wing ever used it as a throughway. Katie waited to see if the girl would come back out, but she did not.

Slowly, warily, Katie started to walk along the sidewalk on Julia Street. She had to find out what Theresa was doing. Maybe she was exploring the old mansion, as Katie herself had often longed to do, or perhaps she was simply taking a shortcut into the backyard of the service wing.

Katie thought Theresa was the most beautiful girl she had ever seen, with her heavy black hair and her green eyes. She had a captivating dimple beside her mouth, and perfect small white teeth. Her breasts were full and high, and Katie only hoped that when she was fully grown she'd have a figure like Theresa's.

She and Theresa used to take walks together down to the riverfront, and the older girl talked about the young men who came to call. Theresa was almost eighteen, quite old enough to be thinking of marriage; yet there was much of the child in her, and Katie often thought

that in some ways *she* was wiser and more resourceful
than Theresa. She certainly knew more about cooking
and housekeeping. But when it came to casting provoc-
ative sidelong glances and tossing her head back gaily
in laughter, Theresa was in a class by herself.

Katie reached the front door of the old house and
stopped suddenly. She had never been this close to a
row house before. She drank in the faded elegance of
the fanlight transom and the wood pilasters that flanked
the door. Forgetting Theresa, she passed her hand
against the sidelights, designed like vertical necklaces of
oval glass, each trimmed with a string of wooden beads,
many of which had fallen off. She admired the fine
grain and the swirling hues of the wooden door, still
beautiful after three quarters of a century.

Cautiously Katie pushed the door. It opened silently,
revealing a mahogany balustrade some ten feet inside.
At the top of the steps was a landing, beyond which the
steps curved and continued up to the second floor.

Now, forgetting why she had come in, she took a few
steps into the living room to the left of the entrance
hall. There was a fireplace, topped with a framed mirror, flanked by corner shelves. The windows ran down
to the floor, and there were relics of inside shutters,
some broken now, some missing. The oak floor, black-
ened over the years, was once golden, as one could
see by untrod areas near the walls.

A noise startled her, and she turned on her heel and
retraced her steps to the foot of the staircase. In the
entrance hall she was about to call Theresa's name
when she heard a voice, a muffled laugh. Intuitively she
silenced herself. The giggle sounded again, coming from
the closet under the staircase. Now she heard a man's
voice, and the sound of shuffling movement, then silence.

"No. Not here." Theresa was whispering.

Katie's eyes opened wide and her skin tightened.

"Yes. Here. And now!" She knew it was her father

who had said the words. Unmistakably. What was it he wanted of Theresa? And why had the girl been laughing?

Katie heard nothing now but soft purring sounds and contented moans. The floor creaked.

Silently she climbed the stairs and followed the curve of the balustrade, lowering herself to sit on the steps in the shadows and lean against the wall until her heart stopped pounding in her chest. Minutes passed, minutes that seemed like hours. At last the door to the stairway closet opened, and Katie heard muffled endearments and kisses. The hair bristled on her head, and she felt a terrible constriction in her throat.

Soon heavy footsteps sounded in the hall below her. Not wanting to know, but having to know, Katie leaned over and peeped through the bars. Just inside the front door her father was buttoning his trousers, then tucking in his shirt and running his fingers through his hair to tidy himself before he let himself out of the door.

Katie could easily have thrown up. Only by the fiercest act of will did she control her feelings. She waited. In seconds Theresa passed below her, and Katie could see the deep cleavage between the white breasts before Theresa pulled the ribbons of her camisole and tied a bow to cover herself. Then she buttoned her blouse and tucked it into her skirt. Her cheeks were flushed and she was humming a tune as she glided into the living room.

Katie could picture her fixing her hair before the mantel mirror as she sang little snatches of song. After an eternity she walked back through the hall and into the courtyard.

For the longest time Katie remained on the stairs, her head resting against the balustrade. She felt revolted, heartbroken, confused. She was not sure exactly what had happened in the closet below her, but she knew that it was immoral and depraved, and it sickened her. She was shocked that her father was having a flirtation, something vaguely to do with love, with someone other than her mother.

The experience had brought back to mind many bits and pieces of information she had gleaned in the past year or two, all related, no doubt, to what had happened here, and to the talk "about life" that she and Frances were to have later on, "when she could understand it better." Now Katie realized that she was beginning to understand it all too well.

Once, when she had taken the children to school, a big boy had winked at her and made obscene gestures with his pelvis, mocking what she knew must be a wicked thing to do. Then, too, she had often seen a word, which she knew must be a bad word, written on walls and fences. Sometimes there were pictures drawn above the word, pictures Katie had chosen not to believe. She remembered now hearing her mother and father, late at night, laughing softly, kissing and moaning contentedly, just as he and Theresa had done today. Her parents had been doing the same thing together. She found it hard to believe this of her mother, and yet Katie knew that it was true. Frances, too, had been guilty. Perhaps she had *had* to do it, Katie considered. Yet the sounds from the kitchen were happy sounds. Katie didn't understand it at all.

What stunned Katie more than her comprehension of the act itself was the sudden realization that both men and women took pleasure in it. Her perception was clearer in that moment than it had ever been before. Little explosions of cognizance were breaking and raining down inside her head like fireworks on the Fourth of July. This whole man-woman thing she had discovered was a force that directed all their lives. It was the reason why men took girls out riding in the country, like the red-faced young man who came to get Janie Macaluso in his rig on Sunday afternoons. It was the thing married women talked about in secret. It was the reason women flirted and painted their faces.

More than that, it was the way babies were made. In that hour, in that dusky stairwell, everything fell together. Of course her mother had done it. There were five children to prove it. How *could* she have? With *him*? She wondered if Theresa would have a baby now that she had given herself to Joe Raspanti. And what would the baby be? Her sister? What would Theresa tell her parents when her belly started to swell? Perhaps one didn't always have a baby. Only time would tell.

In spite of the crushing disappointment that made her ill and weak, the thought did not occur to Katie that Theresa might not be the first her father had taken on a closet floor, or in other hidden places. In her innocence and her total trust she had never noticed the admiring glances he gave Janie Macaluso or Theresa, herself, when they came down the stairs of the service wings, their full busts and small waistlines rigidly corseted beneath white cotton blouses and long, flounced skirts. His eyes would crinkle, his well-clipped mustache would spread, and his lips would part over fine white teeth as he looked them over. Because he was her father, it had never occurred to her that he was a striking-looking man, tall, well built, and sensual.

Neighbors could have told her of his meetings with girls on the waterfront and his wandering hands making intimate caresses. Men could have told her of his visits to the "sporting houses" on Basin Street when he had a few coins to rub together. But until today Katie would not have understood. Until today she would not have believed.

Katie stood up at last on shaky legs. She tightened the garter rolls above her knees and smoothed her skirt. Then, slowly, she descended the stairs and left by the back courtyard to join her mother for morning chores.

Chapter
THREE

Out of the corner of her eye, Frances watched Katie chopping onions for the gravy. The girl's expression was somber and unchanging. She did not talk or laugh or bounce about the kitchen as she usually did. For five days now the child had gone through her chores in stony silence. Clearly something was wrong. Frances had tried to draw her out, but she was not yet ready to speak. Frances stewed about it. She asked Joe what he thought, but he shrugged indifferently.

It was not unusual for Katie to be quiet when her father was home. Big Joe held all his children in mortal fear, especially Katie, who was easily offended by his outbursts. But Frances could not understand Katie's lack of response to *her* questions and *her* pleasantries.

Katie scraped the onions from the chopping board into the frying pan, and the hot oil sizzled. Later, when the gravy was made, she and Frances walked out to the old yard swing. The school clothes had been washed and hung out to dry. The boys had gone into the service alley for a ball game, and the little girls were chanting a jump-rope melody. Katie listened to the dissonant voices of the children.

They called in the doctor,
They called in the nurse,
They called in the lady with the alligator purse;
In came the doctor,

In came the nurse,
In came the lady with the alligator purse.

Leather shoes slapped against the flagstone courtyard as the jump rope hit the ground. The rhythm was
soothing to Katie. It filled her head with nonsense,
which for a moment drove the evil memories away.

"What's the matter with my Katie?" Frances asked
sadly. She put her arm around the child and drew her
to her bosom.

Katie shook her head. She could not talk to her
mother about it, ever, and that was what hurt the most.
There had never been anything she could not discuss
with Frances.

Frances took her daughter's chin between her thumb
and her fingers and looked into the young girl's eyes.

"You know your mama loves you, baby?" she asked.
Katie nodded. The lump in her throat was painful.
"Then why you not tell your mama what hurts you in
your heart?"

"I can't," Katie said.

Frances sighed. How could she comfort her child if
she didn't know the problem? She suddenly wondered if
Katie's depression was a sign of adolescence.

"Katie," she said, "you're a big girl now. In a couple
of years you'll be a woman. Boys be coming around to
call. You be thinking of marriage. It's good to know the
facts of life, and I'm gonna tell you all you have to
know."

"No!" Katie said peremptorily.

Frances was taken aback. "But why?"

"I know all that," she said bitterly, looking away
from her mother. "I know everything."

"But how, Katie? When . . . ?"

"I can't tell you, Mama," Katie said, "but I know. I
know the whole disgusting thing."

"What?" Frances exclaimed. "Why you say that, Katie? The love of a man and a woman, it's a beautiful thing."

"It's horrible!" Katie shouted, startling even her little sisters at play. "Some people may be willing to do that, but *I* never will. Not as long as I live!" she cried, and she left her mother and went into the house.

Frances followed her with her eyes. She was heartsick over her daughter's remarks. How she had learned whatever she knew, Frances had no idea, but whatever she had seen or heard had given her an ugly, tainted picture of lovemaking, and the girl was upset and disillusioned. Frances was aware that Katie considered her own mother as guilty of lewd behavior as anyone else who had ever had sex, and her cheeks burned under her daughter's judgment. She remembered well her own first reaction to the discovery. She, too, had been disappointed with the world. Katie would simply have to grow up. She would eventually accept it all, even embrace it all. It was a bad time for her child, but for the present there was no way Frances could reach her.

Dinner was quiet, as usual. As forks clinked on plates, Frances watched Katie's every move, and she did not miss the look of aversion the child gave her father.

"I need more water," Joe said, handing his glass to Katie.

The girl did not move.

"Katie," he called her to attention. "I said I need more water."

"Then get it," Katie answered coolly.

Five mouths stopped chewing and five pairs of eyes grew round.

"What's that you say to your father, girl?" Big Joe asked the child.

"I said," Katie enunciated slowly, "that you can get it yourself."

Every muscle in her body was in a spasm, but she held her shoulders straight and looked into the big man's eyes, now narrowed in anger. The two smaller girls began to whimper, dreading the blow that would inevitably follow.

Joseph Raspanti put his napkin on the table and pushed back his chair. Without another word he pulled back his arm and slapped the child across the face. A skein of long black hair fell loose with the impact of the blow, and at once redness rushed in where his fingers had left their sting. But she held her head erect and did not divert her gaze from his. She stared at him with loathing, breathing hard.

"Joseph!" Frances cried. "Don't hit her again! *Per favore!* Santa Maria!"

His hand was still upraised, but he lowered it slowly. It was not Frances's plea that restrained him, but the cold, inscrutable message in his daughter's eyes. The kind of hatred they emitted, the words she had spoken in defiance—there had to be a reason. The child knew something about him.

He sat back down in his chair.

"Sit down," he said to Katie. "Everybody, eat your supper."

Obediently the children returned to their plates, unsettled by the frightening scene. Frances's eyes darted from her husband to her daughter.

Katie did not sit down. Quietly, in full possession of herself, she placed her napkin beside her plate, took her shawl from the hook near the door, and left the house.

"Katie," Frances called out, "where you going?"

"Let her go," Joe snapped. "She come back. Sassy witch. Where she learn that kinda stuff?"

Frances ignored her husband and followed Katie into the courtyard. She turned to see the girl running up the stairs to the Macalusos' apartment. Frances was satisfied that Katie would spend the night with Janie, as she often did. At least she would not be out walking alone

in the street at night. She went back inside and began
picking up the supper dishes.

Big Joe got up from the table and walked to the door
for his hat. He turned to Frances and their eyes locked,
but he just walked out without a word. Hours later, the
children were in bed, and Frances was alone. She sat in
the kitchen, wondering if Joe would come home and
take down the mattress from behind the door. Exhausted, she pillowed her head in her arm and slept.

Chapter
FOUR

It was still dark when Katie came down the stairs in the morning. She clutched her shawl beneath her chin as the wind whipped her skirt around her legs. It had not been hard to slip out of the Macaluso apartment because she had slept fully clothed. She had not even washed her face or combed her hair before opening the door and letting herself out onto the balcony. She stopped now in the yard to use the outhouse before dashing through the service alley to Camp Street, and then on toward Poydras.

The market was coming alive when she ended her five-block walk. Mule-drawn wagons from farms on the outskirts of the city lumbered up to the produce section, where merchants were waiting to unload fruits and vegetables.

Katie walked to the place between the two buildings where women gathered to be hired for "day's work." She planned to speak out and tell the ladies that even though she was young, she could work as well as any woman. If she were hired for the day, she'd have a warm house to go to, a meal to eat, and time to think things through.

The wind whistled between the buildings, and she gathered her shawl snugly around her head and shoulders. She sat on the curb and watched the produce merchants disposing of rotten vegetables and throwing buckets of water on the wooden floors and sweeping them. In the other building butchers were arriving at

their stalls. Mr. LeGrand, her mother's butcher, un-
wound the rope that secured the roll of canvas awning,
and it dropped like a wall from eaves to sidewalk, pro-
tecting the butchers from the biting wind. Katie longed
to sit inside the meat market to escape the weather, but
she was determined to be first on hand for work when
the hiring began.

She was cold and hungry and very tired. She wondered how she would manage to do a whole day's work
on the little sleep she had had. She had tossed and
turned in Janie's bed, replaying the scene with her father over and over again. Each time she went through
it, she smelled once again the garlic in the heated room
and her father's body odor. She felt the heat rising in
her neck and her chest heaving as she fought back the
tears. She heard her mother's sobs and saw the fear in
her eyes. It was a moment in her life she would never
forget.

She hated her father. She would never forgive him,
not only for the blow, for it had not been the first, but
for the despicable insult he had dealt her mother. She
suddenly knew she could never live under his roof again
and obey his commands.

Katie knew she must find another place to live. If she
were hired today, perhaps her employer would keep her
permanently, and she could live with the family she
worked for. She would prove to her mistress that she
was a good cook, and she could care for children, too.
Or do laundry. Anything. She'd find herself a place,
and then she'd let her mother know she was well and
safe.

It would be hard for Frances to do without her. She
would have to walk the children back and forth to
school and do all the chores herself. Katie regretted the
added toil and heartache she'd be giving her mother,
but there was no help for it.

The canvas of the sky changed from navy blue to
putty, and the outline of buildings on Poydras Street

etched itself in charcoal against the gray. Business places opened their doors, and proprietors came out to sweep their sidewalks. The aroma of roasting coffee drifted toward the market from the processing plants on Camp Street. Katie's stomach growled.

Seated on the curb, leaning against one of the stone pillars that supported the market arcade, she fell asleep. When she awakened, a half-dozen women had gathered at the "hiring place" and were looking about for employers, calling out their favorite chants: "Day's work! Day's work done! Washin' an' iynin! Any kinda work!"

Katie jumped up from the curb. She took several deep breaths, trying to decide what to do. She was angry with herself for dozing off. She had been there first, and she should have been first to be hired, but what chance did she have now?

The women were all Negresses, burly and black, neatly dressed in gingham dresses and starched white aprons, their heads wrapped in tignons. Some carried mops or scrubbing boards, which they raised above their heads from time to time as a sign of their trade.

Katie stood in the midst of the growing throng of women and felt her face flush as they eyed her and nudged each other.

"Wut you doin' heah, li'l white gal?" one Negro woman asked. "Why don't you go on home by yo' mama?"

The others laughed their rich deep-throated laughter.

"I'm here to get 'day's work,'" she answered, turning to look into each pair of eyes. She frowned at them brazenly, but her heart was racing. She had had little contact with colored women, either as neighbors or as hired help.

"Ho-ho," laughed one of the women. "She gonna git da work of a full-growed woman. Ah'm shore!"

"Den she gonna hafta go git de woman to do it," another jibed, and the crowd burst into laughter.

A buggy pulled up to the curb, and the women milled around it. A door opened, and a lady descended. She looked the women over as they barraged her with a litany of their skills and accomplishments. At last she tapped one of the women on the shoulder and indicated an outdoor seat on the back of the carriage. The Negress climbed up, and the buggy pulled away.

Buggy after buggy pulled up to the curb. Sometimes the ladies in the buggies knew one of the black women and the choice was quickly made. Once the driver hopped down from his perch atop the carriage and made the choice himself, while the lady inside remained unseen. One by one, the women were taken away, each to the security of a full stomach and a day's pay. But Katie remained. None of the ladies seemed to realize that Katie was there for hire. Although she persisted in chanting "day's work," her voice was lost in the chorus of deep-throated cries, just as her figure was lost in their midst.

The wind stopped and the sun seemed to be struggling to come out. It occurred to Katie that as soon as her mother had delivered the children to school, she would come to the market looking for her. She *had* to do something. She must get away.

She combed her hair with her fingers and braided it as well as she could. She arranged her shawl neatly around her shoulders and left the hiring place. Two black women remained there, still hoping to be taken. She walked a half block down Poydras Street in the direction from which carriages had been coming. Then, when she saw a carriage approaching, she stood boldly in the middle of the street and signaled to the driver. The Negro shouted "Whoa!" and pulled forcefully on the reins to bring the horses to a halt.

"Whut you doin' down dere, li'l gal?" he shouted impatiently. "You wanna git yo'self killed?"

"No, sir, but I have to talk with your lady. It's important."

"Wit Miz Eagan? You mus' be crazy. Git outa de way."

"I won't. You'll have to run me down, or let me talk to her. It's life an' death."

A veiled hat appeared at the window of the carriage.

"What is it, Mason?" a voice asked.

"Some crazy white gal wonts to see you 'bout life an' death," the Negro answered.

The head protruded farther, and Katie ran to the side of the carriage where the woman could see her. The child's face was a mask of fear and despair. The woman pursed her lips. She was obviously not pleased to have her errand interrupted. At last, she spoke. "Pull over to the curb, Mason," she said. "Let her in."

Katie sighed with relief. The Negro hopped down and opened the door of the carriage. A step was lowered and Katie climbed into the coupé. She looked about her in awe. It was the first time she had ever been inside a carriage. The vis-à-vis seats were upholstered in maroon horsehair and tufted, and the top of the vehicle was leather, its accordian pleats spread open to protect its passenger against the early morning chill.

"Now," the lady said shortly, "what is it you want?"

The lady smelled of lavender. Her black hair, threaded with silver, had been poofed softly at the hairline, beneath the veiled hat. She was firmly corseted and dressed in fine, black bombazine, with a cameo brooch at her throat. Her slender hands rested on the ivory knob of a walking cane, and her pointed shoes peeped out from the hem of her skirt.

"My name is Katie Raspanti," the child said. "I came to get 'day's work' at the market, but no one will hire me."

"I don't wonder," the lady commented. "You're nothing but a child."

"I'm fifteen, and I can wash and iron and clean. And even take care of children," she added, seeing that the lady was not convinced.

"Goodness, child, you're not old enough for that."

"Oh, yes. Yes, ma'am, I am. I'm the oldest of five, and I help my mother with everything." Katie was on the verge of tears, and her voice broke on the words.

The woman sighed. For the first time she leaned back against the tufted upholstery. "How do you manage that, and go to school besides?" she asked.

"I don't go to school," she said. Her eyes dropped to her lap. She was always ashamed to admit her ignorance, especially now, before such a fine lady. But if her employment depended on it . . . "I stay home to cook and clean with my mother."

"You can cook?"

"Yes, ma'am. My mother taught me. I can make lasagna, fettuccine . . ."

The lady raised her eyebrows in interest.

"Do you use a lot of seasoning in your cooking?" she asked. "My husband likes his food well seasoned."

Katie smiled a full, bright smile. It sounded as if the lady might hire her. "Oh, yes," she said. "We use garlic and oregano, and when my mother makes stuffed eggplants, she even uses crushed mint. We grow it in our garden."

"Good," the lady said. "Now tell me. What will your mother do without you, if you cook for me today?"

"She'll manage. My mother is very smart."

"I'm sure of that. But won't she worry? Does she know where you are now?"

"No, ma'am."

"Don't you think you ought to tell her?"

"Are you really going to hire me?"

"Well, just for the day. And just to cook. I still need a full-grown woman for laundry, if there's anybody left, after all this delay."

"Oh, yes, ma'am. There are still some Negro ladies there," Katie said.

"Which is why you threw yourself in front of my carriage. Right?" the lady asked.

Katie blushed. She fingered the fringe on her shawl.

"Very enterprising young woman." The lady knocked the knob of her cane against the front of the carriage. "Mason," she called out, "please go on to the market." Horses' hooves clopped against cobblestones. The lady turned back to Katie. "I'll take you on for the day on one condition. We're going to tell your mother where you are. I don't plan to get arrested for stealing a child."

Katie nodded unhappily. She wanted that, too, but she was afraid. Her mother might not let her go. Her father might still be home. But if this was the only way . . .

At the hiring place the lady beckoned to one of the women who had been waiting when Katie left. The woman's eyes widened when she saw Katie in the coupé. The Negress climbed to the back seat on top the carriage, grumbling under her breath and frowning at Katie. Katie smiled a small smile, pleased at her victory.

The lady opened the carriage door. "Come on out, Katie," she said. "We'll have to do some shopping if we're going to have a real Italian dinner. Get the basket from Mason. You'll have to tell me what to buy. By the way, I'm Janet Eagan."

The lady lifted her skirt and walked down the aisle of the market as if it were a carpet in Buckingham Palace.

When the carriage turned into the service alley behind Julia Row, children drew back into the courtyard and women hanging their wash stopped and gazed dumbfounded. No carriage like the Eagans' had ever come here before. And when they saw Katie's face at the window of the coupé, they were speechless.

The carriage stopped when Katie pointed out her house. To everyone's surprise Mrs. Eagan ordered Mason to let down the step so she could cross the courtyard to the Raspanti home.

Forewarned by neighbors, Frances came to the door, drying her hands on her long apron. When she saw Katie, tears came to her eyes, and she held out her arms to her child. Katie ran to her mother, and they held each other close.

"I thank you, ma'am, with all my heart, for bringing my Katie home," Frances said. "I was so worried. She spent the night upstairs with neighbors, but when morning came, she was gone. I wanted to go to the police, but my husband say no. He say she turn up. Just now I was getting ready to go to market. I think maybe I would find her there."

"That's where she was," the lady said. "I'm Janet Eagan. May I come in?"

"In here?" Frances asked.

Suddenly she realized that she was blocking the doorway. A half-dozen neighbors were standing in a circle around the two women. Others were watching from the balcony on the second floor.

Mrs. Eagan sighed.

"Oh, sure," Frances said. "I forget my manners. I'm so glad to see my Katie." She drew her child to her again. Then, even as she waved the lady into her warm kitchen, she wondered what her business was and why it was not enough that she had brought Katie home. "Please," she said. "Sit down. How 'bout a nice cup of coffee?"

"No. I thank you kindly. I'm rather in a hurry, but I came to ask you something."

"Oh?"

"I met Katie this morning. She tells me she's a good cook. Is that so?" Mrs. Eagan had taken a chair and was resting her hands once again on the knob of her cane.

"Oh, yes," Frances answered warily. She did not understand why Katie's cooking was of interest to the lady. "My Katie, she cooks like a woman. Anything you want." Then, looking the woman over, she asked, "How you met my Katie?"

"I came to hire a Negress at the Poydras Market. Katie was there, looking for employment."

Frances gasped. "Katie!" she exclaimed.

"I had to get away, Mama. You know . . . ," she said, and tears sprang to her eyes.

Janet Eagan waited. She was getting impatient. Time was passing, and the services of the hearty Negress sitting on her carriage were going to waste. She didn't mind doing the child a favor, but she had no intention of becoming embroiled in her personal life, and she wished for a speedy resolution to whatever family problems Katie and her mother had. She sighed aloud. She tapped her foot.

"Mrs. Raspanti," she said. "I would like to hire Katie to cook for me today. Can you spare her?"

Katie looked at her mother with pleading eyes. Frances frowned and looked at the lady quizzically.

"For money?" Frances asked.

"Oh, yes," Mrs. Eagan answered. "A dollar for the day, and her meals."

"So much!" Frances exclaimed. "Just to cook? You got no cook, Mrs. Eagan?"

"I have a fine Negro cook, but she doesn't prepare Italian dishes, and my husband favors them." She smiled a forced smile, hoping to get the matter settled.

Frances turned to her daughter. "An' you, Katie. This is what you want?"

"Oh, yes, Mama."

"My driver can take her back right after dinner dishes," Mrs. Eagan added.

"Oh, no!" Katie cried out. "Please, ma'am. You've been so kind. I know you'll find a place for me to sleep, so I can work for you every day. I'll sleep anywhere. It This is what you want?" doesn't matter."

Janet Eagan shook her head, wondering how she had gotten into this.

"Suppose we try a few days," she cried. "I have a vacant garret room. It's small, but there's a bed."

Janet Eagan looked from mother to daughter. Frances and Katie were searching each other's eyes. Frances knew that Katie was determined to escape. The child's large eyes sent an unmistakable message. Let me go, or I'll run away again.

"Okay," Frances said wearily. "We try a few days."

Katie threw herself in her mother's arms and kissed her soundly.

"Katie, pack a few changes of clothes," Janet Eagan ordered. "And while you're about it, I'll write my address, so your mother will know where you are."

In minutes Katie was back, with all her worldly possessions in a small bundle under her arm, but the smile on her face made it impossible for anyone to pity her. Mrs. Eagan wrote her address on a calling card she had taken from her handbag and extended it to Frances.

Frances hesitated. She felt as if, in taking the card, she was exchanging it for her child, her precious Katie, her solace, her companion. How strong the premonition was that the child would never live in her father's house again! Katie opened her lips as if to plead again, or was it to beg forgiveness? Frances felt the smooth white velour, and she knew that she'd never touch the card without remembering this moment, when her heart was near to bursting with pain.

"Three days from now, I promise to come by and we'll talk again," Mrs. Eagan said. She shook Frances's hand. "She'll be warm and comfortable, and I won't work her too hard. Don't worry. I have children of my own."

Frances embraced her daughter and kissed her goodbye.

"Don't forget your prayers," Frances said. "And brush your teeth at night."

Katie was embarrassed in front of Mrs. Eagan. "I'll do all that, Mama," she said. "I'm a big girl now." She kissed her mother and whispered in her ear. "I know you don't understand why I sassed Papa, but I had a good reason. I just can't tell you. And I can't live with him anymore."

As tears ran down her mother's face, Katie walked out of the door without looking back. The neighbors had gathered in such numbers that they had to make a path for her to walk through. Mrs. Eagan followed in her wake, and murmurs of admiration rose and fell around her like waves breaking on a shore.

Chapter
FIVE

The carriage rolled past Lee Circle and headed up St. Charles Avenue into an area of town which Katie had never seen before. It was an immensely wide avenue, shaded by huge oaks and graced by magnificent columned mansions set far back from the street. Thick velvet lawns lay in trim squares all along the way.

After a two-mile ride the horses turned into a driveway, and the carriage stopped beside a home of such size that Katie suddenly feared the unfamiliar life of the people who lived there. The driver was down from his seat in one swift, practiced swing. He opened the door for Mrs. Eagan and came around the carriage to open Katie's door. He lowered the step and took her hand to help her down.

She looked about her in awe. The sun had come out, and dewdrops glistened like diamonds on the lawn. They walked up a wide stairway to a gallery surrounded by an iron lacework railing. Beyond the porch a wrought-iron gate gave entry to a vestibule floored with marble. The main door was leaded glass, and Katie could see through its thickness the rainbows it cast on the hardwood floors inside.

She looked up into the face of a fat Negro woman in a gray uniform and a long snowy apron who had admitted them before her mistress had had time to ring the bell.

"Got anything to carry, Miz Janet?" she asked.

"Yes. Thank you, Della. Mason took the carriage

around the back. Go help him take the groceries in, and see to the laundress I hired at the market. Show her where to change, and tell her where the washtubs are. Maybe this one will stay longer than the last."

"Hmp," Della grunted, waddling down the corridor toward the back of the house. "We keep on hopin' dey stay longer, but dey never does. Ah aw'ready tol' mo' nigger gals wheah de washtubs is den you kin shake a stick at."

Janet Eagan walked to the mirrored hat rack and Katie followed, stunned by the vastness of the carpeted corridor. She gazed about her at the chandeliers, the paintings, the towering doors leading off the corridor. Where did they all go? she wondered.

The corridor was lined with mahogany tables and love seats, a grandfather clock, and a small satinwood secretary. The middle of the corridor was spanned by an arch, and at the far end a staircase hugged the back wall and then curved gracefully away into a free-standing spiral.

Janet removed her gloves and took the hatpin from her hat. She hung the hat on a hook beside the mirror, and, studying her reflection, touched the waves at the sides of her head.

"All right, Katie," she said. "I'll show you where you'll sleep."

She walked toward the back of the house, with Katie in her wake. As they passed by open doors, Katie caught glimpses of unimaginable richness in the double parlors to her left and the library to her right. At the end of the corridor they crossed through a dining room as big as the Raspanti apartment. It ran the width of the house, and there were floor-length windows at both ends.

Janet lifted her skirts and climbed the curving staircase. On the second floor Katie marveled at the stained-glass window looking out over the backyard. The panes were of ruby glass, each a petal in an enormous rose. Through the window's opacity she could barely discern the carriage house out back; its beauty was in the rosy light it cast into the stairwell. Standing in that stream of pink sunlight, Katie felt as if she had been transported to another world, where things would never be quite black and white again. Her work and her recreation would all be colored and shaped in new and unfamiliar patterns, structured as much by the house itself as by the people who lived here.

She glanced down the second-floor corridor, but they did not explore it.

"This is where the family sleeps," Mrs. Eagan said. "Your duties will not take you here." Katie understood: to enter was to trespass.

Janet was leading her to the third-floor garret bedroom which had been partitioned off long ago.

"This will be your room," she said. "At least for the next three days."

Katie smiled. The room was bigger than she had imagined, although the ceiling slanted over the bed in conformity with the roof. It was a brass bed, with a patchwork quilt so beautifully made that her mother's would look coarse by comparison. Besides a bed there was a redwood chest, a chair, and best of all, a mirror.

Never in her life had she expected to have such a room! Oh, she must do well, so that her mistress would keep her on. Her joy in her new quarters brought tears to her eyes.

"I love it, Mrs. Eagan," she said. "I promise I'll work so hard you'll never want to let me go. I . . . I . . ."

Katie swallowed hard, knowing that she must not cry. At every crisis in her life, until now, there had always been Frances to run to. Frances had shared her joys and her sorrows, but Katie had just relinquished that comfort. She had chosen a new kind of life, and in that moment, in that garret room, she grew up. She was a working woman now, and her crying days were over.

"Don't become too attached to things, Katie," Mrs. Eagan cautioned. "We'll take this a few days at a time. I know you have problems at home. Perhaps they'll work themselves out, and you can go back."

"Never," the girl said vehemently. She threw her gaze to the floor.

"We'll see," the woman added noncommittally. "If you stay on, you'll work with Della in the kitchen. You'll help her with the cooking and set the table. Della always serves. You'll do the dishes and keep the silver polished." She put her finger to her cheek, thoughtfully. "I may try you at doing the marketing. Della hates it.

"Della will teach you what she knows, good old New Orleans cooking, red beans and rice and okra gumbo." The lady turned to leave the room. "Hopefully," she added, "she'll learn what _you_ know, although I wouldn't count on it. Della is like an old dog. She doesn't like new tricks."

Chapter
SIX

From the kitchen Katie could hear Della in the yard, arguing with the vendor from the Pot of Gold Lottery Shop. Katie opened the screened door onto the back gallery so she could lean over the railing and listen. Six weeks had gone by since she had met Janet Eagan at the Poydras Market. Her first three days with the Eagans had led to three more, and three more, and by that time Katie had become a member of the Eagan household staff.

"Whut you mean, you cain't take no gigs on fo', eleven, an' forty-fo'?" Della asked the vendor irritably.

"The boss said, 'Don't take any washwoman gigs,' " the vendor explained. "The last time that gig hit, every washwoman in town had a bet on it. It broke the bank, and we can't take a chance on that happening again." He shook his head wearily, as if he had been explaining the same thing all morning. "Why don'tcha play your dreams, Della?" he asked.

"It ain't fair," she grumbled. "Dat gig hits once a year, an' it's due to come up now. It just ain't fair." But even as she fussed, she pulled a limp little book from her apron pocket and leafed through the pages. "Ah dremp ah seen a Chinee, an' he was fallin' down de chimney. Now, what Ah'm gonna play? De Chinee gig or de chimney gig?" she asked.

"Play 'em both. Nickel each."

"What you think, Ah'm rich?"

"Come on, Della. Everybody knows you got bags of money hid in your mattress."

"Don't you go sayin' dat, white man," she said. "You'll have every burglar in town rootin' through mah bedroom. Gimme my list, an' git outa heah befo' Miz Janet sees you again."

Della waddled up the steps, studying her list. Katie watched her walk across the kitchen and take her composition notebook out of a drawer. She pasted her list in the book and compared it to other lists for frequency of appearance of numbers. Katie picked up her knife and resumed her chopping. Della stirred the soup on the stove.

"Della, tell me about the lottery," Katie asked. "What's a gig? How do you win the money?"

"If Ah knew how you win de money, Ah'd be able to retire, baby," Della said, chuckling. "But Ah kin tell you 'bout a gig. A gig ain't nothin' but three numbers dat you bet gonna come out of the drawin' all on de same day. You put a nickel bet on 'em, an' if they shows up on de list, you win."

"What about the dreams?"

"Well, it's all in de dream book. Dey's a gig fo' almos' anything you dream."

"You think I could play a gig, Della?"

"Oh, you too young, li'l Katie," Della said. "It mus' be against de law, Ah'm sho.' "

"Then *you* play it for me. How much can I win?"

"Nine dollars. Heh-heh," she laughed. "Whut a li'l gal lak you gonna do wit all dat money?"

"I'd give it to my mama, so she could buy a coat."

"Aw, ain't dat nice?" Della said, coming over to hold the child close.

Katie enjoyed the black woman's embraces. She always smelled clean and starched, bittersweet and earthy.

"Go run an' ketch dat white man," Della said. "Tell 'im Della wants to make another bet. He cain't be far."

Katie ran out on St. Charles Avenue and brought the vendor back. She picked three numbers at random, and Della placed her bet. After the vendor left, Katie took a small change purse from her pocket and gave Della back her nickel. She always kept change in her pocket, just as Della did, in case a vendor came by with Roman taffy or powdered waffles.

Katie loved Della. The black woman had been kind and generous with her, teaching her all the details of her job patiently. She had never resented Katie's invasion of her kitchen.

Della had taught Katie how to write her letters and numbers and how to read the headlines of the newspapers, when they had a quiet hour together in the afternoons. Now it was possible for Katie to read the grocery lists Miss Janet wrote and the hasty notes she scribbled as she left the house. Sometimes there was a word she could not make out, and she took the note to Della. The Negress was used to Miss Janet's handwriting.

In the past weeks a work pattern had evolved. Katie had taken over the grocery shopping, much to Della's relief. Della had never enjoyed the windy two-mile ride to the market or the shuffling and jostling with "no-'count niggers" around the stalls. Katie, on the other hand, found the market an exciting diversion. She enjoyed watching the vendors water their produce and arrange it in the stalls. She was stimulated by the noise and confusion of the traffic.

Best of all it gave her a chance to see her mother. The first time she'd gone to market with Della's detailed instructions, she had seen her mother at the butcher's stall. They had hugged and kissed and cried so long that the gruff Mr. LeGrand had had to interrupt them to get the rest of Frances's order.

Since then Katie had come to market three days a week, which was all that was necessary in a house with an icebox that held two hundred pounds of ice and kept

meat fresh for at least three days. Miss Janet set the
shopping days on Monday, Wednesday, and Friday,
and as soon as she was satisfied that Katie was a relia-
ble shopper, she made arrangements with Mason to
take the carriage out right after breakfast on those days
to drive the girl to market.

On their second meeting her mother asked her to
come to the house for coffee when her shopping was
done. Katie hesitated, then agreed. Both Frances and
Katie were chauffeured back to the service wing by
Mason sitting atop the carriage with his gray top hat
and his wooden expression.

The women in the neighborhood shied away from the
carriage, intimidated by Mason. The old Negro, with a
twinkle in his eye, pulled his little drawstring bag of
Picayune tobacco from his coat pocket and rolled a cigarette while he waited for Katie.

Frances knew that the women wanted to be invited
in to hear Katie's news, as it wasn't every day they had
a visitor from St. Charles Avenue. But Frances wanted
her daughter to herself. Their time together was too
precious to be shared, and there were things Frances
hoped to discuss in private.

She started the water boiling for coffee before she
took off her shawl. Out of the corner of her eye, she
watched Katie looking around to be sure her father was
not at home, then sighing and smiling at her mother.

"Mama, tell me about Jenny and Lala. How are they
doing in school? Do they miss me?"

"We all miss you, Katie. Even the boys. They ask
about you every day, how you are, what you're doing."

Neither one mentioned Joe Raspanti.

"Now, *you* tell me, Katie. You happy? You like it
there, with Mrs. Eagan?"

"I love it, Mama."

"Mrs. Eagan, she's good to you?"

"Very good."

"And what about the papa. You see him?"

"Mr. John? Oh, yes, he comes down to breakfast every morning with his celluloid collar and tie, and a dark worsted suit with a handkerchief in the pocket."

Frances looked impressed.

"He used to do electrical work," Katie explained. "When they first put electric lights in people's houses, he was in charge of all that. But he doesn't do that anymore. He's a very rich man. His father left him a fortune, Della says. He 'sees about his other interests now.' That's how Della says it."

"Who is Della?"

"She's the Negro lady I work with in the kitchen. She's really good to me, Mama. She knows how to read and write, and she's teaching me how."

Frances touched her daughter's face. "I'm so glad, Katie," she said. "You always wanted to read. Your brothers, they never had time to teach you."

The water was boiling. Frances got up and poured it slowly through the coffee. Soon the room was filled with the delicious aroma Katie knew so well. Boiled milk, simmering on the stove since breakfast, was added. Katie brought spoons and cups and sugar to the table, and they continued their conversation.

"You serve Mr. John his meals, Katie?" Frances asked.

Katie shook her head no. "Miss Janet says I'm too young to serve."

"Miss Janet?"

"That's what the servants call her. She says I can set the table and cook and do dishes and make groceries. And there are lots of little things I do, like cleaning the stove and the pantry. She says when I'm sixteen, she'll buy me a maid's uniform, and I can serve. If I'm still there."

Frances had never heard her child talk so much before. She was full of smiles, and her face was transformed. Katie had always been quiet and serious; how could she have been otherwise? She had had no childhood, working from morning till night, deprived of the fun and games other children enjoyed. Although her days were still spent working, she had discovered a whole new world of elegant living. She was not allowed to enter it, but she could view it close up, and it enthralled her. As she talked, she tilted her head and laughed with an air of carefree adolescence. Yes, Frances thought, she was happy.

"And what about the children?" Frances asked. "You walk them to school?"

"I don't have to. They have Mason to drive them, but he only takes Warren. Warren is fifteen. He goes to Jesuit High School. Charlotte goes to Newcomb College, and she has her very own automobile. She drives it and repairs it and everything. Charlotte's very beautiful, Mama. She's nineteen. She made her debut last November."

"What is that, day-bew?"

"I don't know exactly. But it's very important. It means she 'came out.' "

Frances rolled her eyes. She sipped her coffee. "Where she came out from, Katie?"

Katie giggled. "She didn't come out from anywhere, Mama. That's just the way they say it when a young girl is introduced to society."

Frances nodded. "And what other children Mrs. Eagan got?" she asked.

"Well, Stephen is the oldest. I haven't seen him yet. He goes to Tulane University, and he lives in a fraternity house. He'll graduate in June. Della says he always comes home for holidays. He'll be spending a few days home for Mardi Gras." She sipped her coffee. "And then, I told you about Charlotte and Warren. That's all."

"Does he talk to you, this Warren?"

"No, Mama. I said hello once, and just looked at me.

Della says it's best to leave the family alone unless they call for you."

"Oh," Frances remarked soberly. She didn't like the sound of that. Katie was a poor girl, but she had pride and sensitivity, and Frances didn't want her to be hurt. The woman stirred her coffee. "Tell me about your room," she said.

"Oh, Mama, it's so wonderful. I have a big bed all to myself and a chest of drawers and a mirror. And there's a chair to sit on when I put my stockings on." Taking another breath, she started again. "And wait till you hear this! There's a bathing room right in the house, with a tub and a toilet and a basin, all made out of porcelain."

"*Inside?* But Katie, how can that be? How do they clean out the toilet?"

"They don't have to. There's a chain that hangs over the toilet, and you pull it, and everything flushes down underground. Della told me about it."

Frances gasped. "What they gonna think of next!" she exclaimed.

The only style of refuse collection the Raspantis were familiar with was the ignominious "honey wagon" that came through the service alley with odiferous regularity, wearing a layer of flies like a living garment, disgorging men to invade the outhouse, shovel excreta into barrels, seal the barrels, and roll them onto the wagon. As long as Katie could remember, when the wagon turned into the alley, neighborhood children ran screaming up to the balconies, holding their noses.

"Of course, I don't use *that* bathing room," Katie said. "That's just for the family."

"No? Then what *you* do, Katie?"

"I bring hot water to my room. I have a pitcher and a basin on the commode, and good chamomile soap, and it's nice and warm in my room. And I have a slop jar that stays inside the commode. And, Mama, I don't even have to empty it."

"No? Who, then?"

"There's a maid who empties all the slop jars, even mine. And she rinses them well with hot water."

Frances clapped her small hands to her face. It was too much to believe. Her daughter lived like a princess, for all that she might be considered a maid.

"And Della? She lives on the third floor, too?"

"Oh, no. No Negroes live in the big house. They live in another house in the yard. They call it the servants' quarters. Mason lives back there, too. And a new upstairs maid called Treece. Her real name's Theresa, but she calls herself Treece."

Frances sipped her coffee and placed the cup in the saucer. The time had come for her to broach the subject. "You never gonna talk to your papa again, Katie?" she asked.

Katie became rigid. "I can't, Mama. And I can't tell you what he did."

"I know what he did, Katie," Frances said. "He did it before." But still she did not look at her daughter.

"And you stay with him? You *sleep* with him?"

The question shocked Frances. The word and the stress her daughter gave it left no room for doubt that Katie knew what she was talking about. Frances had waited too long to talk to her about sex. Katie had found out on her own, just as she had told Frances that day on the swing. And somehow she had discovered her father's infidelities, too. Whatever Katie had seen or heard, Frances would never know, but at least now she could confide in her as she would in another woman.

"What else am I gonna do, Katie?" she asked. "I got four children to feed. We got the rent to pay. If I put him out, where I'm gonna work?"

"In a house, like I do. Cooking and cleaning. Miss Janet could find you a place. Maybe one of her friends would need a housekeeper."

"No, Katie. Lala, she's just a baby still. I got to walk

her to school. I got to watch her when she plays. She needs me."

Katie frowned. She felt a pang of guilt that the duties she had abandoned now fell to her mother. She felt even worse that her mother was forced to stay with such a man because of a brood of kids. As she watched her daughter contemplating the situation, Frances reached for Katie's hand. "I know it's hard for you to understand," she said, "but I don't *want* your papa to go. It's not only the money." She was trying to light a spark of understanding. "I love him, Katie."

"How can you?" Katie asked. "After what he did?"

Frances shrugged. "Sometimes, when a man gets older, he needs a young woman to tell him he's handsome, he's strong, he's young. He begins to doubt himself. He thinks life is passing him by. Your papa is like that. But he loves *me*, Katie. Only me. He always comes back to me."

Why would you want him? Katie wondered. But she did not want to hurt her mother more than she already had, so she asked, "How do you know that, Mama? That he'll always come back to you?"

Frances's eyes narrowed thoughtfully. "I'm his . . . security." She nodded her head at her choice of words. "I take good care of his kids. I cook his dinner. I make him a good home. That makes him proud. I pretend I'm happy. He thinks *he* makes me happy." She drew her fingers together in a familiar gesture. "And *that* makes him feel important. He needs me, Katie. Your papa, he's a weak man."

Katie shook her head, trying to comprehend the mystery of her mother. She had always thought she understood her mother well. She had believed her to be simple, one-dimensional. How very wrong she had been! Frances Raspanti was a woman whose heart had been broken by a husband she adored, not once, but many times. She knew about his transgressions and she forgave him, over and over again, because of the children and because she loved him. Her life was a bed of nails, and Katie had never known. Katie, too, had fallen for her mother's pretense of happiness.

She got up and sat on her mother's lap and put her arms around her neck. Tears fell from her eyes, and her mother rocked her with her body and patted her back in long, tender strokes.

"Thirteen years ago we came to this country, your papa and me," she said. "It was 1893. All we had then was you, Katie, a baby two years old. Little Joe, he was on the way, and I was feeling bad all the time. In Palermo we sold everything we had to get on a ship. Still all we could afford was a cabin in steerage. The room was half the size of this kitchen, and we were seven people in that room for sixteen days. Your papa's brother, your Uncle Dave, he came, too, with his wife and two kids.

"The sea was rough. There were bad storms. I vomited and the children vomited, and there was no way to clean the mess. At last we reached New York. A week it took us to get through customs. We spoke no English then, and nobody came to help us. The other Sicilians, they tell us New Orleans is a big port. They say your papa can find work selling vegetebbles in one of the markets or unloading ships on the dock. Your Uncle Dave, he come along with us, but not for long. He no like the dampness here. He took his family to Los Angles. It's like Palermo there. Warm, sunny days." She said it with obvious nostalgia.

As her mother spoke, Katie could picture the young couple arriving, finding a place to live, her father getting a job selling produce at the market. A few months later, her mother said, Little Joe was born, and a year later, Davey.

Their first two years in the city the young Raspantis lived in fear. Sicilians were the most despised members of the New Orleans community. A few years before they arrived, the chief of police, David Hennessy, had been assassinated by the Sicilian Mafia because he had so vigorously investigated the activities of the organization. Nineteen Italians were arrested, but the citizens of New Orleans were appalled when the jury failed to convict them. A mob gathered outside Parish Prison. With a battering ram they broke through the wooden door to the jail. Eleven of the Italians were seized and lynched, two left hanging on display on Rampart Street. Others were shot within the prison walls, some who had nothing to do with the Hennessy trial. At last the public thirst for vengeance was slaked.

In the years that followed New Orleanians categorized all Italians as ignorant, dirty, and dangerous. As such they were insulted, avoided, feared, and threatened. Such prevailing attitudes led the Raspantis to the service wings of Julia Row, where there were other Italians to talk to, and at least as much physical comfort as they had been accustomed to in Sicily.

In 1895, an epidemic of Yellow Fever swept the city. Three hundred people died. Wagons passed along Canal Street, dropping barrels of tar at every corner, to be burned at night in a glare that lit up the city. Joe Raspanti came down with the fever, and there was no doctor to be had, even if they could have afforded one. The newspapers told the people what to do, but Frances could not read English. It was the parish priest who came around to translate for his parishioners. Following these instructions, Frances covered Joe's bed with mosquito netting. Her neighbors helped her screen the windows. She poured kerosene and oil into the cistern, and she burned sulfur in Joe's room. She put cold cloths on his forehead and gave him hot footbaths. At last the fever left.

Frances told Katie how joyful she had been when Joe recovered. Without him she would have had to put her children in an orphan home. She would have been all alone in a foreign country where she did not even speak the language and her heart would have been broken.

Although Joe recovered, his job was gone, as was every penny that they had saved. He got a new job then, unloading ships at the Jackson Wharf. He was a teamster. With his good looks and forceful personality, he was soon foreman of the wharf.

"One day a hogshead of sugar got loose," Frances said wearily, "an' broke your papa's leg. Again we spent all our money. While your papa stayed home, I went to work, keeping house, like you said, an' we got by."

Frances sighed heavily as she relived the hardships of the past. She looked into her daughter's eyes. She touched her cheek tenderly.

"We been through a lot together, your papa an' me," she said. "We belong together."

"Does *he* know that, Mama?" Katie asked.

Frances took her daughter's hand in hers. "You can't forgive your papa, Katie?" she asked.

"No, Mama, I can't. I'm glad if you can, because you have to live with him. But *I* don't. Not anymore. Don't be sad because I can't love him, Mama," she asked. "If I thought I was making your life just one bit harder, I couldn't bear it."

"I won't be sad, Katie," Frances said, knowing she was making a promise she could not keep.

"I'll tell you what, Mama," Katie said, brightening. "I'll come every Wednesday after I do the marketing and spend the rest of the day with you. And the children can come home for lunch, so we can all be together."

Frances's face lit up. "Oh, Katie!" she said. "Can you do that? Is it okay with Mrs. Eagan?"

"Oh, sure. It'll be my day off. Miss Janet and I have never settled on a day off. I might see you in the market on Mondays and Fridays, too, if you go shopping then."

"I'll go," Frances said.

"Well, I guess I better leave now, Mama."

They got up together and walked to the carriage in the alley. Neighborhood ladies gathered in the yard and around the carriage. Katie kissed them all and told them her mother would give them the news, since she was already late. Then Mason opened the door of the carriage, and Katie drove away, all alone in the coupé, like a fine lady on her way back to St. Charles Avenue.

Chapter
SEVEN

When Katie started working at the Eagans, Janet Charbonnet Eagan was forty-one years old. Her jet-black hair, now striped with bands of silver, was startling against her milk-white skin which had never lost the freshness of youth. Her gray eyes were fringed with thick black lashes, and she held her long, patrician nose and her pert mouth at an angle of regal disdain. She was considered a beautiful woman.

Although her waistline had never thickened, she was always corseted to keep her breasts high and her stomach flat. She wore wide-brimmed hats, which complemented her delicate features, and suits with fitted jackets and frilly jabots. She was wealthy, fashionable, and pampered.

Janet had been blessed with abundant good health and stamina, both of which had been tested in her recent preparations for her daughter's debut. It was an event she had anticipated since Charlotte was born, and one into which she plunged herself energetically. In the Eagan home Janet had staged the most elaborate debut ball that good taste would allow.

The sliding doors between the double parlors had been thrown open, as well as the floor-length windows giving out onto the gallery, creating a dancing area larger than that in most of the city's hotels. A stringed ensemble played for the guests, and potted palms were everywhere. Carriages stopped at the door, depositing members of the city's first families. Gentlemen in tails and ladies in shimmering gowns danced and drank champagne and nibbled hors d'oeuvres until long past midnight. In preparation for the soiree the maids had attacked every chandelier, painstakingly polishing every prism. The house had been decorated by Bim's Florist, and Janet had hired a photographer, a dozen extra maids, four butlers, and four men to take care of the carriages.

Months earlier Janet had given top priority to the matter of Charlotte's debut gown. She had engaged the finest couturier in the city to design a dress of white point d'esprit over taffeta. It had been made with an off-the-shoulder neckline, gathered at intervals with sprigs of lily of the valley. The bodice had tapered to her tiny waistline like a corset. The gown had struck the perfect balance between innocence and décolletage. But it was Charlotte who had brought the dress to life.

Charlotte was the only woman in any gathering whose beauty rivaled her mother's. She had her mother's wide gray eyes and porcelain skin, but there were always roses in the hollows of her cheeks, and her thick auburn hair was the color of old, burnished copper. Her face was fuller than her mother's, and dimpled, and her mouth was unforgettable: wide cut and sensuous, with straight white teeth. She was a tall girl, slender and small bosomed, but she walked with her shoulders erect, as if proud of her figure, and carried herself with such grace and confidence that one was soon convinced that whatever Charlotte didn't have, she didn't need.

The first time Janet saw her daughter try on the gown, wearing her long white gloves and with her auburn curls draped gracefully over her shoulder, she felt a quickening of pride. She wished her mother could have shared the moment with her. If only Bonnie Charbonnet had lived to witness a debut where money was no object! Janet smiled wanly, remembering the machinations her mother had set into motion to finance *her* debut back in the 1880s.

Without a penny in her purse Bonnie had strutted like a peacock into Worth's, the most expensive establishment of its kind in the city, and purchased her daughter's debut gown on credit. The day after the party, she had returned it, claiming it "did not fit." All the spots had been carefully rubbed out with soap and water. The orchestra and the florist had been paid with checks that bounced, and neighbors on Esplanade Avenue might have noticed wagons pulling up to the Charbonnet home and carrying out a baby grand piano and an antique armoire, which were sold to pay the more pressing expenses. But when the party rolled around, there were champagne fountains, imported caviar, and sculptures of pâté. Both Janet and Bonnie had floated through the evening on gossamer wings, unconcerned with such mundane affairs as how the bills would be paid.

There were ways to stage less expensive debuts. The languid Creoles whose ancestors had founded the city were, more often than not, financially embarrassed when their daughters came of age. Many held a simple presentation in the family's opera box on the opening night of the season. Announcements were mailed, flowers sent by well-wishers, and visits paid to congratulate the debutante at intermission. This was a totally acceptable debut. But not to Bonnie Villere Charbonnet. The Villeres and the Charbonnets were among the oldest families in New Orleans, and for generations their homes had been gathering places of the elite of the city. Janet's antecedents could be traced back five generations on each side and included such notables as Governor Claiborne and the Spanish Territorial Officer Duralde. No debutante of this caliber could have anything less than the finest debut party simply because her family happened to be "slightly short" at the time.

How relieved her mother must have been, Janet often thought, when she accepted John Eagan's proposal of marriage. After the initial shock that her only child would be marrying a man almost old enough to be her father, how ecstatic she must have been that Janet would be rich! John Eagan was the catch of any season. He was the darling of New Orleans, the electronics prodigy, the former associate of Thomas Edison himself. Ever since Eagan had returned from Menlo Park and erected a dazzling electrical display for the Cotton Centennial Exposition, the newspapers had made his name a household word. He was besieged with invitations for dinner parties and galas, this handsome bachelor with the resonant voice and the fascinating past. His unaffected exuberance was exciting to Janet compared to the lethargic dispositions of most of her young Creole gentlemen. He had already inherited a dizzying fortune when his parents died, and the night he proposed to her on her front-porch swing, she knew instinctively that he would be much, much wealthier. He was a brilliant physicist who would be a leader of the world of the future. The world would be run by electricity, her father had said so. Both she and her mother were more than pleased to forget that he was the son of a German immigrant with no social background whatsoever.

Now that Charlotte and the rest of the 1906 debutante coterie had been introduced to society and presented to the members of the Boston and Pickwick clubs, a less restrained kind of revelry was about to break loose. The Mardi Gras season was upon them, and on January 6, it was touched off with the Twelfth Night Revelers Carnival Ball at the French Opera House. All the debutantes were in a fever of excitement over the prospect of attending their first carnival ball. They set about buying evening dresses, tiaras, long kid gloves, dancing slippers, and beaded reticules. Everything had to be new, never seen before, and elegant. After a four-month round of parties and dinners, they discarded their old extensive (and expensive) wardrobes. Everything had to be put aside as the girls entered a whole new plateau of clothes buying.

Debutante fathers went into shock when the bills arrived. Many put new mortgages on their homes or borrowed against life-insurance policies. Yet even the fathers were proud of their blue blood and were anxious to show off their daughters. There was no better way to establish social identity and even improve business standing in New Orleans than for a man to reign as king, or to have his daughter reign as queen, of one of the city's exclusive Mardi Gras organizations.

John Eagan was a notable exception among debutante fathers. He was as proud as any man of his daughter, but he considered the whole panoply a ridiculous and infantile display of wealth and pedigree. He sat back quietly, however, and let it happen. If it made Janet happy, it was worth the trouble and expense.

The carnival clubs were called "krewes." In the week before Mardi Gras they held annual costume balls, at which the mock royal court was taken very seriously. Crowns, ermine trains, and royal garb ran into fortunes, and were paid for by kings and queens who had been "invited" to reign for the day. Besides the royal monarchs there were maids and dukes, ladies-in-waiting, pages, and a captain whose job it was to direct the pageant.

After the entertainment the captain blew a whistle and "call-out" dancing commenced. Young ladies were "called out" by name to dance with a masked member of the krewe, whose identity remained a secret. She *did* retain a memento, however, a krewe favor, which the masker gave her when the music stopped. It was always a token of value, a vanity case or a musical jewelry box, inscribed with the name of the krewe and the date.

The year Charlotte made her debut, five organizations staged carnival balls: the Twelfth Night Revelers, and the krewes of Momus, Proteus, Rex, and Comus. Charlotte was paid the highest compliment that could be given a debutante. She was invited to reign as queen of Comus, the oldest and most prestigious of the carnival organizations. She received invitations, of course, to attend all the other balls, each enclosing a blue call-out card; and Janet was always invited to sit in a box seat, where she and the other mothers might preen as their daughters paraded around the dance floor.

Katie's work was not affected by any of this, except that she could feel the vibrations that traveled through the household. Trips to the seamstress for fittings increased in number. There were more errands to Rouge-lot's for fine French lace and to specialty houses for satin shoes and ivory fans and jeweled combs. Many dresses were needed, for neither of the Eagan women would be seen in the same dress twice in a social season. It soon became necessary for Janet to buy a circular rack for evening gowns, which she installed in Stephen's vacant room.

One afternoon, when Janet was seated in the carriage, ready to leave on a shopping expedition, it began to drizzle. She called out to Katie, who was on the gallery, to go up to her bedroom for her parasol. Katie took the inside steps two at a time and started down the second-floor corridor toward Janet's room. Suddenly she caught a glimpse of the dress rack in Stephen's room. She stopped in her tracks, awestruck at the glitter and splendor of the sight.

She slipped into the room and scanned the rack. One of the dresses had hundreds of seed pearls sewn onto the bodice. Another had rows of lace encircling the throat and running vertically down to the waist. The skirts were narrow, but draped to the side, and one was split to reveal a ruffled underskirt. Satin shoes to match each dress were arranged in a row on the floor, and gloves and jewelry had been laid out on top of the dresser.

Katie was breathless with admiration. She reached out warily to touch the shining cloth. Her fingers trembled as they brushed across a beaded bodice. She had never seen such dresses in her life. She had never been in stores where they were sold or seen pictures of them in books. It was as though she had entered another world, and she stood gazing far longer than she realized.

Suddenly the door swung open.

"Just what are you doing here, Katie?" Janet Eagan asked in a sharp voice.

Katie spun around and sucked in her breath. The expression on the woman's face was one Katie had never seen before. Suspicion was written there, and Janet Eagan was suddenly a woman Katie did not know at all.

"I . . . I came for your parasol . . . ," the girl began.

"And you decided to do a little snooping."

"No, ma'am," Katie said, and tears came to her eyes. This was a mistress she feared—and had never expected to fear. "I was passing by . . . I noticed the beautiful dresses . . . I came in to look. I shouldn't have. I'm sorry," Katie mumbled. "I'll get your parasol." And she passed Janet on her way to the corridor.

"Never mind. I have it," the woman said harshly. "I got tired of waiting. But hold on there. I want to talk to you."

Katie turned back to her mistress, her head lowered. The woman was standing in the doorway to Stephen's room, Katie in the corridor.

"Naturally you are curious," Mrs. Eagan began. "You are a child. Which is the reason why I was never sure you were right for this job."

"Oh, but I am!" Katie interrupted. "It won't happen again. I had just . . . never seen such dresses . . . ."

"Or jewelry, I'm sure."

Katie's jaw dropped and her cheeks flamed. At last she realized what was in the woman's mind. She couldn't believe it! How could Janet Eagan question her honesty or her loyalty? She could not speak. She could not form the words to deny a guilt that did not exist. She stood rigid, waiting to be dismissed. She felt angry, belittled, and shamed. She felt a single tear roll down her cheek, and she did not lift a finger to brush it away.

Janet Eagan seemed to soften at the sight.

"I'm sorry, Katie," she said. "I know you meant no wrong. I'm very nervous these days, what with fittings and preparations, and then Stephen's coming home Friday night. Forgive my hasty words, and get on back to work."

Katie turned and ran to the kitchen, without a word or a sign that she had accepted her mistress's apology. She ran into the pantry, where she proceeded to straighten the shelves. She needed to be alone to sort things out. The scene had been a revelation to her, a lesson that she would not forget.

Janet Eagan was her mistress, not her guardian, not her mother. She had imagined a relationship that did not exist. Gratitude fled from Katie's heart; resentment took its place. Always respectful and obliging, she had obeyed orders, asking neither favors nor privileges because of her youth. Mr. Eagan himself had called her into the dining room time and time again to compliment her excellent cooking.

She felt her heart hardening against Mrs. Eagan. Yes, it would be "Mrs. Eagan" now. She could no longer call her "Miss Janet," which had been a term of affection. Janet Eagan had relegated her to the class in which she belonged. The dresses of wealthy ladies were of no concern to her, unless she were asked to iron them, or to stitch a ripped hem. Vascillating between anger and self-pity, she considered packing her things and leaving the house. But where was she to go? Back to her father?

She straightened her back and drew in a deep breath, knowing that she would stay. She would follow Mrs. Eagan's orders and stay away from the family quarters. She would keep to herself and expect neither compassion nor understanding. They were mistress and servant, and so it would be.

She returned to the kitchen. Katie turned her face away from Della's questioning expression, rolled up her sleeves, and proceeded to wash the dishes in the sink. Somehow she managed to get through the cooking and the table setting, and she started scrubbing pots.

"Ain't you gonna eat?" Della asked.

The Negress had served two plates of food from the stove and put them on the kitchen table, as she always did after they had taken care of the family.

"Not hungry," Katie said.

"What's de matter wit you, baby?" Della asked.

"Nothin'. I just don't feel good. I'm going to do the dishes and go to bed."

"Cain't go to bed wit'out eatin'," Della mumbled. Katie didn't turn around, but she could picture the kind black face beneath the red tignon. "Shouldn't never go to bed wit'out eatin'."

She wanted to tell Della what had happened, but how could she? Della would never think ill of Mrs. Eagan. She might even suspect Katie of thievery herself. Even if she didn't, she couldn't very well comfort Katie without being disloyal to her mistress.

That night Katie knelt beside her bed and prayed for comfort, but comfort would not come. Pulling the quilt from the bed, she wrapped it around her shoulders and sat up in bed, resting against the headboard.

A thought . . . a word . . . something that had been said . . . when? . . . by whom? . . . something was fighting to emerge from the jumble of memories. It was a small bright spot in the midst of the gloom, and she wanted to remember it. It was something Mrs. Eagan had said. Oh, yes. She had said that Stephen was coming home.

Katie did not know why this excited her. She had never even seen Stephen Eagan, but she had studied his picture on the mantel in the dining room. His hair was dark and curly and parted in the center. He was not smiling in the picture. His lips were sealed tight against his teeth, self-consciously, in the expression boys assume when they're having their picture taken. Katie liked to think he had the same fine white teeth that Charlotte had. One asset she had not missed was the handsome cleft in his chin. Suddenly she could not wait to see him.

When Stephen would come, she would remember to keep her place. She would certainly not talk to him. But perhaps he would give her an order. "Katie, tell Mason to bring the carriage around." No, he wouldn't take the carriage. He'd go in Charlotte's car. "Katie, ask Charlotte to let me use her car." Why would he ask her to do that? He'd ask Charlotte himself. He probably wouldn't even know she was in the house. He would only be home for four days.

She lowered herself to the pillow and tossed and turned until she fell asleep.

Chapter
EIGHT

Mardi Gras at the Eagans was nothing like Mardi Gras on Julia Row. Before she left home, Katie and her brothers and sisters used to walk to Lee Circle on Mardi Gras with a bag of sandwiches and sit on the steps leading up to the statue. There they watched the parade as the *papier-mâché* floats wound their way up St. Charles Avenue, around the circle and toward Canal Street. The children yelled, "Throw me somethin', mister," like everyone else in the crowd, and caught a few necklaces and trinkets that the maskers tossed their way.

Each night for a week before Mardi Gras the servants at the Eagan residence gathered on the gallery to watch the family leave for the carnival balls. The ladies would come out of the front door in long velvet coats with ermine collars and long white gloves, their hair piled high in elaborate coiffures. They draped their trains over their arms to keep them dry and clean, descending the steps carefully in their pointed satin shoes. Mr. John was elegant, too, in his top hat and tails, and his patent-leather shoes. Then Mason would drive them to the opera house.

On the Friday night before Mardi Gras Stephen came home. Charlotte had telephoned him to offer to pick him up in her automobile. She was never too busy to stop at his fraternity house where she might "accidentally" run into some of his friends. But Stephen said that a friend would drop him off.

Katie and Della had been cooking since morning, preparing Stephen's favorite dishes. The dress rack had been taken from his room. Treece had cleaned his bedroom, changed his linens, and laid out fresh towels. Everything was ready.

At five o'clock Stephen jumped over the side of his friend's car, swinging his suitcase after him. He ran up the steps and through the corridor to the back of the house.

"Where is everybody?" he called out, pushing open the swinging door to the kitchen.

Katie hid herself in the pantry when she heard him coming. She could hear him laughing and running to Della for a motherly embrace.

"How dey feedin' you at dat faternity house?" Della wanted to know. "You lookin' thin these days."

"I'm not thin, and they feed me very well," he laughed.

"Dey don't cook as good as Della, Ah bet," she said playfully.

"Nobody does, you know that, Della," he answered.

Katie could hear Della laughing her hearty belly laugh. Stephen was her favorite, and nothing made her happier than his homecoming.

Later, when the family was seated at the table, Della served, and Katie, perishing to see what Stephen looked like, peeked into the dining room when the pantry door was open. He was sitting on the opposite side of the table, where she could see him well. He was talking animatedly. How handsome he was! Her heart raced at the sight of him.

He spoke incessantly, unlike Charlotte and Warren, who were self-contained and boring. His hair was parted in the center, as in the picture, and neatly combed in a wave to each side. His teeth *were* perfect, just as she had known they would be. And the cleft in his chin! What a beautiful man!

After dinner the family retired to the parlor where

Della served them coffee. Even from the kitchen Katie could hear them chattering away, making plans for their annual Mardi Gras party. Once in a while Stephen's voice rose above the rest and his laughter floated back through the house.

Katie trembled as she washed the dishes. She had eaten almost nothing when she sat down with Della, and her flushed cheeks made Della smile. There was no doubt in Della's mind that Katie had big eyes for Master Stephen.

Katie rushed to finish in the kitchen, so she could run and hide in her room. She had a feeling that if she met Master Stephen face-to-face, she would stutter and blush like a simpleton. But there was to be no early retirement for the servants that night. The family had reunited and they were celebrating. The kitchen was on call.

After coffee Mrs. Eagan rang her little bell and asked Della to serve the éclairs they had bought in the afternoon. More dishes were piled in the sink. Then Mr. Eagan had his brandy and invited his son to join him. Stephen was twenty-one, and soon to be graduated from Tulane with a degree in electrical engineering. His father's dream was realized, and it merited a toast. But to Katie it meant more dishes. Her hands shook as she handled the delicate crystal stems and, for the first time she broke an expensive glass. She was distraught.

"Go to bed, li'l Katie," Della said, smiling. "Miz Janet, she won't never know de glass is broke less'n dey have mo' den twenty peoples drinkin' brandy at de same time, an' when dat evah gonna be?" And she laughed a quiet, jolly chuckle.

Katie reached up and kissed the loving face. She took off her apron and ran through the pantry to the stairwell. She glanced down the corridor, and to her horror she saw Stephen coming full speed in her direction. Her knees went weak. She tried to move them, but they had turned to water. Seeing her, Stephen smiled and came toward her.

"And who are *you*?" he asked not unkindly. His smile put her a trifle more at ease.

"I'm Katie, Master Stephen," she said, trying to curtsy with her feet on different steps. She almost fell, and he took her elbow to support her.

"I'm not Master Stephen," he said. "Just Stephen. Please."

Katie nodded.

"Where did you come from?" he asked.

"Julia Row."

He chuckled. "I meant, what are you doing here?"

"Working," she answered tremulously. "Cooking."

"My mother must have gotten *you* out of grammar school."

"Oh, no. I asked for the job."

"But why?" He was still smiling.

She shrugged. She looked at her feet.

"All right. Don't tell me if you don't want to."

She looked over his shoulder to see if his mother was coming.

"What are you looking for? Are you afraid of someone?"

She shook her head no. "I have to go to bed now."

"Where? Where is your bedroom?"

"On the third floor."

"In the garret?"

She nodded. She looked down the corridor again, and without even a good-bye dashed up the stairs to her room.

Chapter
NINE

"Don't put dem devil eggs in dat dish, honey," Della told Katie. "We got a devil-egg dish."

Katie stopped arranging the eggs and waited for Della to lead her to the pantry where serving dishes were kept. The heavy woman lifted her skirt and climbed two steps up a ladder to reach for the cut-glass dish.

Katie was learning that there was a dish for everything. A berry dish, a pickle dish, a celery dish, now even a devil-egg dish. Della was teaching her, as the need arose, what to serve things in and where the serving dishes were kept. Now, as she rinsed and dried the dish and began once again to arrange the eggs, she wondered if Della's name for the eggs was accurate. She had vivid memories of Charlotte's laughter the night she had used one of Della's terms of reference.

That evening Mr. Eagan had called her to the table to tell her how good the vegetable was.

"We cooked them with swimps," the child had answered, beaming at the compliment.

Charlotte had laughed aloud for the first time in Katie's memory. "My God, she talks just like Della," Charlotte said.

The blood rushed up into Katie's face. My name is Katie, she wanted to say. Don't talk about me as if I weren't here. But she said nothing.

"Charlotte!" her mother reprimanded, but she was having difficulty repressing her own laughter. Then, turning back to Katie, she had said, "It was delicious. You must fix it for us again soon."

Katie curtsied and turned on her heel for the kitchen. But even as she left, she could hear Warren saying, in a muffled voice, "Yes, and be sure to use swimps." And he and Charlotte screamed and laughed hysterically.

Since that mortifying night Katie had always listened to Mrs. Eagan's pronunciations and repeated them over and over again, so as not to be drawn, through propinquity, into Della's Negro patois.

She glanced at the eggs looking up at her from the small declivities in the dish, like big yellow eyes, speckled with pimiento and pickle. They were eggs, not "aigs," she knew *that*. Now, she had to find out about the "devil" part.

Mardi Gras had come at last, after a weekend of guests and parties and last-minute preparations for the Comus Ball. Since the Eagan residence was on the parade route of the krewes of Proteus, Momus, Rex, and Comus, friends and relatives, many of whom the Eagans saw but once a year, "dropped by" to view the parades from the Eagan gallery. There, they were not at the mercy of the weather and could sit rather than stand.

It was a weekend when kitchen work never ended. Mrs. Eagan had ordered hundreds of sandwiches and hors d'oeuvres from a caterer, but Della still had to make gallons of holiday punch, and Mason had been asked to set up a bar in the library for the men. Dirty dishes accumulated in the kitchen, and, of course, throughout the weekend meals were still expected to be served on schedule.

Even late at night, when the kitchen was at last in order, Charlotte would think nothing of charging in with a crowd of noisy college friends to "raid the icebox," which meant devouring whatever delicacies Della had made ahead for the following day. Sometimes Della chased her out, taking liberties no other servant dared, but more often she stood in the doorway, fists on hips, breathing heavily, watching the girl and her friends go through the beautiful trays of food.

By Tuesday morning every muscle in Katie's body hurt, and she could tell by a lack of chatter that Della was aching, too.

"Now, we gonna serve boo-fay style t'day," Della told her, planting her fists on her hips. "Put de good white tablecloth in de dinin' room, wit de Mardi Gras 'rangement in de middle." Katie recalled the yellow, green, and purple arrangement of fresh flowers that had been delivered the previous day. "Now, den, we gonna 'range all de dishes round de edges of de table: san- wiges, potato salad, devil aigs, purple cole slaw, pickles, olives, all lak dat. Den we gonna stack de china plates at one end, wit de silver an' napkins 'long side, an' each one he'p hisself."

"Then no one will sit down at the table, Della?" Ka- tie asked.

"No, sirree. Ain't no room, when you got all dem people. Dey just has to juggle dey plates or sit on de po'ch wit it."

"How many will there be?"

"Oh, ah dunno. A hunnerd, maybe."

Katie gasped. "Won't they be dropping the china, with no place to put it down?"

"No, dey won't. Dat's de fust thing sassiety people learns is how to juggle china, settin' 'roun' at tea parties an' boo-fays. Dey useta dat. You gonna see."

Katie smiled. "When should we start putting things out?"

"Rat now. It's nine o'clock. Take us a good hour to git set up. By den, comp'ny start comin'. Parade passes by 'roun' eleven. G'wan. Git started." Katie took the dish of eggs and was about to leave the kitchen. "Wait. Ah'm gonna ask Miz Janet kin you serve t'day, out on de po'ch when de parade be passin.' Ah cain't do all dat servin' by mahse'f. Besides, who knows? You might jus git to see de floats go by if you should happen to look up."

Katie put the plate down and ran to give Della a hug. Then her eyes grew big. "What will I wear, Della? I have no uniform and cap."

"Hmmm." Della put her finger to her cheek. "Tell you whut. You serve de nuns an' de ol' ladies on de gallery upstairs. Dey don't care whut you wears."

"Okay," Katie agreed, and she was off to set the table in the dining room.

Every Mardi Gras Day Janet invited the Little Sisters of the Poor, a dozen nuns from an order of mendicants who lived nearby, to view the Rex Parade from the second-floor gallery. Also a ritual was the arrival of ten or twelve old ladies from the Maison Hospitalière, a retirement home for old Creole ladies.

An hour later, when she had finished setting the table in the dining room, Katie called Della for an inspection. Then she prepared a tray of sandwiches and potato salad for the ladies on the upstairs gallery. With Treece close behind, carrying plates, forks, and napkins, Katie carried her tray up the stairs and through the corridor to the porch. She riveted her eyes straight ahead, remembering well not to glance into the bedrooms. Not even a dress of solid diamonds could have tempted her to gaze into those forbidden areas.

She left the darkness of the corridor and stepped out onto the sunlit balcony. She and Treece were greeted with a chorus of ooh's and ah's. The old people were ready for food, though it was not yet eleven o'clock.

From a corner of the porch a raspy voice asked, "What is it? Who's there?"

Katie put the tray on a wicker table; then she glanced in the woman's direction. In the shade of the roof supported by columns sat a little old gnome of a woman, whose eyes were covered with an opaque film.

"It's a tray of sandwiches, ma'am," Katie answered respectfully. "And potato salad. I'll fix you a plate if you like."

"Oh, yes. That's a good girl." The blind woman rubbed her bony hands together.

Why had she come? Katie wondered. The Rex Parade was to *see*. Perhaps she wanted to hear the sounds of merrymaking and drink in the ambience of a joyful day. She probably just wanted to sit on someone's porch on a balmy day with her blanket around her knees and remember a time when she had romped with the crowds.

As Treece was passing around plates of food, Katie served the blind woman and stood before her in case she needed help. All conversation ceased as the ladies enjoyed their repast.

"Best potato salad Janet ever made," one old lady stopped to remark.

Katie smiled inside herself. She wondered if "Janet" could make a dish of potato salad if her life depended on it.

"Hope she didn't put onion in it," another said. "Onion gives me cramps."

The blind woman was having difficulty, so Katie sat beside her and offered to help. As she fed the old woman, she listened to the conversation of the others.

"Guess Janet'll get her picture in the paper, like always," an old lady remarked, pinching her lips and pressing a double chin into evidence.

"Well, Charlotte will, for sure, bein' in Comus. An' they'll name Janet an' John as her parents."

"An' the article will say how Janet *Charbonnet* Eagan once again demonstrated her charity be inviting the nuns and the ladies from the Maison Hospitalière to enjoy the comforts of her home on Mardi Gras," the heavy lady went on caustically.

"That's nothin' new," was another comment.

It amazed Katie that those who visited the Eagans, and the Eagans themselves, for that matter, spoke in her presence as if she were not there. She wondered what the old ladies thought she was doing there. They had to know that she was a servant. Didn't they care that she might repeat what she had heard? Hearing them speak so frankly, she began to understand how Della and the Negroes across the avenue knew everything about everybody. All they had to do was listen, and exercise discretion.

"Tell me what you see down there, girl," the blind lady said to Katie.

Katie stood and shielded her eyes from the sun. There was a wide vantage point between two giant oaks, providing a picture-frame view of the crowds. Beginning at the wrought-iron fence of the Eagan home, masked couples, groups, and families, milling in throngs as far as the eye could see, formed a veritable sea of people.

"There's a Dutch boy and a Dutch girl," Katie said, "and a devil and an angel. Oh, and there's a whole group of clowns or something with bells on their caps and their shoes."

"Those are court jesters, honey," one of the sisters interjected. Smiling, she turned her veiled head to one of her companions. "Nice child," she whispered. "Wonder where the Eagans got her. She's too young to be a servant."

The sound of brass and drums increased in volume as a marching band came down the avenue.

"Parade comin', girl?" the blind lady asked.

"No, ma'am," Katie said. "Not yet. Just a bunch of men playin' music."

"Are they niggers?"

"Yes, ma'am. They're wearing white trousers and dark coats and hats like streetcar conductors."

The ladies tittered.

Katie stopped talking when the Negro marchers, having wound their way in and out of the crowd, stopped close by the Eagan house and played a foot-tapping tune. Couples began dancing in the street to the compelling "tin-panny" syncopation. Loosened by drink, relieved for the day from the rigid restraints of society, the Negroes played their own kind of music. It seemed to come from deep down inside them, and it sounded as if they were making it up as they went along. Once in a while the melody emerged, but most of the time each instrument wandered off on its own, keeping time with all the rest and finding its way back at the end. Yet the many sounds all fit together in a delightful rhythmic whole. Katie felt as if she, too, could have danced, if she only knew how.

"That's Stalebread Charlie Lacombe and his Razzy, Dazzy Spasm Band," a male voice said, and Katie's head spun around to see Stephen Eagan.

"Well, now, thank you, Stephen," one of the nuns said.

"Well, if it isn't Stephen Eagan!" another piped up.

"How are you, Stephen?" an old lady asked.

He answered politely, but he was looking at Katie. It was Katie to whom he had addressed his remark. Her heart was in her throat, and she felt a weakness overtake her. She was glad that she was sitting, or she would surely have crumpled in a heap. Why does he affect me this way? she asked herself. She smiled weakly. She wanted desperately to speak to him, to answer him. Yet she knew that if she tried, she would stammer and make a fool of herself, as she had Friday night. She could feel her cheeks coloring as her eyes met his. He walked over toward her.

"Do you like ragtime, Katie?" he asked.

She glanced at the street and then at Stephen. That must be what the music was called—ragtime.

"Oh, yes. Very much," she said.

"So do I. It started right here in New Orleans, you know." He took a sandwich from the tray and took a bite. "But now it's getting popular all over the country."

He smiled, and she smiled back. His gentleness, his kind, friendly manner were putting her at ease. Why had he come here? she wondered. Had he come up just to see the nuns? Or the old ladies? She hardly thought so. But surely not to see her!

Stephen wondered once again about the pretty little Italian girl. Where was she from? Why did her parents let her stay here and work? At her age she ought to be in school. He had not seen her since Friday, and what with company and parades and carnival balls he hadn't really thought of her again till this morning. Then he had gone looking for her, and Della told him where she was. He wanted to tell her hello, to see if she was as pretty as he had remembered.

Fifteen or so, he guessed, from the full, round contours of her figure beneath the blue calico dress and the long white apron. Her blue-black hair was braided and twisted in a coil at the nape of the neck. A few wisps had escaped, and they spiraled gracefully in front of her ears. Fair skin, tinted pink from the chilly day, set off the huge, dark eyes. They were like doe's eyes, looking up at him. Oh, yes, he had remembered her well. She *was* a beauty.

A siren interrupted their separate meditations.

"The parade's comin'," one of the ladies called out.

The crowds in the street cheered and pushed and jostled for positions along the curb, and policemen on horseback, ten abreast, cleared a path for the parade to follow.

"Come, Katie," Stephen said, taking her hand.

He led her to the corner of the porch where they could stand in the sun and watch the parade. "We can see it well over here, and maybe I can catch something for you."

Katie could not believe that Stephen Eagan was going to watch the Rex Parade with her.

"Won't you be missed downstairs?" she asked timidly.

"No. Mother and Dad have their friends, and Charlotte and Warren have theirs."

"And what about you?"

"I didn't ask any guests for Mardi Gras. I wanted to be free to come and go."

Katie nodded. She dimpled and her heart pounded.

"Will *you* be missed downstairs?" he asked.

"No. Not yet."

"Good. Then we'll watch the parade together."

Katie had to force herself to look away from Stephen's face and watch the activities in the street below. Old men on horseback and in open carriages followed the police vanguard.

"Those are veterans of the War between the States," Stephen said. "Confederates, of course," he added, smiling.

Katie smiled self-consciously. She had no idea what he was talking about. She only hoped he didn't know that. In that moment she made a resolution. She would learn to read at once. She must learn all about the War Between the States. She must find out who the Confederates were. She was such an ignorant girl! If he knew what a stupid girl she was, he wouldn't waste a minute with her.

The title float, pulled by a pair of brawny mules, was an enormous representation of the Boeuf Gras, the bovine symbol of feasting and frolicking that would go on in the city throughout the day and well into the night. Across the top of the float was the theme, spelled out in glittering, silvery letters.

"Children's Nursery Rhymes," Stephen read.

Katie studied the letters, and the way they were grouped. She would remember the words.

Next came the king's float, rising to the height of the gallery, so that Katie and Stephen were on a level with Rex, His Royal Majesty, the king of Misrule. Seated high above the crowds, his ermine train cascading down the back of the float, the king gracefully swept his scepter out over his loyal subjects. The mobs pressed around the float, seeping into the open spaces as it passed by.

A high-school band followed, playing the carnival theme song, "If Ever I Cease to Love," and Stephen sang out the silly lyrics in a rich, fine voice. "If ever I cease to love, if ever I cease to love, may oysters have legs and cows lay eggs, if ever I cease to love."

Katie giggled.

"Haven't you ever heard the words before?" he asked.

She shook her head no.

"Have you ever seen a parade before? Are you from the city?"

"Oh, yes. I've always lived in New Orleans."

"But you said you were from Julia Row. Where is that?"

She giggled again. Then it struck her. He had remembered!

"I used to live on Julia Street," she said. "The block was called Julia Row, because of the row houses."

She saw his eyes looking beyond her thoughtfully. He was picturing the street. She was sorry she had told him.

"Julia Street? Past Lee Circle? The one on the way to Canal Street?" he asked.

She nodded.

He smiled wanly. The girl was poor, he was thinking. Her family needed the money. That was why she was working here. For this lovely, delicate child there was no time to be young. It upset him. He was groping for a way to console her, without offending her.

Seeing the slight frown of pity, Katie changed the subject. "Every Mardi Gras my brothers and sisters and I used to go to Lee Circle to watch the parades. We caught a lot of trinkets there."

"Are you the oldest?"

Katie nodded. "Yes, and then there's Little Joe and

Davey and Jenny and Lala. I miss Lala the most. She's so lovable and cuddly. Like a little kitten."

"Why didn't you go there today? Mother would have let you off."

"I was needed here. I set the table for the buffet. And I'll be needed for washing dishes later. Besides, my mother will take them."

"But you miss them."

"Yes." She wrapped a tendril of hair around her finger thoughtfully, in a way that Stephen thought adorable. "But I see my mother several times a week at the market. And on Wednesdays I spend the day with her. Sometimes we ride the St. Charles streetcar all around the belt. When I spend the day with Mama, the children come home from school for lunch, and I get to see them."

Stephen watched her eyes sparkle as she talked and her pink lips part over small white teeth. He'd heard his friends at school talking obscenely about how they'd pinched their maids or grabbed them in the pantry for a feel or a kiss. Somehow his sentiments about Katie were not like that at all. Exactly what they *were* like, he wasn't sure himself.

The first of the floats went by, preceded by a sign bearer. "Little Red Riding Hood," the placard read. There were a dozen maskers on the float, some dressed in red caps and capes of the storybook heroine, others in hairy, woolen animal suits, their snoots protruding and jaws hanging open. Their eerie, expressionless celluloid masks looked out over the crowds. All were busy, throwing glass beads and trinkets from bags resting at their feet on the floats.

Some of the maskers tried their skill at sailing strings of beads through the air to the Eagan balcony. Stephen caught many, which he proceeded to slip over Katie's head. By the time the parade ended, she was weighted down with the shiny baubles. Delirious with pleasure, Katie made the rounds of the ladies on the porch, giv-

ing them each a necklace as a remembrance of the day.
Then she whispered to Stephen: "I'll save the rest for
my brothers and sisters. They never catch this many.
I'll put them in my room now and get on back to the
kitchen. Della will be needing me."

"I'll help you with the tray," Stephen said.

"No, don't!" Katie cautioned. "Please go now. I
don't think your mother . . ."

She didn't have to finish. Stephen knew the rest. He
wouldn't have hesitated to tell his mother he'd choose
his friends wherever he liked, but he knew he'd be
going back to the fraternity house, and Katie would still
be here. He knew she needed the job, and he didn't
want to make things difficult for her, so he left then.

Katie floated through the rest of the day. She scraped
dishes and stacked and washed them. She cleared the
dining room. She made gallons of coffee, and cut
brioche into squares for serving. When she was alone,
she tried to remember the tune of "May oysters have
legs and cows lay eggs," but she was not gifted musi-
cally, and it eluded her.

An hour after the parade ended, the crowds in the
street had dispersed. Mason took the nuns and the old
people home in several carriage trips. Mr. John helped
out by driving a few of the braver souls in Charlotte's
automobile.

When everyone had left, the family retired for a late-
afternoon nap, for the climax of their activities had not
yet been reached. Mardi Gras night, Charlotte was to
reign as queen of Comus. She would sit in the reviewing
stand at City Hall with the maids of her court as the
parade went by. When the parade was over, she and her
maids would be taken to the French Opera House,
where the courts of Rex and Comus would meet, and
dancing and pageantry would go on until midnight,
when the season of Lent officially began.

Bone tired, but too happy to feel pain, Katie retired
to her bedroom for a nap, but her mind was too full of

Stephen to let her sleep. She might not see him again today. He, too, would be going to the ball, in his full-dress suit and his ruffled shirt. He would wear a great-coat with a cape, and a top hat. How she would love to see him dressed like that! The young ladies at the ball would be weak with admiration. Their caps were set for college men with name and money. To them Stephen would be the best catch of all, with his rosy face and the cleft in his chin.

Katie rested on top of her quilt, with her shawl across her shoulders. She lay on her back and closed her eyes to think of Stephen. She saw him arriving at the opera house in the family carriage and entering the ballroom. In her mind's eye the ballroom had gleaming golden hardwood floors, like those downstairs, and chandeliers even larger than those in the corridor.

It was a circular dance floor she envisioned, with windows that ran to the floor, draped with velvet por-tieres of scarlet fringed with gold. On one side of the ballroom sat the king and queen of Rex, on the other the monarchs of Comus, each surrounded by maids of the court. And at the far end of the room Stalebread Charlie Lacombe and his Razzy, Dazzy Spasm Band were playing ragtime music.

Stephen entered, the music stopped, and every girl in the hall reached out to touch him as he passed, begging him to sign her dance card. But Stephen held his head high, aloof, ignoring them all, awaiting the lady of his heart, for whom he had saved all his dances. And then he saw her, at the other end of the floor, in a dress with a hundred ruffles. She was wearing long white gloves and crystal beads around her neck. She wore a coronet of diamonds and she carried a fan of ostrich plumes. Her black hair fell loosely down her back, and every-one gasped with admiration as she walked across the floor to him.

"Why, it's Mary Katherine Raspanti!" they whis-pered.

"Katie!" Della called from down below, and Katie shot up to her feet. She had been daydreaming, not sleeping at all. And now it was time to get the ladies ready for the ball. She brushed back the loose hairs from the front of her head and secured them with hairpins as she ran down the steps to help.

Chapter
TEN

Somehow they all got through Mardi Gras. Charlotte waved her royal scepter over the crowds, and the king of Comus toasted her in champagne. And while the Eagan family was basking in her glory, Katie and Treece and Della were doing their best to restore the house to order. Every bedroom looked as if it had been hit by a hurricane. The women made beds, hung up clothes, and picked up supper trays. Then there were dishes to wash and the endless job of putting away the hundreds of glasses and plates that had been used throughout the day. Everything must be done before they retired. Tomorrow was Ash Wednesday. The season of Lent was beginning. The family would be up and dressed for seven o'clock Mass in the morning. A whole new regimen would be underway.

From the garret bedroom Katie heard the Eagans returning from the ball. For at least an hour they laughed and chatted in the bedrooms just below her. She heard doors opening and closing, outbursts of laughter, and then, nothing. She tried to distinguish sounds that would tell her Stephen was leaving, but she could not.

She awoke at six to dress for the day. By the time she got down to the kitchen, he was gone. How long would it be till he came home again? The Easter holidays. Six long weeks. She felt as if all the light had gone out of her world.

* * *

The weeks of Lent brought frigid winds to rattle the shutters of the house. Days were consistently gray, and Treece came in from hanging wash, cupping her chilled fingers to her mouth to warm them. Early each morning Katie skipped down the stairs, her thick black hair tucked securely in place, her long dress and apron crisp and flat-iron smooth. At the second-story landing she always stopped to stand in the rose-colored light that poured through the stained-glass window. She felt as if she were bathing in its pinkness, entering another dimension where things were tinted rose, where people were kind to one another, and there was no suspicion or humiliation or fear.

Strengthened, armed for the day, she skipped down the rest of the steps to the dining room, and then walked sedately through the pantry to the kitchen.

For the servants Lent was a welcome respite from the grueling demands of carnival. Each morning Mason took the carriage around the front of the house, where Janet, Charlotte, and Warren waited, bundled up in overcoats, scarves, and gloves, to be driven to seven o'clock Mass at Holy Name of Jesus Church.

Della and Katie were allowed to take turns accompanying them, since there was room for only four in the new two-seater barouche. Katie was glad when it was Della's turn to go and she stayed home in the warm kitchen, preparing a Lenten breakfast of coffee and toast for the family's return.

Della was far more at ease on an outing with the Eagans than Katie. Katie could sense a tenseness in them when she was in their company that they did not feel with Della. Of course Della meant more to them than she did, in terms of familiarity and affection. They loved her and respected her for her tenure of service. The old Negress felt free to offer advice and make criticisms whenever she chose. But Katie noticed that the advice was never heeded, and that they gave her criti-

cisms a deaf ear. Katie, on the other hand, never spoke
unless she was spoken to; yet they could not ignore her.
She was a new and uncertain addition to their household. Although she was of common stock and background, they knew that she would, in time, chafe under
the harness Della willingly wore.

To Janet, the girl's presence in her home was an embarrassment. It was hard to explain to her friends that
employing the child was a charity, both to the girl and
to her family. Janet's friends wondered aloud why the
child wasn't in school, as if *that* were any of their concern. They asked Janet why her parents allowed her to
do such menial work, equating her with their own pampered offspring in the only way they knew how. They
passed remarks that implied that the Eagans could support the whole Raspanti family at no personal sacrifice,
if charity were the only motive for employing her. No
child should be doing a woman's work, their disapprov-
ing looks declared. Yes, a white child in a Negro woman's job was a humiliation to the mistress, and Janet
yearned to be rid of her.

But Janet could find no cause to let her go. Katie
worked hard, she followed instructions intelligently, she
kept herself immaculate, and she smiled politely whenever Janet passed. She spoke to no one except to follow
orders. She was punctual, and she never complained.

Every Wednesday morning, after Mass and breakfast,
Mason drove Katie to the Poydras Market, tethered the
horses, and followed her down the pungent aisles, a
basket on each arm. When shopping was done, he put
the baskets in the carriage and dropped Katie off at her
mother's house for the day.

The weekly appearance of the gray barouche in the
service alley became an event to the ladies of Julia
Row. Frances Raspanti, satisfied now that she'd have
her child to herself for the rest of the day, began inviting her neighbors in for coffee when Katie arrived, and
their Wednesday-morning gatherings were the highlight

of the week. They waited to see if Katie would show up in a new calico dress, and they nudged each other and nodded their heads when she asked Mason to call for her at four in the afternoon.

Mason tipped his hat and answered, "Sho' will, Katie."

Mason loved Katie, as all the servants did, for she treated them all as equals and was ready to fill in for them whenever the need arose. She alone, of all their white acquaintances, put no color line between them and made no distinction.

Once settled in the Raspanti kitchen, their coffee cups in hand, the neighbor ladies barraged Katie with questions. Like children listening to a fairy tale, they gave her their rapt attention as she obligingly described everything that fell under her scrutiny, from Charlotte's ball gown to the silver punch bowl on the dining room table. They fingered Katie's dresses and asked the price of everything, and Katie told them, as well as she could remember. At last they left, their curiosity satisfied, their discontent inflamed.

When Katie and her mother were alone at last, Katie reached inside her stocking and pulled out a neat little roll of three one-dollar bills, half her weekly salary.

"Buy something for the children," she always said, handing her mother the money.

"No. No, Katie," Frances said, shaking her head and pushing Katie's hand gently aside. "The kids, they got all they need. Plenty of food. Nice warm house. Keep your money. You work hard."

The argument continued until Frances took the bills. Katie watched where she put them, in a sugar bowl in the pantry. After a few weeks Katie began putting them there herself, saving her mother discomfort.

She saved her own money in a stocking, which she hid behind a loose brick in her bedroom fireplace. She had bought herself a few inexpensive dresses. Outside of that, she spent only a few nickels a week for taffy when the vendor came or for an occasional lottery bet.

It was impossible for Della's obsession with the lottery not to rub off on Katie. There was no way to ignore the woman's narratives about her dreams and her "gigs." She was also constantly perusing the composition notebook of lottery lists. Katie fell victim to the "rags-to-riches" dream that turned contented housewives into avid lottery fanatics. She, too, began studying Della's lists to see how many times ten had come "top" in the last month, and how often the "blood gig" had hit.

For Katie there was a tremendous fringe benefit. It was by studying these notebooks that she learned to recognize her numbers on sight. And it was by placing bets that she learned to add up her losses and keep track of them in writing. Now that her interest was aroused, she borrowed her brother's arithmetic table card and went through the day singsonging the multiplication and division tables as she chopped seasoning. Soon she was able to take the cost of an apple at the Poydras Market and multiply it by a dozen in her head.

Heretofore she had trusted everyone, knowing they would never cheat her. How nice it was to double-check and find she had been right! Katie discovered she had a gift for figures. It amazed her that her sisters and brothers complained so much about them.

Her appetite for learning had been whetted. Now, following the promise she had made herself on Mardi Gras Day, she determined to teach herself to read. She *had* to learn about the War Between the States and all about the Confederates before Stephen came home for the summer. And there was so much more to learn. She wanted to know everything there was in books everywhere, everything *he* could possibly talk about, so she'd never be an ignorant girl again.

Her very first week at the Eagans', Della had taught her the alphabet and even made her memorize some words from the newspaper. But when the letters were arranged in words, unless it was a word she had memorized, she was lost. There *had* to be a key to it, a way to sound out letters, but Della didn't know the answer.

"Della, what was the War Between the States?" she asked one day in despair. There just wasn't time to study everything. Maybe people could *tell* her things, and her education would go much faster. She was sitting on a stool with an agate pan in her lap, shelling lima beans. Della was washing the shelves of the kitchen cabinet. She stopped and turned to Katie.

"You mean the Civil War? Baby, you don't know dat?" Della asked in amazement.

Katie shook her head no. She was never uncomfortable with Della. Della took her as she was and loved her, ignorance and all.

Della put her rag aside and leaned against the counter.

"De Civil War ended the year Ah wuz born. Dat be forty-one years ago. Mah daddy tol' me all about it." She folded her arms beneath her bosom. "You see, de United States was split right in two, de North aginst de South. In de South de plantation owners wanted to keep dey slaves, to pick de cotton. But de North say no, dey should let de slaves go free. Dat's wut de war wuz all about. It lasted fo' long years. Now Ah guess you don' know wut slaves is." Katie shook her head. Della came over and took a chair beside her. "Honey, slaves wuz black folks lak me, who done de work on de plantations. Mah daddy an' mamma wuz slaves. Dey lived on a plantation in Palquemines, Louisiana. Dey useta pick cotton dere. Dey master had bought 'em together."

"They used to buy *people*?" Katie asked, astonished.

"Why, sho'. Das whut slavery wuz. White people buyin' black people."

"But that was terrible!"

"Dat's for sho'." Della shook her head sorrowfully. "Well, anyway, when mah mama was expectin' me,

President Aba-ham Lincoln signed a paper freein' all de slaves, an' my mama an' daddy come to New Orleans. Dey wanted me to be born free, away from dem slave quarters wheah dey useta live."

"Well, who won the war?" Katie asked.

Della looked at Katie in surprise. "Why, de North, honey. Das why dey ain't no slaves no more."

"And who were the Confederates?" Katie asked.

"Dey wuz de South, an' de Yankees wuz de North. Das how dey called 'em."

"Della, where can I find a book about it?"

"I guess dey be one in Mr. John's liberry, or maybe Miz Charlotte got a school book on it." She turned a suspicious look in Katie's direction. "How you gon' read dat? You cain't read. Why you wonts to know all dat stuff, anyhow?"

Katie shrugged. She didn't have to tell Della everything.

"Write 'Civil War' on a piece of paper for me," Katie said.

"Whut fo'?"

"Never mind. Please write it."

Della dried her hands, frowning warily. She found a piece of paper and the stub of a pencil and sat at the kitchen table. Laboriously she wrote the words, mumbling under her breath and giving Katie sidelong glances. Katie folded the paper and put it in her apron pocket.

An hour after the family had retired, Katie put on her slippers and her shawl. Then she tiptoed down the steps and through the corridor to the library. She had brought along a candle and a match, and the piece of paper Della had written the words on. Stealthily she opened the door to the library and closed it behind her.

She dared not turn on a light so she struck the match and lit the candle, and in its flickering light she tried to match the titles on the book bindings with the letters on the paper. There were C's in some titles, but they were all in the wrong places, and the same was true of the other letters. She sighed with frustration. There were hundreds of books in the library. She might look for hours and never find a book about the Civil War, assuming that there *was* one. Perhaps the book was called by the other name, the War Between the States.

Suddenly she realized that she might be caught and accused of thievery again. Her mouth went dry. But she persisted. Taking the shelves one at a time, she looked for the word "Civil" only. If she could find that one word in any title, she would take the book and run back to her room as fast as she could go.

Beads of sweat broke out on her forehead, although it was a cold night. She took off her shawl and laid it on the sofa. After an hour of looking, she decided to try one more shelf. If it wasn't there, she would give up her search, at least for tonight. Suddenly, in the middle of the last shelf, she saw the word! Civil. As plain as day. She checked the paper for the second word: War. It was there, too, on the book binding. She grabbed the book, blew out the candle, and scampered up the spiral staircase like a squirrel scaling a tree.

In her room she closed the door softly and turned on the light beside her bed. She gave herself a few seconds to catch her breath. Then she opened the book on her lap, thumbing through it and scanning pictures of soldiers in uniform and generals on horseback. Beneath each picture was a caption in heavy print, but the words were as meaningless to Katie as hieroglyphics.

She hugged the book to her and smiled. Oh, she *would* learn. She'd find out how to read one way or another. And this book would open the door to her learning. All she had to do now was hide it well and pray that Mr. John wouldn't need it or look for it for a very long time.

Chapter
ELEVEN

"Katie! Katie!"

Katie could hear White Man's voice calling her name as he drove his bicycle up the carriageway. He was shouting aloud, though it was not yet eight o'clock in the morning. She looked for her shawl on the rack beside the door. Not finding it, she took Della's and ran from the kitchen onto the back gallery.

"Keep quiet, White Man," she called out. It was the only name she knew him by. It was the way Della always addressed him. "You want to wake up the neighborhood?"

The lottery vendor adjusted the kickstand of his bicycle with his right foot and headed for the stairs. As always he wore his derby hat, celluloid collar, and tie, gray sweater buttoned up against the cold, and black trousers held securely around the calf by metal bands, to prevent them from getting caught in the wheel.

"Katie! Your gig hit. Three, eleven, and thirty-three. In yesterday's drawing. Take a look!"

Katie reached out for the list the vendor was handing her. Her eyes scanned it from top to bottom in an instant.

"How much did I win?" she asked.

"Nine dollars, honey," the man said kindly. "Now open your hands, and I'll cross your palm with green."

Katie extended her palms, dropping Della's shawl as the vendor took a roll of bills from his pocket, licked his thumb, and counted, "One, two, three, four, five, six, seven, eight, nine." He laughed with Katie. "How's it feel to be a rich lady?"

Katie's eyes were misty, thinking of the winter coat she would buy her mother.

"Wonderful!" she managed to answer. Then, remembering what Della had done when she won, Katie drew her leather change purse from her apron pocket and handed the vendor a quarter.

"For a tip, White Man," she said.

"Not from *you*, Katie," he said, patting her head like a kindly father. "And my name is Frank Herbert."

"I wish you would take it," she said, still holding out the coin.

Her eyes were earnest, and the sweet smile around her mouth was fading. Her feelings would be hurt if he refused.

"All right, then, lottery lady," he said cheerfully. "And what're you gonna do with all your money?"

"I'll tell you another time, okay?" she said. She was not prepared to share her plans with anyone.

Katie didn't have to tell Della about her good fortune. Before she put Della's shawl back on the hook, the Negress had the lottery list in her hand. She saw Katie's numbers, and she let out a whoop of joy. Grabbing the girl's hands, she danced her around the kitchen, and they both enjoyed a kind of exuberance Katie had had little occasion to feel.

"You done hit, baby! Dat gig paid off! Ah'm sho glad fo' ya. Now you kin git dat coat fo' yo' mama, right?"

Katie nodded.

"Now you hurry on an' git yo' marketin' done, an' Mason kin drive you down to Canal Street. Dey got good sales at de d'partment stores de end of Febrary. Evahthing marked down. You'll git you a *beau*tiful coat fo' nine dollars. Den, you kin bring it to yo' mama t'day. It's Wednesday."

* * *

The gray barouche pulled up into the service alley, and Katie handed a big package to Mason before she got out of the carriage. The women gathered around, trying to riddle out the contents of the package, hoping they'd be allowed to know. Mason gave the box back to Katie, hopped back up to his seat, and waved good-bye.

Frances stood in her doorway, her arms open wide to her daughter. Seeing the box, she dropped her arms to her sides and frowned quizzically. When Katie reached the building, she kissed her mother's cheek and handed her the box. The ladies gathered around them like bees to honey.

"Come in, everyone," Katie said. She had decided to let them share the surprise and let her mother show off her gift.

Frances's smile faded, but a soft pink colored her cheeks. Slowly she slipped the cord off the ends of the box, checking Katie for a sign, for permission to continue. Katie nodded her on.

At last the box was open, and the folds of silk paper turned aside. The women gasped and raised their hands to their faces in awe. Never had they seen such a coat! It was moss-green wool, soft as a rabbit's belly, with a dark green velvet collar and smoked pearl buttons down the front. The sleeves were leg-of-mutton, the cuffs and lapel wide in the latest fashion.

"Katie!" Frances said. The word was like a prayer. The woman's eyes welled with tears, and she took a handkerchief from her pocket to daub at them. She slipped her hand into her daughter's. "Where I'm gonna wear this, Katie? I don't go nowhere good enough for a coat like this."

"Wear it everywhere," Katie said. "To Mass on Sundays, to Canal Street, to market . . ."

"To market?" Frances exclaimed. The women echoed her question.

"Of course," Katie said, and all eyes turned to her.

"A coat is to keep you warm. Wear it whenever you go out. In all the years I've known you, Mama, you've never had a coat."

"But, Katie, it's too dear," Frances argued. "I bet it cost you everything you got."

"No, Mama, I won the money. I won it on the lottery. And the coat was on a half-price sale."

Once again the kitchen was abuzz with exclamations. Gambling was not to be encouraged, especially among young girls. But, on the other hand, lottery was so widespread in the city, it was a part of everyday life. There was not a woman among them who had not placed a bet at one time or another, and while their sentiments were tinged with envy, they were happy over their friends' good fortune.

"It's getting spring now, Katie," Frances went on with her objections. "In a few more weeks I don't need a coat."

"And how about the next ten years?" Katie asked.

"The children. They got no coats."

"There's enough money in the sugar bowl. Buy them some." Katie was ready for all objections. "But wait till the fall. It *is* late in the season. They'll grow a foot by September."

It was settled then. Frances Raspanti had a new coat, and she would have to adjust to it, but she was not at all happy. When the news of her new coat spread around Julia Row, the women would be envious, and she would feel guilty that she was warm and they were not. Her first impulse was to bring the coat back and exchange it for coats for her children. But the coat was Katie's gift, and Katie meant for her to enjoy it. A frightening thought struck her. What would Joseph say? Would he let her keep it? He would be furious, and he would never doubt that Katie had bought it to shame him. What a package of trouble Katie had brought her mother, wrapped neatly in silk paper!

When Katie left, Frances shoved the package under the little girls' bed, where it was to stay until it was later disposed of, or discovered.

Katie returned home at five, her heart light at the end of a happy day. It was so good to be able to do something nice for her mother. At least now she would be warm and comfortable. Not for a moment did Katie consider that she might have added to her mother's many problems with her gift.

She was no sooner in the kitchen than she realized that something was awry.

There was fear in the expression Della wore, and the wide eyes warned Katie to proceed with caution.

"What is it, Della?" Katie asked. "What's the matter?"

"Miz Janet, she wonts to see you in de liberry, de minute you gits back," Della said, nodding her head toward the front of the house. "Better go on."

Katie took off Della's shawl, which she had borrowed for the day, not being able to find her own. She smoothed her hair at the sides of her head and straightened her skirt.

"What does she want?" Katie asked.

"She tell ya." It was all Della would say.

Katie left the kitchen and walked through the dining room and down the wide corridor to the library at the front of the house. She sucked in her breath and swung the door wide open.

"And if you think I'll keep a th—" Mrs. Eagan's voice halted with Katie's appearance in the doorway.

Katie looked around the room. Mr. John was standing at the floor-length window looking out. Mrs. Eagan was in the wing-back chair, sitting stiffly. And Warren sat in the Morris chair, his knickered leg flung over the arm. All eyes turned toward Katie for an instant. The hair on her scalp prickled and her mouth went dry.

Her eyes had caught a detail that made her grab onto the doorknob to steady herself. Janet Eagan's hand rested on Katie's shawl in her lap, and beneath the shawl was the book, the one she had stealthily borrowed from Mr. John's library.

She watched the veined hand close slowly on the shawl, the huge diamond on her third finger catching the light of the lamp beside the chair. How had it all come together? What did they know? What did they *want* to know?

"Well, Katie. You've come home at last," Janet said.

Katie knew it was no later than she came home any other Wednesday, when her mistress showed little or no concern if she was in the house or not.

"Perhaps you can explain this," Janet went on, lifting the shawl from her lap.

"I don't understand," Katie said.

"It was in the library this morning, along with a few drops of melted wax on the carpet . . . so you must have come to the library last night. Surreptitiously, of course."

"Janet, really!" John exclaimed. "You sound like the police."

He turned his back again, but he did not leave. Katie was grateful. Warren did not turn his head to catch her expression. He swung his leg back and forth where it hung over the chair.

Katie swallowed. She felt her face go crimson. Never in her life had she been treated like a criminal before others, and she was smothering with mortification. Even when Janet had rebuked her for ogling the ball gowns, she had not been humiliated before others.

"I came down during the night," Katie said. It was as though she were listening to someone else speaking. There seemed to be no coordination between her brain and her voice. "I borrowed a book so that I could teach myself to read."

"Borrowed?" Janet shrieked. "This book?" she shrieked again, holding the heavy book high, as if it were the evidence to hang her by. "And when someone 'borrows' something, does she hide it beneath her mattress for fear it will be found? Does she steal like a thief in the night, with a candle instead of a light? What else have you 'borrowed,' dear girl? Perhaps the contents of the stocking hidden behind the brick?"

"Oh, no!" Katie shouted aloud. "That's *my* money. I've saved every cent of it."

"And never pilfered from the market change? Not even once?" Janet asked with a malevolent smile. "Oh, John, what a fool I was to take in a child with no breeding and no morals. Better a Negro by far than a low-born da—"

"Enough!" John cried out. It was the only time Katie had ever heard him speak rudely to his wife. "Let the child explain herself, for God's sake! What crime has she committed? She borrowed a book and hid it under her mattress." Then, turning to Katie, he spoke in gentle tones. "Now, tell us, Katie, why you want the book and why you didn't ask me for it directly."

"I've never been to school," Katie answered tremulously, "but I taught myself my numbers and I memorized the times tables. Now I want to learn to read. Della taught me the alphabet. Now I want to try to figure out how the letters go together."

Warren giggled. Silenced with a glance from his father, he went on laughing soundlessly.

"But why the Civil War, Katie?" Mr. John asked. "Or did you know it *was* the Civil War?"

Janet frowned. She was fuming at the exasperating interview.

"Yes, sir, I knew." She cast her eyes down at the Aubusson carpet. "On Mardi Gras Day, the Confederate soldiers rode in the parade." She swallowed. "Someone said they had fought in the Civil War. I wanted to know more about it."

Warren turned toward her and smiled knowingly. Had he seen her with Stephen on the gallery? Had he told anyone? Katie knew he would love nothing more than to see her dismissed. Perhaps he was saving it up, for a time when it would serve him better.

Mr. John clasped his hands behind his back and strode the carpet.

"Very commendable, Katie," he said when she had finished. "Everyone should try to better himself." He pressed his handlebar mustache with his thumb and forefinger as he sought his wife's narrowed eyes. Then he noticed the smirk on Warren's face. "I think it might be a good idea if Warren gave you an hour a day of his time, to help you with your reading. He seems to have time enough to spare."

"Oh, no, sir," Katie begged. "I'll get along just fine. And I don't need the book. I'm very sorry I borrowed it. It won't happen again."

She longed to leave the room. She felt herself close to tears, and she would die before crying in Warren's presence. She despised his scorn, and she would never give him the satisfaction of shaming her.

"On the contrary, I think it *should* happen again," Mr. John said. "I personally give you free access to this library. It's the one room in the house I consider mine, so I have the right, I think. Please help yourself. And Warren is to come to your room at eight o'clock each night to instruct you in phonetic reading, until you are able to show me you can sound out any passage I present to you. Then I will know you can read anything."

"Thank you, Mr. John," she said. Her voice was that of a little girl, hurt and then consoled. She would have preferred physical punishment to Warren's company, but apparently she had no choice.

"John," his wife interjected, "have you lost your mind?" She looked from Warren to Katie, her mouth a thin, tight line. "If you recall, we were discussing the advisability of sending Katie home . . ."

"Oh, no!" Katie cried out instinctively.

". . . where perhaps she should have gone long ago. I don't know how I got into all this."

"I think you were exercising a bit of *noblesse oblige* that morning, my dear," he said wryly, "and for once it did someone *else* good."

Janet stood and looked at her husband with venom.

"No, I think we'll keep Katie around for a while," he said. "I like the way she cooks. Go on now, Katie, and have your dinner. Warren will be up for your lesson at eight."

Warren stood in her doorway, arms folded, head cocked, mouth drawn to one side. She had opened the door to his knock, jarred out of a fitful, uneasy nap. She had not expected to fall asleep, after the scene that had just taken place, but she was exhausted after the long day that had begun before dawn.

Still in a torpor, and disgruntled by the prospect of an hour with Warren, she waved him into the room. Where were they to sit? she asked herself. There was only one chair and the bed. Why had Mr. John suggested *her* room? Why not the kitchen or the parlor? No doubt, he was directing them away from his wife's attention. Shrugging her shoulders, she sat on the bed, close to the light of the lamp. Making a face, Warren sat beside her.

He had brought chalk and a slate, which he rested on his knee. Then he began what was obviously a painful assignment. This gave her satisfaction, but she decided to pay close attention and graduate herself in record time.

Warren turned out to be a capable teacher. He started with the phonetic pronunciation of each of the letters in the alphabet, and when she had repeated them several times, proceeded to vowels and consonants, and the long and short vowel sounds.

"Next time, I'll give you some rules, about when a vowel is short and when it's long," he said. He took his watch from his pocket and opened the case. "Time's up," he said.

Katie repressed a laugh. He was a replica of his father with his pocket watch. The only thing he couldn't do like his father was groom his mustache with his thumb and forefinger. Oh, he thought himself so grand!

Before she could gather her thoughts, Warren put his slate and chalk on the bed beside him. He reached over and cupped Katie's full round breast with his left hand and took a firm hold of her buttocks with his right. He pushed her back onto the bed and rolled over on top of her and kissed her. In an instant she could feel the hardness of his manhood pressed against her body. She was astounded, caught off guard. At first she wanted to laugh, but she felt smothered by the weight of his body. She thought he had always hated her. So it was lust, nothing more, the same kind of lust her father had had for Theresa.

Suddenly she reached out for the slate, and, with a strength she did not know she had, struck him across the side of the head. Looking up into the face so close to her own, she saw his eyelids close, and she felt his hands go limp. Slowly his body slipped off hers and slid down to the floor, and he rolled backward to a sitting position against the wall. Dear God! she thought—I've killed him.

In no more than a minute Warren moaned and put his hand to his head. He pinched his eyebrows together, and finally he opened his eyes.

"You damned little witch," he said in a menacing whisper.

"Get out of here, Warren," she said evenly.

"Not yet, I won't," he said, standing up. "I have to come teach you, and believe me, I'm finding it pretty damn difficult . . . Now, you just better do what I say, or I'll get you shipped back to that tenement you came from."

"How're you gonna do that?" she asked. "Your father wants me here."

"I'll tell him about you and Stephen holding hands on the balcony on Mardi Gras."

Katie's eyes narrowed with anger. She had not been this angry when Warren had touched her and insulted her, because he meant nothing to her. But Stephen! Just the name aroused a feeling that made her skin flush. This little beast had seen them together, just as she suspected, and he would use it against her. And if Janet Eagan ever had reason to believe her son was fond of her servant girl, it would mean the end of her employment, and there would be nothing Mr. John could do about it.

"Let me tell you something, Warren," Katie said. She stood up, too, to give her words more force. "You might tell your mother, and you might get me fired, but before I go, I'll let your father know that you grabbed at me and tried to have your way with me, and I hate to think what your life will be like after that."

Warren continued to breathe heavily, but he did not answer.

"And I'll tell you something else," she added with her hands on her hips. "You're going to teach me to read, whether you like it or not, you little weasel, because I *have* to learn. And if you don't come every night, I'll tell your father what you tried to do. So you see, the quicker you teach me, the better for both of us. And don't ever put your hands on me again."

Warren stomped out of the room, his anger inflamed, his passion unquenched, and his attraction to Katie taking on frightening new dimensions. Although she resented Warren's audacity and his intention of "using" her, she had nevertheless responded to his kiss, and this confused and upset her. He had threatened to tell his parents about Katie and Stephen. Could it be that he was jealous and wouldn't admit it? Maybe he didn't even realize it himself.

Katie had difficulty sleeping that night.

Chapter
TWELVE

Spring arrived overnight as it usually did in New Orleans. One day it was cold and damp; the next day the sun rose hot in a clear blue sky, and everyone knew that winter was over.

Just as quickly as spring had come, summer would follow. In a week windows would be open all over the city, perspiration would be rolling, and the sound of palmetto fans swatting the air would drift toward the *banquettes* from galleries all along the avenue.

One morning a bluebird skittered along Katie's windowsill. She threw the window open, frightening the bird into flight. The smell of new grass and rosebuds rushed up to greet her, and Katie filled her lungs with the fragrance.

Robins and bluebirds sat in rainbow patterns along the gutters of the eaves, on eye level with Katie's garret window. Sparrows chittered on the roof of the carriage house and argued on the rim of the birdbath.

It was so good to know that spring had come. Lent had been cold and rainy, with fasting and abstinence the order of the household. Breakfast and lunch were mere collations, with meat at the main meal only. For almost six weeks there had been no bacon or sweetbreads on the buffet at breakfast, or fried fresh yard eggs like golden suns. Katie missed the beignets, those crisp doughnut squares powdered with confectioner's sugar. She had become accustomed to having them with her coffee. Dry toast and coffee didn't satisfy the appetite she had acquired since her arrival at the Eagans'.

But the end of Lent meant something more to Katie. The Easter holidays meant that Stephen would be coming home for four full days. Della would cook his favorite dishes, and his mother would cater to his every wish.

Katie was light-headed with anticipation. She was not foolish enough to think that Stephen returned her feelings; a man like Stephen could have his pick of all the beautiful, rich society girls. In her daydreams she could still feel the touch of his fingers against her throat as he slipped the strings of carnival beads over her head. Her pulse raced, and she lost her breath remembering.

Such happiness was new to Katie. On Julia Row she had known little moments of quiet contentment, when she quilted with her mother in the evening or walked to market on a sunny day, but this was a kind of joy that coursed through her body like a current, making her giddy, giving her endless vitality.

She closed the window, made her bed, and skipped down the steps to breakfast. By the end of the week he would be home. All she asked was to look at him, and that would be enough. She was exhilarated. She felt as if she could cook for an army. She could scrub every wall in the house. She was tireless. Stephen was coming home!

She attacked the breakfast dishes with a vengeance, singing an old skip-rope favorite of her sisters', giving competition to the birds at the kitchen window.

"My, my, somebody sho' is happy t'day!" Della remarked. "Whut song is dat you singin'?"

"It's a little song my sisters used to sing when they jumped rope in the yard." She hung the dish towel on the rack and came to sit beside the black woman. "I miss them so much, Della. Seeing them once a week is so little. I used to dress them and walk them to school, and help Mama wash them at night. And we all three slept in the same bed. I was more of a mother to them than Mama was."

"An yo' brothers, you miss dem, too?" Della asked.

"I miss seeing them, and the noise and commotion, but they were so independent, you know how boys are. They never let anybody help them."

"I don' know 'bout dat," Della said, picking up a potato. "Now Master Stephen, he don' want nobody to wait on him, 'cause he's jes' too sweet. He rather wait on *dem*." She stopped and looked at Katie. "But dat other one"—she pointed to the front of the house with the potato—"he let you carry him down Canal Street on yo' back."

Katie giggled. She picked up a potato, found a knife in the kitchen-table drawer, and proceeded to help Della.

"How you gittin' on wit de readin' lessons, honey?" Della asked.

"Oh, fine. We had to get a few things straight at first, but since we understand each other, we're really making progress."

Katie smiled to herself. Ever since she had whacked Warren's head, their relationship had been exemplary. He had had a classroom desk, one that had been stored away in the attic, moved into Katie's room. He had also managed to find a floor lamp which gave her more light to read by. Now, at eight each evening, he knocked at her door, then, with Katie at the desk, and Warren in the straight-back chair beside her, the lesson would begin.

Warren was very bright and a born teacher. He seemed to be of a mind with Katie about one thing: the sooner he taught her to read, the sooner she could demonstrate to his father that she could sound out words, the sooner the lessons would end. Not that it had been all *that* disagreeable, she admitted to herself. She had worked very hard, and it was gratifying to see such speedy results. She knew that he was still physically aware of her; she caught him sometimes staring into her eyes or sweeping her body in a glance, but she knew that he would never touch her again.

Spring cleaning began on Monday of Holy Week. Katie was glad to be occupied so that the days would not drag until Easter. On Wednesday afternoon Katie heard Stephen's voice in the corridor.

"Mother! Della!" he called out.

"Stephen!" Janet exclaimed. "My darling! Your father and I were going to come for you. We were waiting for your call."

"It was easy to get a ride," Stephen answered. "Everybody was going home. How are you, Mother?"

Katie could picture him kissing his mother and embracing her.

"I'm fine, darling," Janet said. "Put your things down. How about some tea?"

"Yes. Good. Let me go tell Dad hello. Is he upstairs in the bedroom?"

Sounds in the corridor were muffled then. Janet was talking to Charlotte who had come home at noon for the beginning of Easter holidays. Katie heard Stephen running up the stairs to greet his father.

The ringing of Janet's little bell made Katie start. She suddenly realized that she'd have to carry the tea tray. She was shaking so, she'd be sure to drop something. Janet always did her own pouring, but the cups and things had to be assembled and brought into the dining room.

If only Della were there! Della had gone to visit a friend who worked across the avenue. Treece was in her room above the carriage house. Katie would have run to get her, but there wasn't time. Janet liked her summons answered promptly. Katie pressed her cool fingers to her flaming cheeks, smoothed her apron, and walked into the dining room.

"Katie," Janet said, "get the tea things. There'll be four of us. Master Stephen is home. Oh, and we'll have it over by the window. Put the tray on the marble-top table."

"Yes, ma'am," Katie said, blushing and trembling.

Trying to restrain her emotions, Katie carried the silver tea tray from the pantry to the kitchen. She put a pot of water to boil, cut lemons in wedges and poured cream into the silver pitcher. Mrs. Eagan would want the good china, which meant another trip to the dining room. Heart thumping, she peeked into the dining area and, finding it momentarily deserted, raced to the china closet for the things she needed. Back in the kitchen, she completed her preparations. Then, like an answer to a prayer, Treece walked into the kitchen from the back gallery.

"Oh, Treece! Thank God you're here!" Katie said, brushing a strand of hair from her forehead. "I want you to take this tea tray into the dining room when Miss Janet rings again. Put it on the table by the window."

"Oh, no! I ain't never served tea befo'," Treece objected.

"You don't have to *serve* it, silly," Katie snapped. "Just carry it out there. Miss Janet does her own pouring." She looked at the tray. "Dear God, have I forgotten anything?"

"Whut's de matter wit you, Katie? You looked all flustrated."

"Never mind," Katie answered. "I'd better fix a dish of lady fingers. Everyone's fasting, but anyway . . ." She arranged the cakes on a china plate.

The bell rang and Katie let out a little cry. Treece looked at her quizzically and shook her head.

"Well, go on, Treece," Katie said, "before she comes in here to see what's keeping us."

Katie followed Treece as far as the pantry and listened at the door. She said a prayer that Treece wouldn't drop the pot of tea in Mrs. Eagan's lap. She heard Stephen's voice, and she found herself breathing so fast, she was threatening to black out.

"The math exam was the hardest," Stephen was telling his father. "Physics was easy, and French, well . . ."

The Eagan children all spoke French fluently. Della had told Katie that Janet's mother spoke nothing but French till the day she died, and the children conversed with her in French from the time they were toddlers.

"I wish you knew German that well," Mr. John was saying. "It would be a big help when you get to Europe."

Europe! Stephen was going to Europe! Katie wondered when and hoped frantically that it wouldn't be soon.

"Anyway, it's a relief to have those quarterlies behind me. It won't be long now before it's all over."

Katie opened the pantry door a crack and watched the family gathered around the tea table. Treece had managed to set the tray on the table without dropping it. Stephen was sitting with his back to the pantry.

"Hello, Treece," Stephen said. "It *is* Treece, isn't it?"

"Yassah, Master Stephen. Treece. Das it." She giggled.

Katie watched Janet tighten her lips over her teeth. Janet did not subscribe to chitchat with servants, especially when it interrupted family conversation.

"Where's Katie?" Stephen asked.

Katie's heart gave one giant thud. Feeling faint, she lowered herself to a chair.

"Do you know Katie?" Janet asked, astounded.

"Of course," Stephen said, popping a lady finger into his mouth. "She was here when I came home for Mardi Gras. Is she still working here?"

"Yes," Janet said, frowning disapprovingly. "She's still here."

It was the only time that day that Katie saw him, and then only the back of his head. But it was enough. He had asked for her! He remembered her! He was in the same house she was in, and everything had taken on a brighter color, a sharper line, a whole new freshness. She kept out of the family's way, remaining in the kitchen and her bedroom.

On Good Friday she caught a glimpse of him from the gallery outside the kitchen. The family was leaving in the carriage to visit the St. Roch Cemetery for the outdoor Way of the Cross. He was dressed in a suit and tie, and his dark hair was neatly combed. She studied every detail of his appearance, so that the glimpse would be enough to last her until summer. She would take no more chances trying to see him again. She would be mortified if they came face-to-face and she acted like an idiot. Besides, Mrs. Eagan might see her behavior and recognize it for what it was.

On Easter Saturday morning Katie left her kitchen prison with a basket of cuttings she had brought from her mother's spice garden. She wanted to get them into the ground before they died. There was thyme, rosemary, marjoram, and mint. She had always wanted a spice garden here, to use for her own cooking. All morning long she had not seen Stephen. She decided he had probably gone to visit friends, and it was safe to do her gardening. She skipped down the steps and into the garden beside the carriage house.

It was a glorious day, all blue sky and bright sun. The air was cool and invigorating. Looking around, she discovered a small corner of the yard that had not been planted and knelt in the grass before it. She hummed as she worked, scooping out little mounds of soil with an old spoon and placing her precious cuttings in the holes.

Suddenly she was aware that Stephen was standing beside her. She saw the tennis shoes first, then the grease-stained trousers. Her eyes traveled up the height of him, almost afraid to come to the face, for fear that it would be gleaming with a great, white light.

"Katie! I'm glad to see you!" he said. "Where in the world have you been?"

She looked up into his eyes, like a swimmer taking his first cold plunge of the season. He was smiling broadly and his hair was tousled and falling over his forehead. He was wearing a work shirt and holding some kind of tool in his hand.

"I've been in the kitchen, working," she managed to answer. She knew that her cheeks were scarlet, but all in all she felt that she was holding herself together pretty well.

He sat down on the grass beside her. "Well, you shouldn't make yourself so scarce. I like talking to you. We had such a fine time on Mardi Gras. Remember?"

"Yes, we did."

Did she remember? Did he want her to tell him how the weather was, how many people were on the porch, every word he had said, what he was wearing that day?

"What are you doing there?" he asked, nodding toward the garden.

"Planting spice plants," she said, smiling. "My mother has a spice garden in her yard. She uses them for cooking. I thought I'd like to do that here."

He smiled. He raised one knee and laced his fingers around it.

"You look like a storybook character, in your checked dress and apron, planting your spices. Mary, Mary, quite contrary." He chuckled. He watched her, fascinated. The sun was shining on her blue-black hair, and her cheeks were like roses in bloom.

"Are you contrary, Little Mary?" he asked.

"Sometimes," she said. She sat back on her heels and smiled. "And what are *you* doing, all greased up like a mechanic?" she asked, surprised at her own boldness. Something about the way he talked to her relaxed her inhibitions.

"Trying to fix Charlotte's car. I think I've found the

trouble. That's what I really am, you know. A mechanic. A tinker, like my father."

"A tinker?" Katie asked, going back to her planting.

"Yes. Of course, I'm paying myself a compliment, saying I'm like my father. But some day, hopefully, I'll invent something, or improve on some other invention. That's what a tinker does. He tries to figure out what makes things work, how they're put together, and if they could be put together better." He smiled. "That's what Mr. Edison is."

"Did your father really know him well?" Katie asked.

"Oh, yes. They worked together for ten years at Menlo Park. My father stayed with him until the Central Station in New York turned on the city's electricity. Then he came home to try to get a franchise for the Edison Electric Company in New Orleans."

"And did he?"

"He certainly did. My father's still on the board. So is Mr. Edison, but he never comes here. I've never met him myself."

Stephen watched Katie patting the tiny mounds around her plants.

"Why didn't you get a trowel out of the carriage house, and a pair of garden gloves?" he asked.

"I didn't know there *were* any," she said. "Besides they aren't mine to use."

"I should think you could use whatever you like, if it would make your job easier. By the way, how's Lala?"

Katie couldn't believe it. He had remembered her baby sister's name. Their time spent together on Mardi Gras had had meaning for him, so she wasn't the only one who had treasured it.

"That's nice of you to remember her," Katie smiled up at him. "Lala's fine, and so are the others."

She patted the last mound of soil with her fingertips. She brushed her hands off and got up. She stooped down to retrieve her basket, and when she stood up again, she was looking into Stephen's eyes. He was much too close for comfort. Hastily she started to walk toward the house, with Stephen close behind.

"Don't go," he said. "I'm afraid I won't see you again while I'm here."

He caught her by the elbow as they reached the stairs.

"You probably won't," she said. "I stay in the kitchen, mostly."

He didn't answer. Giving in to a compulsion she could not deny, she turned and looked into his eyes. They were so deep and dark and green, with flecks of brown. Her eyes traveled over the deep, delicious cleft in his chin. She wanted to touch that face, to place her finger in the cleft. She loved him, more the pity for her. Her heart was bruised with joy and pain, so tightly intermingled that she could not tell one from the other. She wanted to drink in the sight of him, to keep it and hold it forever.

Stephen watched the dark doe eyes studying him. What a refreshing and adorable girl she was, so innocent and natural and free of affectation. How different from the spoiled, self-centered girls he'd always known! She was like a storybook child, indeed, who had come to life in his very own home while he was away.

He looked down at his hand and realized that he was still holding her arm. He didn't want to let her go. They locked eyes again, with a depth of feeling he had seldom known before. A vibration passed between them, sweet and unmistakable.

Recovering herself, Katie looked about her with that frightened look Stephen had seen the first night he met her.

"I have to go now," she said. She slipped away from him and rushed up the stairs to the sanctuary of her kitchen.

Chapter
THIRTEEN

"Well, Stephen's college days will soon be over," Janet said at the dinner table one evening. "What we ought to do, John, is have everything ready to go to camp before the commencement exercises. Then, as soon as graduation is over, we can all leave for Milneburg. Oh, I'm really looking forward to it this year."

There was a chorus of agreement as Katie pushed the swinging door into the kitchen.

"Della, what's Milneburg?" she asked.

"Oh, dat's where de family got dere camp. It's on Lake Pontchartrain, on the outskirts of town. Dey spends dey vacations dere, Miz Janet an' de chirren. Mr. John, he just goes out on weekends."

"Is a camp like a house, Della?"

"It *is* a house," Della said. "Dey got a big po'ch runs clean aroun' de place. An it's always cool in summer, 'cause it's right on de lake, wheah de breezes kin knock you down. Dey got rockin' chairs lined up on de po'ch facin' de lake, an' dey all sits dere an' watches de sun go down. I *mean*, it's purty, fo' a summer house."

"You mean, it belongs to the Eagan family?" Katie asked, surprised that one family could own more than one house.

"Sho' nuff. Dey got fo' bedrooms an' a gret big kitchen an' a livin' room wit cahd tables. Only two things wrong in de country. Miskeeters an' slop jars. De winders ain't screened lak city houses, an' ev'ry bed hafta have a miskeeter net, or you jes' git bit up alive."

"I'm surprised Mrs. Eagan goes there," Katie said, thinking aloud.

"Oh, she love it," Della said. "Evah since she was a li'l girl. Dis her father's camp. Course, he daid now, *long* time. When she git dere, she put on a bathin' dress an' cap an' some li'l rubber shoes, jes' lak the young folks, an' she has de time o' her life. Dey all does. Dey goes swimmin' off de beach, an' dey ketch crabs an' fishes off de pier." Della finished scouring a frying pan and put it in the dish drainer. "Sometimes dey has crab boils out on de beach, or wiener roasts. An' dey plays ball out dere, wit a net Mr. John puts up."

Katie listened. She sat with her elbows on the table, resting her chin in her hands. "Do you go, Della?" she asked.

"Oh, sho'. Ah cooks an' cleans an' sweeps out sand every day. An' dey's always de slop jars to do." Della smiled. "Das mah vacation," she added.

It was hard for Katie to tell how Della really felt about that. Did the remark convey a kind of cynicism no one ever saw in Della? Or did she really appreciate the chance to get away? This was the only vacation she ever had, sitting out there on the porch at Milneburg, watching the sunset. The Eagans were her only family.

"Where do you sleep over there?" Katie asked. She had never gotten used to Della's exile in the servants' quarters.

"Dey lets me sleep on de po'ch," Della said. "Dey ain't but one house."

Big of them, Katie thought. She wondered if *she*'d go to Milneburg, too. The thought of seeing Stephen every day was so overwhelming that she felt dizzy. But if she was not needed there, she wouldn't get to see him for three long months. She decided not to ask anyone. She couldn't bear to know the answer.

In the first week of May Katie took up her courage and asked Warren to tell his father she would read for him that night. All day she practiced reading while Della did the cooking. She read the morning paper from front to back. She read an old magazine she had found in the carriage house. She read instructions that had come with the meat grinder. She read big print and small print, captions beneath pictures and even Della's grocery list. By five o'clock in the evening she felt as if her eyes would cross if she read another word.

She was glad there was supper to fix and a table to set to get her mind off the ordeal that lay ahead. At last the dishes were done, and Katie sat in the kitchen, waiting for Warren to come for her. She had not eaten a bite.

"Katie," Warren called out, coming through the swinging door. Katie jumped and let out a little cry.

"What's the matter?" he asked. "He's not going to eat you up."

"I know," she said.

Warren sat beside her at the kitchen table. "I want to tell you something," he said. "It's about that first night I came to your room. I'm sorry I acted like such a rat."

"That's okay," Katie said self-consciously. She twisted the tendril of hair in front of her ear. "You made up for it since."

"No, it was pretty low of me. Not only what I did, but some of the things I said. I guess I was just showing off, being a smart aleck."

Katie shrugged. She didn't know what to answer.

Warren looked at her and smiled, and for the first time she noticed his dimples.

"You sure knew how to take care of yourself," he said. "I feel sorry for the guy who tangles with you."

Katie laughed. "I grew up in a tough neighborhood," she said.

"Well, I'm sorry if I hurt your feelings, Katie," he said. "You're a real smart girl. You learned how to read like a whiz. I really mean it."

Katie beamed. "Thank you, Warren."

"I hope we can be friends."

"Sure," Katie said. "That'll be nice."

"Well, come on, then. Dad's waiting."

Katie dragged herself up out of her chair and followed Warren to the library.

John Eagan was sitting in the Morris chair, his pipe between his teeth, reading the evening paper. Janet looked up when Katie entered, giving the girl a cold, detached stare over her pince-nez, then returning to her needlepoint. The screen she was working on was stretched across a large frame on a stand, and Janet sat before it, on a high cane-back chair.

Katie curtsied. She felt as if her heart would come through her chest.

"Well, Katie," Mr. John said. "Warren tells me you're reading very well, and there's no more need for lessons. Do you agree?"

"Yes, sir." She curtsied again.

"For goodness sake, stop curtsying," Janet said. "You're giving me motion sickness."

"I've marked a passage in the Bible," Mr. John said. "I'd like you to read it for me."

"Yes, sir." This time she did not curtsy.

He handed her the volume and she saw the passage he had penciled off.

"Now Jesus," Katie began to read, "full of the Holy Spirit, returned from the Jor-dan, and was led by the Spirit about the . . . des*sert* . . . ?"

"*Des*ert," Mr. John corrected.

"*Des*ert," Katie repeated. ". . . for forty days, be-ing temp-ted the while by the devil. And he ate nothing those days; and when they were com-ple-ted, he was hungry."

"Excellent, Katie, excellent," Mr. John commented.

Katie smiled and her eyes were shining. Warren was smiling, too. He was proud of his student. She was so pretty, he thought, blushing that way, with her long black lashes and her shiny hair.

"Why, you've learned in two months what it takes a student three or four years to accomplish," Mr. John went on.

"Well, after all, John, she's fifteen years old," Janet said. "That *has* to make a difference."

"I don't care. She's a very bright girl, and she should have a reward."

He rose from his chair and walked over to the bookshelf, where he withdrew a volume with his finger. It was the book about the Civil War that Katie had taken without permission on that terrible night.

"I'm giving you this book, Katie," Mr. John said. "It was the one you wanted to read. You *can* read now, and it's yours. If you need help, I'm sure your teacher, here, will be glad to come to your aid." He patted her on the head.

"Really, John!" Janet remarked. "Reward, indeed!"

Katie did not care what Janet said. She had learned to live with her remarks. She could read, and she had a book of her own, given to her by Mr. John. She would learn about the Civil War and the Confederates, and Stephan would soon be home. Her heart felt near to overflowing.

"You may leave now, Katie," Mr. John said, seeing the child's awkwardness. He smiled.

"Oh, before you go," Janet said to Katie.

Katie had turned to leave. She spun back around. Her skin tightened.

"Stephen's class will be graduated on June seventh. The family will attend. We will all be packed to leave for our summer camp in Milneburg, where we'll be spending the summer. I'm sure Della told you about it."

"Yes, ma'am," Katie said.

"Well. Della will be coming with us, as always," Janet said, not looking at Katie but squinting through her glasses at her needlepoint. "I would like you to be here. You and Treece. Treece will clean house and you will cook, and I'll know that Mr. John is well cared for during the week. He'll join us there on weekends." She turned to look at Katie to see what effect her words had had. "Do you think you can manage that?"

"Yes, ma'am."

Katie left the room. She did not remember leaving or climbing the stairs to her room. She was surprised to find herself sitting on her bed, with the book still tucked under her arm. She undressed herself, slipped into her nightgown, and began undoing her braids as the tears rolled down her cheeks. She would not be with Stephen at all this summer. She would be here, all alone. "All alone" had taken on a whole new meaning for Katie. Now it meant "without Stephen." She turned out her light and slipped beneath her quilt.

For hours she watched her feet in the shaft of moonlight from her garret window. At last the pain in her heart eased as fatigue won out, and she fell asleep.

Chapter FOURTEEN

Just as the family was about to start dinner, the doorbell rang, again and again, insistently, and as Katie carried the meat dish to the buffet, she could hear a man's voice calling her name. It was more of a cry than a call. The voice was pleading, anguished, muffled, like the strangling sound of a man in pain. Katie was paralyzed with fear.

"What on earth . . . ?" Janet said, a frown pinching her eyebrows.

John put down his napkin on the table, pushed out his chair, and walked down the corridor.

"You want me to git dat, Mr. John?" Della asked.

"No, Della. You'd better let me see . . ." His voice trailed off and his steps quickened. Charlotte and Janet followed cautiously, and Katie trailed behind them. When the leaded-glass door was opened, Katie could see through the wrought-iron gate of the vestibule the tall figure of her father. She grabbed onto Della to stop herself from falling.

"Where's Katie?" Joseph Raspanti asked.

"Tell him to go around the back, John," Janet snapped irritably. She turned to walk back to the dining room.

"Good God, Janet," John said, "the man's distraught. Can't you see that?" Turning back to Joe Raspanti, John asked, "What can we do for you, sir?"

He opened the gate and let the man into the vestibule.

"My daughter. She work here. Katie Raspanti. She gotta come home."

Suddenly Katie's heart leaped in her throat. Something had happened to her mother! She ran down the corridor and into the vestibule. She grabbed her father's arm. "Is it Mama?" she asked, her voice breaking on the question.

"No," he said. "Not your mama. It's Little Joe."

"What about him?" she shouted.

"He's dead." The big man sobbed aloud. *"Mòrto!"* he cried.

"Dead? He can't be. How can he be dead? What happened?"

Katie was crying too, but she released her hold on her father.

"He drown in the river," Joe Raspanti said. "Your mama, she always tell the boys, 'Don't swim in the river,' but still, they go. He dive from the dock, he hit his head. He no come back up."

The man's sobs came in convulsions and still Katie did not embrace him. Her own silent tears fell down her cheeks, but she kept her control. She passed back down the corridor, between statuelike Eagans.

"I'm so very sorry, Katie," John said. "I'll have Mason bring the carriage to take you and your father home. If there's anything else we can do . . ."

"Thank you," Katie said, smiling wanly at her employer.

Janet said nothing, considering her husband's condolences sufficient for the family, but her expression had softened. Warren and Charlotte stood aside with respect, to let her by. But it was Della who opened her arms and embraced the child, sobbing with her.

"God gonna take care o' y'all, Katie," she said. "Go on to yo' mama, and remember, Della gonna be prayin' fo' ya."

As if in a dream Katie climbed the stairs to her bedroom. She removed the loose brick and withdrew her stocking of savings. Her parents would have no money for a coffin or a burial place. In a large paper bag she packed her three gingham dresses, underwear, stockings. Back in the corridor she was surprised to find the Eagans exactly where she had left them. They had not returned to the table. They were stunned. Perhaps, in their own cold fashion, they cared.

"Stay as long as you need to, Katie," Janet said. "Your mother will want you home."

Katie was touched by the simple words of kindness.

"I'll have Masses said for your brother," Janet added.

Katie nodded. "Thank you," she said. She bit her bottom lip.

The ride home in the barouche was interminable. Katie and her father did not speak. From time to time a sigh, broken by sobs, came from one or the other. Katie tried to bring her brother's face into focus, the dark curly hair, the fair skin and large dark eyes so much like her own. He had been mischief incarnate, but he had loved his mother and been affectionate, and that made him very special to Katie. She pictured the child when his body was brought to the surface, his face blue and drawn from the final bursting effort to keep on breathing, to keep on living. How he must have suffered! She cried aloud.

Instinctively Big Joe raised his arm to enfold his daughter, but she saw the move and pulled away from him. Joe's eyes narrowed. He would not beg her to share his grief. She hated him, for what he did not know. There was much to hate, he admitted to himself, but Katie knew nothing of that.

He glanced at the silhouette of his daughter, outlined against the streetlight at the corner. He could not believe his eyes. Her body had softened into that of a woman. She looked like Frances when he first knew her. In a few short months her small frame had taken on curves and contours. She had responded to the news with maturity, too. Joe had been proud of his daughter.

When the carriage turned into the service alley, Katie jumped down without waiting for Mason to stop and ran to the Raspanti apartment. Dropping her things in the bedroom, she rushed to her mother, who was sitting in a rocking chair in the kitchen. She looked so small and sad, her face resting in her hand, her elbow on the rocker's arm.

"Mama," Katie whispered.

She knelt beside the woman she loved so dearly and put her arms around her. She felt her mother's arms trembling as they enclosed her. She felt the body in her arms rocking with deep, heartrending sobs.

"Katie! He's gone! Little Joe, he's gone!" The tears streamed down her cheeks.

For the longest time mother and daughter cried together and held each other close. At last, strength gone, they sobbed softly and wearily, letting their cries die away in the lonely kitchen.

"Where are the kids?" Katie asked, drying her eyes and blowing her nose.

"Miz Macaluso, she got the girls. Davey, he went to stay with Father Rafferty."

Frances began to talk, then, finding comfort in relating the events to her daughter, and Katie was able to piece the story together.

When Little Joe had failed to surface after diving off the Jackson Street Wharf, a dock worker had rushed to the scene, attracted by the commotion of a group who had gathered there. The man went under the water again and again until he found the boy's body, wrapped around a piling, held fast against it by the current. He dragged the child to the surface and stretched him out on the dock, where he tried to revive him, pressing his ribs to expel the water. But it was too late.

Big Joe Raspanti came soon after, alerted by the other teamsters. He lifted the child in his arms, bellowing his anguish like a wounded bull, crying aloud and rocking the boy in his arms. The rescuer called the police, and the body was taken home in a police wagon to his mother.

A simply funeral had been arranged, and a burial in a Catholic cemetery for the indigent. The body, laid in a wooden coffin, would be slipped into one of the long rows of aboveground receptacles called "ovens." It was a tenement for the dead. Even for the poor, the law forbade burial in the moisture-laden grounds. The priest had called on the undertaker and returned with him to Julia Row to remove the body, so that it might be prepared for burial.

At eight o'clock Father Rafferty and the undertaker brought Little Joe's body home. Katie gasped when she saw him, daubed with stage makeup to give him back the color of life, and rouged to simulate health. It was absurd! Little Joe had never had rosy cheeks in his life. His life! His life was over, almost before it had begun! Tears sprang easily to her eyes. Little Joe was dressed in a white shirt with a soft bow tie at the neck. His hair was plastered with pomade. All Katie could do was stand and shake her head, wishing she could wash his face and brush the gel from his hair, make his curls rough-and-tumble, the way they should be. She shivered when she realized the color his skin would be beneath the makeup.

Neighbors began to arrive, each bursting into wails at the sight of the child in the coffin. Then they offered lavish compliments to the family on the way he had been arranged. Katie, it seemed, was the only one who was upset about his appearance. Each neighbor came with a plate of food or a pot of soup or some wine. No one would go home hungry or totally sober.

A florist's wagon pulled up into the service alley. The driver carried a wreath draped with a black crepe, a card with Katie's name tucked into the foliage.

Our sincerest sympathies on your great loss. Both
you and your parents will be in our daily prayers.
The Eagans

The card was taken from Katie's hand and passed
around the congregation, and a murmur of appreciation
followed its progress. With the swelling crowd of mourners, there was so little room in the apartment that Katie left the wreath on its stand in the yard, where it was
duly respected by all.

Katie had pushed the two beds against the same wall
in the bedroom. The coffin was placed on a bier against
the opposite wall, leaving a passageway wide enough
for a line of incoming and outgoing mourners. From the
bedroom the line queued to the kitchen, where Frances
still sat in her rocker. She had not come to look at her
boy in the coffin. She had not had the strength. Each
new visitor brought forth a fresh stream of tears from
the disconsolate woman, and a repetition of the same
story from Big Joe, who lingered in the kitchen near his
wife.

Katie eyed him scornfully. At least he was at her side,
she thought, even if it took his son's death to get him
there. She had nothing but bitter thoughts for her father; even shared grief had not given her compassion.
To her he seemed to be enjoying the role of bereaved
father, narrator, and host. This was a crowd of friends
whom, ordinarily, he had neither the money nor the in-
clination to entertain. He drank as much wine as any of
his guests, and soon, the story of his son's death was
accompanied by boisterous sobs, which elicited hugs
and kisses and words of consolation.

At last the mourners left, and Katie was alone with
her parents. Big Joe had drunk himself into a stupor.
He sat slumped across the kitchen table. Frances remained in her rocker and Katie sat beside her to keep
the vigil with her. From time to time she patted her
mother's hand or kissed her lightly on the cheek. Her

mother neither moved nor spoke. Katie had to kneel to see if her eyes were open or closed.

Once, seeing her awake, she spoke to her.

"Mama, I've learned to read. Did I tell you?" she asked. Frances did not answer. "I'll read to you if you like. Father Rafferty left his missal here for the prayers tomorrow. Maybe if I read some prayers to you, it might help."

Still no answer. Katie sat beside her mother and opened the book to the page the priest had marked with a leather bookmark. She read:

> The Lord is my shepherd; I shall not want. He maketh me to lie down in green pastures: he leadeth me beside the still waters.
> He restoreth my soul: he leadeth me in the paths of righteousness for his name's sake.

Frances sobbed, and Katie put her arm around her mother. She knew her mother did not understand the words, but they had a comforting sound, and her heart was easily tapped.

"Read," Frances said, waving her hand. "Read."

> Yea, though I walk through the valley of the shadow of death, I will fear no evil: for thou art with me, thy rod and thy staff they comfort me.

Frances buried her head in her daughter's shoulder and cried, and Katie cried, too.

The neighbors accompanied the family to the cemetery, though they all had to ride in the streetcar after Requiem Mass at St. Patrick's. The sun beat down mercilessly on the black-clad group following the coffin down the narrow paths of the graveyard. Father Rafferty led the way, with Davey, serving as altar boy, both wearing cassocks and white surplices. The sweat rolled in streams down the boy's face, mingling with his tears.

At a corner of the cemetery the priest stopped and motioned the pallbearers toward a niche in the wall that had been opened in preparation for the burial. Into the black hole went the wooden box, scraping along the brick edges.

A cry of exquisite pain went up from Frances, and the women moaned aloud in anguish. Big Joe put his arm around his wife, and Katie stooped over to take Jenny and Lala in her arms. Davey handed the holy-water vessel to the priest.

A wooden door was used to close the vault. Father Rafferty took the sprinkler from the vessel and swung his arm three times, showering the burial site.

"May he rest in peace, in the name of the Father, and of the Son, and of the Holy Ghost. Amen."

The crowd turned and slowly left the cemetery. The lone wreath, sent by the Eagans, wilting now from the stifling heat, was set before the grave.

Somehow, in the days that followed, life went on for the Raspantis. Big Joe left early for work each day. Katie made breakfast and sent the children, now on summer vacation, out to play. She cleared the breakfast dishes and planned the supper, discussing meals with her mother as if the stunned and vacant woman were responding. She made beds and cleaned floors, as she knew her mother would have done, in the unbearable heat of the two small rooms, and she did not complain. When there was shopping to be done, she left her mother in Davey's care and took the little girls with her.

Big Joe was always there to lay the mattress early in case Frances wanted to retire. But Katie suggested her mother take Davey's bed, and Davey share the mattress with his father. Two pairs of dark eyes radiated hostility when the suggestion was made, but Katie outstared her father. She had not missed the thickening around her mother's waist, and she dared not address her father, for fear that the words she would say would be words neither of them would ever forget. Frances was to bear him another child, this wronged woman, this vessel of sorrow. The knowledge weighed on Katie's heart like a great immovable stone.

Frances did as Katie said, content not to have to make decisions. By day she sat mutely in her rocking chair, face cupped in hand. By night she lay in her bed in a pool of sweat, not even lifting a hand to fan herself with her palmetto fan. Sometimes Katie awoke at night and fanned her mother, and the woman sighed as the unexpected breeze flowed over her.

Ten days after the funeral the gray barouche pulled into the service alley, and John Eagan descended. Katie was hanging wash in the courtyard when he approached.

"Mr. John," she called out. "Good morning." She smiled for the first time since her brother's funeral.

"Katie, how are you?" he asked.

"I'm well. We're getting along fine."

"And your mother?"

"Not so well, Mr. John."

"Of course. That's natural. It takes time, Katie."

"I wanted to thank you for the flowers. They were the only ones we had."

John Eagan lowered his head for a moment.

"I would have written you a note, but I don't write very well yet. So I waited to tell you in person."

Eagan cleared his throat.

"I came to tell you not to feel you must rush to get back to us," he said. "The family has all gone to the lake house. And I have Treece at home. She can manage very well till you get back."

The family was gone! In her grief and her preoccupation with her mother Katie had forgotten the time. She had let the days go by, and the precious time had passed. The graduation was over! The packing was over! They had gone! Stephen was gone, not to return for three long months. She had missed him altogether!

She swallowed hard and her chin quivered. "How was the graduation?" she asked, trying to pick up the conversation.

"It was fine. Very simple. Not a lot of frills."

She forced a smile. "And they've all packed and left?"

"Yes. Janet and Charlotte went out on the Smoky Mary. It's the only time of the year they ride on a train. Mason and I took the luggage out in the wagons, and Stephen drove Charlotte's car."

Katie looked around. She put the clothespins back in the basket. She felt awkward, as if she should be extending a courtesy, and there was none to offer.

"I'd like to ask you in," she said, not meaning it. She would have died before letting Mr. John see the inside of the apartment. She had not felt that way the first time she brought Janet here and begged her for a job, but she hadn't known then how people like the Eagans lived. "But my mother might be resting," she finished her excuse.

"No apologies, Katie," her employer said kindly. "I just wanted to see how you were, and if you needed anything. Oh!" he said as if remembering a part of the errand he had forgotten. "I have two envelopes for you. One is your pay."

"But I haven't worked," she objected.

"Still, you need your money. Call it vacation, though I know it isn't much of one."

Katie had never been on vacation, so its absence was a matter of indifference to her. The fact was, she had not expected to be paid.

"The other envelope is an offering for your brother. I know how much it hurts to talk about it, but when close friends pass away, it's customary to have Masses said or to send flowers."

"But you've already done that."

He pressed the envelope in her palm and closed her fingers around it.

"This is to help with funeral expenses," John said.

"But . . ."

"Please, Katie, don't be proud. God wants us to help one another. I've grown very fond of you. It would please me very much if you'd let me do this for you."

She nodded. She was not even aware that tears were falling foolishly down her cheeks. John Eagan bent down and kissed the girl on the top of her head.

"Come back whenever you're ready. Your job will be waiting. But don't feel that you must rush on my account."

He squeezed her hand and left the courtyard, and she followed the barouche with her eyes till it was out of sight.

Chapter
FIFTEEN

Katie gave the streetcar conductor a nickel and walked down the aisle to take a seat. The car rocked and shifted on its tracks, and Katie had to grab onto one of the brass handles on the slatted seats. Handle over handle, she pulled herself forward, her shopping bag hanging from her wrist, until at last she slid into a seat at the front of the car.

It was three weeks since her brother's death, and she was returning to her job. Her mother had become dependent on her, and Katie knew that she would not come out of her lethargy until there was no one around to do things for her. Then, too, Mr. John continued to pay her wages, whether she was working or not, and she could not go on accepting his charity indefinitely.

She sat at an open window and let the wind hit her square in the face, taking her breath away, but drying the perspiration at her hairline. What a scorching summer it was going to be! Ninety-three degrees in June! How would they survive when August came? She ran her fingers inside the high neck of her dress. She lifted the bodice away from her body, shaking it lightly so the dampness would evaporate in the breeze.

She felt guilty going back to live in the cool house when her mother and Davey and the girls had to sweat out the summer in the service wing. She closed her eyes, picturing the Eagans' cavernous dining room, the butler's pantry, the huge well-equipped kitchen, the back gallery, the carriage house, and her own garret bedroom, high up in the treetops with the birds. She would have the whole house to herself this summer, just as if she were, indeed, the mistress of the mansion. She experienced a quickening of anticipation with every turn of the trolley's wheels, and a mounting revulsion for the poverty, the odors, and the congestion of Julia Row.

The face of her dead brother came to her as it did at least once a day, to squeeze at her heart and wring out tears. She lowered her head to her hand and sobbed softly into her handkerchief. Then, the companion thought, the heartsickness for her mother, grieving for the child that was gone, as a new one stirred inside her. Predictably the seizure of hatred for her father followed. Oh, why couldn't he leave her mother alone? Weren't things bad enough already, without another baby to nurse and change and make room for?

She had left these heartaches behind to return to the comforts of St. Charles Avenue. And yet it had not been a totally selfish move. Half of everything she earned went to her mother, and the money was badly needed. Katie had spoken privately to Father Rafferty, begging him to accept payment for the niche in the cemetery wall where her brother had been placed, but he had convinced her that the wall was church property intended for the needy, and that her money would be better spent providing for her mother and the children.

She shook her head to clear away all the depressing thoughts and concentrated on the lovely ride down St. Charles Avenue. Azaleas were ablaze in shades of pink and salmon and fuchsia alongside the streetcar tracks in the neutral ground. They grew in thick banks against the mansions which lined the street. Dark green lawns, edged with white impatiens, lay like carpets before the gracious homes. Crape myrtles, in every hue of pink, grew in rows between the houses; and huge oaks, spreading their umbrellas, met high above the avenue, lending a cool, green shade to all the galleries. The area was called the Garden District, and it lived up to its name.

Katie breathed in the perfume of jasmine and sweet olive that saturated the neighborhood. She couldn't help contrasting it to the aroma of roasting coffee and molasses from the sugar refinery that descended heavily on Julia Row. Growing up with the sickly sweet aroma in her nostrils, she had never been aware of it till now.

When the streetcar passed Napoleon Avenue, Katie reached up and pressed the button that rang the conductor's bell. At the corner she stepped down from the car and stood for a moment, after it had passed her by, looking at the Eagan mansion. Tall and white, it stood with its proud columns, its black wrought-iron railings on the double balconies, and its wings curving gracefully to the rear. Oaks and sycamores rose to shelter the house with shade.

She felt proud to be part of such an establishment, even if she were only *in* it, and not *of* it. She shifted her shopping bag, crossed the street, and walked down the carriageway to the back gallery.

She rang the doorbell, and in a moment Treece opened the door. The Negress shouted her welcome and took Katie in her arms, stepping back quickly, embarrassed at her own exuberance, hoping she had not offended the girl.

"Hi, Treece," Katie said, smiling. "It's good to see you."

"It sho' *is* good, Miz Katie!" Treece said.

Katie pinched her mouth. "Since when do you call me 'Miz Katie'? I'm Katie. Just Katie. I work here, same as you. We'll be the only two here all summer, so let's be friends."

She passed by Treece and deposited her belongings on the kitchen table. The long windows were open. She left the porch door open, too, to create a draft.

"Boy, does it feel nice and cool in here!" Katie said.

Treece smiled shyly and stood on one foot, rubbing the other behind it.

Treece was a skinny, light-colored Negro in her middle twenties, with enormous energy and a great desire to please. She "knew her place," according to Janet. She never spoke unless she was spoken to, and she was always cheerful. She lived in the servants' quarters out back, along with Della and Mason. She had been married once, and had a baby, too, but the way Della told it, her husband had left her and the baby had died of "crib death." Katie had asked her what "crib death" was. Della had rolled her eyes and pursed her thick lips. At last she answered: "Crib death is when you put de baby in de crib fo' de night, an' den in de mawnin' he's daid." Katie had let it go at that.

Treece watched as Katie pulled her long apron out of her shopping bag and tied it around her waist. Then, hungry for company, she followed Katie into the pantry, where Katie looked over the supply of staples, and to the icebox, where she found nothing but a lonely head of lettuce and a spotted apple. What on earth had Treece been feeding Mr. John? She didn't ask, but she knew she had to get to market right away, so she could prepare something really special tonight. She checked the drawer in the kitchen cabinet where grocery money was kept. There were several five-dollar bills. Mr. John must have put them there, she thought.

"Where's Mason keeping himself these days?" she asked, counting out the bills with an air of authority.

"He be in de cahage house, groomin' down de hawses. He go back an' fo'th 'tween heah an' Milneburg. He take Mr. John out dere on Fridays."

"Why didn't Mr. John keep Charlotte's car, and take himself back and forth to the camp?"

"Oh, dey need Miz Charlotte's car at de camp, for goin' to de yacht club. Mr. John, he got a sailboat dere."

"You ever been to the camp, Treece?"

"One time, when Della was sick, dey took me. It's real nice. Dey's a big bunch o' camps on stilts like, out over de water? It's all connected like. It look lak a great big spider, de whole thing do. It be real cool at night on de big screen po'ch. Dey swims an' dey crabs an' dey takes de boat out fishin'.'"

Katie thought of Stephen swimming in long even strokes, suntanned and handsome. She could see him standing on the deck of the boat, with white trousers rippling in the wind.

She sighed. "I'm going to ask Mason to drive me to market. We don't even have flour or salt in the pantry, let alone meat and vegetables for supper."

"Think Ah could come along?" Treece asked shyly.

"Don't see why not. There's nobody here to ask, so we'll just do to suit ourselves."

She flashed Treece a smile, full of enthusiasm and warmth. Treece returned the smile. She had one gold tooth in the front, of which she was inordinately proud.

"Ah'll git my shoppin' basket an' my straw hat," she said, and she was off with a burst of energy.

Treece enjoyed the outing. To Katie it had become routine, but Treece rarely left the house, and to her it was a holiday. She was entranced with the colorful display of produce. Katie treated her to a chocolate coconut praline from the Negro mammy, and she thought the girl would have a fit of apoplexy.

"Mornin', mammy," Katie said, fumbling for her change. "Hot, isn't it?"

"Mawnin', Katie. It sho' is!"

Mr. LeGrand greeted Katie by her name at the butcher's stand, and Treece was impressed. On the way home she commented on it.

"Yo' sho' is a big shot in dat mahket," she said. "Katie dis, an' Katie dat. Um-ump, dey sho' do know you."

Katie grinned. How childlike and innocent Treece was to be so pleased over such a simple recognition! She thought about the change that had come over her.

Not long ago a vendor's greeting would have meant a lot to her. But today she felt mature, capable, in control of things, so that she need not ever depend on anyone again.

She had suffered the first great loss of her life when her brother died. She had taken over control of her mother's household at the time of the funeral, cared for the other children, handled the finances, and seen to her mother's comfort. She had met her father eye to eye, not in fear but in defiance, and he had backed down. He knew the reason for her contempt, she was sure, and he had reacted like a chastised child. He had stayed close to home, treated Frances with attention, and done his best to stay in Katie's good grace as long as she was there. This from the father she had feared! It had given her a feeling of power.

Her return to the Eagan household had reinforced her confidence. There, for the rest of the summer, she would be alone with Treece and Mason, and already she could feel that they respected her authority and did not resent her for it.

The weeks slipped by, and Katie was content. She was up early in the morning to fix Mr. John's breakfast. He loved grillades and grits, which took an hour to prepare the way Della had taught her. Sometimes she fixed a simple breakfast of coddled eggs and ham, or pancakes with maple syrup. There was always fresh squeezed orange juice and hot black chicory coffee with boiled milk. This was Creole cooking, which Della had learned as a teen-ager and which she had passed on to Katie.

When Mr. John left for work, Katie and Treece had breakfast, and then went their separate ways, Treece to straighten Mr. John's room, to change his linens or scrub the bathing room on the second floor, Katie to plan the dinner for the evening, to see to the kitchen, the butler's pantry, and the dining room. Katie worked energetically. She was proud of her cooking and took pleasure in embellishing her art. She could now cook French, American, and Italian dishes, and prepare many complicated recipes from memory. Long cooking, like stews and dumplings and gumbos, she did early in the morning, leaving salads for the late afternoon.

Treece's duties included washing and ironing. At the end of the week there were only Mr. John's shirts, but on Sunday nights Mason came back from the camp with a bundle of laundry. For two days Treece was busy at the washtub in the yard, and later in the kitchen, sprinkling and ironing clothes. Katie always gave her a hand, and by Tuesday afternoon, unless it rained, Mason had a wagonload of clean, folded clothes to bring back to the vacationers.

Katie smiled back. She loved to listen to Mr. John. His voice was as mellow as honey. She felt relaxed with him, and she was eager to hear about his childhood.

"The best investment he ever made was in land," Mr. John said. "He bought twenty-five acres of swamp land in Morgan City, and it turned out to be rich in oil. That was the basis of his fortune.

"Well, Katie, here was this energetic little German merchant who thought his son would follow in his foot-steps. He always hoped I would take over his busi-nesses, or that I would be a doctor or a lawyer, some-thing he could brag about to his German friends." He shook his head sadly. "I wasn't any of those things. The day he dragged me home from school, he asked me what I wanted to be. Do you know what I told him?"

"What?"

"A telegraph operator. Can you imagine how he felt? I wish you could have seen the look on his face."

"Why did you want to be that, Mr. John?"

"Well, it wasn't my *real* ambition, but at least it was in a related field. What I *really* wanted to do was to outfit a laboratory in the basement of our home and work all of Faraday's experiments, but I knew my father wouldn't let me do that. I wanted to study things like why electricity produced energy and how sound was transmitted over wire."

"Well, those things must be important, too," Katie said.

"In those days people knew nothing about electricity, Katie. Papa couldn't stand to see me wasting my time doing experiments and daydreaming about things that would never earn me a living. You see, to my father, unless you worked or went to school, you were nothing but a bum. I guess I can understand how he felt, now that I'm older."

"But what about when you met Mr. Edison? He must have been proud of you then."

John laughed. "When I met Edison, he was nothing but a poverty-stricken twenty-year-old telegraph operator, like me."

"He hadn't invented anything yet?"

"Nothing that had been patented. A lot of knick-knacks, like his roach electrocutor." He laughed again.

"Was he living in New Orleans?"

"Just passing through. At least he thought he was passing through. He was on his way to Brazil to string electric wire in the jungle. He and a few friends had bought tickets on a chartered steamer leaving out of New Orleans. It was right after the Civil War." He looked at Katie. "Remember, you wanted to read the book about the Civil War?" Katie nodded. "Did you ever read it?" he asked. She nodded again, though she couldn't bring herself to talk about it; it brought back such bitter memories. "Well, anyway," he continued, "after the South lost the war, some Yankees called car-petbaggers came down here and started making life in-tolerable for the Southerners. A lot of ex-Confederates had already taken their families by boat to Brazil to work on plantations. There were riots every day in New Orleans against the new laws and the new administration. Well, what happened was, the governor seized the chartered ship that Edison was supposed to leave on and used it to bring in federal troops to put down the riots."

Katie felt proud that she knew who the Confederates were, and the Yankees and the carpetbaggers. How wonderful it was to have learned all these things from books!

"So Edison was stuck here in New Orleans, with no money," Eagan went on. "He had to go to work. One day I walked into my office at Western Union and there was this friendly new face. Edison had just been hired to work the transmitter beside me." Eagan smiled. "I didn't know it then, but that was a big day in my life."

"Did he stay here long?"

"Only a few weeks. He kept trying to get another ship. Then word came back from Brazil that the Americans there were facing great danger and hardship. Edison changed his mind and went to New York instead."

"Did you go with him?"

"I wanted to. I knew by then what a genius he was. I wanted to follow him wherever he went, because I knew he was going to do important things. But my father was dying at the time, so I stayed at his bedside. Well, my father passed away. And later, when I wound up his affairs, I joined Edison in New York. In a few years he set up his laboratory in Menlo Park, and I worked with him there for ten years. I was there when the first incandescent lamp burned for forty hours. I helped him lay the mains for the first Central Station in New York. After that I came back to New Orleans."

"What happened to your mother?"

"She died while I was at Menlo Park."

"Were you an only child, Mr. John?"

"Yes. My parents married late in life. My father was almost fifty when I was born, and my mother was forty. They were much too old to understand me, Katie. To them, I was just a rebellious youth, a rich man's son who wouldn't follow his father's guidance."

Katie shook her head sympathetically.

Eagan took his watch from his vest pocket. "My goodness, it's five o'clock. I *have* been bending your ear. There must be something else you wanted to do."

"Oh, no, sir. I wanted to listen to you. If you think of any other stories, please tell them to me. I'm often here in the afternoon."

"I'll remember that, Katie."

On Wednesdays Katie still visited her mother, and Treece took over the cooking chores. But Frances no longer met her at the market, as had been her custom. After Little Joe's death, Katie would find her mother, sitting at the kitchen table, not moving, almost comatose. She had lost weight, and her face was drawn. Her hair was never combed. Katie bit her lip to see her mother sitting there in the heat of the kitchen, not even raising a window shade, as if she knew nothing of heat or cold, as if she had lost all contact with the world. She remembered the cheerful woman, so beloved by all the neighbors, and it broke her heart.

The rain began that summer in July and did not let up until late August. At first it was no more than a shower every afternoon, which was not unusual for New Orleans. Natives were accustomed to the combination of extreme heat and humidity. But rain usually came in a series of showers, followed by a period of drought, when swimmers and golfers took advantage of the sunshine. The summer of 1906 did not follow that pattern. There was only rain, rain, and more rain.

In the afternoons, when their work was done, Katie and Treece played cards at the kitchen table while the rain beat steadily on the windows. They would open the kitchen door that led out onto the back gallery, and the smell of rain on the grass was fresh and astringent. Katie taught Treece to play games her brothers had taught her. Sometimes Katie read aloud to Treece, which usually put the girl to sleep.

Taking full advantage of the library, since neither Janet nor Charlotte was there, she spent every spare moment of her day perusing book titles which stood shoulder to shoulder in the ceiling-high bookcases. And each night in her room she read for hours.

One afternoon, after selecting a book, she was leaving the library deep in thought when she bumped into Mr. John.

"Oh, excuse me, Mr. John," she said. "I wasn't looking."

"It's my fault, Katie," he said, smiling warmly. "Here. Let me see what you're reading these days."

Eagan took the book from her hands and glanced at the title. "*David Copperfield,*" he said with astonishment. "Quite an ambitious project for one so new at reading!"

"Oh?" Katie looked disappointed. "Do you think I shouldn't read it, Mr. John?"

"I don't mean that. But will you understand it, that's the question."

"Well, I read another book by Mr. Dickens," she explained. "*Christmas Carol.*"

"You did? Did you understand the words?"

"Not all of them. Sometimes I'd stop and look them up in the dictionary. But if I was enjoying the story, I'd skip over the words, and I still understood enough."

"Why, that's wonderful, Katie. I'm proud of you. Now, if you can read *David Copperfield*, I'll say you're as good a reader as anyone I know. The main thing is, your interest hasn't flagged. Learning to read wasn't just a whim with you."

"Oh, no, sir. I'm planning to read for the rest of my life."

"Come back into the library, Katie," he said, "and let me show you how my books are arranged."

He guided the girl across the floor to the stacks of

books. Explaining how the books had been grouped according to subject matter, he pointed out the sections on history, politics, science, and physics. Then he came to the section Katie had found all by herself: the novels.

"Have you read them all, Mr. John?" she asked.

"Not all the novels, but most of the others," he said.

"Did you love to read when you were my age?"

John Eagan laughed. "I hated it. I read nothing but physics and science. I thought everything else was a waste of time."

Eagan sat in his Morris chair. "Sit down, Katie," he said.

Katie sat on the hassock at his feet and watched him light a cigar. He took a few puffs, and the room was filled with the aromatic fragrance. Katie inhaled the fine, masculine smell. She waited for Mr. John to speak.

"When I was a boy, I used to read all my textbooks in the first week of the school year. Not because I loved them, but just to get rid of them, so I could spend the rest of the year studying science and physics."

"Did you read those science books in class?" Katie asked.

"Yes, I did." He smiled mischievously, remembering. "Of course, my teachers didn't take too kindly to that. I guess they figured I was addled," he said, touching his forehead. "But they let me alone, just so long as I passed my subjects and didn't annoy the other students."

"But didn't they realize how smart you were, that you could do that?"

Eagan laughed. "I'm afraid they didn't look at it that way." He took a puff on his cigar. "Well, I got away with it all through grammar school. But when it came time to go to high school, it was another matter. In high school you had to conform to the rules, or else you were expelled."

Katie drew in a gasp. Mr. John settled comfortably in his chair, happy to have an attentive audience. It wasn't often that anyone in his household listened to what he had to say.

"The principal called my father into his office. He told him I had been reading other books in class and not paying attention. Well, that very day my father dragged me out of school by the ear, and that was the end of my education."

"Really, Mr. John? I thought you were a college man."

"Oh, no, my dear Katie. I was a terrible disappointment to my father." He blew a smoke ring and gazed through it intently. "When he and my mother came over from Germany, he opened a store near City Park. He imported German food, German clothing, and handmade clocks and novelties. Later he added a restaurant and beer garden. He worked long hours and he saved his money. And then he began investing. He took a trip to Morgan City, Louisiana, and bought an icehouse for servicing shrimp boats and a lumberyard; there were thousands of acres of cypress in the area. Oh, he was quite an entrepreneur. There's a good word for you, Katie," he said, smiling.

Immediately, when she arrived, Katie would begin straightening things, trying to put some organization back into the Raspanti home. Her brother Davey and her sisters spent their days in the street or in the service alley, playing. When they were hungry, they helped themselves to bread and butter or to something left over far too long in the icebox. No one watched over them. No one cared.

For weeks Katie detained Mason on Wednesdays long enough to make a shopping list for her mother's house and take her back to the market. Then, she'd set about cooking and cleaning and putting away groceries. The sweat rolled down her body. Frances's clothes were stuck to her, too, but she seemed not even to notice.

One afternoon, when they were alone in the kitchen, Katie reached out for her mother's hand where it lay on the oilcloth cover. She rubbed the small hand gently, Then she spoke.

"I know your heart is broken, Mama," she said.

Tears brimmed in Frances's eyes.

"But you have to come out of this . . . this state you're in."

Frances closed her eyes and shook her head, waving her hand before her face.

"Listen to me, Mama. You have three other children who need you. Do you hear me?"

Frances opened her eyes, with a surprised look on her face, as though she had just remembered them.

"They're in the street all day," Katie said. "Now that may be all right for Davey. He's old enough to take care of himself. But Lala is only eight years old. Do you know where I found the girls this morning?"

Childlike, Frances shook her head.

"At Lee Circle. Do you realize how far away that is?"

Frances looked both hurt and astonished. "I didn't know," she said.

"That's just it, Mama. You don't know. And they're running wild, thinking you don't care. They could get run over by a wagon, or they could run in front of a streetcar." Frances was crying now, her head on her daughter's shoulder. "And they're eating like beggars, whatever scraps they find lying around. How can you let them do that, Mama?"

The accusation had the effect of an electric shock. Frances wept for a minute. Then, backing away from her daughter, she blew her nose and smoothed the wisps of unruly hair at the side of her head. It was the first feeble attempt to make some order out of the chaos in her life.

Katie continued. "They need someone to cook for them the way you used to, and I can't be here to do it,

Mama. I have a job, and we need the money. You need it and I need it. I want my independence. I've grown used to it, and it means a lot to me."

Frances looked into Katie's eyes, trying to make some dim, recessed connection between what Katie had said and her hostility to her father.

"You never gonna forgive your papa, Katie?" she asked, in a pleading, tearful voice.

Katie decided to lie. She could not be so stonehearted as to deny her mother this one concession.

"Yes, I'll forgive him, Mama," she said, touching her mother's face affectionately, "if you'll promise me to try to come out of this trance you're in."

Frances nodded gratefully. It was more than she had hoped for.

"I want you to get up every morning like you used to," Katie said, "and make your plans for the day." Frances nodded. "Do your shopping, your cooking, your cleaning. The neighbors all used to say you had the cleanest house on the block."

"You right, Katie. You right," Frances answered.

"I want you to get back to your gardening and your quilting. Look at that garden out there. It's all turned under. I can't even see the beds. And I'll bet you haven't touched the quilt since I left."

Frances shook her head.

"Okay. Now don't forget about the girls. Keep them close to home. Take them to the market with you. Teach them how to quilt. It'll give them something to do at home. And play cards with them. The next time I come home, I'll bring a new deck of cards."

"Katie, you good girl," Frances said. She leaned over to kiss Katie on the cheek. It was the first time Katie had ever smelled stale perspiration on her mother. "You stay tonight and have supper with your papa."

"No, Mama," she said a bit too quickly. "I . . . I have to get back. Mason is coming for me at five. I'm needed at the Eagans'."

She hated herself for wanting to be back in her clean, cool room, where the sheets were slick and she had an electric lamp to read by. Most of all she wanted to get away from the odor of sweat and outhouses and the cloying sweetness of molasses and roasting coffee.

"Okay. Okay, my Katie," her mother said.

After awhile Katie put on her hat and picked up her purse.

"I think it might do you good to take a nice long walk every day, Mama," she said. "I heard Mrs. Eagan say that it was the thing to do when you're expecting."

"Take a walk?" Frances asked.

"Yes. And drink some milk every day. And please try not to lift anything heavy."

"Okay."

"Are you still sleeping in the boys' bed? Or have you gone back to the mattress in the kitchen?"

Frances didn't answer. She kept her eyes lowered.

"Mama!" Katie scolded. "How can he let you sleep on the floor? In your condition?"

"Go on, Katie," Frances pleaded. "You better leave now. You be late." Frances had visions of Joe walking in and getting into an argument with Katie. "I tell your papa I want to sleep in the boys' bed."

"And let Davey sleep with him," Katie added.

Frances nodded.

"It's better for your back," Katie said, ". . . and for other things."

Mother and daughter looked away from each other. Both women blushed.

Katie was happy to be on her way back home. She didn't know when it had happened, but she realized that she had come to think of the Eagan house as "home." She loved her mother and the children with all her heart, but going back to Julia Row had become a duty to her, and a heavy, depressing one.

Chapter
SIXTEEN

One day in July the sun shone, and Katie and Treece threw open all the windows to let the fresh air sweep through the house, taking all the dampness with it. Treece decided to take a walk down the avenue in the midafternoon.

"Why don't you come wit me, Katie?" Treece asked. "We ain' been out dis house in weeks."

"I'd love to, Treece, but I'm at such a good part in my book, an' I've been waiting all day to have time to read."

"You an' yo' books!" Treece chuckled and shook her head. "Okay, g'wan an' read. Ah'll say hello to the flowers fo' ya."

At two o'clock Katie curled up in the velvet Morris chair at the end of the dining room and stretched out her legs on the ottoman. She sighed with contentment. Behind her head, curtains billowed in the windows. The dining room was the only room that ran the entire width of the house, and the cross ventilation was delightful. She looked around at the lovely room where the family gathered and where they did their entertaining.

At each end of the room was a black marble fireplace, flanked by floor-length windows, now thrown open to the spring air. The huge walnut oval table was in the center of the room, beneath a gasolier of frosted glass globes in a circle of brass. Near all the windows there were easy chairs and ottomans, where the ladies might have tea or do handwork by daylight. Near the end of the room where Katie was sitting was a player piano, which only Stephen played. A china cabinet sprawled against one wall, a mirrored buffet against another, and a server, with its Georgian tea and coffee service, stood catercorner near the entrance to the butler's pantry.

Though the family was gone, it had taken Katie two weeks after coming back to her job to get up her courage to sit in the dining room and read in the afternoons. She knew she was overstepping her bounds. The dining room was not hers to use. From kitchen to garret bedroom was her territory. She expected no more, and she was grateful for what she had, but it *did* seem silly to let the lovely, cool, dining room go to waste. At last one afternoon, weeks ago, she had decided to sit there with her book, and now it had become routine. When her work was done, she came to the dining room to read.

Oh, how she looked forward to her reading! She was well into *Jane Eyre* now, to the chapter where Jane was about to meet Mr. Rochester. She was sure they would fall in love.

Afraid to soil the ottoman, Katie leaned over and unbuttoned her high-topped shoes and placed them beside the chair. Then she lay back against the satin pillows and opened her book to where she had marked it with a strip of palmetto. The marquisette paneling floated in the air over her head, and the breeze wafted across her chair. She began reading, and soon the words began to blur. She was sleepier than she had imagined. She had been up since six, and she had scrubbed and cooked and ironed. Before ten minutes had gone by, the book fell to her lap and she slumped down in the chair, fast asleep.

Charlotte's car pulled into the carriageway, and Stephen ran up the back steps and into the kitchen. Through the butler's pantry, he walked swiftly, and then on into the dining room, where he stopped short at the sight that greeted him.

Katie lay like a figure in a Renoir painting, her body that of a woman, her face imprinted with the innocence of a child. The soft cotton dress fell into the curves of her breast and followed the line of her shapely hip. One hand was tucked beneath a satin pillow, which set off her delicate profile like a cameo. Stephen stepped quietly to her side.

She was like an angel, fair of face, lids fringed with thick, dark lashes. Her lips were full, her cheeks pink from sleep. She lay on her side, her feet in their dark stockings protruding from beneath the skirt, her shoes on the floor beside the chair.

Stephen smiled. Suddenly he wanted to touch her tenderly, to brush the stray hairs from her forehead with his fingertips, but he didn't want to wake her. He felt something new stirring inside him. What a vision of peacefulness and beauty she was! He had an outrageous urge to pick her up in his arms and kiss that childish mouth. He felt like an intruder, inspecting her as she slept.

She moved. Her eyelids fluttered. She suddenly stiffened, as if she were aware of his presence and frightened to death. Her eyes flew open, and she lay unmoving, transfixed.

"Stephen!" she said in amazement.

"Hello, Katie," he said. "How are you?"

"I'm fine."

Katie smiled. Then, realizing that she was in a reclining position in his presence, she sat up and fumbled to put her shoes on.

"I'm so sorry," she said, not knowing what to do first to right her appearance and her behavior.

"What for?" he asked.

"Well, for resting in your mother's chair . . . and for having my shoes off . . . and for being in the dining room . . ."

Stephen laughed. "And what else?" he asked. He pulled up a chair and sat watching her.

She looked up into his eyes and saw that he was joking. She smiled.

"That's better," he said. "Why shouldn't you be resting in the afternoon, anywhere you like? You've got the whole house to yourself."

"No. It isn't my place . . ."

"Place! What an antiquated idea! You have needs just like anyone else. I don't want to hear about your place."

He leaned over to pick up the book that had dropped to the floor when she stood up.

"What are you reading?" he asked.

"*Jane Eyre*."

"You like it?"

"Oh, yes."

"I didn't. I don't believe a man would lock up his crazy wife in a tower."

"Oh, Stephen. I hadn't read that part yet," she said.

"I'm sorry," he apologized. "Now I've ruined it for you."

"It doesn't matter."

"Oh, but it does. I'll have to make it up to you."

She was wishing she hadn't chastised him. It really didn't matter, not when she had Stephen with her here, alone, in the flesh. Nothing he could say or do was wrong. She had finished buttoning her shoes, and she stood before him, hands folded, as if she were awaiting orders.

"Sit down," he said. "Relax. Let's talk a little."

She sat where she had been before, facing him.

"I didn't know if you were still working here, until we got to the camp. Della talks about you all the time."

"Della and I are great friends," Katie said. Katie had always loved Della, but never so much as now.

Stephen looked around him. "What do you do by yourself all day?"

"Oh, I'm not alone, I have Treece. She's just gone out for a walk. And then at night, I have your father."

"I see. So what is your day like?"

"Well, I cook and clean and I go to market. And in the afternoon, I read."

"How lonesome for you!"

"Oh, no. I'm happy here."

"But you're young and pretty, and you should be having fun. I wish you could be with us at the camp. Would you like me to tell you about it?"

"Please do." She wanted to picture him there.

"It's lovely out there in the summer. Other families we know have camps near ours, and we get together and do things. The other night we all went floundering."

"How do you do it?" she asked, her smile widening.

"Well, the flounders come close to shore at night, you see. So you have to wade in shallow water. And you take a lantern and a little spear, and when you see a flounder in the water, you try to spear him. There's nothing better in this world than fresh flounder, the way Della fixes it."

"With lemon and butter sauce?" Katie asked.

"I forgot, you're a gourmet cook." Stephen smiled.

A flood of emotion swelled up inside her, and she felt that she would burst from it. She wanted to take his face between her hands and kiss that mouth and touch that cleft in his chin.

"Did you . . . catch many fish?" she asked to stop herself from looking at him with love.

"Enough," he said. He, too, was distracted. He had felt the wave of love coming from the girl. He was aware of an enormous attraction to her. It was absurd, he knew. This was only the third time he had seen her, talked to her. And yet it was enough. He had never been in love before in his life, but he was sure that what he felt was the beginning of love.

"How old are you, Katie?" he asked.

"Fifteen."

"I'm twenty-one."

"I know." She knew everything about him. She realized perhaps she should not have admitted knowing. She turned her face away, blushing.

"Look at me, Katie," he said.

Slowly she looked into his eyes. How green they were, with the small brown flecks! Like a sea she would gladly have drowned in.

"I'm going to Europe in the fall," he said.

"Why must you go?" she asked. She couldn't believe her own boldness, but if he had confided in her, he wanted her to know.

"My father is sending me to London and Paris and Berlin. He wants me to observe in the laboratories of some experts in the electronics field. My father says electricity is going to shape the world. He wants me to learn all there is to know about it."

"He must be right," Katie said.

"He plans for me to be there a year or two. He says I should get a worldwide picture of the whole movement."

"That must be exciting."

"Yes, I *have* been excited about it." Till today, he wanted to add. Now that we've just found each other, we'll be apart again, for maybe two long years. Perhaps he was being impulsive. Maybe it was just summer madness.

"Stephen," she said, "why did you come here today?"

"I had almost forgotten," he said. "I came for the volleyball net. It's up in the attic. I'll get it."

He left her then and ran up the stairs to the second-floor corridor. She heard him pulling down the folding stairs to the attic. Then, noises of boxes being moved. She prayed Treece would not come back for just a little while. If only she could see him off alone!

In minutes he was back, brushing the dust from his

shirt and trousers. He was carrying a net that had been rolled up and tied with a rope. He stopped before Katie.

"Come on out in the back and say good-bye," he said.

"I haven't offered to fix you anything," she said. "Some tea, maybe. Or lemonade."

"No thank you, Katie."

She knew that he was looking at her eyes and her hair and her bosom. She wanted to turn away. Her cheeks were on fire.

"Kate," he said gently, "give me your hand."

She swallowed. Slowly she extended her trembling hand and he took it firmly in his own. He walked her through the kitchen onto the back gallery. It had begun to drizzle and the air was perfumed with sweet olive. He put the roll of netting on the floor beside him and looked into her eyes. She could not look away. He took her face between his hands and kissed her soft, warm lips.

"I would have died if I hadn't done that," he said.

Katie felt a wave of heat, like a desert breeze, flush her skin. She drew in a breath to steady herself, and Stephen knew that she, too, was overcome with fresh new love. He gathered her in his arms and kissed her tenderly, covering her mouth with his. Her breath was like crushed rose petals, and her lips were like a child's lips, soft and moist. Then he drew away and held both her hands in his.

"I think I'm in love with you, Katie," he said. He brought her hands to his lips and kissed them.

"No," she said. "You can't be. You just think you are, because I'm . . . well, you know, different."

He paused for a moment, weighing what she had said. "You think I'm trifling with you? That I consider you a novelty?"

She looked at him and knew that it wasn't so. She shook her head no. She flew into his arms again and held him close. Oh, God, she prayed, is it possible that this man could love me?

"I'll write you, Katie, when I'm away," he said.

"No, don't. Your mother will know."

"You're right. But I'll find a way. I promise."

He took her hand and walked her down the back steps to the car.

"I wish you could be coming with me to the camp," he said.

Katie nodded. A tear rolled down each cheek. Stephen lifted her chin and brushed them aside.

"We'll be back after Labor Day," he said. "Please don't work too hard."

He reached out for her and kissed her once more before he got into the car and started the motor. Katie stood in the carriageway and waved as the car backed up onto St. Charles Avenue and started the journey back to camp.

He would be back after Labor Day. Then what? He could never acknowledge his love for her, if love was what he truly felt. Then he'd be gone again for two long years. And after the two years were over, what would happen then? No doubt, he would long since have forgotten he had ever said the words. And even if he remembered, what could he do about it? Such a match was unthinkable for Stephen Eagan.

She turned and walked back to the steps. She would treasure this day forever, just as she had treasured Mardi Gras Day. But it was just another leaf in a book of hopeless dreams.

Chapter SEVENTEEN

A horn sounded in the driveway. It was Charlotte's car. They heard the groan of luggage-laden wagon wheels on the brick drive leading to the carriage house.

"Hoo-ray! De family's home! Come on, Katie!" Treece shouted. She rushed from the kitchen, slamming the door and scooting down the back stairs, eager to lend a hand to carry a valise or an armful of laundry.

Katie sat frozen, her fingers motionless in the pan of beans she had been shelling. How could she look at Stephen without giving everything away? Trembling, she put the pan on the table and walked to the door. She could hear the sounds of car doors slamming, of Treece shouting welcome, and the family giving orders. She *had* to go down and help.

On shaky legs she walked out onto the back gallery and down the stairs.

"Treece, take that bag and the cardboard box," she heard Janet say. "Mason, you'd better get the heavy things. Warren, come back here. Give us a hand and let's get this wagon unloaded."

Katie did not raise her eyes till she was at the foot of the stairs. Then, suddenly, she was swept up in Della's commodious embrace.

"Katie, how're ya doin', honey? Ah sho' been missin' you."

Katie's eyes were shining. "Oh, Della, it's so good to have you back."

She looked at Janet and Charlotte in their surprisingly casual attire. Neither of them were coiffed in their usual meticulous fashion. Their hair hung loose from a central part and was tied at the neck with a ribbon. They looked windblown and healthy, and Katie came as close to liking them as she ever had.

"Welcome home, Mrs. Eagan," she said, smiling. "Miss Charlotte." She turned to the younger girl.

"Here, Katie, help me with this," was Charlotte's reply. She was trying to work a straw valise out of the back of the car.

Katie pulled at the valise and it gave. The weight of it spun her around and she found herself facing Stephen. She felt a sudden explosion in her chest. He was smiling broadly, his fine white teeth even whiter beneath the brown mustache he had grown. How glorious he was, with his tan skin and his chestnut hair bleached copper by the sun! Her heart was beating so hard that she could hear it in her ears.

"Hello, Katie," he said. "Here, let me take that."

"No! No!" She looked at him fearfully. "I've got to help." And she rushed up the stairs with the valise.

She was terrified that Janet might notice that Stephen was coming to her assistance. What would she think? It was imperative that he treat her as he always had. Dear God, let him understand that, she prayed. She had not even dared to answer his greeting. Perhaps she was wrong in going to the other extreme. A simple "hello" would have attracted less attention than her frightened words and hasty exit. Fortunately everyone was much too occupied to notice.

Would it be like this from now on? she wondered. Would she always be pulling in one direction, trying to avoid a look or a word that might reveal too much, while he was pulling in another, trying to let her know that he still cared? She didn't know if she could handle that. She would have to stay away from him entirely, or she'd surely give everything away.

It was good that he'd be gone again in a week, so

that she could relax. But the thought of being without him for such a long time left her desolate. What hope was there for such an impossible love?

For the rest of the day the family settled back into the household. Everyone wanted a tub bath. The ladies dug through boxes that had been hurriedly packed, looking for a hairbrush or a particular pair of shoes. Treece helped them unpack and carried laundry downstairs, while Katie and Della spent their day catching up on news and getting meals together.

At dinner John Eagan looked radiant with his family gathered around him once again. He was glad that Labor Day was behind them and summer was officially over. He and Stephen had much to talk about because in a week Stephen was to take a train to New York, and then an ocean liner to Europe.

"I've reserved accommodations for you in Paris," John said. "I want you to make your first stop with a man named Marais. I've written him that you're coming."

"Marais?" Stephen asked. "Is he the same Marais that experimented with photographing motion?"

"He is. He was a pioneer in the field. Do you know him?"

"Oh, yes. I mean, we studied him at Tulane. He published a book on analyzing motion, like running and falling."

John smiled and sipped his wine. "I'm surprised. It seems such a short time ago that he did those experiments, though I guess it's over twenty years."

"Well, everything in the field is new, Dad. That's what's so exciting about it."

"And the books will be changing every year, with so many new theories and discoveries."

Stephen buttered a dinner roll. "It'll be great to meet someone I studied about. I remember one day in class we were discussing how so many inventors were working on the motion-picture camera and projector at the same time, in the United States, France, and England."

"And they all succeeded, almost at the same time," John said. "I remember that. But Edison got the credit, which he deserved."

"How's that?" Stephen asked facetiously.

"Well, he perforated the film on the edges," John explained, "and his machine had a sprocket that engaged those perforations and . . ." Catching on, he gave his son a look of mock disapproval. "You know all that. Why are you asking *me*?"

"To see if *you* know." Stephen laughed. "Do you ever hear from Mr. Edison, Dad? Do you know what he's working on now?"

"Well, he always used to talk about putting the phonograph and the motion-picture camera together, so that one day we would have talking pictures. I know he won't give up till he does that."

"Daddy!" Charlotte chided. "You're teasing, of course."

"Not at all!"

"I know you think Mr. Edison is second only to God, but talking pictures! Really!"

"It *does* sound like a fantasy, John," Janet said.

John pinched his lips. "Dear ladies," he said, with forced patience, "it's only a matter of time. It's a mechanical obstacle, nothing more. Sound and image must both be recorded on the same strip of film. Twenty years ago scientists knew it was possible. With a few more technical developments, someone will make a projector that can reproduce both images and sounds. And it will probably be Edison. Please don't go around expressing absurd opinions. You make me look ridiculous." He turned back to his son. Charlotte and Janet looked at each other and shrugged.

"When you're in Paris, Stephen, register for some courses at the Sorbonne," John said. He cut his meat and speared a piece with his fork. "That's the place to study German. Find some students who speak the language, and practice talking with them. It will be important when you get to Berlin."

"Who will I study with in Berlin?" Stephen asked.

John touched his napkin to his lips. "You'll work with Bergman there," he said. He smiled, remembering. "He and I worked together back in 1881, making meters and sockets and switches. Then, when the franchise came through to electrify New York, I helped him make tube conductors and junction boxes for the underground mains."

"He speaks English, then," Stephen said.

"Oh, yes."

"What is he doing in Berlin?"

"That's his home. Lots of men came from Europe to work at Menlo Park. Bergman was a bench worker for Edison in the old days. He made everything from chandeliers to phonographs, and he can tell you how it's done and introduce you to some promising young inventors over there. He's the chief owner of electrical works in Berlin today."

Della served and picked up the dishes, depositing them in the butler's pantry just outside the dining room. Katie collected them there and brought them into the kitchen, but she lingered each trip to listen to Stephen's voice and to catch snatches of his conversation with his father. She closed her eyes and let the words wash over her, like music, understanding nothing of their meaning.

The days went by, and she awakened early, both heavy and light of heart, buoyed with anticipation, of what she did not know, and weighted down with despair. She came downstairs early and retired late, staying always in the kitchen, where Stephen had no cause to come.

One morning Della had gone to the carriage house and Katie was alone in the kitchen when the swinging door opened and Stephen stood in the doorway. He scanned the room well, and then quickly crossed the kitchen floor and took Katie in his arms.

Her eyes grew wide, looking over his shoulder, and her cheeks flushed. She was rigid with fear, but the touch of his palm on her back sent a wave of heat through her body.

"Stephen, you mustn't," she whispered. "Your mother might come in."

"She's gone shopping with Charlotte," he answered huskily. He covered her face with kisses. Her knees went weak but he held her firmly in his arms.

"Della will be back," she argued, but he shut off the words, covering her mouth with his. Little explosions went off all over her body.

"I love you, Katie," he said. "I have to see you alone."

"There's no way," she answered. "Go, now. Della's coming."

"Say you love me."

"I do. I love you." Her eyes were moist with happy tears.

He left her then, his hand sliding sensuously along her arm, squeezing her hand in parting. The door was still swinging after him when Della came in from the porch. Katie turned her blushing face toward the cupboard, as if she were in search of something. She was drained from the encounter. Della looked first at the swinging door, and then at Katie's trembling form. She rolled her eyes, and the whites were larger than ever.

Wednesday came, and after breakfast Katie went to her room to dress for her visit with her mother. On the lamp table beside her bed, in a water glass, was a fragrant sprig of jasmine. It was the variety that grew in Janet's garden, called night jasmine. Katie smiled with delight as she walked over and bent down to sniff the delicate little flowers. The blossoms were tiny and fresh, and seemed to fill her small room with perfume.

She lifted the dripping stem from the glass and lay back across her bed, holding it to her bosom. She closed her eyes and sniffed its delightful aroma. She held it up above her, studying the cluster of starlike flowers. A drop of water fell on her nose and she laughed aloud. Stephen had cut the flowers for her and left them here for her to enjoy. She kissed the sprig, inhaling the sweetness. She wished she could wear it inside her clothes so it would be close to her heart all day. But instead she opened her Civil War book, placed the flowers in its center, closed the book, and returned it to the shelf. She would look at the sprig every night and enjoy its fragrance as long as it lasted; but even after that she would keep it forever and ever.

How light her heart would be when she visited her mother today! She would think of him all day, and her heart would be leaping in her bosom. Hurriedly she dressed, and she remembered to bring the glass back to the kitchen before she went down to the carriage house. At least, when she got to her mother's house, she could spend the day without constant fear and agitation.

When she descended the stairs, Mason was waiting for her with the carriage, sitting on his perch. She opened the door and climbed in, and the chestnut mares clopped down the driveway toward the avenue. Suddenly the carriage stopped, and Stephen was standing beside it, talking to Mason.

"I'll take Katie to her mother's house," Stephen said. "I'm going to Canal Street anyway, to buy a few things for my trip. No trouble. No, Mason, I insist."

Katie lost her breath. The men changed places and the carriage rumbled down the drive and onto the avenue. A few blocks down St. Charles, Stephen turned the carriage around and headed for Audubon Park.

He drove down a road in the park between rows of ancient oaks. They passed alongside magnificent buildings still standing from the Louisiana Cotton Centennial

Exposition of the '80s, and at last the carriage came to a stop in a secluded spot near a lagoon. Stephen got down from the driver's seat and opened the door to the carriage. He got in beside Katie and took her in his arms.

"My dearest!" he whispered. "My love!"

He kissed her hungrily, and she wrapped her arms around him, savoring the moment. *This* was what she had lived for all her life. This was what made all the agony worthwhile, all the deprivation, all the hatred she had harbored for her father and the shame she had known at Janet's hands. Oh, if Janet knew! Her son was holding Katie in his arms. He loved her. He had told her so.

Eagerly she surrendered herself to the sweet, unbelievable moment. He crushed her body to his, achingly aware of her breasts pressed against his chest.

"I've been so miserable and lonely," he said, "ever since the day I found you resting in the dining room. There were some days I thought I would fly apart. Oh, I *do* love you, Katie. I really do."

He kissed her cheeks and her smooth, white throat.

"My darling, how can I leave you now?" he asked. "I need you, Katie."

His voice broke with emotion at the hopelessness of their situation. She touched his head, and the warm, crisp chestnut curls sprang back around her fingers. How long she had dreamed of touching that head! And the cleft in his chin! She backed away now to look at it, and she saw that his eyes were misty.

She brushed away his tears, as he had once done hers. With the tips of her fingers, she caressed his cheek, following the contours of his face like a blind woman, memorizing every curve. And then she placed her index finger in the cleft in his chin.

"I've always wanted to do that," she said.

He put his hand behind her neck and drew her to

him. He kissed her mouth deeply, greedily. They sighed aloud, and Stephen's hand followed the line of Katie's hip. Then, suddenly, he broke away from her.

"I can't do this to you," he said.

"I love you, Stephen," she said as if that were all he had to know.

He sat away from her and straightened his clothes. "If you were a Creole girl," he explained, "you'd be under the eye of a chaperon, day and night, with no chance of a wild lover spiriting you away in a carriage and kissing you and touching you."

"Then I'm glad I'm not a Creole girl," she said.

He shook his head. He would not be distracted. "If you were a few years older, you wouldn't need a chaperon. You could protect yourself. But don't you see, the way things are, you're too young to know better, and you have no one to watch over you. So what I'm doing is taking advantage of you."

"Then take advantage of me," she said. "It's the only happiness I've ever known."

"If I care for you, and God knows I do, I've got to look out for you. But it's just that we never have a chance to see each other. We can't even talk alone. And what I feel for you is so intense, I can't eat or sleep. And I'll be gone such a long time."

"Oh, Stephen," she said, throwing herself back into his arms, "do you really love me? Is it possible?"

"I adore you." He cradled her head against the curve of his shoulder. He cupped her face in his hand, and gently, slowly, kissed her flushed cheeks and her thick, black lashes, wet with tears.

"I'll go to Europe because I must, but I won't be gone forever. When I come home, you'll be seventeen, and old enough to marry. Will you marry me then, Katie?"

Katie's mouth fell open. After a moment she shook her head slowly and sadly.

"It can never be, Stephen," she said. "Your parents would never allow it. And they're right."

"How can you say that?"

"I'm only a servant, Stephen." She saw that he was about to object, and she put her hand over his mouth. "I have no education, no background, no social standing, all the things that are so important to your family."

"And so unimportant to me," he said. "You weren't born a servant. That's just an accident of the economy."

Katie laughed in spite of her misery.

"You're a beautiful, wonderful girl," Stephen said, "and you're smart, and I love you. Do you love me?"

"Oh, yes. Oh, Stephen, I love you."

"And do you want to marry me?"

"More than anything in the world."

"Then, when I come home from Europe, I'll tell my parents we love each other, and we're going to be married. If they object, I really don't care. If they want to disown me, then let them. I'll be able to support you."

Katie knew that she could never let him do it. She would never be the cause of his losing a fortune and the affection of his family, to say nothing to the respect of other families in his social circle. But somehow she knew that this was not the time to say what was in her heart. So many things could happen in two years. She would not spoil this brief moment, which would be all they would both have to cherish.

"Promise me something," she said.

"Anything."

"Don't come to the kitchen looking for me the rest of the week."

"How can I promise that?" he asked. "All I do is think about you."

She moaned with delicious contentment. It was so wonderful to know he was going through the same agony she was enduring.

"But you must promise. We'll say our good-byes

now, and you won't look for me again. I've been as nervous as a cat, for fear of what you'd do."

"I promise."

They kissed again, and a wave of passion so overwhelming swept over them that Katie pulled away and lowered her head to her hand.

"I think you'd better take me to my mother's now," she said.

Stephen didn't speak. He knew he could not guard her innocence much longer. His body was on fire. He waited until he had gained control of himself, and he climbed back up on top of the carriage.

Only then did Katie realize that she had not even thanked him for the night jasmine.

Chapter
EIGHTEEN

The wind whipped the sides of the house, slapping the branches of sycamore trees against the windows. Katie paced the downstairs corridor. She stood at the leaded-glass door, peering out beyond the vestibule and the gallery into the darkness of St. Charles Avenue. From time to time a carriage rolled by or a street car clanged its way toward town. She could hear children singing Christmas carols somewhere in the neighborhood.

The parlors were dark, but the dwindling fire in the hearth lit shiny surfaces of ornaments on the Christmas tree. She walked into the first parlor and began putting empty anisette glasses on a tray. The Eagans and their guests had had liqueurs before departing for the evening. They were attending a soiree for the season's debutantes, and their guests had come early to visit first.

Katie picked up the tray of glasses, wiped the walnut table with her apron, and headed for the kitchen. She was so worried about her mother that she felt her insides trembling. When would that baby come? Frances was a week late already, and still no labor pains. Katie prayed this was not a sign of trouble brewing. Her mother was thirty-seven years old, not young to have a baby, and she had never been well since Little Joe died.

In spite of Katie's advice Frances had never eaten properly and never taken walks, considering the last suggestion of no value whatsoever. Katie wished with all her heart she were with her mother now, just to give her comfort and to wait on her, which no one else ever did. But she had asked for two weeks off *after* the baby was born, when her mother would be in bed, and she would be needed to care for the other children. How could she ask for more time now? Suppose the baby didn't come for another week? What good would it do to sit there looking at her mother?

In the kitchen she ran the water, added soap chips, and began washing glasses.

Della and Treece had retired to the servants' quarters, and Warren had gone to bed. She was glad to be alone with her thoughts. The telephone rang. Katie rushed through the corridor, drying her hands on her apron. She picked up the phone.

"Eagan residence," she said.

"Katie?" It was Davey.

"Yes." It was all she could say. Her knees turned to jelly, and she sank into the chair beside the telephone.

"Mama's having pains," the boy said. "I went for Mrs. Noonan, like you said. She's on her way there now, so don't worry."

"Thank God for that. Where are you now, Davey?"

"At the rectory."

"Well, stay there. I'll let you know when there's news. I'll be leaving here right away. Mason will drive me home. Is Mama suffering bad?"

"I don't know. She moans a lot."

"Oh, God. I'll be right there."

Mason answered to a knock at his door and said he would hitch up the carriage at once. Katie rushed back to the main house for her coat and shawl and the shopping bag she had packed days ago for her stay with her mother.

The wind blew and a light drizzle fell against the carriage window. Katie shivered. All along the avenue Christmas trees stood in parlor windows, their candles making little yellow blurs of light. Sometimes a door would open and the sounds of music or laughter would pour out onto the banquettes. It was the night before Christmas Eve, and the city was in a holiday mood.

Katie was sick with fear as she neared the alley behind Julia Row. She moans a lot, Davey had said. She must be suffering so much! Frances was not one to give in to pain. But, Katie recalled, her mother had lost all resolution since Little Joe's death. She would have no will to be strong now, Katie thought. Thank God Mrs. Noonan, the midwife, was with her to ease her pain, if it were possible.

A scream from the service wing ran through her like a knife. She jumped from the carriage and ran toward the house, forgetting her shopping bag. Mason ran after her with it.

"Thank you, Mason," she said. "Now, for God's sake, don't forget to tell Mrs. Eagan where I am, the minute she gets back, no matter what time it is."

"Don' worry. Ah be waitin' up fo' 'em."

Katie ran to her mother's bed without taking off her coat or her shawl. Her heart sank when she looked down at her mother. She was puffed beyond recognition and her skin was blotched. Her eyes were closed and her face was distorted with pain. Fists clenched down hard on the bed; she was suffering a horrible contraction.

How could women endure such pain? Katie wondered. Why should they have to? So that men could have their moments of pleasure? She looked across the bed at Mrs. Noonan. The kerosene lamp flickered on the table at her mother's side, casting crazy shadows across the midwife's face. She seemed to be smiling, then frowning, her eyes hooded and dark.

"Where is my father?" she asked.

"He was here when I came," the woman answered. "But he said he'd best be gone while the baby's comin'. He's right, I think. Men are just in the way at such a time."

Katie took off her coat and shawl and hung them near the door. She carried a kitchen chair and sat at her mother's side.

"I don't think he's right," she said. "I wish he were here to see it all. I wish he could hear her scream and see her suffer. I'd like him to know what he put her through."

Mrs. Noonan put her hand to her mouth. She was shocked to hear Katie speak so frankly.

"And where are Jenny and Lala?" Katie asked.

"Davey brought them upstairs to Mrs. Macaluso. She says they can spend the night. No need to worry."

"Good."

"Katie," Frances called to her, reaching out her hand for Katie to hold.

"Wait, Mama, my hands are cold," she said.

She walked over to the heater, turned up the wick, and cupped her hands around the metal cylinder till they were warm. Then, she came back and took her mother's hand in both her own.

"How do you feel?" Katie asked.

"Bad, Katie. I feel real bad."

Katie felt the panic growing inside her. This was so unlike her mother.

"Is there anything you can do, Mrs. Noonan?" Katie asked.

"I gave her some laudanum when I came," the woman said. "I'll give her more later on, but she's got to be able to help her pains or the babe'll never come. She's groggy now."

"Katie," Frances moaned, her eyes still closed. "Don't be mad at your papa. It's not his fault."

Katie resolved not to say anything more about her father, no matter how long the birth took. Frances had enough to suffer, without being torn emotionally between her daughter and her husband.

"Why is she puffy like that?" she asked Mrs. Noonan.

"She has a kidney disorder, I'm afraid. Her legs and feet are swollen, too." The midwife pulled the blanket up over one foot and pressed her thumb to the swollen calf. The depression remained. "There's water retention there."

"So what can we do for her?"

"Nothing now, more's the pity. She should've gone to a doctor months ago. He would have put her on a diet to control the condition."

Katie looked at her mother. Her eyes were still closed. The laudanum was making her doze between contractions. She signaled the midwife to come into the kitchen so they could talk. She lit the overhead gas lamp in the kitchen and struck a match to the wood in the stove. The room was colder than a grave.

"What's going to happen to her? Do you know?" Katie asked.

"She'll be all right, Katie dear," Mrs. Noonan said. "She'll deliver same as usual. It's just that she mustn't take too long, or her blood pressure will go up."

"What happens then?" the girl asked, wide-eyed with fear.

Mrs. Noonan bit her lip and turned her back to the girl. Katie grabbed her arm and swung her around.

"What happens then?" she shouted.

"Sometimes, they get convulsions."

"What else?"

"They go into a coma."

"What else?"

The woman gave a little cry. She was afraid of Katie. "Sometimes they die," she said.

Katie realized that her fingers were digging into the woman's arms. She could feel her own body trembling with a spasm of shock and pain. She wanted to slap the colorless face, to tell her to do something to save her mother.

Hesitating, fearing the girl's anger, the midwife said, "The position is not good. The seat is coming first. But if we wait awhile, the babe may turn, or I may be able to turn him, when she's dilated better. All we can do is wait, Katie."

"No. That isn't all," Katie said. "I'm going to get a doctor."

She grabbed her coat and shawl from the nail in the bedroom.

The wind whistled as she opened the door.

"Where will you be goin'?" the woman asked.

"To the rectory to use the telephone. Father Rafferty will help me get a doctor. Now don't you leave my mother for a minute. I'll be back as soon as I can."

Into the darkness Katie ran, with the rain and the cold wind in her face. She arrived at the priest's house, and as soon as she had made her mother's condition known, Father Rafferty dialed the number of the doctor who took care of the priests of the parish. Katie stood beside him, wringing her hands.

"I wanted her to see a doctor all along," Katie said. "I *told* her to go. I would have paid for it gladly. I should have *made* her go. But she wouldn't. She was too ashamed."

"Didn't she ever have a doctor for the others?" Father asked.

"Never. Only Mrs. Noonan."

"And she's never had trouble before?"

The girl shook her head. She was beside herself with worry. She lowered her face to her hands and wept.

"Is Doctor Mullins in?" she could hear the priest asking. "No? When do you expect him? Yes. It's an emergency. You can't? Well, how long will that be?"

At last he replaced the receiver. "I'm sorry, Katie," he said. "The doctor is out of town visiting his daughter for the Christmas holidays. Even if he could be reached, he's too far away to get here in time. He doesn't plan to return for two more days."

"Dear God! Please help me," she prayed.

"Have you no doctor of your own? A family doctor?"

"No, Father," she said, sobbing. "We've never really been sick. For colds and things, Mama always took us to the druggist."

"I'll call my sister," the priest said suddenly. "She has a wonderful family physician. He'll come. I'm sure of it."

But the doctor was not in. He was at the Hotel Dieu Hospital, caring for the influenza victims. There was an epidemic in the city that had already claimed the lives of hundreds, and more were being brought into the hospital each day.

"Call him there," Katie said peremptorily. "At the hospital. He'll come. My mother is in agony."

She said it as if the priest were having difficulty comprehending the situation. Indeed this is what she thought. People had influenza, and they lived or died. But they didn't suffer the tortures of the damned.

Moved by the power of Katie's will, the priest looked up the number of the hospital and argued with the nurse in the office until she put the doctor on the line.

"You must come, Doctor," Father Rafferty said. He turned his back to Katie, so that his explanation would not embarrass her. "It sounds like the woman is having a breech birth, and I don't think she's progressing at all. What? Wait, I'll ask."

He turned to Katie. "How long has your mother been in labor?"

"I don't know. Maybe four hours."

Father Rafferty relayed the information. He waited. He turned to Katie.

"How far apart are the pains?"

"About five minutes, I think. Let me talk to him, Father," she said, taking the receiver from the priest's hand. "Doctor, I beg you to come and help my mother. I've never seen anyone suffer like that."

"It's always like that in labor, child," the voice said.

"No. Not like this. I remember when my sisters were born. It was never like this. She'll die if you don't come."

"You're distraught, young woman. You shouldn't have the burden of all that. Is there no one at all to care for her?"

"There's a midwife with her," Katie said, sobbing. She felt herself becoming hysterical.

"A good one?" the voice asked.

"She delivered all my mother's children."

"Well, then, I'm sure she'll do just fine. Listen to me. After a while your mother will dilate sufficiently for the woman to be able to turn the child. Do you understand what I'm saying?"

"But suppose she can't turn it? My mother could die."

"That could happen even if I were there."

"No. You could operate."

"Not in her house, I couldn't. And it's too late to move her now." Katie's silence gave him time to try to reason with her. "Listen to me, miss. I've got people dying all around me here. I can't get away."

Katie hung up the receiver, tears streaming down her face. It was so unbearable to be helpless when someone you loved was suffering. She had to get back. To do what, she did not know. Her mother could have died since she left home, or the baby could have come. She had to go. She grabbed her coat like a wild woman, not knowing which way to turn, not thinking if she would walk or ride or run.

"Katie, wait," Father Rafferty said. "I'll take you back."

She grabbed the priest by both arms.

"We *must* do something," she said. She shifted her gaze from the floor to the walls, as if the answer would be written there. "I know," she said, gripping the man's arms harder. "Mr. Eagan, my employer. He'll know a doctor, I'm sure of it. He'll find a doctor and bring him to us." She rushed to the telephone, then stopped. "But he isn't home. They're out for the evening. It may be hours before they return, and I don't know where they are."

"Wouldn't *anyone* be home? Someone who'd know?"

"Warren. Warren is there. I'll call."

With trembling fingers she dialed the number and waited, but the phone just rang and rang. She knew that Warren was sleeping. She hoped he would hear the ring at last and come downstairs to answer the phone, but after a dozen rings she replaced the receiver.

"Would you go there, Father?" she pleaded.

"Of course. You know I will."

"I'll write the address for you. Wait on the front gallery. When the family comes home, explain about my mother. Ask *Mr.* Eagan, not Mrs. Eagan. He'll get us a doctor. Then go to the doctor's house, Father, wherever it is, and bring him to us. I have no choice but to ask this of you. There's no one else."

"That's what priests are for, Katie. To help, if there's a way."

She put on her coat, and the priest took his own coat and hat from the closet.

"Let's go, then," he said. "I'll drop you off, and go on to the Eagans' to wait for them."

"God bless you, Father."

Katie could hear the scream from the service alley, and she jumped from the carriage, even before it had come to a complete stop. She raced across the yard and swung the door open to her mother's bedroom. Leaning against the closed door, she gasped and put her hand to her mouth.

There, in the bed, her mother writhed in agony. By the light of the kerosene lamp, she turned her mountainous body, trying to find some escape from the pain. Her belly rose like a huge tight knot. She pressed her hands to the bed, to support the pain that had taken control of her. Her face was drenched in sweat, and her eyes seemed to have sunk into deep, black holes, but they were wide and wild and tortured.

Mrs. Noonan threw back the covers and examined her patient. There was no time for modesty, even if Katie were there. Katie's eyes followed the woman's hands. The opening was quite wide now, perhaps three inches wide. If the baby's head were there, she could be giving birth now, Katie was sure. But, instead, the baby's bottom was slightly protruding.

"Push, now, Frances, you've got to push. You're dilated big enough."

Frances screamed and threw herself to the side of the bed.

"Jesus, God in heaven!" Katie whispered. She felt as if she would faint or throw up. She had never seen a baby born before.

"Now, Frances, you've got to stop throwin' yourself around," the woman said, "or you'll be hurtin' the baby. Lie straight, an' push when the pains come. You know that, Frances. You've been through this before."

"Never like this," Frances shrieked.

In a minute the mound of her belly softened, and she relaxed. She seemed almost to sleep. She was exhausted.

"Maybe you shouldn't make her push till you turn the baby around," Katie told Mrs. Noonan. "She'll never get it out, the way it is."

Mrs. Noonan frowned and pursed her lips. "When you can't turn the baby aroun', you try to birth it whatever way you can," the woman said.

"A doctor may be coming later," Katie said. She offered no explanations.

"Katie," her mother said with such relief that tears came to Katie's eyes. Her mother thought her worries were over now. Katie was here, and she had sent for help. Katie would give her comfort. Everything would be all right now.

Oh, God, Katie prayed, please let someone come. Please help this angel who lies here in agony before You. She has known nothing but suffering all her life. What mercy is there, that she must go through this?

Katie was to ask those questions many times in the hours that followed. The pains came, and the screams came, but no doctor arrived. The baby did not turn, and the midwife could not turn it. At each seizure of pain Katie suffered with her mother, and cried out with her, in desperation and anger. She held her mother in her arms and helped her push or pressed against her stomach to force the baby down. She could not imagine that the baby could ever pass from her mother's body, seat first, without tearing her apart. But Mrs. Noonan had said to push, and she did. Hours passed, and no one came. No doctor, no priest, not even Davey with a message. Where had they all gone?

As the night dragged by, Katie could feel her mother's strength waning, her ability to fight slipping away. At intervals Mrs. Noonan gave her laudanum, and for a time she was relieved. Katie was glad of this, but the labor was slower then, and she wondered if a doctor would have approved of the laudanum, or of the pushing, with the baby in this position. But Katie had no choice but to hope that the woman knew what she was doing.

Just after the church bell chimed three o'clock in the morning, a knock came at the door. Katie had fallen asleep on one side of her mother's bed, and Mrs. Noonan was dozing on the other. Katie rose with a start and ran to the door.

"Miss Raspanti?" the gentleman asked. He was wearing a dark overcoat and a bowler hat. His woolen scarf was around his ears and his nose, and his voice was muffled.

"Yes?" Katie responded.

"I'm Doctor Cooper. Mr. Eagan sent me, and Father Rafferty is outside in the carriage. He wants to know if you need him."

He wants to know if she's dead, Katie thought. He wonders if I need him for the last sacraments.

"No. Tell him to go. But come in, Doctor. Quickly," Katie said.

The doctor signaled the priest to leave. Then he came inside and took off his coat and hat. He asked where he could wash his hands and Katie led him to the kitchen, crying with relief and exhaustion.

"Oh, Doctor, I'm so glad to see you," she said. "My mother's been in labor for hours. She's suffered so much. And I don't think she's made much progress at all. The baby's coming seat first, and my mother's very weak and worn out."

"I'll do everything I can," he said. "Try to rest. Get the woman who's helping to boil my instruments."

Katie followed instructions, and then she and Mrs. Noonan retired to the kitchen so the doctor could work with her mother. They had a cup of tea and they waited. Hearing no screams, Katie rested her head on her arm on the kitchen table. Try as she would to stay awake, she dozed.

The sun was streaming through the kitchen window when Dr. Cooper touched Katie's arm. She jumped up and was wide awake immediately.

"What time is it?" she asked.

"A little after seven," the doctor answered.

"How's my mother?"

"Well, she made it through the night."

Katie frowned. Had he thought she wouldn't? "Is the baby born?"

"No, Miss Raspanti. Your mother is in a very critical condition. Her blood pressure is extremely high. It is possible she could go into convulsions at any moment."

"Dear Jesus! What can you do? Can't you operate?" Katie cried out, grabbing at the man's arm. Mrs.

Noonan had been sleeping, too. Katie's cries awakened her and she sat up, listening.

The doctor shook his head. "Surgery at this point is impossible. Your mother would die. She would go into shock. Her heart is weak. She's exhausted."

"Is there anything else you can do to save her life?" Katie begged.

The doctor didn't answer. He knew he could destroy the fetus and it was possible the woman could survive. But it was not within his province to save the mother's life by killing the child. If only the baby were dead! But he could still hear the heartbeat.

"There is!" Katie shouted. "You can kill the baby. You must!"

"I can't do that, young woman," he said irascibly. "I live and practice by the rules set down by the Catholic church. I cannot take one human life to save another."

"But she's our mother," Katie argued, the tears falling down her face. "We need her. Don't let her die."

"It is not a situation I have created. Ask God to help you."

"Then you're just going to wait around till they're both dead," Katie said with spite.

Before he could answer the accusation, a thump sounded in the bedroom. All three ran into her mother's room, but Katie stopped in the middle of the floor. Frances had stiffened straight as a board. She let out all the air in her lungs in one audible exhalation. Then she stopped breathing.

"She's going into convulsions," Dr. Cooper said. "Here, Mrs. Noonan, put this between her teeth," he yelled at the woman, handing her a tongue depressor. "Get out of here, miss," he shouted at Katie.

Katie's feet seemed rooted to the floor. She was transfixed by her mother's appearance. The blotches were darker now, against the stark white face, and her eyes were like two black cavities. She seemed to have lost weight overnight. While Katie stood there, her mother's body snapped in a quick, convulsive movement, rattling the springs of the bed.

"The baby's coming now," the doctor said, throwing back the sheet that hid his patient's body. "I'm going to have to pull it out. Please get out of here, young woman!"

Katie ran to the kitchen. She knelt beside the table and prayed aloud. She tried to drown out the sound of springs squeaking when her mother's weight came down on them in hard, repeated jerks. She tried to drown out the grunts of a man wrestling in a terrible physical maneuver. She put her hands to her ears to blot it all out.

"Dear God, let my mother live," she begged. "If you do this for me, I promise . . ." She tried to think of the hardest thing to promise. "I'll speak kindly to my father, and I'll . . . forgive him." She thought of the endless, agonizing night her mother had endured with no sign of her father, and she seethed with hatred for the man. "But You'll have to help me, God."

She let herself sink to the kitchen floor, where she leaned against a chair and waited. She heard no sound from the next room. No moans. No baby's cry. There was muffled movement as if the doctor and Mrs. Noonan were changing linens and rearranging things. She had no strength to move. At last the doctor opened the door. His expression told her there was no hope.

"You may want to see your mother," he said.

"Is she dying?" Katie asked.

"Yes. She's in a coma now. I delivered the baby. A little girl. She was born dead."

Katie flashed the doctor a cruel look. The baby had died anyway. If he had destroyed it even an hour ago, her mother might have lived. He knew all the messages her look conveyed.

Katie walked to her mother's side. She put her arms around her mother's neck. The body beneath hers did not move. She was warm and her heart was beating, but she was unconscious. She knew her mother would never open her eyes again. Hot tears rolled down Katie's face and onto her mother's.

Faintly, as if in the distance, a knock resounded and Father Rafferty entered. He had brought his black case with the crucifix and the oils and holy water for the last sacraments. Davey was with him, in cassock and surplice. There were tears in Davey's eyes. Mrs. Macaluso followed them into the bedroom, having seen the priest arrive.

Father Rafferty questioned the doctor inaudibly, and the doctor shook his head. The priest came over to Katie and laid a hand on her arm.

"I knew when so much time had gone by and we heard nothing," he said, "that your mother must be gravely ill. I brought the last sacraments with me."

He said it as if he were asking permission. Katie nodded. "Gravely ill," he had said, not "dying." But he had spoken to the doctor, so he knew. The priest kissed the end of the stole and put it around his neck. He began to pray as he took the crucifix from his case. Tears spilled down Katie's cheeks as she listened to the Latin prayers. Mrs. Macaluso and Mrs. Noonan stood at the foot of the bed, crying into their handkerchiefs.

For the first time Katie noticed a tiny bundle, wrapped in a blanket, on the other bed. Even the face had been covered over. Perhaps it had been disfigured in delivery. She would allow herself no feeling for the baby.

"Can Frances be awakened?" Father Rafferty asked the doctor.

The doctor shook his head.

"Why?" Katie asked.

"So she can confess," Father said.

"My mother has no sins," she said. "She's a saint. God's waiting for her in heaven. If there *is* a God, and if there *is* a heaven."

"Please leave the room," the priest said to Katie. Katie looked up as if she had been struck. "God's sacraments are being administered here, and your words are sacrilegious. I'll hear your confession later."

Katie left. She sat at the kitchen table, her eyes narrowed with bitterness. She heard the mingled sounds of Latin prayers and her brother Davey's sniffling. Then silence. Father Rafferty appeared at the kitchen door, tall and black robed, the Messenger of Death.

"Your mother's gone," he said.

Katie let out a cry of grief that filled the room. The priest put his hand on her shoulder.

"Don't cry, Katie," he said. "She'll never suffer again. She's with God now. She'll live with Him in eternal happiness. She died doing God's work."

"God's work!" Katie screamed, rising to her feet in fury. "Is it God's work to bring another baby into the world, to be cold and hungry and raised like an animal? Is it God's work to suffer the kind of agony my mother went through last night? What kind of a God could want that?"

"It's hard to understand sometimes . . ."

"It isn't hard at all. It's not God's work that killed her. It's man's work. A filthy man. My father."

"Don't ever say that, Katie," Father Rafferty admonished her.

"I will. I'll say it to him. I hate him."

She clenched her teeth and tightened her lips against them. Hatred ruled her emotions, replacing grief, at least for the moment. She was consumed with loathing for her father. Where had he been for the last twenty-four hours while her mother was dying an agonizing death? The fire of hatred roared through her, threatening to smother her. Then, exhausted by her own venom, she let out a sigh.

"Where is the doctor?" she asked Father Rafferty.

"Gone. His work was finished here."

Where had he gone? Katie wondered. How was she to pay him? She didn't know, and she didn't care.

"Sit down, Father," she said, lowering herself heavily into a chair. "I want to talk about the funeral."

"Would you like to confess first, Katie?" he asked.

She looked at the man, as if she didn't understand, didn't make the connection. Then she remembered. She had been sacrilegious.

"No," she said. "I wouldn't."

Something had happened to Katie. She felt hard and mean. She knew she would never be young again, never patient again, never shy or demure or self-deprecating. Never again would she humble herself or beg forgiveness. Never would she allow herself to be vulnerable to the point of self-destruction. Life was too cruel. God was too cruel. He took those He wanted, sparing them no pain. And sparing no pain to those they left behind. What had she done to confess? She had spoken the truth, and to say she was sorry would be a lie.

The priest sat beside her, an expression of disapproval written clearly in the tight line of his mouth.

Katie spoke. "I want to buy some burial property in the cemetery where my brother is buried. I am not destitute. I have saved quite a bit of money. I want a double vault, and I would like for you to arrange to have Joey moved to my mother's side. As for my mother, she will be buried with the baby in her arms. Now," she said, preparing to launch into another topic. The priest studied the girl and the frown left his brow. She had become the keeper of the house. She spoke with authority, and he could not help but admire her ability to function at such a time. "I plan to have a wake here tonight," she continued. "If you will call McCormick-Lyons Funeral Home for me and have someone come out to get her as soon as possible, I'll let them take her to be embalmed, but the coffin will be closed. No one is going to look at my mother in curiosity to see what a night of torture did to her."

"But, Katie, they know how to fix a body . . ."

"Yes, with makeup and rouge and all the things my

mother never used. She'll look just like Joey did, like a painted freak. I won't have it."

"Shouldn't you ask your father what he thinks?"

"My father?" She laughed a hard, satirical laugh, and the priest looked at her with pity. "I have no father," she said.

"You're bitter, Katie," he said, "but you mustn't be. It isn't his fault that she died."

"Oh, but it *is*," she said, still smiling her cynical smile. "He didn't have enough, rutting with every whore in town, he had to take my mother, too."

"Katie! Don't use such language! Ask God to forgive you. You don't know what you're saying. Men and women marry to reproduce, as God commanded."

"Then God is the murderer!" she shouted, her eyes blazing.

"I'll leave you now to meditate on what you've said, Katie. I'm sure you'll realize how displeased Our Lord must be with you. I'll go back to the rectory now to make the calls you wanted. If you wish to confess later, I'll be back."

"I'll be leavin' now, too, Katie," Mrs. Noonan said. "I'm real sorry about your mother." She sniffled. She came over to Katie and kissed her on the cheek.

Katie had forgotten the woman was in the room. Both the midwife and Mrs. Macaluso had listened to Katie's outburst and the sharp answers she had given the priest. They had not joined in or offered opinions, for which Katie was grateful. No doubt, they both knew her father for what he was. She was glad the little girls were still upstairs in Mrs. Macaluso's apartment and Davey had gone outside. She listened now, and she could hear the squeaking of the yard swing. Davey was waiting there for Father Rafferty.

Katie stretched her back and walked over to the kitchen window. Davey was sitting in the swing, crying for his mother. When he saw the priest coming, he was torn between staying with Katie and going with Father

Rafferty. Katie watched him look in both directions. Then he followed the priest. She knew he would.

After a few words of sympathy Mrs. Macaluso walked to the door.

"Please keep the girls upstairs till they come for Mama," Katie asked.

The tears fell freely down her cheeks. Mrs. Macaluso took Katie in her arms, and they cried together.

"Don't worry about the girls, Katie. I'll keep them all day. Why don't you let me fix you some breakfast?" the woman asked, patting the girl's back.

"No, thanks, I couldn't eat," Katie said. "Maybe later on. But I guess I ought to come upstairs and tell the girls about Mama."

Mrs. Macaluso nodded, touching her eyes with her handkerchief. She led the way to her apartment and Katie followed. They found Jenny and Lala on the second-floor balcony, waiting for someone to come with news of their mother.

Katie took them in her arms and sat on the steps with them. Her chin quivered.

"Mama's gone to heaven with God," she said, though the words felt like thorns in her throat. The little girls wept into Katie's skirt and she rocked them with her body. "Her baby was born dead, too," she said in a breaking voice. "But I want you to remember that Mama will never feel pain again. She'll never be cold again or hungry or frightened or tired. She'll watch over you from heaven, and you can pray to her."

They all sobbed freely and Mrs. Macaluso leaned against the railing and wept.

"Can we come down now, Katie?" Jenny asked. "We want to be with you."

"No," Katie said, more sternly than she had intended. She was thinking of the still body lying in the bedroom down below them. "Stay here with Mrs. Macaluso till tonight."

Back down in her own apartment Katie tried to keep

herself occupied. She straightened the two rooms, which were disorderly after the long night of labor and the delivery. From time to time she glanced over at her mother, who lay, hands crossed over her breast as Father Rafferty had arranged her. She had died while he was with her, and Katie had not had the courage to come close to her since her death. When the rooms were clean, and there was nothing left to do, she washed herself in the kitchen and dressed herself neatly. She drank some tea and when she had put it off as long as she could, she went to sit beside her mother.

Frances Raspanti's eyes were closed in death and her mouth was set in a peaceful expression. Katie lit the lamp so she could look at her well. She turned up the wick and sat back down and took her mother's hand. It was cold, and she dropped it at once. It fell woodenly, and the realization that her mother was dead struck her forcefully.

"Mama!" she cried, pressing her head to the bed beside her mother. "Oh, Mama!" Her sobs were loud and hard. "How can I live without you, Mama?" she wailed from the depths of her grief. "You made life bearable for us all." She looked up, her face streaked with tears. "No. You made life beautiful for us all."

Sobs came again, and she felt as if she could not catch her breath. "I loved you more than anyone in the world. I wanted to make life good for you, my angel Mama, and I never had the chance."

For hours Katie cried at her mother's side. She slept off and on, and at last the shadows closed in around her. It was late afternoon, and the undertaker had not come. Christmas Eve. A hard day to get services of any kind. She was glad Mrs. Macaluso had not sent the little girls down.

While Katie was crying, Joe Raspanti opened the door and then stood in the obscurity of a far corner, his stocking cap in his hands. When, at last, Katie rested, her face on the bed, he walked around to the other side of the bed, looking down at his wife and waiting for Katie to notice him.

Twenty-four hours ago he had left the house, as Frances always requested when she was in labor. She didn't want him to hear her cries, and he was glad to go. He was a coward and he knew it. He couldn't bear to see her suffer. The midwife would be there. Katie would be there. She wouldn't be alone.

At first he had walked the waterfront. Then, seized with panic, he went to church and prayed. He lit every candle in the rack and begged God on his knees for his wife's life, promising fidelity, gentleness, anything he could call forth from his repertoire of promises. Then he walked to the Red Lion and had a drink with some friends.

For hours he sat in Lafayette Square, in the wind and the cold, punishing himself, when he could have been in church or in a saloon.

At three o'clock in the morning he rang the bell at the rectory. Father Rafferty told him what a terrible time Frances was having. He had just returned from bringing Dr. Cooper to Julia Row. The priest told him not to go home yet. He invited Joe to sleep on the couch in the parlor, where it was warm. There Joe had slept away the morning.

Father Rafferty had awakened him when he was about to leave for Julia Row with the last sacraments. Joe wept and got up to follow, but Father Rafferty suggested he wait a bit longer, till he came back. Then he would let him know if the baby had been born and how Frances was. Joe was easily persuaded. When the priest returned, he didn't have to tell Joe that his wife was dead. He read it in the man's eyes.

Now, standing beside his wife's bed, he looked at her face, beyond pain, cold in the sleep of death. He looked at his daughter's head, bent down on the bed that was her mother's funeral bier. There, on the same bed, his oldest son had lain six months ago. What curse had the

Lord sent his family, that his beloved ones would be snatched from him?

Katie raised her head at the sound of movement and the rancid smell of perspiration. The eyes she looked into across her mother's body were bloodshot. There was a heavy stubble of dark beard on her father's chin.

"You killed her," she said evenly.

His eyebrows came together with a look of pain such as Katie had seen only on her mother's face when she was in the throes of agony. She heard the church bells clang out vespers.

"Merry Christmas, Papa," she said.

Chapter
NINETEEN

Katie looked strikingly beautiful in mourning, more so because she was so totally unaware of her beauty. She had draped the mirror in her mother's house and the one in her garret bedroom, just as her mother had done when Little Joe died. Her reflection was of little interest to her. She was concerned only that she was neatly groomed and freshly clothed.

She had bought herself two black broadcloth dresses with buttons from neck to waist, long straight sleeves, and small white cuffs and collars. Each night she washed one and ironed the other. With these, and her snow-white aprons, she was meticulous and stunning, for the severity of the costume complemented her fair skin, her wide, dark eyes, and the pinkness of her cheeks and well-drawn lips. A few curls escaped the confines of her braided coronet, lending a youthful softness to her self-imposed austerity. She could not have imagined the glances that followed her as she served at parties and dinners for the Eagans. Heads turned in astonishment as she passed quietly among the guests.

After her mother's funeral Katie made it known to her father that *she* was now in charge of the Raspanti household, and that she would also continue to work for the Eagans. Overnight she matured, she grew hard, she gave orders, she became a martinet; and she expected her brothers and sisters to fall in line. It was a hard world, Katie had decided, and there was no room in it for coddling. That was a lesson they must *all* learn.

She laid down orders for the operation of the Raspanti household. Davey, Jenny, and Lala were to bathe themselves at night, and Katie would give them inspection. She yanked at ears and hands and knees in a way that made their mother's scrubbing seem tame. She gave orders for homework and bedtime curfew that no one dared disobey. She herself was taxed beyond her strength; she had no intention of letting the children make her life one whit more difficult. Everyone complied.

Since Katie had to be at the Eagans' at seven each morning, she was up at six and in the streetcar at six-thirty. It was up to the girls to dress themselves, and to Davey to walk them to school. Jenny learned to make oatmeal for breakfast, and Lala to set the table. Surprisingly everyone functioned well.

In the evening Katie returned at five. She and Della had worked out an arrangement: if Katie were in the kitchen before breakfast, Della would start work later and stay until after the supper dishes were done. So at five each evening, Katie, having cooked and cleaned all day for the Eagans, caught the streetcar for Julia Row to cook for her own family. After supper came housecleaning, mending, ironing, and other chores that delayed her bath and retirement until midnight.

If her father was home for breakfast or dinner, she fed him. If not, it was of no concern to her. She never spoke to him. Saturday nights she waited for him in the kitchen, hand extended, and he gave her the weekly allowance for running the house. She never questioned the amount. She used what he gave her, and if she needed more, she used her own. She would have cut out her tongue before asking him for a penny. But she saved what she could from her wages, for the children were always in need of shoes or clothes, and household necessities constantly needed replenishing.

She spent her free day grocery shopping, housecleaning, and cooking for the next several days. She washed and ironed, scrubbed floors, and shampooed her hair, in general getting herself ready for another week. The days were long and grueling, but she was strong. She knew she would survive. She had no intention of giving up her job with the Eagans. Being in their home was her lifeline to Stephen, and her independence from her father was the most important luxury in her life.

She went about her work with a taciturn expression, which the Eagans interpreted as grief. She spoke to no one except for a "Yes, ma'am" or a "No, ma'am." She had turned inside herself to think, and there were not enough hours in the day to get the thinking done. The thinking spun around in a circle, twisted like a vortex around a central eye. And the central eye was Hate.

She hated her father whose infidelity had wounded her mother cruelly and whose unsatisfied desires had finally killed her. She hated the doctor who had refused to sacrifice the child to save her mother's life. Did he sleep well at night, she wondered, knowing he had let two people die? She had never tried to contact him again. She wondered if Mr. John had settled her debt with him. She had never asked.

She hated Father Rafferty for saying her mother had died doing God's work. God's work! She couldn't believe the words. Her mother had suffered the agonies of the damned and died in childbirth. Was that God's work? She hated the church that held such views. She hated God Himself for taking her mother. It was something she would never understand.

Above all she hated herself for not insisting that her mother see a physician during her pregnancy. If she had, he would have known her condition, and there might have been time for a Cesarean operation. And yet Katie knew she could hardly blame herself for that. Few women let male doctors examine them, regardless of the necessity, unless they were shameless or very liberal. Even the rich, like Mrs. Eagan, had midwives for their *accouchements,* as the Creoles called it. Creole husbands would not allow other ~~men~~, even doctors, such close contact with their wives. For a poor woman it would have been almost unthinkable.

There was one memory that helped ease the ache of so much hate. It blew like a balmy breeze, caressing her and soothing away the bitterness. It was the memory of Stephen's lips on hers, and the feel of his strong arms around her. Stephen! Stephen! The name whispered itself over and over in her soul like a prayer. How different he was from her father! How she longed to find refuge in him! Lying in bed at night, thinking of him, she could feel herself swept away from Julia Row and away from the Eagan kitchen. In her dreams she was wearing a long white dress with a wide pink sash. Her hair hung loose down her back and tumbled over her shoulders. She was in Stephen's arms in a grassy field, with the clear, blue sky overhead. "I love you, Katie," he was saying. He was kissing her lips and holding her close. "I want to marry you. It doesn't matter what anyone thinks. We'll go away together. We'll start a whole new life."

The bubble would pop, and the dream would be over. It was only a dream, nothing more. She knew it could never really happen. She could never let him abandon his family for her. She would hate herself for it, and in time he would hate her, too.

He had always been surrounded by luxury. He had grown up in a socially prominent family and been educated and traveled and groomed to take his place in their society. If he married her, an ignorant Italian servant girl, they would disown him, there was no doubt of that. He would never again know the kind of life he had been accustomed to. Oh, she knew he could support her, far better than she had ever been supported. But it was Stephen who would be deprived.

She tried to imagine Stephen taking a streetcar to work and coming home to a small apartment. It depressed her. It was unthinkable! Stephen with his barouche and his chestnut mares. Stephen with his well-cut suits and his gold cuff links. Did he know that a single pair of his cuff links would feed the Raspanti family for a month? Katie was six years younger than Stephen, but so much wiser about what lay beyond his comfortable and exclusive little circle. If he married her, would the day come when he would feel resentment toward her for having cut him off from people like himself?

And what about the help his father would have given him in business? That would be lost. He'd have to start at the bottom, on his own.

There was no life for them together, anywhere. Certainly not under Janet's roof, and God have mercy, not on Julia Row! She lay awake for hours at night, wondering where her darling was, on the other side of the world. Did he, too, kiss her in his dreams, and fret away the night searching for an answer?

All these depressing meditations blinded her to the passing of the cold, damp days of winter and the coming of spring. Her demanding schedule kept her unaware that weeks were melting into months since her mother had died. One morning Katie woke up and breathed in the freshness of April. A week later a heat wave descended upon the city.

Katie mopped her forehead as she went about her chores. She unbuttoned the neck of her bodice and rolled her long sleeves up to the elbow. She could feel the perspiration rolling down her legs, beneath the many layers of stockings and bloomers, slip and dress and apron.

She stood on the back gallery and lifted her skirt, shaking it this way and that, trying to let the air cool her saturated limbs. Even so early in the season the temperature was hitting ninety degrees every day, and the humidity was oppressive. Katie was thinking about getting out of deep mourning and going into second mourning. Then she could wear seersucker uniforms, which would be much cooler than heavy black broadcloth.

She was waiting for White Man to bring her lottery list. He had asked her to call him Mr. Herbert, but she kept forgetting. The gardener had come earlier in the morning, and the smell of fresh-cut grass wafted up on an unexpected breeze. Katie looked at the sky. The glare was so bright it hurt her eyes, but there was no sun. Another gust of wind knocked over a little ceramic flowerpot on the gallery, and Katie picked it up. It was going to rain. She could smell it.

Suddenly she heard something that sounded like a hiss. She looked around the yard and into the carriage house. "Ssss!" She heard it again. Frowning curiously, she picked up her skirts and descended the stairs to the yard and entered the carriage house.

"Ssss!"

She turned swiftly in the direction of the sound and saw, to her surprise, a young man about twenty years old, standing behind the Victoria, hidden in its shadows. He was neatly dressed but apparently nervous.

"Who are you?" she asked. "What are you doing here?"

"Come here," he whispered. Curious, she walked over toward him. "I've come to bring you a letter from Stephen," he said.

Katie thought her knees would buckle under her, and inadvertently she reached out to hold onto the young man's arm.

"My name is Thomas LeJeune. I live a few blocks from here on Napoleon Avenue. I was studying in Paris at the Sorbonne, and Stephen and I happened to run into each other. Well, you can imagine how surprised we were, I mean to find each other in Paris. Why, Stephen and I have known each other all our lives. We went to . . ."

"Please," Katie begged. "The letter. When did he give it to you?"

"About two weeks ago. Just before I left to come home. I'd had enough of Europe. You see, I've got a sweetheart here, and . . ."

"Mr. LeJeune," Katie interrupted, "tell me. Is he coming home? Is Stephen coming home?"

"No. Not yet. He was going on to London and then to Berlin. But he's going to send me a letter for you every week. He wants me to bring it here. He told me not to let anyone know. Are you here every day?"

"Every day but Wednesday. Don't come on Wednesday. And never leave the letter with anyone but me. Please!" she asked with fear in her eyes.

The boy knew how important this was to her. "Don't worry," he said. "And if you'll forgive me, miss, I . . . certainly can understand why Stephen is so moonstruck."

He smiled. It was a boyish smile, full of innocence, ingenuous.

"Thank you . . . Thomas." She lowered her head and dimpled. "Is he really moonstruck?"

"I never saw a man so much in love."

Katie felt the blood rush to her face. Her joy was so complete that she was sure she would die from it. "The letter?" she said again. "May I have it, please?"

He gave her the envelope, bent and crumpled from its two-week voyage across the ocean. She said a hurried good-bye, never asking Thomas's address or when she would see him again, hardly thanking him for what meant so much to her. She ran up the steps to the gallery, and then up the inside staircase to her room. She sat on the bed, panting, and tore the envelope open. Her fingers trembled as she counted the pages. One, two, three, four. She was ecstatic. She had to brush the tears from her eyes so she could focus on the words.

My dearest Kate,

She crushed the letter to her bosom and closed her eyes. My dearest Kate. No one had ever called her Kate. It was *his* name for her.

> I'm sending this letter by an old and trusted friend, who will be our intermediary from now on. Please write me, and give your letter to him. He'll know where to send it.

Write you! How can I? she asked herself. She had never learned to write, except for the ugly misshapen letters Della had taught her. Stephen had forgotten that. But she'd learn now. She'd learn right away. She'd practice all day, every day.

> I have very comfortable lodgings in a boarding-house for students of the Sorbonne. At first, I took a fancy apartment in the Isle de la Cîté, but I decided I preferred to live the way the other students live, so I moved to the rue D'Allemagne. I catch the omnibus each morning. It's a double-decker bus pulled by horses. I like to climb up the tiny corkscrew staircase at the rear of the bus and sit on the roof. From there I can see all the shops along the way, the crowds in the streets, the elm trees. The bus crosses the Seine, where the two arms of the river are outstretched, and I can see the islands, the monuments, even the towers of Notre Dame. Paris is a glorious city, especially in the spring. I wish we could live here together some day, my love.

Katie stopped reading and let the tears fall from her eyes. He really wanted to marry her. Suppose they *did* live in a distant city like Paris. Then it wouldn't matter if they were of different bloodlines and backgrounds. No one would know, and no one would care. Stephen didn't care. He had left the comfort of the better part of the city to live the way the students lived. Perhaps she had not done him justice, presuming that the only way he could be happy was if he were surrounded by luxury.

My studies are enjoyable. In electronics, they are no further advanced here than we are in America, but it is interesting to hear the subject taught in French. It is a real challenge to be studying German under a French *maîtresse*! She pronounces the consonants much too softly, but she is an excellent teacher.

My work with Monsieur Marais has been exhilarating. I have learned more from him about the photography of motion than I could have learned on my own in a decade. The man is truly a genius. It makes me realize how much I have yet to learn. I look forward to my sojourn in Berlin.

So he's going to Berlin, Katie thought. No hope that his travels would be cut short. He had gone to Europe, not for his parents' sake, but because he *had* to know whatever anyone could teach him in his field, and his eagerness to learn had not diminished. She was proud of him for that, but disappointed that their separation was to be prolonged. She sighed.

I wish you could know the German students I have befriended in this boardinghouse. They have come here with nothing but the clothes on their backs. They take any kind of work to make a franc or two to buy food for a few days. They live on almost nothing, yet they are talented and witty, the most charming people I have ever known, and they are all helping me to learn their language. One plays the piano accordian which he brought with him from Frankfurt. They put on plays in

their butchered French. Then they serve tea and
cakes with as much pride as if it were a banquet.
They are the salt of the earth, and I admire them
more than I can tell you.

Oh Stephen, my Stephen, you love them for what
they are: stouthearted, ambitious, courageous. It
doesn't matter to you that they are without money,
without background, without anything but raw determination. Oh, yes, my love, there is hope for us!

And now, my Kate, let me say what is in my
heart. I love you and I want you to be my wife.
Where and how we will live and who will accept
us is of little concern to me. It would be fine if my
family would welcome you with open arms, because you deserve to be cherished and treasured.
But I am a realist, and I know my mother. I do
not expect her blessing, and I do not need it. I
need only you.

It will be another year before I come home.
You will be seventeen by then and of marriageable
age. Plan to be married next April, my love. It will
give us both something to wake up for each morning.

Write to me, dear Kate. All my love,

Stephen

Katie lay back across her bed and gazed at the ceiling. To love a man so much and be loved in return was
a kind of ecstasy she had never expected to know. And
such a man! Brilliant and handsome, gentle and kind.
In that moment she knew it was possible that they
would marry and spend the rest of their lives together,
somewhere. She knew Stephen more intimately through
his letter than she had ever known him in their few
brief conversations. She knew that he measured people

not by their wealth or background, but by heart and courage and determination to overcome obstacles.

It would be a year. She could get through it easily now. Every task would be a joy. No labor would be too exhausting, no day too long, no heat too unbearable.

Katie reached across her bed to pull out her Civil War book. Sitting on the side of the bed, she opened it to where she had pressed the flower. She lifted it from the page and sniffed it. The sweet perfume of the night jasmine was dying but not gone, like a fading photograph, or a dream one forgets in time. She pressed the petals to her lips and put it back in the book. She felt as if she had touched Stephen today. She had read his letter and savored once again the fragrance of the flower he had given her long ago. No matter what the future held in store, no one could ever take these things away from her.

Chapter
TWENTY

"Get out of my way, Warren," Charlotte cried out irascibly. "Can't you see my arms are loaded? Any minute now, I'm gonna go head over heels down these stairs. I don't know what good it is to have servants," she went on mumbling, "if you have to do all the work yourself."

Katie looked at Treece and made a mouth. Katie was weighed down with a corrugated cardboard box filled with lawn-tennis equipment; Treece was carrying an enormous paper bag in each arm. Katie wondered how much more "the servants" were expected to carry at one time.

Moving day for the summer months at Milneburg was always a scene of general confusion. It was like transferring a household. There were barbecue grills for fish fries on the beach, ice chests and extra cots, linens and pots and pans, to say nothing of clothes for four people, bathing dresses and caps and shoes, crab nets and fishing poles. The back gallery was a mountain range of boxes and packages, as the human conveyor belt kept chipping off at the stacks and transferring parcels to the wagons.

It looked like nothing but work to Katie, and she wondered if it was really worth the effort. Of course she knew she was seeing only the labor involved, and the short tempers of moving day. What she never got to see was the fun that began when the neighboring camps started filling up and friends got together on the beach for swimming parties and picnics.

Katie heard them all laughing sometimes at the dinner table over a joke a friend had told when they had sat around the campfire roasting marshmallows. There was a story Warren liked to tell about the time his friend Willie got lost and went into the wrong camp and spent the night on a cot on the porch. They probably enjoyed themselves in their own way, Katie thought, but she wouldn't have joined them there expecting to have fun. She would have to be born all over again to do that, she told herself. They were a different breed of people, except for Stephen, of course, and Mr. John.

What a relief it was to see the last wagon rolling out of the driveway! They were gone for the summer. What a blessed exodus! Katie knew she'd miss Della, but now she and Treece could fall back into that easy routine they had established the summer before, and life would be pleasant for three whole months.

With only Mr. John to cook and clean for, the days were delightful. There was lots of free time, and she could spend it all practicing her penmanship and writing letters to Stephen. Every Thursday for the past eight weeks, she had received a letter from her darling, always with picture postcards enclosed so she could see the beautiful buildings and the rivers and monuments he was visiting in Paris, and now in London. He had sent her pictures of the Eiffel Tower and the Hall of Mirrors at Versailles, of Buckingham Palace and the Tower of London.

The day after Thomas LeJeune had delivered Stephen's first letter, Katie had used the excuse of shopping day to have Mason drive her to the five-and-dime on Canal Street. There she had selected a tablet of paper for practicing her writing, a dozen pencils with erasers, a pocket pencil sharpener, some scented stationery, and a book on penmanship. Thus armed, she returned to her garret room and began her self-instruction.

She set herself up at the schoolroom desk Warren had brought her and laid her supplies on the bed beside her. She threw her window open and took off her dress and slip. Then, in her camisole and bloomers, she sat at her desk and began. She decided to take a letter a day, capital and small, and practice it till it was perfect.

Tongue pressed against her upper lip, she pinched her fingers around the pencil and tried to write an A. She followed the instructions Della had given her months ago.

After half an hour a dozen crumpled sheets had accumulated on the bedroom floor, and Katie slumped in her desk in disgust. Writing wasn't easy at all. Most people made it look so simple, but she was sure they had forgotten how difficult it was when they began. What she really needed was someone to show her how to hold the pencil. Her little sister Jenny! She'd ask Jenny to help her. Jenny was eleven now and very bright in school. Her handwriting was beautiful. The inspiration revived her.

At five o'clock that evening, sitting at the kitchen table in the Raspanti apartment, Katie discovered how much easier it was when someone showed you how.

"Don't grip the pencil so tight," Jenny said, putting her hand over Katie's. "Here, let me show you."

It went along superbly after that. Katie was so engrossed in her new skills that she didn't notice the time going by until nine-year-old Lala started fixing scrambled eggs with ham for supper.

"Here, Lala, let me do that," Katie said.

"No, Katie. Go on with your writing," Lala answered.

Katie smiled at both her little sisters and gave them each a hug. They were growing up so beautifully. They were neat and well mannered, and capable of doing any household chores. And never a complaint about schoolwork or housework. She loved them with all her heart, and she vowed that she would keep them with her when she married, until they found good husbands to take care of them.

"We're going to do nice things together this summer," Katie told the girls.

"Are we, Katie?" Lala asked. Lala had light brown hair, like Davey, and the same sprinkling of freckles across her nose. She looked more Irish than Italian. Good for her, Katie thought. Maybe she won't be called "dago" or "wop" so often. "What are we going to do?" Lala wanted to know.

"Well, you'll be on vacation, so you can get the house in order, and I can come home early since it's only Mr. John there now. He's an angel. If I cook in the morning, he doesn't mind if Treece serves him his dinner, and I can take off once in a while. Then we can go on outings together. We'll take the Smoky Mary all the way to Lake Pontchartrain. But maybe we ought to go on a Wednesday, when I have the whole day off, and bring a picnic lunch."

"Oh, Katie, how wonderful!" Lala cried.

"Can we manage, Katie?" Jenny asked. "Is there enough money?"

"Of course there is. I have some money saved. And we deserve to have some fun. We can go to West End Amusement Park, too, and swim off the beach."

"But we haven't any bathing dresses," Jenny objected.

"Hmm," Katie said, drumming her fingers on the table. "Well, I guess we can rent some at the bathhouse. Mrs. Macaluso did that for her kids last summer."

The little girls giggled excitedly. They clapped their hands. "Oh, Katie, let's do it," they begged.

"We will. We positively will." And she laughed along with them. "What about Davey?" Katie asked. "Will he want to come?"

"No. No, just us," they both begged. "Besides he'd rather be with Father Rafferty," Jenny added.

"Would he really?" Katie asked soberly.

She got up and took the knives and forks from the

table drawer. She cleared the papers and pencils from the table.

"Yes, he would," Jenny said. "All he ever wants to do is serve Mass and follow Father Rafferty around. He'll prob'ly be a priest."

"Has he said so?" Katie asked.

Davey was able to answer the question himself. He pushed the kitchen door open, pecked Katie on the cheek, and walked over to the sink to wash his hands.

"I haven't told anyone yet, because I wanted you to be the first to know," Davey said. He whipped a dish towel from the rack and dried his hands. Then he pulled a chair up to the table and sat, and Katie sat beside him. "I *am* going to be a priest, Katie."

She drew in a breath and her face saddened. Her brother seemed so old for thirteen. They were all so mature, so serious. They had done so much shifting for themselves. Suddenly her heart was filled with love for them. She took Davey's hand affectionately.

"Now that I'm out of grammar school," he went on, "I can go right into the seminary. Father Rafferty has arranged it for me. I won't have to pay anything. There are scholarships for boys who can't pay their own tuition."

Katie hated charity. Most of all she didn't want the boy to be a priest. She didn't want him to grow up in the image of Father Rafferty, narrow and unbending and holy and self-righteous when it came to spending other people's lives. He would live out his life in the dark recesses of musty confessionals, listening to the made-up sins of pious old ladies. What a waste of a young man's energies! She wanted more for her only brother.

"Why do you want to be a priest, Davey?" she asked.

"Why?" he asked, surprised at the question. He frowned, and then, suddenly, he smiled. "I never wanted to be anything else in my life. I love God with all my heart, and I want to spend the rest of my life serving Him. Besides it's what Mama wanted me to be."

She looked into his light brown eyes, so handsome beneath the well-defined brows, and she knew his life was set. There was as little chance of changing his mind as there was of talking her out of loving Stephen. Such a short time ago they had all been children here together, sleeping in the same room. Now they were setting their feet on different paths that would lead them away from one another.

Katie leaned over and kissed the boy's warm cheek. She had never let the children know that she no longer attended Mass or said her rosary; she had no intention of spreading her bitterness around. Let them have the comfort of their religion. They would be disillusioned soon enough.

After ten days of practice, Katie could wait no longer. She was ready to write her letter to Stephen. She decided to make it short and to use no difficult words, and nothing with z's or q's. She copied the letter a dozen times before she finally wrote it on her good blue stationery. Then she read it again and again before folding it and sealing it in an envelope.

Dear Stephen,

I guess you are wondering why I have not sent any letters yet. It is because I had to learn how to write first. This is my very first letter, so please excuse mistakes.

There is so much I want to say. There is so much in my heart. I think of you every day. I think about Paris and your apartment and your friends, and how lucky they are to be with you.

The family has gone to Milneburg for the summer. I guess you will miss going to camp, but I'm sure it is more exciting to be in Europe. It is hard to believe that a whole year has gone by since you

came home from the camp last summer to get the
volleyball net. That will always be one of the best
days of my life.

Treece and I are alone here every day, and your
father is home at night. I have lots of time to read
and spend with my sisters.

I love hearing all about Paris and seeing the
picture postcards. Most of all, I love hearing about
you. I am always afraid we will be found out.
Your mother would never forgive me.

I miss you, Stephen. Two years is a very long
time.

                                        Love,
                                          Katie

She wanted to say "I love you, Stephen." She ached
to shape the words and look at them on her blue-
scented paper. She wanted to tell him how happy she
was that he still wanted to marry her, and she was beginning to think that it might be possible. But she didn't
have the courage yet to say such things in writing. She
still wrote so poorly that her script would make the
words seem foolish, even childish. Perhaps when her
handwriting improved, the words would seem more mature, and she would think of a better way to say them.

Katie did not tell Stephen about her mother's death;
she felt she could not form the words on paper that
were still so raw in her heart.

Chapter
TWENTY-ONE

Quietly she opened the library door and turned on the light. She let her eyes wander across the walls of books. It was her favorite place in the world. She had never quite grown used to being here, surrounded by the works of learned writers. She sighed contentedly and smiled, relishing her solitude and her sense of belonging. Mr. John had given her *carte blanche*, as Janet called it, and it made her feel important.

For the first time in her memory she was all alone in the Eagan house. There had been no need to go home to Julia Row tonight. Mrs. Macaluso had invited Davey and the girls to dinner, so Katie had decided to stay at the Eagans' and read. Treece had gone to the servants' quarters for the night, and Mr. John had taken the horse and buggy and gone visiting after dinner.

Katie walked briskly to the shelf of novels. She had been so busy with her writing in recent weeks that she had not looked over Mr. John's latest acquisitions. She scanned the shelves. All the old book covers were so familiar to her that she noticed the new ones at once. She passed her fingers lovingly along the bindings. *Conquest of Canaan*, by Booth Tarkington. She loved Booth Tarkington. She remembered how much she had enjoyed *Beautiful Lady*. *The Call of the Wild*, by Jack London. She pulled the book from the shelf. On the cover, sketched in ink, was a picture of a dog pulling a sled. She put the volume back. *The Jungle*, by Upton Sinclair. She didn't like the sound of that. *The Seven*

Darlings, by Gouverneur Morris. Was he really a governor, she wondered, or was that his name? She pulled the book out with her index finger, and opened the cover. Chapter One. Page One.

> Six of the Darlings were girls. The seventh was a young man that looked like Galahad and took exquisite photographs.

Katie walked over to the encyclopedia resting open on its stand. Galahad. Galahad. She licked her finger and turned to the G's. There, looking up into the heavens, was a beautiful young man in a metal suit with a sword hanging at his side. He was standing beside a snow-white horse, holding a helmet under his arm. His face seemed to glow with inner goodness, and there was a nimbus of light around his head.

> Galahad: the purest and noblest knight of the Round Table in the legends of King Arthur. He took the lead in the search for the Holy Grail, the cup from which Christ drank at the Last Supper. Sir Galahad is pictured as the ideal young man, set apart by his strength and purity.

She looked at the face again. It could have been Stephen, even to the cleft in the chin. And wasn't Stephen like Galahad? The purest and noblest knight of them all? She closed the encyclopedia and went back to *The Seven Darlings*.

> Their father had died within the month and Mr. Gilpin, the lawyer, had just faced them, in family assembled, with the lamentable fact that they, who had been so very, very rich, were now astonishingly poor.

She wanted to look up "lamentable" in the dictionary. It was her way of improving her vocabulary. But she was sure she had caught the general meaning in context, and she was anxious to find out what happened to the Darlings. She took the book to the softest chair in the room, which was Janet's chair. She pulled the cord that turned on the floor lamp and settled down to read.

Hours later Mr. John opened the door to the library and Katie gave a little cry of fright.

"Oh, I'm sorry, Mr. John," she said, rising. "I was so absorbed in this story, I didn't realize the time."

"No, *I*'m the one who's sorry," he said. "I didn't mean to frighten you. What are you reading?"

"*The Seven Darlings,*" she answered, smiling. "It's a very good book."

"Really? Well, tell me about it, Katie. I haven't read it yet."

"Oh, it's not a book for *you*, Mr. John. It's just a light love story at a summer resort," she explained, mispronouncing the last word.

John Eagan tugged at his mustache, restraining a smile. He hesitated. Then, he decided she was smart enough to take correction.

"That's a summer re-*sort,* Katie. It's a place where people go on vacation."

"Oh? I did it again, didn't I?" Her laughter was tinged with embarrassment. "But I knew what it meant, the re*sort,* I mean. I looked it up in the dictionary."

"You did?" he seemed pleased.

"Yes, sir."

"Do you always do that?"

"When I don't know the word. Yes, sir."

"Well, I'm very proud of you, Katie. You're doing a wonderful job of educating yourself. You're a very ambitious young lady. You would have done splendidly in college."

Katie beamed. It meant so much to her to have Mr. John's approval.

"Oh, no, sir," she objected. "I'll never be smart enough for that."

"Nonsense. You're smart enough already. Have you learned to write yet?"

"Yes, sir. I've taught myself."

"Here. Show me," he said. He walked over to the secretary and pulled down the desk extension. He drew a sheet of white paper from one of the pigeonholes. He dipped a pen in ink and handed it to Katie.

"May I use pencil?" she asked. "I've never practiced with a pen holder and pen point."

"Of course."

Katie sat in Janet's rosewood chair and opened the book she was reading. She began copying a paragraph. She pressed her tongue to her upper lip and let the pencil lie loose against her knuckle as Jenny had shown her. All her practicing had not been in vain. Even she was pleased when she had finished. The lines of script were neat and uniform, and all the letters slanted in the same direction.

"Beautiful, Katie!" Mr. John exclaimed. "You really are a wonder. You manage two households, take care of two families, and you still have time to teach yourself to read and write."

"Thank you, Mr. John. I really thank you, sir. But I know it can never be the same as a real school education."

"You don't think so? Let me tell you a little story, Katie."

He sat in his Morris chair, and Katie took the hassock at his feet.

"You know the man I admire more than anyone alive today?"

"Yes, sir. Mr. Edison."

"Right. Well, Thomas Edison was seven years old when he started school. He went to school for three months, and that was all the formal education the man ever had."

Katie's jaw dropped open, and her mouth formed an O. Eagan nodded to emphasize the point.

"There were many who thought the boy was dim-witted," Eagan said, "but his mother knew better. She knew he was gifted, and she taught him at home. She was a schoolteacher, you see."

"Oh."

"By the time he was twelve, he was reading very advanced literature. But his real love was science. He was never any good at math. I say that because I never was either, and it makes me feel a little better.

"All the time we were growing up, Edison and I, we were being driven by the same desires. I don't mean to compare myself to Edison, but I'm trying to make a point about formal education. Neither one of us had much, you see. Edison was in New Jersey and I was here in New Orleans. We didn't meet till we were grown. But all through our childhood, our lives followed the same pattern. We both loved physics. We both used every cent we could get to buy chemicals and try out experiments. We both had laboratories in our basements, and we both liked to tinker with inventions. When we finally met, in the telegraph office here in New Orleans, we were like long-lost friends who had found each other."

Katie smiled, enjoying Mr. John's conversation.

"It didn't take me long to realize that I couldn't hold a candle to Al, but as long as he was willing to have me tag along, I intended to work for him, because he was the kind of a man you meet once in a lifetime, *if* you're lucky."

Eagan laced his fingers across his waist and rested his head against the back of the chair. He closed his eyes and smiled. Then, remembering, he opened them again. "He visited here once, when Janet and I were first married."

"In this very house?"

"He sat in this very chair," Eagan answered proudly. He pulled his watch from his pocket and got to his feet. "My goodness, I didn't realize how late it was, Miss Kate," he said jocularly.

The use of the nickname startled her. Stephen was the only one who ever called her Kate. Could Mr. John have seen one of Stephen's letters? No, it wasn't possible. She kept her letters on Julia Row, where they could never be discovered. She felt suddenly very dishonest to be chatting away with Mr. John, all the while concealing the fact that she was in love with his son. But what was she to do? She had no choice but to wait until Stephen came home before telling anyone at all.

"You'd better be off to bed, my girl, or you'll never be able to get up in the morning."

"I'm used to it, Mr. John. I never go to bed till midnight when I'm home on Julia Street."

Eagan's gray-brown eyebrows came together. "Why is that, Katie?"

"Oh, there's so much to do. Laundry and housecleaning, and supervising my little sisters' baths and studies."

"You work too hard, Katie," Eagan said kindly. He scratched his chin and paced the floor as though figuring out what he could do about the problem. Katie waited. "I'll tell you what," he said. "I want you to take a week's vacation, starting right away."

"I have no place to go," Katie said.

"Stay home with your sisters. Sleep late. Take the little girls for a ride in the streetcar, or out to the beach. Make a picnic lunch. Go swimming. Go to a moving picture show. There are lots of things to do right here in the city."

Katie lowered her head. "Mr. John, I can't do without the wages, sir, and I don't need free time. I'm happy here."

He placed his hand on her shoulder. "I'm glad you're

happy here, but everyone needs time to himself once in a while. I'm planning to pay you, Katie. I wouldn't ask you to take time off without pay."

Katie tried to check a sob in her throat, but it sounded quite loud in the enormous room. She made an involuntary step in Mr. John's direction. She longed to hug the man, because he was so good and she loved him like a father. But she stopped herself and lowered her head.

Eagan knew what was in the child's heart. He opened his arms to her, and she came to him. He held her fondly, as he would a daughter.

Katie pressed her cheek to his vest. He smelled of clean serge and Havana cigars and brandy and horses, and she filled her nostrils with the aroma.

This was the man who would be her father-in-law, and he would be proud of her. To him she had always been a person, not a servant, and deserving of respect. He was first-generation American, just as she was herself. Because of his father's enterprise he was a very wealthy man, and his wealth had been his entrée into society. As a man with a keen and inquiring mind, and a disciple of Edison, he was sought after and respected. But he had never lost sight of what he was. He was the boy who had been expelled from high school and despaired of by his father because he had dared to aspire to something different. He was only what he had made himself by sleepless nights and determination and an all-consuming love for the work he did.

In John Eagan's eyes Katie's marriage to Stephen would not only be possible but desirable. But the thought of Janet's expression when Stephen would at last tell her of his feelings made her shiver in Mr. John's arms.

"What is it, Katie dear?" Eagan asked.

"Oh, nothing, sir. I'm just so happy. That's all."

He smiled. He held her away from him, placing his hands on her shoulders.

"After your week of vacation, Treece will have hers. And then we'll begin a new schedule. The two of you will alternate working here in the summer. Three days on, three days off, or however you want to work it. But a full-grown man shouldn't need the services of two women to survive. It makes me feel decrepit." He raised his finger. "Full wages, of course." A full smile widened beneath the mustache.

Katie's eyes were shining. "Mr. John, I think you're the kindest, loveliest man I've ever known," she said.

She picked up *The Seven Darlings* and left the room.

Chapter
TWENTY-TWO

It was Katie's best summer ever. As she planned activities with her sisters, she was aware of a metamorphosis taking place inside her. She was shedding the shrewishness she had put on as an armor against the world that had hurt her.

To Jenny and Lala it was a summer they would always remember. Frances had always tried to help her children find pleasure in little things, for she had nothing else to give them. She had tried to create a happy atmosphere for them to work and play in. But never before had they had the kind of experiences they had that summer with Katie.

At West End Amusement Park they walked the boardwalk built over the water and had lunch at the outdoor restaurant. They sat on a bench and listened to a band concert. They rode the Ferris wheel and the scenic railway, and they took a ride in the Tunnel of Love and watched a young man kiss his girl friend in the car in front of them.

Another day they boarded the New Orleans-City-and-Lake Railroad for Spanish Fort, where they rented bathing dresses and waded in the water. They had brought a picnic basket with them, and after their "bath," they spread a tablecloth on a redwood table beneath a pavilion and ate their sandwiches. They giggled, and their long wet braids dripped into their lunch, and they had the time of their lives.

As Mr. John had suggested, Katie took them riding

on streetcars all over town. She discovered places in the city she didn't know existed. One day they went to Canal Street, and walked in and out of stores like grand ladies on a shopping spree. The stores on Canal Street were painted full across the front with advertising in bright, enormous letters a story high. They read like lines in a newspaper:

MOODY'S SHIRTS
GENTS FURNISHING GOODS
AGENCY OF THE TROY SHIRT COLLAR MANUFAC-
TORY
THE NEW ORLEANS SHIRT EMPORIUM——HOSIERY
AND GLOVES

Moody's shirt store was on a corner, and the advertising wrapped around the building.

Another storefront boasted:

TYLER'S
WATCHES AND JEWELRY
SILVER AND PLATED WARE

The signs were garish and lively, in keeping with booming business, and nobody knew or cared if they covered up magnificent dentiled cornices and cast-iron pillars with ancanthus-leaf capitals, buried now, like the nineteenth-century architects who had labored over them.

After walking the length of Canal Street, the girls paid a nickel each at the box office of the Acme Theater and entered the darkened building. They rested their feet as they watched *Rescued from the Eagle's Nest*, a one-reel film that lasted nine minutes. Over and over again, the brief plot unfolded, and the girls watched for almost an hour. They loved the piano playing of a vigorous young woman who watched the movie screen and took her cue from the pace of the action. Even though the film split and they saw number fives and circles running up and down the screen, they had a thoroughly delightful time.

The weeks that followed Katie's vacation were almost as enjoyable as the vacation itself. She now spent three days at a time on Julia Row, and left the house in such good condition and with so much food cooked that it was not necessary for her to return for the next three days.

When she was at home, she and her sisters worked on the quilt and in the garden. The first time she took the quilt from under her mother's bed, and found the moss-green coat there, Katie cried, and Jenny and Lala comforted her. The little girls did not cry so easily for their mother. They were so much younger, and they had never been as close to Frances as Katie had. It was just as well, Katie thought. The emptiness she felt for her mother was a deep and painful thing. If they were spared that, she was glad.

Once, after three days away from the Eagans', it occurred to Katie that she might have missed her rendezvous with Thomas LeJeune. She hoped that he had not let himself be seen or given the letter to Treece. He wouldn't do that, she assured herself. She had warned him sternly enough. But she must be sure to be there the next time he came, or he might do something foolish. She realized that she didn't even know his address. Napoleon Avenue, he had said, but what number?

She arranged her schedule with Treece so that she would always be at the Eagans' on Thursdays, which would be her meeting day with Thomas. That would be easier than making a new schedule with him every week, and worrying whether or not he would remember it. The next time she saw him, she wrote his address in her notebook. She almost hugged the boy when he handed her *two* letters from Stephen. What a treasure trove! She would read them slowly and savor them. She would try to picture where he was sitting when he wrote them and how he was dressed and how he was holding the pen. In her fantasy she would take the pen from his hand and press his hand to her cheek. She wanted to reach across the ocean and touch her lips to his. Oh, God, she loved him so!

September brought the Eagans home, in their usual disgruntled and sunburned condition. Davey entered the seminary that fall, and it left Katie depressed for weeks. She felt that he, too, had been taken from her and there was nothing left of her family now but her sisters. Her father seldom came home anymore, but he still sent her money or left it there in her absence.

Mrs. Macaluso had told her, when they had a private moment together, that he was drinking more and more. She said she had seen him one day with her own eyes, stretched out across the sidewalk before a saloon, and she had had to pick up her skirts and step across him to continue on her way. Katie felt ashamed for herself and for her sisters, but not for him. Her hatred for her father was already so intense that nothing could make it deeper.

She wondered how he managed to work, intoxicated all the time. Perhaps Mrs. Macaluso was exaggerating.

Why was he drinking? Katie wondered. Was it to numb the memory of his wife lying dead in her bed? Or was it the memory of Katie's accusation he was trying to forget?

During the Christmas holidays the servants were called together in the library. Mr. John paced the floor, grinning happily and rubbing his hands together. Janet sat at her needlepoint screen and watched her husband. She, too, was obviously delighted.

"Della, Treece, Katie, Mason," Mr. John began, "we're going to have a most unusual guest in our house." He brought his palms together resoundingly and laughed aloud.

"Dat's got to be Mr. Edison," Della said, grinning as widely as her employer.

"No, Della, if you can believe it, it's someone even more important than that."

"Den de onliest man dat kin be is de President."

"That's exactly who it is," John Eagan announced. He stopped pacing and checked their expressions.

Silence fell over the room.

"Aw, Mr. John," Della said, "you mus' be funnin' us." She put her hands on her hips and assumed a scolding expression.

"Not at all, Della," Eagan said. "Mr. Teddy Roosevelt is going to visit the city, and at the request of my good friend, Thomas Edison, he'll be having dinner here."

"My Gawd in heaven!" Della exclaimed.

The rest of the servants were speechless.

"Mistuh John, suh," Della pleaded, "Ah cain't cook no dinner fo' no President of the Yewnited States. No, suh. Ah jus' cain't do it."

"Please don't carry on, Della," Janet said tightly, pulling a needle through the crewel screen. "I'm going to supervise everything."

Eagan resumed his nervous pacing, and the smile returned to his lips. He was an unsophisticated man, and he was genuinely delighted.

"Mr. Roosevelt is a man of very simple tastes," he said. "He's an outdoor man. He's probably cooked many a meal over a campfire. We're not going to go through any elaborate preparations. If you just prepare simple Southern Creole food, I'm sure he'll enjoy it immensely. Now don't worry. Just get the house in order, and be sure you all have new uniforms."

"How much time we got?" Della asked, frowning with puckered lips.

"A week," John said.

* * *

If John Eagan thought for a minute that Janet Charbonnet Eagan was going to have the President of the United States to dinner and offer him simple Southern Creole cooking, he was very much mistaken. If he thought that the chief executive would be invited to sit at Janet's table without elaborate preparations, he was the most naïve man who ever lived.

The day after the announcement Janet was in the library at the crack of dawn, her glasses on the bridge of her nose, poring over cookbooks and menus, seating arrangements and table settings. She made notes at her secretary, scratching out and adding to the menu until she had arrived at what she considered an acceptable formal dinner, but she decided to keep her mind open to changes till the very last minute.

Her dinner would include:

> Celery and Olives
> Turtle soup au sherry
> Grilled pompano
> Roast duck à l'orange with wild rice
> Spinach soufflé
> Hearts of lettuce salad with French dressing
> French bread
> Bread pudding and hard sauce
> Café brûlot

There was to be champagne in silver coolers. Bordeaux wine, Benedictine, brandy, and cognac, and the finest Havana cigars.

Janet put the pen in its holder and called Della to help her. Out of the armoire came the thirty-foot linen tablecloth and the two dozen lace-edged napkins from Bonnie Villere's trousseau. Down from the attic came the Sèvres service plates, the fingerbowls and the silver champagne coolers and goblets. From the china cabinet

came the Sèvres "Old Paris" service for twenty-four
and the Waterford crystal. And from the buffet the
Georgian silver flatware.

The silver epergne would be polished and brought to
the florist for an arrangement of winter roses and chry-
santhemums. Red roses, perhaps, Janet thought, and
blue and white mums. An American-flag arrangement!
How splendid!

She left the rest of the china counting to Della and
returned to her secretary. She made a note for the florist at once. Then she copied her menu in her very best
script for the *Daily Picayune*. The society eidtor would
be delirious to publish what Janet Charbonnet would be
serving the President of the United States for dinner.

Midmorning, Janet dressed herself in a walking suit
and a sailor hat and ordered Mason to come to the
front door with the carriage. She was on her way to
Galatoire's to order the dinner and to hire a half-dozen
men who were experienced at serving formal banquets.
She had never for a fleeting moment intended that any
member of her household staff come near the dining
room during the presidential dinner.

From the restaurant Mason drove her through the
narrow streets of the French Quarter to Tyler's Jewel-
ers, where she purchased two dozen china napkin rings
with matching china place cards in red, white, and blue,
several cut-glass decanters, a half-dozen crystal vases, a
dozen silver-rimmed ashtrays, and two dozen demitasse
cups in cobalt blue.

The next stop was the office of the *Daily Picayune*,
facing Lafayette Square. The society editor had gotten
wind of the coming dinner for the President, and he
greeted her warmly, pulling out a chair and rubbing his
hands together. Janet Charbonnet was always good
copy, but never so good as now. She took off her gloves
and loosened the strings of her reticule, drawing out the
menu. Beaming, the editor asked pertinent questions:

time, date, names of the guests, decorations. Janet presented her guest list and her program for the evening. Publicity was nothing new to the chatelaine of the Eagan estate.

The guest list had caused her many a fretful moment. She knew that society matrons all over town were sitting on their front porches waiting for the sight of Mason bringing them the hand-written invitation to be present at the dinner in honor of Mr. Roosevelt. It was impossible to invite them all. There would be twenty-four people at table. She could have invited two hundred. Many would never speak to her again while others would be her devoted slaves for life. There was nothing she could do about it.

Near Lee Circle she completed her intinerary for the day. She stopped at Bim's Florist Shoppe with her order for the presidential arrangement. Then she went directly home, removed her corset, and fell into bed exhausted.

The pace was to continue throughout the week. Each day new ideas came to Janet. She visited her seamstress with bolts of cotton in red, white, and blue, and ordered a bunting to be made. It was to be draped over her front porch in honor of Mr. Roosevelt. In truth, it was to announce that she, Janet Eagan, was entertaining the President, if there was anyone left in the city who did not already know it.

She hired a Pierce Great Arrow touring car to call for the President at the St. Charles Hotel, where he would be staying during his visit. She stared at the bedroom ceiling throughout the night, hoping she had not forgotten anything and came to the breakfast table in the morning with dark smudges beneath her eyes from lack of sleep.

The servants soon realized that they were to have no part in the affair. It was both a relief and a disappointment. Even the "new uniforms," which Mr. John had so innocently suggested, were not to be seen by anyone at all. After a day or two they sensed that it would be wise to keep out of Janet's way when she came charging through the house and into the kitchen.

They polished the prisms of the chandeliers. They cleaned silver and washed china and crystal. They scrubbed windows and laundered curtains and polished baseboards. They rubbed lemon oil into every piece of furniture in the house.

Early on the day of the presidential dinner, wagons from the restaurant, the florist, the liquor store, the jeweler, and other secondary establishments began to flow in an endless procession into the carriageway. When Katie arrived in the kitchen, Della was ecstatic about the article in the morning paper. Mr. John had brought it with him to breakfast and left it for the servants.

"Jes' wait till you read dis, Katie," Della said, beaming. "It tell all 'bout whut we gonna have fo' dinner an' ev'rything."

Katie smiled and took the paper. She read aloud:

PRESIDENT THEODORE ROOSEVELT TO ARRIVE TO-DAY
CHIEF EXECUTIVE WILL INSPECT CITY PORT FACILITIES
MAYOR AND GOVERNOR WILL WELCOME T.R. AT CITY HALL
PROMINENT CIVIC LEADER TO ENTERTAIN PRESIDENT AT DINNER

At 10 o'clock this morning, President Theodore Roosevelt will arrive by boat at the foot of Canal Street. The chief executive will be visiting the city as part of a nationwide tour in which he is inspecting port facilities.

The President will be greeted by a parade of automobiles and marching groups, which will be his escort to City Hall. There, he will be welcomed by

Mayor Martin Behrman and Governor Luther Hall. The governor will present him with a key to our fair city.

Several of our high-school bands will be on hand to parade before the grandstand, which has been erected in front of City Hall, and Mrs. Anita Baird of Esplanade High School will present the President with a bouquet of American beauty roses.

The President will spend the afternoon inspecting the docks of the city. He will also be shown through the cotton warehouses on the riverfront.

Later this evening our beloved chief executive will be feted at the home of one of the city's most prominent social and civic families, that of Mr. and Mrs. John Bernhard Eagan. Mr. Eagan will be remembered as a close friend and associate of the Wizard of Menlo Park, Mr. Thomas Alva Edison. Mr. Eagan's magnificent electrical display at the Cotton Centennial in Audubon Park in the 1880s is still talked about as one of the most outstanding electrical exhibitions of the period. In 1886, when the first franchise for street lighting in New Orleans was obtained, Mr. Eagan supervised the laying of the mains. Mrs. Eagan is the former Janet Charbonnet, long a society leader in our city.

Mr. Roosevelt will be staying at the St. Charles Hotel and will depart the city at noon tomorrow from the L. & N. Railroad Station on Canal Street. All citizens are invited to be present to hear a few parting comments from the hero of San Juan Hill, our popular chief executive.

On another part of the page Janet's menu was boxed and given prominent attention.

"Della, this is wonderful!" Katie said. "The article

says more about the Eagans than it does about the President!" They all laughed jubilantly.

"Das how it goes in dis town. If you is sassiety heah, you is better den any President. Heh-heh-heh."

Treece was giggling, too, listening wide-eyed as Katie read. They were all as excited as children. The President of the United States was to be in their home that very evening, and they might catch a glimpse of him when the waiters were going back and forth to the kitchen and the doors were open. At least they wouldn't have to worry about spilling soup in his lap. That would be somebody else's problem.

Tension ran high throughout the day. Charlotte had a magnificent new gown, and Katie was called up to her room to pin up the skirt and hem it. She tried not to show how the dress took her breath away. It was made of white mousseline, décolleté at the neckline, shirred at the hips and bust, with a wide violet sash and violet velvet straps at the shoulders. There were long ruffles over the arms and bust, and a small bunch of violets at the waist. Out of the corner of her eye Katie could see Janet's dress hanging on the back of the door. It was of dubonnet watersilk taffeta with a yoke of Cluny lace that rose to a stock neckline.

Katie hemmed quickly, eager to return to the kitchen. Tempers were running short on the second floor, and poor Mr. John was pacing the floor, wringing his hands, wondering what manner of event he had created.

Her sewing done, Katie skipped down to the first floor and walked out onto the back gallery, eager to watch the traffic jam of wagons coming in and backing up. Although it was January the weather was as balmy as spring and as beautiful. The sky was robin's-egg blue with a few wisps of white clouds drifting by.

Suddenly a figure in the crowd arrested her attention and stopped the breath in her throat. Thomas LeJeune!

She could not believe her eyes. One driver was telling him to get out of the way. Another was asking him to help carry boxes. The idiot! What was he doing here? But, of course, it was Thursday, she remembered, and Thomas was not one to miss a meeting. She had never thought him bright, but Dear Lord, hadn't he read the papers? Didn't he know what was going on here? How could he take such a chance?

She looked over her shoulder and felt fairly certain that no one in the house had seen him. She dashed down the steps, dodging delivery men and wagons till she came face-to-face with the boy.

"You shouldn't have come," she said. "You'll be seen. Give me the letter and please get out of here."

Looking dazed and bewildered, Thomas reached in his vest pocket and handed her a letter. Katie discovered she had no apron and no pocket to put the letter in. She was unable to shove it down her bosom without unbuttoning her bodice. She folded it in her fist. Then, eyes downcast, she climbed the stairs back up to the porch.

Reaching the top step, she raised her eyes and found herself looking into the face of Janet Eagan. The fearsome gray eyes pierced daggers into hers. Katie's mouth went dry. Weakness washed over her.

"I'll take that," Janet said quietly but with venom.

"What?" Katie asked.

"That letter. I've seen that young man loitering about here before . . . meeting you on the sly. I'd like to know what kind of trash he writes you. This may be proof enough for Mr. Eagan that you're not the kind of person we like to have in our home."

"I won't give it to you," Katie said, almost inaudibly.

She folded the letter even smaller and slipped it into her cuff. Janet reached out and grabbed the girl's wrist with her left hand and withdrew the letter with her right. Slowly, looking all the while at Katie, she unfolded the envelope. Then she scanned it. Astonishment struck her like a blow. Her face became ashen.

"This is from Stephen," she said. The words were said in a normal voice, as if there had to be a rational explanation, but her pallor divulged her fear.

Katie lowered her head. She did not answer. In all the scenes she had imagined of Janet's "finding out," never once had she been alone in her plight. Stephen had always been with her, her rampart, her strength. How could she explain to Janet? How could she come out other than ugly, common, beneath contempt?

"Never mind," Janet said. "I don't want you to tell me now. The most important event in my life is about to take place, and I refuse to let you ruin it for me. I will wait to read this until after the President has gone. Then I'll call for you, my girl, and you'd better have an explanation."

Chapter
TWENTY-THREE

Treece and Katie sat huddled together in a dark corner of the butler's pantry, trying to catch a glimpse of the great T. R. through the swinging door to the dining room, as waiters went in and out, carrying steaming trays and returning with the remains of the last course.

Katie got a good look at the President, the light from the chandelier striking the silver rims of his pince-nez, his well-known mustache spread in a joyous grin, his huge white teeth very much in evidence. He was a great talker, and respectfully everyone listened.

"Yes, indeed, I'm very much at home in the company of young people," the President said. (Was he talking to Charlotte and Warren?) "I have quite a vociferous family of my own. Reporters call them the White House Gang. Heh-heh-heh." Everyone at the table laughed. "I got word last week that they were planning to attack the White House. Well, sir, I sent them a message through the War Office. That settled them down pretty good. Heh-heh-heh." He laughed at his own joke, and the dinner guests politely guffawed.

Once, when the door swung wide, Katie caught a glimpse of Janet at the far end of the table, her white face underlined by the arrangement in the silver epergne, like Lady Liberty herself, rising from the bed of red, white, and blue flowers. She was the perfect hostess, beautiful, convivial, quick to laugh at the witticisms of her guests, head tilted gaily to one side, all the while calculating the temperature of the wine and the

readiness of the food, the length of time between
courses, and the deftness of the waiters. Her eyes swept
over the serving men, missing no detail of their personal
grooming. Her attention returned unerringly to her
Guest of Honor, her bell-like laughter marking her as
lighthearted, cordial, ingenuous.

How well she does that! Katie thought. How discip-
lined she is! Who would believe that an hour ago her
world was shattered by the possibility that her son and
heir, her pride and joy, her beloved firstborn was having some kind of a fling with the cook? Who would
have thought it possible, watching her lift her fork so
daintily to her lips, that even now she was rehearsing
the scene that would follow in the library? Inside the
dark head, striped so strikingly with silver bands,
coiffed in an enormous poof that framed her face, the
words of the coming interview were already written.
The questions were there, and the retorts to Katie's retorts. Perhaps Mr. John would have a kind word to
say in her behalf. It was her only hope.

If only she knew the contents of the letter, she would
know what charges to answer. Perhaps it was only a
news letter. Stephen wrote that way sometimes. It
would be foolish to reveal anything Janet didn't already
know. Maybe he hadn't referred to their wedding plans.
Katie wouldn't refer to them either. She would answer
only what she was asked, nothing more. But of course,
he would open, "Dearest Kate." He always did. She
dropped her head to her hands and sobbed soundlessly.

Treece put her arm around her friend and Katie
turned her head into Treece's shoulder. Both Treece
and Della had witnessed the scene on the gallery. When
Katie had come back into the kitchen, Della had given
her a mournful look, sensitive and full of understanding
but lacking hope. Treece had taken her in her arms and
petted her. She supposed they were wondering why she
hadn't left right away.

"Now, that big ditch we're digging down in Panama . . ." the President was saying. He spoke with broad A's, making the word sound like Panamah. The discussion of the Panamanian revolt against Colombia and the treaty to build the canal was lively. Everyone congratulated T. R. on recognizing Panama's independence.

They chatted about the Wright Brothers launching the Air Age and the airplane craze that was growing into mania. Then voices became more somber as the topic changed to the disastrous earthquake in San Francisco the year before and the many lives that had been lost.

"Mr. President," John Eagan said, "I hope you won't think me presumptuous if I congratulate you on winning the Nobel Peace Prize for mediating in the Russo-Japanese Peace Talks."

"No, no, my friend," the President said, laughing. "Nothing presumptuous about that. What good is it to win a prize, if no one talks about it? Heh-heh-heh."

The President spoke in the tenderest terms about his baby granddaughter, Edith Derby, and he laughed aloud when he related his children's pranks at the "Little White House" at Sagamore Hill.

Katie tried to let the gaiety of the extraordinary gathering distract her, but it was as if all emotion had died in her when Janet had pulled the letter from her cuff and set her trial for after the President's visit. The fact that she was listening to the voice of Teddy Roosevelt meant no more to her than if it had been White Man from the lottery.

Stringed music wafted into the dining room from the first parlor. A trio of musicians had been hired to play while the men had their port and cigars in the library. They were playing "After the Ball is Over," one of Katie's favorites. Janet suggested that the ladies retire to the second parlor.

"Thomas Edison is the most remarkable man I've ever met," the President was saying. Katie could see

Mr. John smiling broadly, as if the President had complimented his very own son. She wondered if Mr. John knew about the letter and the coming confrontation.

Somehow the evening ended. Topcoats and hats, gloves and canes suddenly appeared, and the men who had served as waiters doubled as butlers, helping the guests with their wraps and calling for their carriages or automobiles.

The noise drifted out onto the porch and dimmed to a scattered sidewalk chatter. Then silence fell. Katie's heart thundered in her breast.

Katie and Treece had stationed themselves at the kitchen sink when the party exited the dining room, Katie washing dishes, Treece drying. Della scraped plates and stacked them, and did her best to find containers for leftovers. They had all been forewarned to take special care in handling the delicate crystal and china. The patterns were no longer "open" and could not be replaced. Katie was glad to be occupied, while waiting for her summons.

Lightning flashed across the sky, an orange split in the blackness framed by the kitchen window.

"Ain' it gran' dat de President done gone befo' de rain stahts?" Della asked.

"Sho' is," Treece answered.

They were both as nervous as Katie.

The stacks of dishes kept coming. There was no end to them. Salad dishes, bread and butters, dinner plates, soups, finger bowls, berry dishes, serving trays. The water in the sink had to be changed a dozen times to keep it clear.

"Wasn't dat some fine music! Mm-mmp!" Della said.

"Sho' was!" Treece agreed.

Both shot sidelong glances at Katie.

Maybe she won't call me tonight, Katie thought. Maybe she'll let me suffer till tomorrow. Maybe she's too exhausted to go through another ordeal.

Katie shifted from foot to foot, rubbing the back of one foot with the other. She remembered kneeling for a whole hour during Forty Hours Devotion at St. Patrick's Church, and thinking how endless the time was, with her knees marked from the hard kneeling benches. Her head throbbed and there was a sour burning feeling in her stomach, but the weakness passed and her strength returned.

At last the dishes were done. Della had washed the stove and the tables and mopped the kitchen floor. The stacks of china and the hundreds of crystal stems now stood on the dining room table to be put away tomorrow. Exhausted, the three women looked at each other.

"Ah'm 'bout daid on my feet," Della said. "Ah'm goin' to bed."

She said it sorrowfully, as though she were abandoning Katie in her hour of need.

"Go on, Della, please," Katie said. "You need your rest."

"Guess I'll go, too," Treece added.

Katie patted the girl on the shoulder. She took off her apron and left it in the pantry. Then, cautiously, she climbed the curving staircase to her garret bedroom. On the second floor she glanced down the corridor. The doors to the bedrooms were closed, and there was a strip of light beneath each door. She could hear conversation, but it was pleasant chatter, such as couples enjoy after a social evening. She could hear no cries, no accusations.

Inside her room Katie lay on top her quilt fully dressed, in case she would be called. She tried to read, but the words all ran together. At last she fell asleep, without having loosened her stays or undone her braids. She slept with the light still burning, exhausted from fear, and she did not awaken until the sparrows started arguing on her windowsill for breadcrumbs she had strewn there yesterday.

In the pearl-gray dawn she sat bolt upright, trying to

remember why she was still dressed. She turned out the lamp on her nightstand. Janet had never called for her! She couldn't understand it. Was she too tired last night? Too ill?

No, Janet was making her suffer for the effrontery of falling in love with Stephen. She was dragging it out, letting her wait to hear the insults and accusations.

A loud knock resounded. Katie jumped and let out a little cry. She rose from the bed and approached the door.

"It's Warren," she heard the boy say. Quickly she opened the door. "Oh. I'm glad you're dressed," he said. "Mother wants to see you in the library."

"What time is it?"

"Seven. I've got to eat my breakfast, so I won't be late for school. Mother says come right away."

"Wait, Warren. Is your father with her?"

"I don't know." He shrugged. "She was in the bedroom when she asked me to come up."

"Okay."

Katie locked the door and made her morning ablutions. She washed herself and brushed her teeth and braided her hair. She changed into a clean uniform and apron, all the while breathing so deeply, she threatened to black out from hyperventilation. At last she was ready. She pulled the crepe from her mirror and checked her appearance. She was ghostly white, but clean and fresh. Touching her hands to her hair, and smoothing her dress at the waist, she left the room and descended the staircase.

The house was deadly quiet. Warren and Charlotte were probably having breakfast in the kitchen. They would be leaving for school without coming through the front of the house. She knocked softly at the library door.

"Come in." It was Mr. John. She thanked whatever God there was that she'd have someone on her side.

Janet was sitting in her chair, no handwork to distract her. She was neatly dressed and combed for such an early hour. Mr. John stood at the window in a vested suit, a collar, and tie. He had not taken a seat beside his wife. Nebulously Katie understood that he had not wished to make it appear a tribunal. Katie stood before Janet and waited.

"I have read the letter," Janet announced. "I have been ill the entire night. In truth I shall probably never be quite well again."

John did not speak. He groomed his mustache with his thumb and forefinger. Katie stood rigid before her accuser. It was not yet time to answer.

"To think that a girl who needed shelter, who begged me to take her off the street . . . could return my kindness with such deceit and treachery . . ."

Katie felt the water rise under her tongue. Never had she asked to be taken "off the street."

"I didn't need food or shelter," Katie answered evenly. "I had to get away from my father. He had . . . sinned . . . against my mother. By accident I . . . saw him . . . with a girl."

Katie was mortified to have to admit it in Mr. John's presence, but there was no help for it. She felt her face burning.

"You have learned something from him, then," Janet said. "You have betrayed my trust, and no doubt you have committed the same sin,"

Katie looked at Janet and drew in a sharp breath. "Never!" she said. "Never in my life!"

"Janet, I'm ashamed of you," John said. "You have no grounds whatsoever for such an accusation."

"Really, John," Janet said. "You are incredibly naïve. What other reason is there for a young man of Stephen's background to become infatuated with a common little girl from the slums? I am thoroughly disappointed in his lack of discretion. If he chose to satisfy his lust, which is what I suppose we must expect from all men"—her lids were hooded in disdain—"he could refrain from putting anything in writing. And to speak of marriage! Really! Such promises are not necessary for these people." She extended her hand in Katie's direction, as if she were devoid of feeling. Her eyes remained focused on her husband.

"I won't let you speak of Katie this way," he said. "I know her far better than you do, and I know her to be a fine, clean young woman."

"So, she's won you over, too, has she?" Janet shrieked. "It makes a person wonder what happened here all summer, when the two of you were alone."

"Janet!" John gasped. "How dare you? How dare you accuse me, and this innocent child, of acts that are so far beneath our dignity? I came here to listen to what you had to say. You are my wife and I owe you that. But you have just canceled that obligation, my dear. If you can so lightly accuse *me* after twenty-four years of faithful marriage, then I'm not surprised at anything you'd say about Katie."

Janet's eyes shifted. Her expression relaxed visibly. She's going to try another tack, Katie told herself.

"But he says he *loves* her, John." She was pleading now, trying to win him with persuasion, since she had failed to shame him into agreement. She drew her handkerchief from her sleeve. "He wants to *marry* her! A boy with six generations of Creole New Orleans society behind him. A young man of wealth and promise. Are you going to let him throw all that away? Can you look at this girl and tell me she's for Stephen?"

John looked at Katie. She was the most beautiful young woman he had ever seen. Her lovely face wore a plaintive expression, and she was white with fear, but even this reflection of her suffering added to her beauty. He thought of her industry and her energy, and her love for her younger siblings. He remembered her determination to teach herself to read and write. He knew her to be bright and strong and loyal. Above all, he knew her to be a lady.

"I think Stephen would be lucky to have her for his wife," John said.

Katie turned her face to her employer with a look of gratitude. She had always loved Mr. John, but never so much as now. She wanted to hug him warmly, but she dared not move from her place on the carpet, as if the spot had been marked off for her, like an actor in a play.

"I cannot believe my ears," Janet said slowly. "You are so befuddled by this child that you are willing to lose sight of everything we have ever planned for Stephen. He is our boy, John, whom we've educated and raised with such delicacy, among people like himself. To what avail was it? We might just as well have sent him to public schools, or let him wander in the streets with wild companions, if we abandon him now to a common, unschooled Italian . . ."

"Why do you bring her nationality into it?" he asked impatiently.

"If Stephen marries this girl, he'll never be accepted in the homes of our friends. Or even our family. He'll have to find a job on his own, without your influence."

"The best thing in the world for him. It was the way I got started."

Janet narrowed her eyes. "You did exactly what Stephen is doing, John. You abandoned your parents who had worked so hard to make life easy for you. You could have been a professional man, anything you wanted, but you had to get thrown out of school and take a ridiculous telegrapher's job."

John smiled a crooked smile. This was the first he had ever known of Janet's sentiments on the subject. "I didn't do so badly," he said.

"Don't take any credit for that, John. Your father was a very rich man. There was a fortune waiting for you whenever you got tired of your gypsy life."

"And there'll be one waiting for Stephen," John said.

"Oh, no!" Janet said, rising to her feet. She squared

her shoulders. "Oh, no!" she repeated. "If Stephen marries this girl, he will never set foot in this house again, and I will see to it that he gets control of *nothing* as long as I live."

Katie turned and quietly left the room. No one called her back. As she opened the leaded-glass door into the vestibule, she could hear the voices of her employers rising in argument against each other now, instead of against her. She had heard all she had to hear. If Stephen married her, his world would end. There would be no money, no acceptance, no opportunities for success in the business world. How could she ever have believed that she could deprive him of all that? She had had to hear it said aloud to know how totally impossible the marriage was. Her face was hot with shame that she had tried to drag her beloved Stephen into such an unworthy marriage.

She ran across the porch and down the steps to the street. She would go home to Julia Row where she belonged and never again return to the Eagans'. Leaving all her possessions behind, she crossed over and stood at the streetcar stop. In the pocket of her apron was her leather coin purse, from which she took her last remaining nickel. With this coin she would travel from one world to another, from one life to another, back to Julia Row and as far from Stephen's world as any domicile could be.

Even as she sat in the streetcar, she was aware that she must see Thomas LeJeune no later than tomorrow so that he would not come to the Eagans' house again. Janet would be waiting for him, eager to take the letters, to scrutinize Stephen's most intimate thoughts and plans. She would take the streetcar to Thomas's house tomorrow to tell him what had happened. She hoped he would continue to exchange letters for them. Stephen must not find out, not now. She would not have him interrupt his studies and come home, only to find out she had decided not to marry him; nor did she wish to

come between Stephen and his parents. Her letters to
Stephen would now become fewer and fewer, and later
on she would tell Stephen that she no longer loved him.
Then he could go on about his life, just as if he had
never known her.

Tomorrow. Yes, tomorrow she'd take the streetcar to
Thomas's house.

Chapter
TWENTY-FOUR

"May I help you, madam?" Katie asked.

The lady tilted her head back far enough to see Katie from under the brim of her straw hat.

"Are you a saleslady?" she asked.

"Yes, ma'am," Katie answered, smiling.

"They're hiring them so young these days," she mumbled, settling herself into one of the seats welded to the floor before the counter. She rested her parasol against the counter's edge. "Where's the regular lady? Miss Greishaber?"

"She's on vacation, ma'am, but I'll be glad to serve you."

"Oh . . . well." She was obviously disappointed. "I was looking for a pair of white kid gloves. Three buttons. Size six and a half."

"One moment, please," Katie said.

Katie turned to a wall of glass boxes behind her and pulled out a box marked "6½." She selected a pair of gloves and showed them to the customer. The lady nodded. Katie shook talcum into the right-hand glove. The customer placed her elbow on the counter, and Katie worked the glove onto her fingers.

"Now. How does that feel?" she asked.

"Fine. That's fine. I'll take them, dear." She looked at Katie's hair. "Tell me, darling, how do you do your hair that way?"

Katie blushed. She had started wearing her hair in a "poof" the day she applied for work at D. H. Holmes

Department Store, hoping she would look older. She was still not sure she was doing it right. She raised her hand to her head.

"Well, I tease it with a brush, then I lay it over flannel rats, all around the hairline. Then I bring all the hair together on top my head and twist it into a coil right here in the center. Does it look all right?"

"It's lovely."

The customer took out her lorgnette and looked at Katie as the girl fingered the loose curls at her neckline. Her hair was sooty black and soft as a halo around her lovely young face. She wondered how old the girl was. She was full bosomed in her white cotton blouse, and she had a wasp waist and full hips under the molded black skirt. A black grosgrain ribbon circled her throat on top of the stock neckline and was secured in front by a cameo brooch. She wore no other jewelry. Her cheeks were as pink as roses, and it was easy to see that she did not "paint," as some of the other clerks did. The lady studied the clear, dark eyes and the fresh young complexion enviously.

She took a five-dollar bill from her handbag and handed it to Katie. Katie completed her sales slip and put the bill and the slip in a metal capsule which shot up in a pneumatic tube. In minutes the capsule was back from the office with a receipt and the lady's change, which Katie counted out.

"Thank you so much," Katie said "Please come again."

"What is your name, child?"

"Katie. Katie Raspanti."

"I'll ask for you next time." She picked up her parasol and carried her rigid body down the corridor to the door.

Katie returned the glass box to the wall and busied herself straightening the counter. She enjoyed the feeling of space around her, and the churchlike quiet of the huge main floor. She worked inside an oval-shaped counter in the center aisle, where she saw every customer come in and go out of the store. It was interesting and exciting. She loved to look up at the larger oval-shaped balcony on the mezzanine, and beyond it, the second-floor ceiling with its lighting fixtures in clusters of glass balls on long brass chains.

The thing she liked most about her job was that it had given her financial independence at last and the wherewithal to provide for her sisters without her father's help.

Two months had gone by since Katie had last seen her father. He had come one day to bring her weekly money, instead of sending it to her. The circles beneath his eyes were dark, and there was a two-day growth of beard on his chin. He looked intoxicated to Katie.

"How do you keep your job, the way you drink, Papa?" she had asked.

Tears had sprung to his eyes. "I don't drink no more, Katie," he said. "I been sick."

Pity clutched at her heart. But quickly she girded herself with the memory of her dead mother which revived her hostility.

"Don't bring me any more money, Papa," she said. "I can support the girls with my wages from the store. And Davey's in the seminary. He's no expense to me now. Just take care of yourself. See a good doctor. Do you"—she had choked on the words—"want to come back here to live?"

"No . . . no," he answered. "I'm okay. I got a place. Don't you worry, Katie."

He had extended his hand in her direction, in a gesture of . . . what? Love? Appreciation? He had not extended it far enough to touch her, and she had not inched closer to bridge the gap.

She knew she should have felt sorry for her father, prayed for him perhaps. But she never even thought of him. He was out of her life, and she was glad of it. How good it was to be independent! How nice to wear pretty

blouses and skirts to work and to see her sisters in good
leather shoes!

Jenny and Lala had been beside themselves when
Katie bought three brass headboards and beds from
D. H. Holmes Department Store on her employee's discount. When her mother's bed was removed from the
flat, much of Katie's grief for her miraculously went
with it. Since then she had known nothing but health
and optimism. She had felt brisk enough to go shopping
for chests of drawers in the secondhand stores on
Dryades Street. She had found three chests, exactly
alike, and spent several Sundays stripping them down
and varnishing them. She made new cotton curtains and
sewed them to brass rings that hung from wooden rods.
Then, with the girls' help, she painted the bedroom and
hung pictures from the five-and-dime. The redecorated
bedroom was as glamorous to them as a princess's boudoir.

Katie was seventeen now, her sisters twelve and ten.
The younger girls cooked in the evenings and did the
grocery shopping, for Katie did not get home till six-
thirty from the store. They did their chores willingly,
for their home life was easy and joyful, now that Katie
was with them for good. Together they shared a peaceful home, without arguments, fears, or heartaches, and
because of their older sister's fine new job, without
want.

Her thoughts slipped back to the morning she had
come to apply for the job. She had been sitting in the
outer office of Mr. Schoen, the personnel manager,
when she overheard his conversation with another ap-
plicant.

"I'm sorry, Miss Robinson," he said, "but you must
be eighteen to work at D. H. Holmes. No, I'm sorry,
not even with your parents' permission. It's a policy of
the store."

"But I left school to make a career in the mercantile
field," the young woman insisted.

"Then you aren't a high-school graduate?"

Katie had heard nothing then.

"Oh, then I'm sorry, my dear, we couldn't have hired you anyway."

Katie's eyes opened wide and she jumped from the chair and left the room. Without a moment's hesitation she walked three blocks to a stationery store and, pretending to be a teacher, bought a half-dozen report cards. She always bought more writing materials than she needed, expecting to make mistakes. Then she took the streetcar home.

She sat at the kitchen table, with Jenny's and Davey's report cards before her, and filled out a senior report card, copying names of courses, and manufacturing a teacher, a high school, and a fictitious city. She held the finished product before her and nodded her head with pride.

The next thing that needed fixing was her birth certificate. She rummaged through the kitchen pantry till she located the envelope where her mother had always kept family records. With no qualms of conscience she pulled out her birth certificate and neatly made herself one year older.

The following day she styled her hair in a "poof," like the clerks she had seen in the store, and returned to the personnel office, armed with her report card and her birth certificate. She had not thought to make herself a diploma, but she hoped that the excellent grades she had given herself would convince Mr. Schoen that she surely must have graduated. They did. Smiling with pleasure, he asked her if she would like to sell gloves and hosiery in the center aisle, main floor. She was delighted.

Each day since, Mr. Schoen had passed by her counter and asked how she was getting along. He made Katie uncomfortable, the way his eyes explored her contours, but she had no choice but to be cordial and businesslike. The gentlemen clerks on the floor had taken notice of Katie, too. More than one had stopped by to chat on slow days when they weren't busy. Duane Brady had bought her coffee once in the employee's cafeteria and asked her if he might call, but Katie had declined. She explained that she was engaged and felt the old familiar tightness squeeze her heart.

She had put her plans for marrying Stephen out of her mind, but she had never succeeded in putting them out of her heart. Till the last two weeks she had still picked up his letters at Thomas LeJeune's. His recent letters were full of questions about what had happened, for she no longer wrote to him of love or marriage. She gave him nothing but hard, cold news, and she wrote less often. On the first of April, knowing he was scheduled to return within the month, she had written him her very last letter, telling him she no longer loved him. She cried herself to sleep that night, half hoping he wouldn't believe her.

He would have received it by now, she reflected, sitting on the stool behind the counter. She laced her fingers together in her lap and sighed heavily.

"Hiya, Katie," a young man said. "Will you let me buy you a cup of coffee after work?"

Katie looked up. "Sorry, Duane, I have to get right home. Another time."

The boy looked disappointed but he moved along, catching a glimpse of the floor walker watching him. Capsules zinged through tubes overhead. Katie returned to her thoughts.

Stephen was on his way home. Anytime now, he'd be walking into the Eagan home, running down the corridor to the kitchen, looking for her. If he'd received her letter, he'd want an explanation. In any case he would find out about the scene between Janet and Katie. Who would tell him? What would they say? How would he take the news? Katie was certain Janet had never written him about the confrontation because of the questions in his letters.

Katie wondered if Mr. John would have anything to say in her behalf. Her chin quivered. She wondered why Mr. John had let her go and never come looking for her or asked about her welfare after that morning. She hoped that his feelings for her had not changed, but perhaps Janet had made his life so miserable that he had decided that the only way to live in peace was to accept her decision in the matter. She hated to think that was true, but who was to know what a man or a woman would do to keep peace in a marriage? Her mother had suffered much greater pain and anxiety, keeping a worthless husband at her side.

"Good afternoon, Miss Raspanti. How are you today?"

Even before looking up, she recognized Mr. Schoen's unctuous voice.

"Very well, thank you, sir," she said, busying herself straightening an already straight counter.

"Now, now, Katie," he said, taking liberties using her given name, "you'll wear yourself out keeping order back there. Sit and rest between customers." He reached across the counter and squeezed her hand. The old goat, she was thinking, resenting the fact that she was a captive object of his attentions. *I wonder what Mrs. Schoen would think about his squeezing young girls' hands.*

She smiled innocently. Mr. Schoen patted her cheek and went on down the center aisle. Katie stood up and stretched. She turned around and rested her arms on top of the stock case, absently watching a salesman in the shirt department take pins from a cotton shirt.

"Katie." She heard her name whispered.

Her heart stopped beating for a moment. She knew the voice. All the blood drained from her body and she felt weak. She closed her eyes and drew in a breath.

"Kate. Turn around. It's Stephen. I'm here."

Shakily she turned her body, still not opening her eyes. Tears squeezed from beneath her closed lashes, and when she dared to look, fearing he would vanish before she did, she saw him through her tears. He was dressed in a dark suit, and by contrast, his linens were snowy white. His chestnut curls framed his rosy face, and his lips were parted in anticipation. And there was that precious cleft that she adored!

She wanted to throw herself in his arms and feel those arms close around her body. But there was so much more than a counter standing between them. There was family, and there were insults and warnings. There were dire predictions and threats and prophecies of gloom if they were to reach out and grab the happiness they could give each other. There was a chasm between them of status and education, of bloodline and wealth and everything that seemed to matter so much to others.

Tears fell down her cheeks and thundering love swelled her heart to the bursting point.

"Don't cry, my darling," he whispered. "Dear God, you're even more beautiful than I remembered. I've come to get you, Kate. This is our wedding month, dear love."

She sobbed quietly and let the tears roll down her face. Slowly she lifted a hand and extended it toward Stephen. He grasped it firmly between his strong, warm hands, and they leaned toward each other.

"Stephen. Beloved," she whispered. "Has your father told you what happened?"

"My father is dead," he said.

"Dead?" Katie exclaimed softly. "I didn't know."

She had not read the papers since leaving the Eagan home. She was so busy now that they did not get the paper on Julia Row, so she had missed the death notices.

"He had a heart attack in January. My mother didn't write me to come home. I just found out."

"In January? Then, that was just after . . ."

"Yes. My mother told me everything." His jaw clenched.

"Oh, Stephen, I'm so sorry . . ."

"He had a will," Stephen continued. "He left my mother everything. She has disowned me."

"Because of me," Katie said.

"Because I adore you. Without you I have no life."

"Oh, Stephen," she whispered again. Fresh tears started.

"So if you're willing to marry a penniless electrician, I'm yours."

"My darling," she said, crying aloud. She reached awkwardly across the counter and threw her arms around his neck. He pulled back slightly so he could press his lips to hers. And then he drew her to him again and held her close.

Customers and clerks had begun gathering when the young couple first held hands, and the beautiful young woman had started to cry. Women took out their handkerchiefs. Heads hung over the mezzanine, watching the tender love scene. Silence fell over the spectators, and when Stephen and Katie embraced at last, across a line of immovable seats and a showcase counter, the crowd murmured, then cheered, then broke into a round of applause.

Pushing his way to the forefront of the gathering, Mr. Schoen looked at Katie disapprovingly.

"Miss Raspanti!" he shouted. "I guess you know that such an exhibition is reason enough for dismissal."

"And if that isn't enough, I'll give you a better one," Stephen said, smiling broadly. "She's getting married."

The crowd broke into a rousing round of applause and robust cheers. Katie looked up. She looked around. In Stephen's eyes she could see that he wanted her, and nothing else mattered.

"Come on, Katie," he said, still holding her hand.

She grabbed her purse and came out from behind the counter. Stephen took her in his arms again and held her close. The crowd went wild. Mr. Schoen looked as if he would have a seizure.

"Good luck, Katie," Duane said.

"Good luck, Katie," customers and clerks cried out. "Good luck." She heard it from above and from every side.

Chapter
TWENTY-FIVE

A strip of sunlight fell across Katie's face and awakened her. Even before she opened her eyes, an inner excitement ran through her, and she smiled.

"What are you smiling about?" Stephen asked.

She opened her eyes to see him resting on one elbow, watching her sleep. She smiled again and drew the sheet over her head. Memories of last night crowded in and embarrassed her. She had made love to Stephen so freely and easily that she was ashamed to look at him in the light of day.

He turned down the sheet and slipped his arms around her. He cradled her gently in his arms and kissed her slowly, sensuously, slipping her gown off her arm and fondling her breast. All the passion of the night before swept over her, and they made love again. And then, when they had fallen away from each other in that solemn, peace-filled, resting time, he pressed his lips to her warm, flushed cheek and the curve of her neck and her shoulder.

"Oh, God, I love you," he said. "I missed you so much when you were away that it hurt inside like a sickness."

"It was like that for me, too, Stephen," she said.

"If I had known what was going on, I would have been here months ago. I still can't believe you didn't tell me."

"Don't talk about that now," she said. "Just hold me and say sweet things to me."

He smiled. He leaned up on one elbow and put his arm around her.

"Well, first of all, you have the most beautiful mouth I've ever seen," he said. He traced the edges of her lips with his fingertip. "It's just as if the Lord took a paintbrush and outlined your lips before he filled them in with color."

"Hmmm . . . That's lovely," she said. She ran her fingers through his curly hair and drew his mouth down to hers. Then, after they had kissed, she asked: "What else?"

"What else?" He laughed aloud. "Your hair is as black and shiny as a raven." He took a strand of hair between his fingers.

She closed her eyes and smiled. "What else?" she asked.

"Your face is like a cameo. That little cameo you wear."

"It was my mother's."

Katie was quiet for a time. She turned her head into his shoulder and closed her eyes. She had enjoyed a sexual relation with a man, and she had never believed she would. Years ago she had made up her mind to find it revolting, because of her father's transgressions. And yet she had been transported to another world in her beloved husband's arms. Now she knew why her mother had let Joe Raspanti come back again and again. She could not live without him, any more than Katie could ever live without Stephen now. She laced her fingers behind her head and stared up at the ceiling. She could see a place where she had missed with the paintbrush.

"I've been a fool all my life," she said.

Stephen rubbed her cheek with the back of his fingers.

"Well, it hasn't been a very long life," he said. "Maybe there's still hope."

"No, seriously, Stephen. I couldn't understand, till now, why my mother took my father back in her bed after his unfaithfulness." She looked into her husband's eyes. "I asked her how she could do it. I must have made her feel so cheap."

"You were a child, Kate. Your mother realized that."

"I guess." She turned her face away. "But I feel real bad about it."

He drew her to him and held her close.

"We all feel bad about things we do. That's life. I'm just so glad you understand now why she took him back. It means that last night, and this morning, well, it was good for you. You didn't just endure it, as women say they do."

She wrapped her arms around him. "Oh, Stephen, darling, how can I tell you? I can't say the words, because I'm not that bold, but believe me, I didn't just endure it."

They fell silent and he stroked her hair.

"Stephen."

"Yes, angel."

"I didn't want you to spend your wedding night on Julia Row."

"Why not?"

"Look at it, Stephen," she said, waving a hand at the ceiling. "It isn't much like St. Charles Avenue, is it?"

"What makes you think I judge every place by how much it's like my mother's house?" he asked.

He had said, "my *mother*'s house," not "my house." He claimed no connection with it. It bore Janet's stamp, especially now that his father was gone.

"I wish you could see the places I stayed in in Paris," he said. "They'd make this apartment look like a palace. Dirty little *pensions*. Tiny rooms, hardly big enough for a bed and chest."

She leaned up on her elbow. "But why, Stephen? Surely not for lack of money."

"You get tired of living in the snooty part of town, putting your shoes outside the door to be polished, having a servant bring you a tray in the mornings."

"Hmp! Speak for yourself, dear. *I* wouldn't mind trying it awhile."

"I wanted to live the way the other students lived. I wanted to feel the cold and the heat, and know what it was like to have a hunger pang now and then."

"You're crazy," she commented. "But if you like it so much, I may let you have one right now. I'm not used to cooking anymore. The girls do it, and unfortunately . . . or *for*tunately, they're not here."

"God bless Mrs. Macaluso," Stephen said.

"Say it a little louder and she'll hear you upstairs. The girls will, too."

He cupped his hands to his mouth. "GOD BLESS YOU, MRS. MACALUSO," he shouted.

"Stephen!" Katie cried out. She giggled. "You idiot!" She laughed aloud. "Get some clothes on, husband, and I'll see if I remember how to scramble eggs."

She put on her wrapper, smiling as she walked to the kitchen.

"Delicious!" Stephen said. "Best bacon and eggs I've ever eaten. You know, we used to have a cook on St. Charles Avenue who made bacon and eggs like that."

Katie dimpled. She touched his hand across the table. "You don't mind that I was your cook?" she asked.

"Why should I mind?" he asked. "You still are." They laughed together.

"Can we be serious, Stephen?"

He nodded. She knew he would fall into her mood.

"What are we going to do for money?" she asked. "You dragged me out of the department store, so I guess we can consider that job *fichu*."

"That's French," Stephen said, looking surprised.

"I know."

"That's one of my mother's *bons mots*."

"That's where I got it."

"Do you know what it means?"

"No, but I got the general idea. I had to do that a lot. Your mother and Charlotte spoke French whenever they didn't want me to know what they were saying."

"They did that to you?"

"It doesn't matter."

"It matters to me. It's insulting and humiliating."

"I was only a servant, Stephen."

"Servants are people with feelings and sensitivities."

"Get back to the subject, Stephen, my dear. What are we going to do for money?"

"Monday morning, I'm going to apply for a job as lineman with Edison Electric," he said. "Anything to get started."

"And after you're started?" She spread jam on a piece of toast and took a bite.

"I'm going to open my own electrical contracting business when I've saved a little money."

"And what do *they* do?"

"Wind motors and repair electrical appliances, like fans and toasters. They wire houses, too, new houses just being built. Someday contractors will wire *all* the houses. Edison Electric will just turn on the juice." He finished his coffee. "I have some ideas, too, I'd like to work on, some improvements in electrical appliances. If they work out, I'll get them patented. Who knows? Someday you may have an inventor on your hands."

"Really, Stephen?" she said. "That's wonderful." But her mind was still troubled. "Look, darling, I have to know two things," she said. "I wouldn't ask you how much money you're going to make, but I have to be sure we can support my two little sisters."

"Of course we can," he said. "Now what's the other thing?"

She sighed. "How on earth can we all live here together in one bedroom?"

Stephen pressed his napkin to his lips. "Beats the hell

out of me," he said. Then he took Katie's hand. "But we'll think of something," he said.

A timid knock came at the kitchen door.

"Come in," Katie said.

Slowly, with downcast eyes, Jenny and Lala entered and stood before the newlyweds. They were shy in the presence of their new brother-in-law. They had met him only once, yesterday, just before the wedding in the rectory at St. Patrick's.

"Katie, dear, do you know these two young ladies?" he asked.

The girls giggled. Katie laughed softly as she carried a stack of dishes to the sink. Slowly the children raised their heads to make sure he was really joking. Stephen held his arms open wide, and the girls ran to hug him.

"Here, Katie, let us do the dishes," Jenny said, leaving Stephen's embrace. She took the apron from Katie. "You and Stephen relax in the yard."

Katie and Stephen looked at each other and shrugged. They both knew the girls had come down to offer their services to their sister on her "after wedding" day. Stephen held out his hand for Katie, and they walked to the swing in the yard and sat facing each other, just as Frances and Katie used to do.

"Oh, I almost forgot," Stephen said. "I have a letter for you. I meant to give it to you yesterday, but I guess my mind was occupied with other things."

He leaned over and kissed her cheek. He got out of the swing and walked back into the house. Puzzled, she thought that it might be a letter that *he* had written and hadn't had time to mail. Stephen returned, bending a crumpled letter back into shape. He handed it to her.

"It's from my father," he said.

She gasped.

"I received it when I was in Germany," Stephen explained. "It was inside a letter addressed to me. My father asked me to give it to you in the event of his death.

I didn't know he was . . . dead, until I got home yesterday."

Katie suddenly realized that Stephen had left his mother right after he returned, as soon as he had learned about Katie's dismissal. So Janet was grieving for her husband *and* her estranged son. Katie wasn't sure what sentiments she felt for Janet at that moment.

She looked into Stephen's eyes. He was here, and he was hers. In this place of her beginnings, Julia Row, he had shared her wedding bed, and he seemed as comfortable in these surroundings as he ever had in the opulence of his mother's home.

Katie tore the envelope open. The letter was dated January 15, just four days after she had left the Eagan home. She read it aloud.

My dear Katie,

I am heartbroken to have lost your sweet company, and I share the humiliation you bore to have your character slandered and your dignity besmirched because of such meaningless attributes as heritage and schooling. I apologize for Janet.

Now let me apologize for myself, for not coming to your aid. I spoke up for you, but I did not come to get you and bring you back. I want you to know why. I threatened to tear up my will (in which I had left everything to Janet), unless she would reconcile with you. I threatened to write another will, specifying a certain legacy to each of my children upon reaching their majority. Then, in the event of my death, Stephen could claim his portion of my estate, which is considerable.

But Janet made a counterthreat which I could not ignore. She vowed that if I destroyed the original will, or moved against her in the matter of Stephen's marriage, she would bring suit against me for divorce, charging me with adultery and naming you as corespondent. She planned to use as evidence the evenings we spent alone together last summer.

Of course, she has no proof, because there is none, but I could not risk dragging you through that and making it impossible for you and Stephen ever to get together. Please try to understand.

A tear fell from Katie's lashes. She reached out for Stephen's hand and held it for a moment. She continued reading.

I have written a codicil to my will. It is a valid legal document. It is dated later than my original will, which incidentally, is carefully itemized and includes no mention of the property I am leaving you.

Katie's eyes opened wide. "The property he's leaving *me*?" Her brows knitted and Stephen shook his head and shrugged. She read on.

In 1850, my father, Franz Sales Eagan, built a sturdy home overlooking Bayou St. John, at the end of Esplanade Avenue. From the gallery, you can see the old Allard Plantation, which is now City Park, right across the water.

It is a gracious house with wide galleries and high-ceilinged rooms. There is a carriage house and many lovely pecan trees. It is old now, and in need of repair. There is no indoor plumbing or electricity, but they can be installed. It is a lovely, big home in which to raise a family. I give it to you, Katie, for it is mine, to do with as I please. I inherited it before I married, so Janet can make no claim to it as community property. There is no one I would rather think of, walking down its corridors, than you, whether you marry my son or not.

But marry him, Katie, even without consent. You are the best girl he will ever know. Raise a family together. He will make a name for himself without family influence or money. I did, in some small measure, and he is a better man than I ever was.

Now it was Stephen's turn to brush the tears from his eyes.

After you read this letter, have my attorney, Anton Schwab, open the bank box in the Whitney Bank and verify the legality of the codicil. The key to the house is also in the bank box. Enjoy your home, dear Kate. Janet has never lived in it or even seen it. She does not know that it exists. Something has always kept me from telling her about it. I suppose only God knows what.

My blessings and best wishes are with you always.

Love,
John Bernhard Eagan
January 15, 1908

She dropped the letter to her lap. Her eyes were misty. "He didn't just let me go! He *did* care what happened to me!" she said as if talking to herself. And then, turning to her husband, she said, "I loved your father, Stephen, and he loved me, too, as a daughter, not at all the way your mother said."

"I know that," Stephen said, breathing deeply and staring into space. A look of fury hardened his features for the despicable insult his mother had dealt Katie.

"I can't believe he did this!" she said, raising the letter. "A house! In all my life I never dreamed I'd own a house. And such a wonderful house!" She took her handkerchief from her pocket and blew her nose. Stephen moved over to her side of the swing and put his arm around her. "We had become so close, sitting in the library at night, talking, like father and daughter. He thought it was so grand that I had taught myself to read and write," she said, smiling sadly.

Katie got up from the swing and crossed the yard. She held out her hand to Stephen and he followed. "Come walk with me," she said.

He took her hand and they walked through the service alley onto Camp Street.

"I think my father must have known he would die soon," Stephen said, "to write you a letter urging you to marry me. Doesn't that seem logical? I mean, you weren't to get the letter till after he died."

"That's right," Katie said. "But how . . . ?"

"He may have been suffering chest pains. We'll never know, will we?"

"No, dear, we never will," Katie said.

Stephen was overcome with emotion for his father's death and his generous gesture.

"Somehow, I never thought of your father as such a wealthy man," she said. "Oh, he was always well dressed, but never ostentatious. Is that the word?"

"That's the word." Stephen smiled.

"When my brother died, your father came to offer me sympathy. He had sent a wreath. It was the only one we had. Did you know that?"

"No. I wasn't living home then. I wish I had known."

"He gave me money for funeral expenses and paid my wages till I came back."

Stephen nodded. His chin quivered. He, too, had needed to talk about his father.

"Then, when Mama was in labor, he went after his own doctor in the middle of the night and sent him to us. I'll never forget that. Of course Mama died anyway. I don't want to think about that."

He stopped and took her in his arms again, this time beneath the awning of a typewriter shop on Camp Street. He lifted her chin and looked into her eyes.

"Don't cry, sweet Kate. My father wanted you to be happy. He left you a house. Don't you want to go see it?"

"Oh, yes. Of course, I do."

"I think Mr. Schwab's office is in the Whitney Bank Building. Let's check a telephone directory."

Solemnly they sat in the musty outer office of Anton Schwab, Attorney, waiting what seemed an eternity for the man to see them. At last they were ushered in. Lawyer Schwab sat behind a huge mahogany desk and inspected the pair.

"I'm Stephen Eagan," the young man said, extending his hand. "This is my wife, Katherine."

Katie looked at Stephen and smiled. His wife! How glorious! and Katherine!

The lawyer looked surprised, but with the composure of a legal man he nodded in her direction. Then, turning his gaze to Stephen, he asked: "How may I help you?"

"You were my father's attorney. He was the late John Bernhard Eagan."

"Yes. Oh, yes. Forgive me, I didn't make the connection. Please accept my condolences. Your father was an outstanding member of the community," he said pompously.

Stephen nodded.

"We have a letter written by my father to my wife, just days before he died. In it he mentions a codicil to his will, which he put in a bank box here in the Whitney Bank. He directs us to you to locate it and verify its legality."

"Does he say what change he wanted to make in his original will?"

"Yes, he left my wife a piece of property. She was not my wife at the time he wrote the codicil. She was an employee in my father's household."

"I see," said Mr. Schwab.

The lawyer got up and walked around to the front of his desk. He sat on the corner of the desk nearest Stephen.

"I recall your father's will. I read it to the family soon after he died. Where were you then?" he asked.

"I was in Europe. My mother did not notify me or call me home."

"I see," said Schwab. "Well, as I recall, he left everything to your mother."

"Yes, but his properties were itemized, purposely, and he made no mention of the house on the bayou, the property he left my wife. This is what he explained in the letter he wrote her."

"Well, then," the lawyer said, "let's see if we can find that codicil."

Within an hour the codicil had been located, as well as the keys to a house that had been vacant for over twenty years.

"Now, of course, this posterior will must be probated," Anton Schwab informed them.

"How long will that take?" Stephen asked.

"A few days," the lawyer said. "We will need two witnesses to testify that this is your father's handwriting."

"What about us?" Stephen asked. "Or you?"

"I'm afraid not, Mr. Eagan. Your wife and I are disqualified. *You* may act as a witness, but we need one more. Some member of the family, perhaps?"

"No," Stephen answered, louder than he had intended. He looked embarrassed, but he did not explain. "Have you a partner, Mr. Schwab?" he asked.

"Yes."

"Did he know my father's handwriting? Did he see his original will?"

"Of course. He'll do just fine. Now, we must meet in the judge's chambers. I'll arrange it as soon as possible. Each page of the codicil must be examined and verified, and then signed by the judge. That's all there is to it. After that, you can assume ownership."

"Mr. Schwab," Stephen said, "would it be possible for us to see the house today? We won't touch a thing. I don't think we can wait a few days."

"Of course." The lawyer smiled. "This is all just formality, anyway. The document is clear and not incompatible with the original will. Go ahead." He handed Katie the keys.

Katie hugged the keys to her bosom. "Thank you, sir," she said.

"Is there anything else I can do for you?" the lawyer asked.

"Yes. One more thing," Stephen said. "My mother is not to know about this house. I prefer if she has no idea where we live."

"You have my word," Schwab said.

Stephen and Katie left the office and went to pick up the girls on Julia Row. Together they took the streetcar down Canal Street to Jefferson Davis Parkway, where they got down and followed the curve of the bayou. They walked six blocks, watching the boats on the water and the addresses of the houses along the way. At last, an old frame house rose up above a flight of stone steps at number 17 Moss Street. Laughing like children, they ran up the steps to the gallery.

It was a cypress house, once painted yellow. Specks of paint remained in some spots, but for the most part, the boards were bare. Some of the boards in the porch floor were missing, and Stephen cautioned everyone to watch where they were going.

What wonderful lines the old house had! It was Victorian in design, with the remains of spindled cornices outlining the porch. The trim had once been white and the shutters green. How lovely it must have been, Katie thought. She and Stephen would make it lovely once again.

The girls ran through the house, ignoring Stephen's warning. On the main floor, to the left of a wide corridor, were three rooms with high ceilings and marble mantels: a drawing room, a library, and a dining room. Lace panels still hung in the windows, ripe to the touch, like a fabric of dust. Last of all was the kitchen, as large as the Eagans' kitchen, with iron pots still hanging from wall hooks. A wooden table stood in the middle of the kitchen. A place had been set at the table and never used. Whose had it been? Katie wondered. There was no one alive to ask. She nudged Stephen and nodded in the direction of the place setting.

The bedrooms on the second floor looked out over the bayou with a breathtaking view. Katie could see the tops of trees in City Park across the water. She would raise a family here and bring her children to play in the park. She was delirious with happiness.

They spent an hour in the house, and then locked the door with the big iron key and walked back to the carline. There was one more visit to pay before going home. They took the Canal Car to the end of the line, to the junction of the Two Cemeteries. They crossed the street to St. Patrick's Cemetery.

John Eagan's grave was a huge marble tomb, a resting-place set like a small royal palace on terraced land. Above the door was a sculpted angel in flight. Only the angel's foot touched the pointed rooftop of the little building. John's name had been etched in gold on the tomb and a wrought-iron bench had been welded to the stone approach, facing the edifice.

Weary from the trip, Katie and the girls sat down to rest. Soon Katie got up and started pulling weeds from the grassy mound. She noticed daisies growing wild nearby and gathered a bouquet and placed them in a stone vase before the marble door.

"Next time we come, we'll bring roses," she said. She brushed the hair back from her forehead. "We'll have money to buy some then."

She knelt on the step of the tomb and made the sign of the cross. Stephen and her sisters followed her lead. They prayed an Our Father and crossed themselves again. It was the first time Katie had prayed since her mother died. She hoped God would forgive her her long absence. Now she had so much to be grateful for.

Chapter
TWENTY-SIX

"The paint goes on the house, Stephen, not on your wife," Katie said.

"Yeah, but when your wife looks like the side of a house, you get confused."

Katie's mouth fell open. She put her hands on her hips, paintbrush and all. Then she snapped the brush in Stephen's direction, leaving a line of yellow dots across his face. She giggled. There had not been a painting session yet in which one of the four of them had not wound up dotted or striped.

Stephen took a rag and wiped the spots off his face before they dried.

"I'll get you for that, my lovely," he said theatrically.

He looked at his wife as she stood on the gallery, paintbrush poised. She had braided her hair and tied a bandanna around her head, knotting it at the back. A few spots of paint marked her cheek near her mouth. She had put on Stephen's shirt and pants, since none of her own clothes fit anymore (except her two good maternity dresses), and covered her ill-fitting costume with a butcher's apron. She was a sight, but the kind of sight that he loved best in all the world.

Her pregnancy had never slowed her down, but he worried sometimes that she was doing too much. She had promised not to lift heavy things or to scrub floors now that there were only two more months to go.

It had been fifteen months since she and Stephen had married and taken her sisters to live with them in the yellow house on Moss Street, and only now were they nearly finished with painting and repairs. They had had to do it bit by bit when money was available from Stephen's wages for paint and lumber and tools and curtain fabrics.

They had renovated the inside first, so that they could live in it while they worked. The floors had been scrubbed and the walls divested of cobwebs. Then they had painted the inside walls and hung curtains in the windows. Though months went by with no visible improvement on the outside, Stephen was replacing floorboards in the porch or tiles in the roof or restoring the fireplaces. Even when these jobs were done, they had had to wait till they saved enough money for paint. They had gone a whole summer with half the house a bright canary yellow while the other half remained bare boards. During those months, Katie had experienced a strange imbalance in her emotional equilibrium. She had found herself vacillating between good cheer and depression. At last they were closing up the gap, and Katie breathed a sigh of relief.

The house was a bright yellow landmark overlooking the bayou, with dark green shutters and white railings. Rockers lined the gallery and a porch swing hung to one side. Katie loved the house so much and was so proud of it that when she glimpsed it from the levee of the bayou, seeing it as others saw it on their Sunday rides, her eyes stung with tears of proprietary joy. If she had had the means to build a house of her own, she could never have conceived of one so lovely.

Another trial to Katie's patience were the months she had had to wait before getting pregnant. At first she was glad to be able to put it off for a while. There was so much physical labor needed in the house. She didn't like to admit it, even to herself, but she was terrified of childbirth, after her mother's experience. But as the months went by, and the house took shape, and their lives fell into place, she began to feel the sharpest kind of disappointment when her periods came unerringly on time. She yearned to give Stephen a child, and she began to hunger for the feel of a baby in her own arms. It seemed that in her new life, everything took so long to happen. At last, after eight months of marriage, she was able to tell her husband that he was going to be father.

That night he had held her in his arms with a devouring kind of love and kissed her eyes and her lips and her cheeks. They had laughed like children and made all the delightful, impossible plans parents make for their firstborn child.

They had sat on the porch swing till midnight, and Katie had related the events of the night before her mother died. She sat with her head on Stephen's shoulder, her fingers laced through his, and he had felt her body tremble as she recounted the details of that horrible night.

"Don't cry, my love," he said when she had finished. "We won't let that happen to you. *Or* to our baby. I'll get you the best specialist in town, and your own room in the hospital for as long as you need it."

"Stephen, you really won't mind?" she had asked.

"Of course not."

"They say Creole men never let their wives go to male doctors."

"Then they're even bigger jackasses than I thought." Katie laughed.

"The question is, will *you* mind?" he asked. "*You're* the one who dresses behind the door. What are you going to do? Make him deliver the baby blindfolded?"

Katie laughed a small laugh. It had been worrying her.

"I'll have to force myself, I guess," she said. "I'll offer it up for the Poor Souls."

"That's us."

"I know."

* * *

So Katie had a doctor, and she was to have her baby in the hospital. The Creole ladies on Esplanade whispered to each other as they took their strolls on Sunday afternoons. "On dit" (they would say) that young Mrs. Eagan shows herself blatantly in public. "On dit" that she is actually getting a doctor for her *accouchement*. "No wonder poor Janet was forced to turn them out," the gossips sympathized. "Young people have no modesty at all these days."

But Katie cared little for what people said. She worked outdoors at seven months in her husband's clothing. She went downtown in the street car even now, when according to Creole standards any "decent" woman in her condition would have been hiding behind the curtains until her confinement. But Katie didn't live by convention. Convention was for those who could afford it. She hadn't won her husband on her beautiful home by bowing to convention.

Katie and Stephen and the girls had enjoyed restoring the antique furniture they found in the house. They were constantly discovering old pictures, old clothing; and personal belongings of the original owners. The home was like a time capsule. Katie and her sisters spoke of Stephen's grandparents often as they sat on the gallery in the evenings, watching the boats go by.

"I wonder if Stephen's grandmother was alone here when she died," Katie said. "Her dresses were still hanging in the closets, her jewelry was still in the chest . . . It's a wonder nobody broke in and stole them all those years."

"Stephen says she was alone here for years after old Franz Eagan died and Mr. John went to Menlo Park," said Jenny.

"He must have been a small man, from the size of his clothes and his shoes," Lala said. "Don't you like to think about them, Katie? Imagine coming all the way from Germany and making so much money in a foreign country!"

"He must have been very smart," Katie agreed. "Do you know what I found out about Franz Eagan? The beer garden and restaurant he started was only a few blocks away from here."

"Really?" Lala asked.

Katie nodded. "It was on City Park Avenue, just around the corner and a few blocks down. Stephen pointed it out to me when we were taking a walk. It's not a beer garden now. It's a French restaurant called Lamothe's. And I'll bet the people who own it don't even know about Franz Eagan. Well, anyway, Stephen says we can go there for dinner, just as soon as he saves enough money."

"Wonderful!" Lala said.

"We'll sit outdoors on the upstairs gallery and watch the automobiles go in and out of the park. Oh, I just can't wait."

True to his word, Stephen took the girls to Lamothe's. They requested a second-floor balcony table, and everyone selected a dinner of moderate price. When they had eaten, they called the waiter for the check.

"Is the owner here, please?" Katie asked.

"Oh, yes, madame," the waiter said. "Monsieur Lamothe is always here."

"Then ask him to come to our table, please."

The waiter frowned at this irregularity. The lady was pushy enough to have appeared in public in such an advanced stage, but . . . "If I may convey your compliments to Mr. Lamothe, madame?"

"No. He must come himself. I have something for him. A gift."

Stephen and the girls looked at Katie questioningly. None of them were in on her secret, whatever it was. Grumbling, the waiter went off in search of the owner.

"What is it, Kate?" Stephen asked. "What are you up to?"

Eyes twinkling, Katie opened the drawstrings of a huge handbag she had carried with her. She pulled out a rectangular package tied with brown paper, but she said nothing. At last the waiter and the owner, arguing in modulated voices, came toward the Eagans and stopped at their table.

"Mr. Lamothe?" Katie asked.

"Yes, madame," the gentleman answered stiffly. His vest was draped with a heavy gold chain. He sported a gold tooth in the front of his mouth, and his handlebar mustache curled at the ends.

"I have a gift for you, sir," Katie said. "Open it, please."

Lamothe took the package, feeling awkward unwrapping a gift in the middle of a crowded restaurant, but when his eyes fell on the framed picture Katie had handed him, his face was transformed with delight.

"But it is our restaurant!" he said excitedly. "Many years ago. Perhaps when it first opened." Katie nodded. "There is the gallery and the awnings . . . Madame, where on earth did you get this picture?"

"In an old trunk in our attic. It belonged to the original owners of this place, Franz and Anna Eagan. Here they are in the photograph. They're standing there on the sidewalk."

She pointed to the two figures in the picture.

"Ever since I bought the restaurant," Lamothe said, "I've been trying to find out who the original owner was, but I've had no success. The building has changed hands so many times."

"Well, there they are," Katie said proudly.

"Remarkable! Franz and Anna Eagan. And you've framed it. I'll hang it in the downstairs dining room, where everyone can see it, and I will label it with their names. I couldn't be more pleased, Mrs. . . .?"

"Eagan, too. My husband is their grandson."

"My dear Mr. Eagan," Lamothe said, pumping the

young man's hand vigorously. "My dear Mrs. Eagan."
He took her hand, too, and kissed it. Jenny and Lala
giggled into their napkins. "And these young ladies
are . . . ?"

"My sisters," Katie said.

"Then the Eagan party will be my guests tonight.
Waiter, no bill." He reached across the table and
picked up the check. Dramatically he tore the slip in
two.

"No, please, we can't . . ." Stephen argued.

"Yes, I insist. Your charming wife has made me a
gift that money cannot buy. A dinner is little enough in
return."

"Then we accept gratefully," Katie said, nudging her
husband under the table.

All the way home Jenny and Lala laughed about the
owner with the mustache that curled in a full circle at
the ends. They skipped ahead of Katie and Stephen,
jumping the cracks in the sidewalk.

Their singsong voices floated back to Stephen and
Katie as they walked along hand in hand.

"I just knew whoever owned the restaurant would
love that picture," Katie said.

"Well, if you find any more, don't give them away.
That was the first picture I've ever seen of my grandparents."

"Oh, darling, there are dozens of them in the attic.
All glass negatives. We can take them down and hang
them all over the house. They were the cutest couple.
Your grandfather was smaller than his wife, but he was
very domineering. And she was the perfect wife, a slave
to her lord and master."

"How can you tell all that?" he asked.

"From the way she looks at him. I love them, Stephen. I feel like I know them since I'm living in their
house."

"Your house."

"Our house," she corrected, squeezing his arm. "And

by the way," she said, "don't ever argue with a restaurant owner when he says he'll take your check. He *might* change his mind."

Stephen smiled. "If I'd known he was going to pick up the check, I'd have taken you there weeks ago."

"If *I'd* known," Katie said, "I would have ordered lobster."

Chapter
TWENTY-SEVEN

"Listen to this!" Katie said, not taking her eyes from the letter. Jenny and Lala came over to where she was sitting on the porch swing. Jenny sat beside her, and Lala sat cross-legged on the floor. "It's from Davey."

That in itself was not remarkable, for Katie heard from her brother from time to time, but her expression told the girls something unusual was about to happen.

"He's coming home," Katie said, smiling.

"Here?" Jenny asked. The Moss Street house had never been "home" to Davey, a fact which Katie seemed to have forgotten.

"Yes. For three whole weeks!"

"Oh, dear!" Jenny said. "I wonder how he'll be."

"What do you mean?" Katie asked.

"You know. I wonder if he'll be holy and go around saying his rosary, and if we'll have to be careful what we say."

"Don't be silly," Katie said. "Anyway, what do you say that you can't say in front of a seminarian? He's only fifteen years old. He's just a high-school boy. That's all."

"I know. But he seems like such a stranger. Three years is a long time."

Katie gazed out over the water. "I wonder what he looks like now. I always picture him the way he was when he left home, but I'll bet he's grown a foot. He says he'll be able to spend his vacations with us now, isn't that wonderful?"

No one answered.

"And holidays and special occasions," Katie added. "I guess they figure if he's stayed in the seminary this long, he has a real vocation. They can give him a little more freedom."

"Think he plays ball, and stuff?"

"Sure," Katie said. "He's just a regular boy." She studied the serious faces. "For goodness sake, when he gets here, don't stand around gawking at him as if he were a freak, or something."

When Davey arrived on a streetcar, he was carrying a straw valise. He slowly climbed the stairs, and when everyone had kissed and embraced him and marveled over his height and his changed appearance, a deadly silence fell over the group, and the two little girls watched him unblinking, as if, at any moment, he would perform a miracle or deliver a homily.

"Well!" Katie said, smiling. "How tall you've grown, Davey!"

Davey smiled uncertainly. Katie searched her mind for something else to say, but it was as if they were total strangers. To make matters worse, Stephen was not yet home from work, to help keep the conversation going.

After an eternity of painful silences and awkward forays into conversation, Stephen at last arrived, and Katie excused herself to finish preparations for dinner. Jenny and Lala followed on her heels, and they all sighed aloud when they reached the kitchen.

"What'll we ever do for three long weeks?" Jenny asked.

"It'll get better," Katie promised, and she hoped she was right.

The prophecy was fulfilled that very night. After supper Stephen took Davey and the girls to the City Park for a game of softball. Jenny and Lala were natural athletes, and they often went with Stephen to "throw the ball around" or play a three-man game. Katie had played, too, until a few months ago, when she got so big that she was afraid to fall and hurt herself or the baby. Now she watched from a park bench, enjoying the cool breezes off the lagoon. There was nothing like physical activity and shared enjoyment to bring a family together.

"Good, Lala," Davey called out. "Good catch!"

Lala beamed. "You're pretty good, too, Davey. Do you play at the seminary?"

"Every day."

"What position do you like?" Jenny asked.

Davey caught a ball and threw it back to Stephen. "I like first base, but I play right field if they need me."

"When do you study?" Lala wanted to know.

"At night. And we play ball in the afternoon, at Physical Education."

"You mean, you get regular Physical Education, just like we do?" Jenny asked.

"Sure. I go to regular school, just like you do." Davey winked at Stephen.

After that, tension disappeared. They all played ball every evening, and Stephen taught them Auction Bridge at night. One evening he took them to West End Amusement Park, where they rode the scenic railway out over the water and swam off the public pier. After two weeks they found themselves laughing and giggling like sisters and brothers in any family, more so because they would not be together long enough to get on one another's nerves.

The day before Davey was to leave, Katie sent her sisters on an errand so that she would have time alone with Davey just to talk. She took her basket of embroidery to the porch and asked Davey to keep her company. Together they settled into two of the rocking chairs.

"We'll miss you, Davey," she said fondly, looking at her brother.

He was less freckled now than when he had been a

child, and he had an abundance of curly brown hair. His skin was fair, now pink from the sun, and without a blemish or the sign of a beard. The next time she saw him, he would probably be shaving.

"I've had such a good time, Katie," he said. "I can tell you now I was scared to death to come."

"No more than we were to have you. Remember that first day?" she asked. They both laughed. "Let's never be like that again."

"Never," he promised.

"I've been wanting to talk to you, Davey," she said.

"I know."

"When you left to go into the seminary, I was not at all happy about it."

"I knew that, too, and it made me feel really bad, Katie. But it was what I had to do. It was the only thing I ever wanted to do."

"I was bitter then, Davey. I was mean inside, on account of losing Mama. I wanted to hate somebody for that. I wanted to blame somebody, somebody bigger than Papa. I blamed God, I guess, and I hated Him, too. I didn't want you to give up your life for Him."

Davey nodded. He had always understood.

"But I want you to know I'm over all that, Davey. I have so much to be thankful for. Stephen and I are so happy together, and I'm so lucky to have the girls here with me. Pretty soon, there'll be a baby to bring us even more joy. I wake up at night and think about my life, and I just can't believe it."

"You deserve every happiness, Katie. You've always been so good to everyone."

"No. Not everyone."

Davey frowned, not understanding. Katie put her embroidery in her lap and looked into her brother's eyes.

"There's Stephen's mother. We don't even visit her. Or talk to her. Stephen refuses. It's a long story, but the point of it is, she put me out when she found out Stephen and I were in love, and he can't forgive her for that."

"Then there's nothing you can do. Pray for him. One day, he'll forgive her."

Katie nodded. Such mature advice for so young a head! And he was probably right.

"And then there's Papa," Katie sighed. "I don't even know where he is." She gazed into the clear brown eyes. "I don't know how to feel about Papa. Do you?"

"We don't have to feel anything. He never loved us. He didn't even take care of us. *You* did that, Katie. I know you wouldn't want to see him sick or hungry, and neither would I, but he's not an old man. He can take care of himself."

Katie patted her brother's hand. He had had much time for reflection, and his conclusions were hard common sense. No sermons on the mount.

"Just try not to blame him for Mama's death," Davey added, surprising her. "I know you did, at first. Maybe you still do. It'll only eat you up inside. It wasn't his fault, you know."

Katie *didn't* know. She wondered how Davey could be so sure of everything. She didn't promise to accept his judgment on her father's guilt.

"The thing I feel worst about is turning my back on God for a year," she said. "That was when you left for the seminary, and I thought you were wasting your life. I was wrong about that, Davey. I think you'll be a wonderful priest."

Davey reached over and kissed her cheek.

"I hope God won't punish me for my meanness," Katie went on. "I hope he won't take my baby or put me through a terrible delivery like Mama had."

Davey looked into her eyes and saw that she was scared to death.

"God wouldn't do that, Katie," he said. "God isn't vindictive."

"Do you know Him so well?" she asked, smiling,

tears verging, chiding him gently. "If so, I hope you'll put in a good word for me."

He looked up, and she was smiling, still, the tears spilling down her cheeks. He took the hem of her apron and dried her face. He took both her hands in his and kissed them. She was the dearest person in Davey's world.

"For whatever my prayers are worth," he said, "I'll say a rosary for you every night."

Chapter
TWENTY-EIGHT

For over a year Stephen had been working as a lineman with the Edison Electric Company. He liked working outdoors, climbing poles and dropping lines to the homes of new customers. He also worked underground, repairing junction boxes after heavy rains. He whistled throughout the day, thinking of his Kate and the baby soon to come.

It was nice to meet people and to see their faces when the lights went on in their homes for the very first time. His wages were not generous, but adequate, and since the house was free and clear, their chief expenses were food and clothes, and a savings account for the baby. The Raspanti girls had economized all their lives, so living frugally was nothing new to them. They had never dreamed that they would live in a home like number 17 Moss Street which, to them, was a mansion.

During the first winter of their marriage Stephen set up a laboratory in the basement of their home. He did not know that his father had had a laboratory there some thirty years before, until the day he found a notebook with records of experiments and a cabinet where chemicals, neatly labeled, had been standing for three decades.

That first spring he began working on a guard for the electric fan. It was an invention that required no scientific knowledge and very little imagination. Yet, amazingly no one had ever patented it. People had been known to lose fingers in the sharp, whirring blades.

He purchased his supplies: a blow torch, a vise, and several yards of baling wire. He designed a curved cage in which the fan would be imprisoned in such a way that the blades could spin untouched, but fingers would be protected. By the middle of June he had received his patent from the office in Washington, D.C., for his fan guard. Edison Electric was impressed with his idea, and production of the guards was begun at once on all fans in the manufactory in Gretna, across the river.

Stephen received fifteen cents on each fan, and he was astonished at the number of fans that were turned out every month, not only for New Orleans, but for all of southern Louisiana and Mississippi. Stephen's first invention had been a success.

In 1910, there was still much resistance to change. The desire to preserve the status quo was nowhere stronger than in the languorous South, and especially in old cities like New Orleans, where established traditions were the norm. Sunday rides were still taken in buggies, and gas lighting was still part of a gracious way of life.

Stockholders in Edison Electric were primarily an exclusive group of physicians and surgeons who were becoming weary of throwing good money after bad. Even after three decades of incandescent lighting, few homes in the city were wired for electricity, and most of the business places used only a fraction of the electric power to which they might have subscribed. When the situation reached the point where the infant electric plant might conceivably have to shut down for lack of funds, an Edison agent from New York was sent to New Orleans.

Thomas Edison had written his condolences at the time of the death of his good friend, John Eagan. Now he asked his agent, Sidney Gentry, who was to come to the city to try to stem the tide of financial disaster, to visit John's widow and his son, Stephen, who, he had heard from his European connections, was a promising young electrical engineer.

When Gentry arrived one evening at the door of the St. Charles Avenue home, he was warmly received by Janet Eagan, who listened politely as he explained his reason for being in the city. She wrote out her son's address on Moss Street, which her friends on Esplanade had given her.

The following day Gentry rode the Canal streetcar and then walked along the bayou to the yellow house on Moss Street. He enjoyed the picturesque walk, beneath the cavernous oaks, and he took his time, watching the small craft on the water. At last he looked up to see a lovely house on the terrace overlooking the bayou.

A young couple was sitting on the gallery in rocking chairs, holding hands. Two girls sat on the porch floor, playing jacks. The picture was wholesome and heartwarming.

He climbed the steps to the gallery and introduced himself.

"Please sit with us, Mr. Gentry," Stephen said, pulling up another rocker. "It was so good of Mr. Edison to ask you to look me up."

"He insisted on it," Gentry said. "He says you're a very bright young man. His friends in Europe, the ones you studied with, they wrote him about you."

"I was wondering," Stephen said. "You see, I've never met the Great Man. And would you tell me something, Mr. Gentry? How did you find me, sir?"

"Your mother gave me your address."

Gentry did not miss the exchange of looks between the young man and his wife. No doubt bad blood had passed between young Eagan and his mother.

As it was nearing the supper hour, Katie insisted that Mr. Gentry stay and eat with them. At the table Gentry explained why he was in New Orleans. He was a finan- *i* cial troubleshooter for all the Edison Electric plants. It was his job to visit a city whenever a central station appeared to be going under for lack of revenue. Edison Electric of New Orleans looked that way right now.

"I understand you work for the company as a lineman," Gentry said to Stephen.

"Did my mother tell you that?"

"No. I have access to the records," Gentry smiled.

He wore his hair in a plastered wave in the center of his forehead, and he had a nervous habit of pulling his neck up out of his collar.

"I'd like to know your opinion, Stephen," he said. "You meet the public every day. You talk to people who are having their houses wired. They tell you why they're taking the step, I'm sure."

"They usually do."

"And they tell you why they didn't do it sooner?"

"Sometimes."

"Well, what do you think? Are attitudes changing at all? Do you see any promise for expansion?"

"Very little. It's remarkable how people hang on to the old ways."

"Our only hope of getting by this crisis is to increase our capacity and then take on all available additional business," Gentry said. "I mean commercial business, primarily. We need mass production and mass distribution. It's the only way this company can survive."

"Well, sir, there are dozens of untapped businesses in this city," Stephen said.

"Like what?"

"We have two breweries in town. They ought to have electric refrigeration, but they don't."

"That would be quite a contract."

"And we still have dozens of hotels with hydraulic elevators, operated on steam pumps. And lumberyards still use gasoline engines."

"Unbelievable! You people are living in the Middle Ages, Stephen. No offense."

"Oh, I know it. And the few who are moving forward consider themselves so daring. They're still not sure they're doing the right thing, you know? They don't really see the significance of electricity in their lives."

"Then how can we convince them, Stephen? These are your friends, your neighbors. You know them better than I do."

"You've got to put on a sales campaign like this city has never seen before. Put it on billboards, in newspapers, in streetcar advertising. Everywhere people look, they've got to see a lady ironing with an electric iron, a schoolboy reading by soft electric light, a front door lit up for company. Offer them a whole line of household appliances and make them think everyone else in town is using them, that they can't live without them.

"Maybe we could have a modern house, all set up with electrical gadgets. You could call it the House of Tomorrow, or something like that. People would run to see it. And once the fad caught on, each family would be trying to keep up with its neighbors."

"Does that kind of competition work here, I mean with your lethargic southerners?" Gentry asked.

"Oh, yes," said Stephen emphatically. "You can bet your life it does." Stephen thought for a moment, and then added: "Maybe you could offer them a bargain. A reduced rate per kilowatt hour, over a certain number of hours. Or how about installing some of the new appliances on a trial basis?"

"We're already doing that."

"Then how about letting them pay for appliances on time? A dollar down, a dollar a month?"

"We're not Sears Roebuck, Stephen."

"I know we're not. *They*'re making money."

Gentry chuckled. "You have good sales ideas, my boy," he said. "What are you doing climbing poles for a living?"

"Oh, I'm no salesman," Stephen demurred. "I'm a

tinker, like my father. I was born thirty years too late. How I envy him, being at Menlo Park with Edison."

"So do I. A tinker, are you? Have you come up with anything worthwhile?"

"He certainly has," Katie injected. "He invented a guard for the electric fan. We're getting royalties."

"Wonderful, Stephen!" Gentry said, slapping the young man on the shoulder. "Very good, indeed."

Stephen grinned. "There's something else I'm working on that I think may be much more important. It's a new type of socket that will screw into the outlet."

Gentry frowned. "Instead of the bayonet type?"

Stephen nodded. "I think it will be much less awkward and easier to get a snug fit."

"Interesting. I'd like to see it when you're done. But get your patent first. We tinkers are all thieves, you know." The two men laughed.

"Nonsense. I'll show you what I've got so far."

After dinner they went down to the basement, while Katie and the girls picked up the supper dishes. Later, when they were all out on the porch, enjoying the perfume of magnolias and the view of the moon on the water, Gentry said:

"Can't understand how you got sidetracked into the installation department. You're the kind of man we need in sales. The company's in a real jam, and I need the help of native New Orleanians who know how the people think. How about changing departments and coming to work with me?"

"I don't know. I've never done selling before," Stephen said.

"You do it every day when you're wiring houses. You believe in your product. You talk about it. Of course you can do it."

"He can do anything, Mr. Gentry," Katie said. "He's the smartest man I know."

"Of course, my wife wouldn't be prejudiced," Stephen said facetiously.

Gentry laughed.

The porch swing creaked as Katie touched her foot to the floor and moved her voluminous weight slowly back and forth.

"He graduated from Tulane with honors, and you know he studied in Europe with the very best men in their fields," Katie persisted. Katie saw an opportunity to push her husband into the stratum in which he belonged, and she wasn't going to waste it.

"Did you tell them all this when you applied for work?" Gentry asked.

"Not Stephen," Katie answered. "I asked him the same question, and do you know what he answered? 'What difference does it make if you've got a degree, if you're applying for a lineman's job?' Can you believe that? He just didn't want anybody to know he was John Eagan's son."

"But why not, Stephen?" Gentry asked. "We have so few men with your background. We need you."

"I had my reasons," Stephen said.

He had applied for the job soon after his violent rift with his mother. He wanted no part of the family. He refused to be obligated to the family name for any success he might have with Edison Electric.

"Well, whatever your reasons were, will you work with us now in sales?" Gentry asked.

Stephen hesitated.

"I'll see that your wages are doubled," Gentry said.

"He'll come," Katie said.

Katie's time was drawing near. She was lethargic now and uncomfortable. Her legs were huge with fluid, and the summer heat made her miserable. One evening in August the pains began. She and Stephen took the streetcar on Esplanade Avenue to the Hotel Dieu Hospital. It took all night for her to deliver her baby, but she had a normal birth and she presented Stephen with a handsome eight-pound boy.

The baby had Stephen's eyes, but in every other way he was Katie. His skin was fair and his hair black as ebony, and Katie had no doubt that he was the most beautiful baby in the world.

Chapter
TWENTY-NINE

Every evening after work Stephen stood at the glass wall of the nursery in Hotel Dieu, admiring his remarkable son. The nuns had to remind him not to whistle in the corridors on the way to his wife's room. Since his baby's birth, he was so infused with fresh love for Katie, he was so exuberant, so emotional, that he had to take her in his arms quickly and bury his face in her thick hair so she wouldn't see the tears standing in his eyes. Then he'd kiss her face and stroke her hair and pet her as if she were a baby herself.

"Dear Kate," he said one evening. It was the name that went back to his letter-writing days. "Do you know that the single most wonderful thing you have ever done in your entire life was to give birth to that baby out there?"

"Dear Stephen," she retorted, "do you know that when it got to that point, there wasn't anything else I could do with it?"

He laughed. He kissed her neck and she wrapped her arms around him.

"It's funny," she said. "In delivery, they keep telling you 'Push! Push!' as if there were anything else you could do. There you are, bathed in your own sweat, one big pain from head to foot, with this giant object trying to work its way out of you, and you want it out so bad, you'd die trying. And still they tell you 'Push!' "

Stephen made sympathetic noises. "You speak very frankly these days," he said.

"Once you have a baby," Katie said, "you have no more modesty."

"Was it really bad, Katie?"

"Terrible!"

He chuckled, although he didn't mean to. "Don't you know you're supposed to say, 'Oh, no, darling, it wasn't too bad.' "

"The hell I will!"

"Katie!" Stephen exclaimed. "That's the first time I've ever heard you swear."

"Well, it won't be the last," she said.

"Good! I like a feisty woman." He kissed her again and caressed her arm as he sat beside her. He knew that whatever kind of woman she was, she was the kind he loved. If she was feisty or sweet, angry or tender, she was perfection to Stephen.

"Stephen," she said one day. "Doesn't it seem unnatural that a grandmother lives in the same city as her firstborn grandchild, and she can't come to see him?"

"Yes. Very unnatural." He said it without expression, and he would not look at Katie.

"Then why don't you tell your mother about the baby? And ask her to come?"

"No!" he shouted vehemently. He got up from Katie's bedside and walked over to look out the window. "She made the rules the day she put us out of her life. Cut off forever! That was the way *she* wanted it."

"She was threatening you, Stephen, to try to keep you from making a mistake, or what *she* thought was a mistake. Now she sees her threat didn't work. If she saw us together, she'd see how well we're doing, and how successful you've become on your own. She'd know there's no point in remaining hostile. She'd accept us . . ."

"Accept *us*?" he shouted. "I don't intend to give her a chance to accept us. I don't need her acceptance. The question is, 'Can we accept *her*?' "

"Can we?" Katie asked.

"Can you?"

"I don't know." She stared thoughtfully into space. "Sometimes I remember little ways she hurt my feelings, but then I have to remind myself that I was her servant then, not her daughter-in-law. I guess she was sorry she ever picked me up in her carriage that morning on Poydras Street. She didn't dream that the little waif who was running away from home would one day be her son's wife." She looked back at Stephen. "I guess I can't blame her for wanting the best for you. I have a son now. I'd want the same."

"You *were* the best for me, Katie," he said. He held her hand in both his own. "I knew that the first time I ever saw that sweet face." He stroked her hair and kissed her softly on the lips. "When she threw you out, she threw me out, too, even if I wasn't there at the time, and even if nobody told me about it." The fact that Katie had never written Stephen about that final morning was a sore point between them. "And when she cut us out of her life, she separated herself from all her grandchildren."

"That's pretty hardhearted of you, isn't it?" Katie asked. "How long are you going to punish her? For all generations?"

"I'm not punishing her, Katie. I just won't have her looking down on you or on the way we live . . ."

"Are you ashamed of the way we live?"

"You know better than that."

"I'm not so sure . . ."

"You're just trying to trick me into a reconciliation, and I'm not ready for that. I'm not sure I'll ever be."

He paced again, restlessly. Katie knew she had stirred up conflicting emotions.

It must be terrible, she thought, to be cut off from one's entire family. Charlotte had never sought them out to befriend them, so they could only conclude that she, too, disapproved of the marriage. How could it be otherwise? Charlotte had never considered Katie an equal. She had never spoken to her, when Katie worked for the family, except to give an order. How could she ever reconcile herself to such a match? And as long as she scorned Katie, Stephen would despise her. The society column of the *Daily Picayune* published Charlotte's picture often, as a member of one volunteer organization or another. She still lived with her mother, and she had not married or become engaged. She had never worked. Like Creole ladies of gentility and refinement, she stayed at home, doing her needlepoint and hoping there would be gentlemen callers.

Warren was at Tulane now, studying electrical engineering as Stephen had done. But, according to the newspapers, he spent a lot more time appearing in plays at the Little Theater and acting with other dramatic groups than he did at the university. Stephen had heard that he was living at the fraternity house and that he sported an expensive Pierce Arrow. Katie knew that Stephen was disappointed that Warren had never looked them up. If his mother knew where they lived, Warren knew. Warren surely had no strong family loyalties that kept him from visiting. What it boiled down to, then, was indifference.

Stephen seemed not to suffer from the estrangement, but Katie knew that there must have been times when he remembered the family sitting around the walnut table in the dining room or swimming off the pier at the camp in Milneburg. One didn't erase a lifetime of memories so easily. He must have thought of his mother in her bathing dress, laughing like a girl, and his father setting up the volleyball net. There had to be pain in his heart, for whether they were dead or not, they were lost to him forever.

Stephen stopped pacing and stood at the foot of her bed.

"What about your *own* father?" he asked. "He's the baby's grandfather. What do you intend to do about him?"

"Nothing."

"Now who's being hardhearted?"

Katie sighed. "Oh, Stephen, I don't know how to feel about Papa," she said.

She pulled her hair down over one shoulder and started braiding it, thoughtfully. Stephen sat beside her, watching her, listening, ready to share her burden.

"I used to say I'd never forgive him. I blamed him for my mother's death." She looked into her husband's eyes. "But I was a child then, Stephen, and I've grown up. He loved her, I know that now, even though he was sometimes unfaithful. I can't very well blame him because she had a breech birth. Besides, the last time I saw him, he said he was sick. Maybe he was just drunk, and covering up, I don't know, but I've been worried. I've been thinking of asking Mrs. Macaluso to look him up."

"Do that, Katie, for your own peace of mind," Stephen said. "By the way, what are we going to call the baby? We can't go on saying 'the baby' forever."

"I thought maybe John, for your father. I like the nickname Johnny. What do you think?"

"I like it. And what about Joseph for a middle name, for *your* father?"

She shook her head no, but she didn't speak. Then after a moment she said "All right."

The baby was christened John Joseph Eagan on the second Sunday after his birth at Holy Rosary Church on Esplanade. Jenny stood as godmother. She was fourteen now, and about to begin her second year at Esplanade High School. She held the baby nervously as the priest poured water over his head and put salt on his tongue. With Davey as godfather, everyone knew the child's spiritual training would never suffer.

Weeks later Katie took the baby, all buttoned up in a bunting, on the streetcar to Julia Row. She wanted to show him off to the Macalusos and the Campos. She also wanted news of her father.

The ladies passed the infant around, smothering him with hugs and kisses and showering compliments on Katie. When their exuberance had subsided, Katie asked about Big Joe.

"He ain't been around for a long time, Katie," Mrs. Macaluso said. "Some weeks ago he went in the hospital for the cure." She pantomimed tipping the bottle.

"What hospital?" Katie asked.

"Charity. He has no money."

"How long ago was it?"

"Few weeks. A month, maybe."

"And you have no idea where he's staying now?"

The woman shook her head.

"If he comes around," Katie said, "will you tell him I was looking for him? Will you give him my address? I'll write it for you. Tell him I . . . would like to see him. And tell him about Johnny."

Katie hardened her heart so she wouldn't cry. It depressed her to come back to Julia Row. It made her think of the cold winter mornings and the summer days when the rooms were like an oven. She thought of the backbreaking work her mother had done to make the apartment livable, which she saw now was a remarkable feat. She thought of her father's infidelity. She remembered the day he had struck her and the night she ran away. She remembered the day her brother drowned, and she recalled her mother's agony. Her wedding night was the only happy memory for her to take away from Julia Row. Somehow that almost made up for all the bad things. But she knew that after this visit, she would never come back to Julia Row again.

Chapter
THIRTY

To Katie's great surprise her father found his way to
her steps soon after her visit to Julia Row. She asked
him up on the porch, and he climbed the steps and sat
on a rocker beside her. He was clean-shaven and had
apparently bathed, but his clothes were shabby and his
hand shook when he reached out to touch the baby.
Jenny and Lala came out on the porch and gave him
sidelong glances, only extending their hands to him
when Katie nodded her head.

Big Joe gave Katie a silver dollar for the baby, and
she thanked him. She did not love her father; the best
she could say was that she hated him less. But looking
at him, sitting there abjectly beside her, pathetically
thin, gray of face, with teeth missing in obvious places,
her heart was moved to pity. She remembered how
handsome he used to be. Even now he was only in his
late forties. She wondered if drink had done this to him,
or if guilt or grief had worn him down.

"Are you well, Papa?" she asked.

"Yes. Yes," he said, tilting his head in a way Italians
did when they wanted you to know they were suffering
in silence.

"Would you like to come to dinner Sunday?" she
asked, almost choking on the words. She could see
Jenny making a mouth and Lala cringing.

"No. No, Katie. Another time, maybe."

He gave no explanations, and she did not insist. She

was relieved, knowing how uncomfortable the girls would be. How sad! They didn't even know him.

The next two years were filled with balmy, blissful days when Katie took her little boy, in his curls and long dresses, for walks along the lagoon in City Park. When he was big enough, she sat him on a swing and pushed him high in the air, while he clung, white-knuckled, to the chains. She and Johnny brought stale bread to feed the ducks that promenaded in families along the shores of the little lakes.

When Johnny was two, Katie gave birth to another boy, and they called him Thomas Edison Eagan. Now, when they took their walks, it was Johnny running alongside, holding onto his mother's skirts, and Tommy in the perambulator, gurgling pleasantly. They were both good babies, and they were Katie's life. She was ostentatious in her affection for them, kissing them re-soundingly wherever she happened to be and hugging them till they begged to be let free. She idolized her husband, she adored her children, and she cherished her home.

Davey came each summer to spend a month or two with the family. He enjoyed holding the babies, and taking them to the park. As Katie watched him play with them and feed them and wash their faces, she thought what a wonderful father he would have made. She found herself waiting anxiously for his visits, to ask his opinions about things. Unlike Stephen, who was an extension of her own heart and soul, Davey was objective and brutally frank. She did not always follow his advice, but she listened.

Katie hadn't seen her mother-in-law since the day she left St. Charles Avenue four years before. In the beginning she had tried to get Stephen to reconcile with Janet, but he had refused adamantly. Now she no longer argued. Months went by, and she didn't even think about the Eagans.

After Joe Raspanti's first visit to Katie on Moss Street, he came by three or four times a year, when Katie least expected him, never calling ahead, never staying for dinner. He sat with her on the porch and rocked a bit and talked inarticulately to the babies, holding out a tobacco-stained finger for them to grasp. Jenny and Lala always treated him awkwardly, although Katie had asked them to try to make him feel comfortable.

Katie learned of her father's death from a foreman at the Jackson Street wharf. Months ago Big Joe had been demoted from this position for drinking and failing to show up for work. On the telephone the man explained that there had been an accident on the dock. A steamship had been unloaded, and several draymen had transferred the hogsheads of sugar to their flat wagons. The wheel of a wagon had broken, and before Joe could move out of the way, the hogshead on the top of the load had fallen over on him and broken his neck.

"I'm sorry to give you this news, Mrs. Eagan," the foreman said. "If it's any comfort to you, he died instantly."

Katie didn't cry. She was shocked and full of compassion that he had died such a horrible death. Though it was a consolation to know that his pain had been so brief, she could not pretend love or grief or loss of a dearly beloved. In her secret heart she was relieved that a source of constant worry and guilt would be put to rest.

With Stephen and Davey and her sisters, she buried her father beside her mother and Little Joe. She had a Requiem Mass said for the repose of his soul, and she went on with her life as before.

Chapter
THIRTY-ONE

Stephen had made progress right from the start in his new job, as Katie knew he would. His first real coup was the sale of electric power to the Cosmopolitan Hotel on Royal Street for the operation of their elevators. He had had to agree to the installation of all motors and pumps on a trial basis, without any certainty that his chief would approve. But he was given the "go ahead," and the machinery was installed. A month later the hotel bought the equipment, and the contract was secured. In no time at all every hotel in the downtown district followed suit. Stephen was applauded in the sales office, and he received a sizable raise as well.

Full of confidence now, he decided to approach the Jackson Brewery. For a month he parked on the owner's doorstep, following him to and from work, each day with new arguments as to why the plant needed and could profit from electric refrigeration. His persistence was rewarded and he got the contract. Stephen was soon promoted to account executive, and, after four years in the department, to sales manager. Everyone predicted a vice-presidency.

Stephen's success meant more to him for the recognition he had gained without family connections than for the change in financial status. Sometimes Katie believed that Stephen had forgotten he was born rich. He had grown up attending private schools, riding in luxurious broughams, taking expensive trips. But when he no longer had these things, he didn't miss them. He used whatever substitute was available, with no apparent inconvenience.

He took the streetcar to and from work, and found it a new experience. He had never had a car of his own, so he didn't miss it. He planned to send his children to Holy Rosary School, with two or three hundred other children. Private schools had always seemed stuffy to Stephen, and he was satisfied that his children would be prepared more realistically for life than he had been. For almost three years they did without indoor plumbing, and in that time Stephen watched the "honey wagons" and the men emptying cement containers with the same morbid fascination Katie and her sisters had known back on Julia Row when they were children.

Their home was wired for electricity right from the start, but that was because Stephen had wired it himself, and the monthly charges were low because of his employee discount. He brought home every new appliance displayed in the showroom on Baronne Street, and they used it on a "trial basis." These were the luxuries made possible by his work, and they were the only ones the Eagans had.

But Stephen found nothing lacking in his life for he did a lot of things in his new life that he had never done before. When Mardi Gras came around, he stood in the streets, in the midst of the crowds, with one of his boys on his shoulders, enjoying the parades. All his life he had viewed them from afar, in the grandstand at City Hall or at the Boston Club.

There was no greater pleasure to him than buying knickknacks or furnishings for his home. That had been out of the question on St. Charles Avenue because every room in his mother's house was like a scene from an elaborate play in which they were to act out their lives. No one dared move a piece of furniture or suggest a change. But on Moss Street Katie welcomed his additions eagerly, and together they decided where they would look best.

He enjoyed long walks with Katie and the children, dinners at Lamothe's, movies at the picture show on Canal Street, picnics at the amusement parks, and most of all, making love to his beautiful wife. If Stephen had left anything of value on St. Charles Avenue, he was totally unaware of it.

Chapter
THIRTY-TWO

Shirts, socks, underwear. Warren threw stacks of clothes into a valise he had flung open on his bed. An extra pair of shoes. He walked to his dresser and picked up hairbrushes, a billfold. He stopped to look at a portrait of his mother and father taken before he was born at the Cotton Centennial. His father's hair was brown then; his mother wore a coquettish smile. He put the picture in his suitcase.

He walked to the bathing room and returned with his toiletries. He was about to place them in the pockets of his valise when there was a knock at his bedroom door. He froze. He knew there was going to be a scene with his mother, but he would have preferred it to be later, when he had had a chance to get his thoughts in order.

"Come in," he said, still holding bottles of hair cream and aftershave.

The door opened and Janet entered. Her eyes caught the suitcase, the bottles, then rested on Warren.

"Going somewhere?" she asked.

The young man sighed. He placed the toiletries gently in the suitcase and looked again at his mother. "Sit down, Mother," he said.

Janet took a wicker chair near the window. She placed her hands on the arms of the chair and waited. She watched Warren pace a few steps, scratching his head, trying to find a way to begin. Only occasionally, like now, did she realize how strikingly handsome her son was.

He was no longer a boy but a beautiful young man of twenty. His shoulders were broad and his hips narrow. His custom-made clothes followed every contour of his body. He was wearing flannel slacks and a sleeveless Argyle sweater over a dress shirt and tie. But it was the face that made one look again.

He had Janet's jet black hair and wide-set gray eyes. His cheekbones were high and he had the family's straight white teeth. In addition to all that, he had deep, incredible dimples.

In truth Janet hardly ever saw the boy because he spent all his time working in dramatic presentations in one theater or another. He was also the most popular leading man in the Dramatic Club at Tulane. Whatever time he didn't spend rehearsing or performing, he spent at the fraternity house. He had become a stranger in his own home, which was the reason why Janet had been so surprised to see him when he appeared at the front door the night before, asking if there was anything left from supper, like some common beggar who had no place to eat. He had offered no explanation; he simply ate and went to bed. And now he was packing with a kind of urgency. She wondered if he would have left without telling her if she hadn't found him packing.

"Mother," he said at last, "I know you'll never understand what I have to say."

"Try me," she said.

"You know that I'm interested in acting."

"I guess I *should* know that."

"Well, I've decided to make it my career. At least, I want to give it a try."

"But Warren, this is January," she said, leaning forward. "The middle of the school year. Surely you'll wait till summer. Maybe you can work in summer stock till school opens in the fall."

"I'm finished with school, Mother. I'm quitting."

"You're doing no such thing!" Janet said. "With only a year and a half to graduate?"

"I'll never graduate. I'm failing everything. You might as well know it."

"Failing? But how did that happen? Have you neglected your studies for these idiot plays?"

Warren smirked. "I never expected you to understand. These 'idiot plays,' as you call them, are the works of Shaw and Shakespeare. The people who come to see them are patrons of the arts. These productions are what I live for, Mother. And I'll make them my life's work, if I'm good enough."

He snapped his suitcase closed and buckled the straps. Janet made a tent of her fingers and watched her son.

"You had no intention of asking my consent?" she asked.

He laughed sardonically. "I knew I'd never get it. But I did plan to talk to you, yes." He walked to his dresser and emptied a handful of change from a small cedar box, and put it in his pocket. He looked at his mother. He sat back on the bed and searched her eyes.

"Look, Mother," he said. "I'm not Stephen. I have no head for electrical engineering. And I have no interest in it. It's all over my head and I'm bored to death in those classes. But just because I'm not following in his footsteps doesn't mean I'm simpleminded. In my own field I'm really not bad. You've never seen any of my plays, so you have no way of knowing, but my directors say I have real talent. They say I can be a fine actor with a little experience. So why drag through day after day of misery?"

"For one good reason. So you can get an education and have something worthwhile to fall back on when you get tired of playing around."

Warren fumed. He clenched his teeth and breathed hard.

"You're like all the Eagan men, Warren," Janet continued. "You're restless and footloose and totally irresponsible. It's a good thing your grandfather made enough money to support so many drifters."

"His money isn't supporting Stephen," Warren said.

Janet's jaw hardened. The scorn Stephen had shown for the fortune she had denied him was a very sore spot.

Warren decided to hold his temper. Hotheadedness would get him nowhere. He would swallow his pride and beg, if necessary. Where he was going, he would need money.

"Now, Mother," he began again, "let's not argue and part angry. That's the last thing I want. I had hoped to take away fond memories when I left."

"And a big bag of money," Janet added. She pinched her lips. "Don't play games with me, Warren. I wasn't born yesterday."

Warren checked the urge to fire back.

Janet took a good look at her son. No doubt his head was turned by his own good looks. He could see himself as a matinee idol. Undoubtedly girls must flatter him and throw themselves at him. She could understand why local directors sought him out for leading roles.

He pulled up a chair and sat beside his mother.

"Let me tell you about Hollywood, Mother," he said. "It's the most exciting place in the world. There's a brand new industry out there. A whole new art form. Studios as big as city blocks are making films on stages and outside lots. Every day, hundreds of actors . . ."

"Wait a minute," Janet interrupted. "Wait just a minute. I thought the film factories were in New York."

"They were. Some of them still are, but most of them are in Hollywood now, where there's sunshine all year round for outdoor scenes."

"And what does this have to do with you?"

"Well, I thought you understood. I want to act in moving pictures."

"I can't believe what you're telling me. When you spoke of acting, I had hoped, at the very least, you were referring to the legitimate theater. That, in itself, would be bad enough. But at least you would be studying drama, pursuing some kind of a respectable career. But the nickelodeon! Warren! You cannot be serious!"

"The moving pictures, Mother, and I've never been more serious in my life," he said quietly. He wished he had known her sentiments. He would not have hesitated to lie, to say that he was going to New York. That way, he might have managed to get away with a nice, fat check before she found out where he was.

He started again. "If you'd just let me tell you all I've read about the movies, I know you'd change your mind. You see, most of the studios are on the West Coast now; they've moved there to get away from the Edison revenuers. They're near the Mexican border, so they can make a run for it if they have to."

"Good God, Warren, is that what you want to be a part of?" she asked.

Another detail he should have omitted. "That's just a temporary thing, Mother," he said. "The film industry is booming. Very soon, there'll be no more hope of collecting royalties from everyone who operates a camera. The picture industry will be the biggest thing that ever hit this country, and I want to be in on the ground floor."

Janet closed her eyes and shook her head. "Incredible!" she said. "Grown men making nine-minute films called *The Arrival of the Train*, and *Men Playing Cards*." She turned to her son. "To act in *that*, you would give up your college education?"

"Those one-reel films are finished now, Mother. The industry is growing up. Moving pictures are going to tell stories now. They'll be two reels long, or three, or four, and they'll have a plot, like a stage play."

"No one will ever sit that long."

"They've made a nine-reel film in France, with Sarah Bernhardt. It lasts *two hours*."

"The world is full of crazy people, Warren. Some of

them ride airplanes. That doesn't mean we all have to do it."

Warren sighed. He was getting nowhere. He felt as if he were wading through quicksand, but he had to go on.

"There's a genius out in Hollywood called D. W. Griffith," he said. "I suppose you never heard of him."

"It may surprise you, but I *have* heard of him," Janet said. "I read, you know."

"Then you know what brilliant and innovative things he's doing with films. He's fashioning an art, Mother. He takes a scene, you see, and he splits it into little parts. One part will be a close-up, I mean so close you can see the freckles on the actor's face. Then another part will be a long shot. And after that he reassembles the scene. It's marvelous. He films the whole story, mixing outside scenes with scenes shot on a studio stage, and he carries the plot from one scene to the next, never breaking the thread of action."

Warren had used his hands as he spoke, first as a frame for close-ups, then as a pointer for long shots. He talked animatedly, and his face was flushed with enthusiasm.

Janet's expression was wooden.

"Warren . . . Warren," she said, shaking her head despairingly. "This is the Penny Arcade business, son. You're a rich young man with background and promise. With a little travel, a law degree perhaps, if you don't care for electronics, you could be *some*body in this city. Don't talk to me about studio lots and painted women and celluloid film for the immigrants."

"For the immigrants?" Warren shouted. He laughed a shrill laugh at the absurdity of it.

"Yes, for the immigrants. There are thousands of them here in this country. They go to the movies because they have a nickel to spend and they don't have to understand English. Now just think for a minute about the messages in these films. The evils of drink, women's place in the home, crime and its punishment, virtue is its own reward, and the ennobling effects of poverty. That last one is very important," she said sarcastically. "The movie makers tell us that virtue and poverty go together. Wealth and evil go together, too. These are films to teach the masses, to keep the beggars in line. Then they all go home with a sermon under their belt, and they don't even know they've had it." She looked at Warren with affected surprise. "You mean, you have never thought of movies as a social force?" she asked.

The young man frowned. His mother had given more thought to the industry than he gave her credit for. More thought than *he* had, from certain angles.

"Why do you think these actors won't let their names be published with the films?" she asked.

"The producers want it that way. They'd have to pay the actors more," he said.

"Not so," she shot back. "It's because it's a comedown for any decent actor to be seen in this kind of trash."

"Well, I hate to ruin your argument," he said, "but the films are giving them credits now. The public is demanding it. They want to know who the Vitagraph Boy is and who Little Mary is. Mary Pickford and Douglas Fairbanks and Mae Marsh and the Gish sisters. They get thousands of letters every day. They have fame and fortune and public adulation."

"Is that what you want, Warren? Fame and fortune and . . . public adulation?"

He laughed with a flash of white teeth. "I think I could learn to live with it."

Janet tapped her fingertips together soundlessly, studying them as she did so. Warren sat before his mother, waiting. This was it. He could feel it.

Two pairs of gray eyes stared each other down.

"Mother," he asked, "will you let me draw from my share of Dad's estate?"

Janet frowned. "*Your* share?" she asked. "You *have* no share unless I say so."

"And do you say so?"

"No." She got up from the chair. "Definitely not." She turned to leave the room.

Warren ran to block the door. "Wait, Mother, we haven't finished yet."

"I have."

"If you won't give me an income, write me a check. A thousand dollars. Five hundred. Anything to get me started."

"Nothing," she said emphatically. "I refuse to underwrite stupidity and wasted time. Let me by. I want you to unpack all those things and try to get back into school, if they'll have you."

"I'm not doing that, Mother. You refuse to understand. I'm leaving today for Hollywood."

They stared daggers into each other's eyes.

"I can make my own living," he said.

"Hah!" She walked down the corridor toward the stairway.

"I'm taking the Pierce Arrow," he called after her. She turned and faced him. "You *are not!*"

"The papers are in my name. It's mine and I'm taking it. I have a few hundred dollars of my own and some jewelry . . ."

"Which *I* gave you," she said. She stared at him down the length of the hall. "That will get you from here to Hollywood, the way you live. What then?"

Warren put his hands on his hips and watched his mother descend the stairs at the end of the corridor. Then he went back to his room to get his suitcase.

Chapter
THIRTY-THREE

On the third day of his journey west Warren saw mountains for the very first time. He had never made the Grand Tour of Europe, as Stephen and Charlotte had. In fact the farthest from home he had ever been was Panama City, Florida. He was a flatlander, and to him the towering peaks of lilac and blue surrounding the valleys in which he drove were magnificent and awe-inspiring. For them alone he would have made the trip.

He slept every night in his car and he ate at roadside beaneries, hoarding his cash. When he got to Los Angeles, he would sell the Pierce Arrow, and the price he'd get should keep him solvent long enough to make the rounds of the studios and get started with a few small parts. He laughed when he thought of the offer he'd gotten from a used-car dealer in Houston. A thousand dollars for a brand new George Washington Coach Pierce Arrow was ridiculous. His mother had paid eight thousand dollars for it. Even after the trip to L.A. he'd take no less than five.

Early on the morning of the fifth day he pulled up to a small white frame restaurant hugging the highway south of Los Angeles. He took a deep breath. He had arrived. Grabbing his small leather bag with his toiletries and his valise, he got out of the car and walked through the screened door of the restaurant.

There were no customers yet at the lunch counter or at the three small tables. It was only seven thirty. Through a pass-through window, he could see a cook in the rear getting ready for the day. The aroma of fresh coffee wafted toward him.

To his right, behind a cashier's counter, was a young woman in her early twenties who was looking him up and down as he examined the place. Her lips were a startling red and her eyebrows pencil thin. Her dark hair was arranged in deep finger waves around her face and in corkscrew curls on her forehead.

Warren felt self-conscious with a two-day growth of beard and rumpled clothes, but the girl's expression told him that she found no fault with his appearance.

"Is there a washroom here?" he asked.

She took a key with a wooden marker from behind the counter and held it out to him.

"Outside," she said. "Round back."

But when he reached for the key, she held it tight and placed her other hand over his. Warren could see that she had left the top buttons of her green uniform open, and the cleavage they revealed was deep enough to drown in.

"Where you come from, honey?" she asked.

Warren hated to talk till he'd washed his face and shaved, but he answered.

"New Orleans," he said. He smiled reluctantly.

She still held his hand and the key.

"My, my," she said. "Long way from home, ain'tcha? Whatcha gonna do out here? Be a movie star?"

Warren smiled. "Maybe so. Who knows?"

"Shouldn't have no trouble with those big gray eyes," the girl said.

Warren withdrew his hand and excused himself. Back outside, he shielded his eyes from the sun and walked around to the rear, where he found a small white house. It was cleaner than he had expected. He brushed his teeth, washed his face and hands, and did the best he could to shave with cold water. After changing into a clean shirt, he felt revitalized. He picked up his luggage and started back to the restaurant. But when he turned the corner to the front of the diner, he stopped cold. His car was gone! His beautiful Pierce Arrow! It took only a minute to check all sides of the diner. It was nowhere in sight. Someone had stolen his automobile, his meal ticket for at least a whole year. He ran out onto the highway and looked in both directions, but the road was lost in the folds of rolling hills. He dashed back inside to call the police.

By this time five or six customers were sitting at the counter, ordering breakfast. The girl who had given him the key was taking orders, and sizzling sounds emanated from the kitchen.

"My car is gone!" he said to the girl. "Did you see anyone drive away in a yellow Pierce Arrow?"

"A yellow Pierce Arrow!" she repeated. The exclamation reverberated around the diner. Customers looked up from their newspapers curiously. "Mister, I ain't never seen a yellow Pierce Arrow in my life," she said.

She looked at his handsome, clean-shaven face, and she smiled sensuously as she leaned across the counter. "Listen, honey, don't get yourself all upset," she said. "C'mon in the back and we'll call the cops."

"You do have a phone?" he asked.

"Sure, handsome. This ain't Hicksville. This is Hollywood."

It was Hollywood, indeed, and Warren had a lot to learn about it. The girl dialed the number of the police and Warren could hear her relating the incident just as it had happened, giving the license number he had written out for her. The rest of the day he stayed close to the phone in case the police would call back. Warren discovered that the young woman called herself Mary May Manson, a name that was, no doubt, designed to skyrocket her to stardom. She made frequent trips to the kitchen, bringing him breakfast and coffee and generous glimpses of her generous bosom. On one of these trips Mary May sat beside him and rested her hand on his thigh. She asked if he had a place to stay for the night. Her eyes promised treats beyond his wildest imaginings.

All day she kept him in a constant state of heat, although he was sick with disappointment about his car. He had a strong premonition that the police would do little to help him. He could not believe that he had lost all means of supporting himself on his very first day in Hollywood.

Once, in the early afternoon, he looked up to see Mary May leaning against a table in the kitchen. When she saw he was looking, she tilted her chin forward and slowly passed the tip of her tongue along her upper lip. Warren felt his temperature rise. He felt everything rise. She had him crazy. It was a whole new experience for him to be so aggressively approached by a girl.

With the girls he knew back home, he had to outmaneuver the watchful eyes of aunts or guardians just to get a kiss. Of course there *were* houses on Basin Street, where his friends went regularly. Warren had gone along once or twice, but he had never taken a girl. He was too fastidious. The thought of unclean bodies and odors and possible disease had left him cold.

Only once had Warren made love to a girl, and even that had been interrupted. A college girl he was dating had let him into her bedroom by way of the roof. She had let him undress her, and touch her, and she had said that he could go "all the way." But at the most crucial moment of his life, they had heard her father's voice as he came down the hall to her bedroom. Warren had barely made it to the roof, with his clothes in his arm, when the father entered the room. Stark naked, he had slithered down a tree, and he still had the scars to prove it.

He studied Mary May as she jiggled her breasts and swished her backside coming and going with orders. At five o'clock she dismissed the cook and closed up the restaurant. The place belonged to her brother-in-law, she told Warren, and he was out of town and had left things in her hands.

"Come on to my place, honey," she said. "I live alone. I'll give you a meal and a place to sleep. And don't you worry. The cops're gonna find your car."

They got into a Ford (her brother-in law's, she said) and she leaned over and caressed his thigh. Warren's eyes rolled back in his head. He didn't need any more tactile persuasion.

Mary May drove past miles of orange groves into the heart of the city. It was Warren's first glimpse of Hollywood, and although he was sensually distracted, he made mental note of the route they were taking and the sights along the way. There were mud streets and paved sidewalks in this older part of town where the houses were one-story frame, mostly white or dark green, with screened porches and stone steps.

"Look back behind the houses," Mary May said. "You can see some movie sets."

Warren leaned out of the window and looked. Not more than a block away there were structures five to six stories high, scaffoldings and Egyptian statues high in the air, perhaps the setting for some spectacular film set in ancient times. He laughed with excitement. It was exhilarating to be in Hollywood, where things like this were part of the landscape.

Another mile brought them to a newer, better neighborhood of mission-style stucco houses with red-tiled roofs and wrought-iron grilles on the windows. Mary May parked in front of an apartment house built in a U around a central patio. She took Warren's hand and led him swiftly across the patio to a corner apartment. Once inside, she did not turn on the lights, although night had fallen.

They passed through what appeared to be a sitting room and a kitchen, but she did not stop until she reached the bedroom. Nothing was said about food. Immediately the girl began to take off her clothes. In the meager daylight Warren watched her, transfixed, as she revealed her voluptuous body. Naked now, she turned back the spread and got into bed. She looked at Warren, as though surprised that he was still dressed. In seconds Warren was out of his clothes and under the spread with Mary May.

Never before had a woman offered herself to him, stretched out on a bed, totally nude, and he didn't know what to do with her. Sensing his ineptitude, she guided his hands to her breasts, her smooth hips, her thighs. Warren shivered with anticipation. She seemed not to be dismayed by his inexperience, but rather pleased about it, as though even her tutoring added zest to their lovemaking. She giggled and nibbled at his ear and his neck, as one would fondle a delightful child.

After a whole day of preconditioning, Warren was ready almost at once. In seconds he felt as if his whole body had exploded in little red splinters. The bed undulated beneath him, as wave after wave of passion rocked him. Fiercely he clutched her smooth, white back.

Afterwards Warren lay with Mary May in his arms, his eyes closed. He felt as if he were floating in a warm, buoyant pool. He was weightless, bodyless, painless. Every part of his body tingled with well-being.

And the night was only beginning. Before it was over, Warren was to be quite experienced in the art of lovemaking. He had come to Mary May almost a virgin, but that night, she saw to it that he made up for lost time. She guided his movements and taught him sexual maneuvers he had not known existed. Mary May was a whole new genre to Warren, a woman whose body and mind were free, totally devoid of inhibitions, religious or conventional. He was having a free ride on a sexual merry-go-round, and he wondered if he'd ever be quite the same again. He wished that he would never have to let her go. He would follow her anywhere, wait on her hand and foot, if only she would share his bed.

Warren woke up in the morning with a fly buzzing around his face. He swatted at it sleepily and turned over on his stomach. He reached for Mary May. Her side of the bed was empty.

He came awake and sat up. It was not yet daylight. He pulled the bedspread up to his chest. He was uncomfortable in his nakedness. The sheets on the bed were disheveled. His own clothes were all over the floor, but Mary May was gone. Even her clothes were gone. He listened, but he could hear no sound in the apartment.

Quickly he dressed and ran through the rooms. She was nowhere about. A thought occurred to him, a terrible thought that made his temples throb. Running back to the bedroom, he looked for his billfold and his jewelry. They were gone! Three hundred dollars, all he had left in the world, and his father's gold watch and chain! The bitch! he thought. The miserable thieving bitch!

How could she hope to get by with it? he wondered. All he had to do was wait. She'd have to come home sooner or later. She lived here. Or did she? He opened the closets. They were empty. The chest of drawers. Empty! Not a handkerchief. Not a pair of stockings. Back in the kitchen he opened cabinets, drawers, the pantry. All empty! What a fool he had been! She didn't live here at all. She hadn't used a key, he recalled. Either she had known the apartment was vacant, or someone had left it open for her. He had been so driven by sexual urgency that he had let himself be robbed, wiped out. And he didn't even know her real name.

But he knew where she worked, by damn! He'd go to the diner and find her. That seemed too simple, somehow. No one would rob a man of three hundred dollars and an expensive watch and go back to where she had met him. She wouldn't be there, he knew that. Maybe it would turn out to be a nightmare, where the diner had vanished, or had never been there at all. No, it had been there. He had eaten their food. He had seen the cook and the other customers. If Mary May had vanished, *some*one could tell him who she really was and where she had gone.

His stomach growled. He was starving. There had been no dinner last night. Twelve hours ago, he had been content to live on love, or whatever it was they had had. But now there was such a gnawing in his belly that he searched the kitchen again for a slice of bread, a crust, anything.

Angrily he finished dressing and picked up his valise and his small leather bag. Why hadn't she taken these, too? he wondered, and left him naked in the bed. It was what he deserved for stupidity. Thank God she had left him his clothes. At least he could leave the apartment and look for work. He carried his luggage across the patio.

The aroma of frying bacon drifted toward him. Warren stopped and sniffed. He followed the delicious aroma to an apartment in the opposite corner of the patio. The door was open and a huge woman, obviously of Mexican descent, was singing a Spanish melody as she turned lean strips of bacon with a fork. Warren knocked at the open door.

"Oh," the woman shrieked. "You scared me, mister. What you want here?"

"I'm sorry. I didn't mean to frighten you," he said. "I was wondering if I might ask you a few questions. Where can I find the landlord?"

His stomach growled noisily. Warren smiled sheepishly.

"You hungry?" the woman asked.

He laughed. "Starving. If you'd let me have breakfast, I'd be glad to do some work for you. Whatever needs doing."

"No money, eh?"

He shook his head no.

"Come in and sit down," she said, walking back to the stove.

In minutes a steaming platter of fried eggs and bacon with hash-brown potatoes was placed before him, followed by a cup of black coffee and fresh white bread. He found himself trembling with hunger and tried not to show how ravenous he was as he devoured the food.

"Now," he said, finishing, "what can I do to pay you for all this?"

She smirked. "That's funny. What can you do. A fancy man with expensive clothes and college manners. Bet you never did a day's work in your life."

"No," he said, smiling his fine white smile. "But I can learn."

"God, but you're handsome," the woman commented, sitting across the table from him. "Even dimples, yet. What's your name?"

"Warren Eagan. What's yours?"

"Maria Lopez. Want to go to bed with me?"

Warren laughed. "I'm sorry," he said, seeing the insulted expression on her face. "It's just that I don't even know you."

The explanation sounded childish, but he meant it. In the two days he had been in Hollywood, he had met two women and been offered two beds. Did he look like a stud? (He hoped so, though it was the furthest thing from the truth; it would certainly help his movie image.) Or was it just that all Hollywood women were promiscuous?

Maria Lopez was at least forty years old. She also weighed well over two hundred pounds. She walked around the tiled floor of her kitchen on bare feet, kicking the dog aside as she passed. Her black hair was parted in the middle and pulled slick back to a braid that hung down her back. It was threaded with gray, but her lashes and brows were jet black and heavy, and her olive skin was as smooth as marble. Warren liked her.

"Miss Lopez," Warren began.

"Maria," the woman corrected him.

"Maria." He smiled. "Do you know the lady who brought me here last night? She said she lived here. She called herself Mary May Manson."

Now it was Maria's turn to laugh. "A madeup name if I ever heard one." She shook her head. "Nobody by that name lives here. I'm the landlady."

"She was a pretty girl, about twenty-two, black hair, thin eyebrows? She was very well built." Warren outlined an hourglass with his hands, but the woman did not smile. She came out badly in the comparison. "We were in that corner apartment, directly across the patio," he said, pointing through the open door.

Maria shook her head. "That apartment's vacant. *Been* vacant for a month." She picked up a strip of bacon and took a bite. "Let you sleep there free, if you don't mind my company."

Warren was dangerously close to laughing again.

"I thank you for the offer," he said, "but I've got some unfinished business with that little tramp. She took my money and my watch, and I'm going to catch her before she gets out of town."

"Where you plan to look?"

"At the diner where she works. Oh, do you have a telephone?" he asked.

Maria nodded.

"Would you call the police for me? Would you tell them what I told you? And ask them to look for her at a place called Charlie's Diner on the State Highway coming into L.A. from the south? Tell them I'll get there as soon as I can walk there."

"Okay." Maria nodded. "You comin' back?" she asked.

"I just might, Maria. I haven't a cent. It's good to know there's a place where I can sleep. Thanks for breakfast."

With his suitcases Warren began the long walk down the main street of town, past orange groves, out onto the highway to the diner. The sun baked his back and sweat ran down to his waistline in little rivulets. From time to time he rested, sitting on his valise in the shade of an orange tree. It gave him time to think about Mary May and what he would do to her when he found her.

The little slut had a fine racket going, and he had been dupe enough to fall for it. For all he knew, she could be in partnership with Maria Lopez, who might be waiting even now for her cut of the take. Or, of course, some friend of Mary May's, living there, might have told her about the vacant apartment. It might even have been Mary May who had had his car taken yesterday. Why not? She could have seen it easily enough through the window of the restaurant while he was back in the men's room. Maybe the cook had driven it away, or the unseen brother-in-law.

Jesus! What a blind, trusting idiot he had been! To leave the keys in the car, just as he used to leave them, when he parked in the carriageway at home. Sweet, trusting Warren! To him the world was just bursting with good, honest people, and they all loved him for his body. Christ, what a moron!

He thought of the night of sex he had had with Mary May and, once again, he was aroused. Quickly he reminded himself that the sleazy little tart had robbed him of his very last penny. It had the same effect as a bucket of cold water.

There was one thing he had to give Mary May. He laughed out loud. The girl surely threw herself into her work. How many times was it? Four? She could have robbed him of the same amount of money after just one go round. He would have fallen off to sleep and never known the difference.

There were times in the past, and there'd be times in the future, he was sure, when he'd consider three hundred dollars small pay for the orgy he'd had last night, but as he sat at the side of the road in the shade of an orange tree, his body still tingling, his pockets empty, his feet blistered, he considered it the most expensive lay he would probably ever get. He brushed off the seat of his pants and kept on walking.

Chapter
THIRTY-FOUR

As Warren had expected, Mary May was not in the diner. He carried his luggage directly into the kitchen, determined not to let it out of his sight. It was all he had left.

The cook was busy turning sausages in the skillet, stopping now and then to stir a huge pot of beans on the back burner. He was a small, skinny man with greasy hair and a perpetual toothpick dangling from the corner of his mouth. He wore a white undershirt and dark trousers, covered by a butcher's apron that made its way around him more than once.

"Where is Mary May?" Warren asked the cook.

"Who?" the man asked, not stopping to look at Warren.

"Mary May Manson, the girl who was in here yesterday. The cashier and waitress. For Christ sake, you were the only two people working here."

"Never heard of her." The cook kept on frying.

Warren wanted to grab the man and shake him till his teeth rattled. He put his suitcases under the table. This was going to take longer than he thought. He walked back to the cook.

"Will you kindly look at me?" Warren asked the man.

The cook looked up, and Warren found himself staring into a pair of eyes as badly crossed as Ben Turpin's.

"You *do* remember that pretty, dark-haired girl that

stood in this very kitchen with me yesterday. Now don't tell me you don't."

The toothpick danced a little. The man looked down. He didn't answer. He turned back to the stove and picked up his cooking fork.

"Who owns this goddamn place?" Warren shouted. He could feel the blood pounding in his temples.

"Mr. Charlie Romero and his wife Wendy," the cook answered, taking sausages from the pan. "But they ain't here. They gone down to Mexico on vacation."

Ran behind the border, Warren thought. Wonder if they're selling my Pierce Arrow down there. Maybe they're smuggling in heroin or cocaine, too.

"What about the girl who was working here yesterday?" Warren shouted, his voice pitched almost an octave higher than usual. "She said she was the owner's sister-in-law."

The cook wiped his hands on his apron and turned off the fire on the stove.

"There's a sister-in-law, awright, but it ain't no Mary May," the cook said. "Her name's Jeanie Sawyer. I think that's it."

"Well? Is she the girl who was here yesterday?"

The cook looked back up at Warren. He still didn't answer. One of his eyes was all the way in the corner. Warren couldn't look at him. Warren figured the man was using those eyes to rattle him so he'd get the hell out of there. And it was working.

Taking his luggage, Warren walked to the front of the diner. Five customers, each one alone and angry looking, sat at the counter. There was no waitress today. The cook was serving and cooking and taking orders, too. Warren spoke aloud.

"I wonder if any of you folks can help me," he said.

Five faces frowned. Five pairs of bleary eyes looked at him as if he had insulted them. Then all turned their attention back to their plates or their newspapers.

"Do any of you men know a pretty, black-haired

young lady who was working in here yesterday?" he asked. No one answered. "She had on a green uniform. Were any of you in here yesterday?" He might as well have been talking to the wall. "I've got to find her. If any of you know her name or where she lives, I'd be happy to . . ." He realized he had no money to offer.

There was not an answer in the lot. Not a smile. He walked back to the kitchen and picked up the telephone receiver. The line was dead.

"Shit!" he said. "This damn thing was dead yesterday. She never *did* report the car to the police." He shook his head and laughed cynically at himself. All day long he had sat on his behind, waiting for a dead phone to ring, like a goddamn idiot. He gritted his teeth. He wanted to pitch things.

Raging, he took his suitcases and slammed himself out of the front door. He wasn't going to wait around in the hope that Maria had notified the police. He had no more reason to trust her than he did to trust Mary May. He'd go to the police himself. Maybe there would be pictures he could look at to identify the girl. Oh, he'd get the little bitch one of these days, and she'd pay up every penny she had stolen, *plus* the value of his car; he'd see to that. But for the moment he was facing a long walk all the way back into town and then to the police station, wherever *that* was. His feet were raw with blisters. He decided to try to thumb a ride.

A truck picked him up, and after he attempted a few pleasantries, to which the driver made no response, he rested his head against the back of the seat and closed his eyes. He felt exhausted. He wasn't accustomed to walking long distances carrying his own luggage. Rich boy in fancy clothes. Maria had hit it on the head. But he'd have to roll up his sleeves and dig ditches, if necessary. He was broke, and what was worse, he was hungry again. It was work or starve or go back home, and *that* he would never do.

Halfway between the diner and the orange groves, in an uninhabited stretch of flat desert land, a caravan of trucks and automobiles was winding its way to a predetermined location when Warren opened his eyes. The lead truck stopped, and as Warren watched, a camera was unloaded and placed on its tripod.

"Wait. What's going on out there?" Warren asked the driver.

"Shooting a movie." The driver had black dirt beneath his fingernails and he was smoking a hand-rolled cigarette.

"I'm sorry. Would you mind stopping a moment?" Warren asked. "I've never seen a movie being made."

"I'll let you off, pardner. I'm in a hurry."

"All right. Yes, do that."

Standing at the edge of the highway, Warren could make out the letters on the side of the vans. AMERICAN BIOGRAPH. Biograph! That was Mary Pickford's company. Maybe she was in the movie and he'd get to see her. Even if she wasn't in the picture, he'd see a film being made, which was why he had come all the way to California. Forget the car and the money for an hour or two, he told himself. This was his future, being spread out for him like a birthday party.

He felt his spirits soar as he walked down the slope from the highway and approached the scene of activity. The vans had been arranged in a circle, like a wagon train. From one van, props were being carried to the scene, which was a small clearing in the center of the circle. From another, folding chairs were being unloaded and set up, where actors would be made up for the coming scenes.

Warren stood around watching, still holding onto his luggage. At last he stashed it behind a bush and prayed it would be safe. Then he walked around, trying to keep the smile off his face as he watched costumed actors and actresses getting their instructions from the director. The director was wearing leather boots and a golf cap turned around so that he could take an occasional look through the camera lens.

"All right. Places!" the director called out through a megaphone.

Warren was thrilled. A man and a very small lady made their way to the clearing. They were to stand for this scene, and the director marked two X's with his riding crop in the hard desert sand.

"We want to get this on the first take," he said aloud. "It's hot out here, and I don't want Mary sweating through her makeup."

When the director moved out of the clearing, and the couple faced the camera, Warren got his first look at Mary Pickford. Little Mary, the Biograph Girl! A grin broke across his face. He was ecstatic.

"Clapper boy! Where's the damned clapper boy?" the director roared.

"Never showed up today, boss," someone answered.

"Christ! I wonder what would happen if everything went right, just once!" He took off his cap and scratched his head. He looked around the group. "Any of you extras want to make a dollar more as a clapper boy?"

"I do," Warren said quickly.

"Okay. Come on."

Someone put a pair of boards in his hand and shoved him toward the clearing. He stood before the director holding the boards, eyes wide, waiting.

"Well, you're the clapper boy, ain'tcha?" the director asked.

Warren smiled.

"Well, clap, already!"

Warren looked at the boards. The top board read Scene 12, the bottom board Take 1. They were hinged together at one side. Guessing, hoping, he opened the boards and clapped them together. He waited. That had to be wrong. It was too easy.

"Say, clapper," the director said, addressing Warren. "You mind getting out of the way now so we can shoot the scene?"

Warren almost tripped over his own feet trying to get out of the clearing. He heard a giggle behind him. From the sidelines he turned to look. It was Mary Pickford, laughing. She gave him a reassuring smile. A thrill ran through him. These were the movies, the very same movies that played at the Strand and the Acme in New Orleans. Even if he was only a clapper boy, he was working in the same picture as Mary Pickford. To hell with the car and the money. To hell with everything but this.

At noon a folding table appeared, stacked with box lunches and bottles of orange soda. Warren thought he would have to explain himself to get lunch, but no one seemed to care. After the line had gone by, a few stragglers remained behind, slipping wrapped sandwiches into their pockets. Feeling like a beggar, Warren did the same. At least he wouldn't have to go without supper tonight. Then he sat beneath a tree with two young men to eat his lunch.

"I'm Warren Eagan," he said, extending his hand.

Both men looked at him, frowning, and went back to their sandwiches. Warren withdrew his hand self-consciously. Good manners seemed to have no place out here. He took a bite of his sandwich. With his mouth full, he talked to the pair. He didn't care much if they answered or not. He felt the need to talk.

"How do I get on as an extra in this movie?" he asked. "Is it too late?"

"You mean you're not an extra?" one of them asked.

Warren shook his head, taking another bite of his sandwich.

"Then what are you doing here?"

"Watching. Clapping. Trying to get in the movie." He washed his lunch down with a swig of orange pop.

"Try the casting director. I think he said he needed

another cop for the chase. He's the one in the pink shirt over there. Don't get too close, though." He laughed with his companion. "He'll like you."

Warren wiped his hands on his paper napkin and crossed the clearing to where the casting director sat in his canvas chair, his legs crossed, his expression languid and affected.

"Excuse me, sir," Warren said. "I heard you needed another extra."

The man smiled slowly and with obvious admiration. "I need *you*, handsome. I can tell you that."

The man's nails were polished with a clear lacquer, something Warren had never seen in his life. He was smoking a cigarette in a long silver holder.

"Go on over to the wardrobe truck and get yourself a policeman's costume, honey," the director said in a voice that was like caramel. "You'll be in the chase."

"What do I do?" Warren asked.

"Just run where the other policemen run. There's nothing to it. Now what's your name?" Warren hesitated. "For payroll," the director explained. "You *do* want to get paid, don't you?"

If he was dreaming, Warren hoped no one would wake him up. For better or worse, he was going to be in a movie. In the twenty-four hours he had been in Hollywood, he had been robbed, laid, lied to by a cross-eyed cook, and hired by a queer director. But, by damn, he had made it into a movie, and that's what he had come for. He was in!

American Biograph made two movies the first week Warren was in Hollywood, each a two-reeler, and Warren was hired as an extra in both. As long as he smiled nicely at the casting director with the shiny fingernails, he got a ticket that entitled him to a costume, a box lunch, and one dollar and fifty cents at the end of the day. Warren decided he was willing to make lots of concessions.

The second film of the week starred Dorothy Gish and was shot inside the Biograph Studios. Warren was like a tourist waiting to enter the building. A dozen extras were herded through the barnlike structure with its thickly padded walls and ceilings ablaze with lights. They passed through a property shop, where everything from furniture to artificial cobwebs was being produced on call. They passed by stages, where artists were putting the finishing touches to scenes of mountains or churches painted on backdrops. The trek ended in a corner of the studio, where a set had been arranged to look like a telegraph office. They were told to sit in folding chairs and wait while the present scene was in progress.

"Now we want a medium long shot on this," the director shouted to the cameraman. The camera was rolled to the desired position. Warren read the name on the back of the director's chair. D. W. Griffith! This was the same man who had hired him as a clapper boy a few days ago!

"Camera! Action!" Griffith shouted.

The clapper boy smacked the boards together. The camera whirred. Actors on the stage began to move. Warren didn't know what to watch first. In the scene about to be filmed, a telegraph operator lay unconscious on the floor of the office. Now his daughter was entering. It was Dorothy Gish. She was coming to bring her father his lunch. She saw her father. She gasped. Her hands went up to her face. She put down the lunch and tried to revive him. She untied his hands. She threw water in his face. He revived. End of scene.

"Take five minutes," Griffith announced through the megaphone.

The extras were taken into the makeup room, where each was scrutinized by a makeup man and attacked like an artist's canvas. No "How do you do. I'm Warren Eagan," this time. He had learned his lesson. It just wasn't done like that out here.

For the first time Warren saw himself with painted lips, penciled eyebrows, and mascaraed lids. If Mother could only see me now, he thought to himself, looking into a mirror with a napkin still draped inside his collar.

Wardrobe came next. This time it was western garb, a cowboy's outfit. Within an hour they were all back on the set. The telegraph office had become the inside of a log cabin, and a barn dance was in progress. At last he was informed that he was to be one of the dancers. Warren knew nothing at all about square dancing, but fortunately, about two steps after the scene began, the dance was to be interrupted by the entry of the now-recovered telegraph operator and his daughter, still carrying the lunch basket. He had come to tell them all that there was to be a robbery, and the whole party was then led out of the room. End of scene.

It troubled Warren that he did not know how the movie ended. The last scene was to be shot outdoors the following day. But he was to find that rarely would he know the whole plot of any movie unless he was the star. He learned to live with bits and pieces, in and out of sequence.

Reluctantly he took Maria Lopez up on her offer of free room and board in exchange for personal services. He saw no other choice. Though he notified the police of the robbery on the second day he was in Hollywood, Warren was never to see the car or Mary May again. After a week had gone by, he began to wonder if the police were not also in on the conspiracy. One thing was certain: Maria Lopez was not.

His first sexual experience with Maria was physically and emotionally disconcerting. From the beginning he was extremely reluctant to make love to this gargantuan woman. Holding her in his arms was like wrestling with a bear. The first night they slept together, he wanted to laugh aloud, even as he was approaching culmination, a process which overtook him with remarkable speed. The end came much too quickly to suit Maria, who asked if they might not try again. Warren thought about breakfast in the morning, and he agreed.

"And try to go slower, my darling," Maria said, touching his face and kissing him with sweet, full lips.

Warren was grateful that when it was over, Maria returned to her own apartment, leaving him the whole bed to spread-eagle in, for a good night's sleep. He was grateful to Maria for many things. As long as he was under her roof, which turned out to be his first two months in Hollywood, she did his laundry and served him delicious, filling, Mexican-style meals, never asking for a penny or even a promise that he would return in the evening.

Such an arrangement freed him from the need to find a regular job, and he was able to make the rounds of the studios each day looking for work as an extra. Vast new studios were blossoming in the quiet town beside the dusty roads and behind the rows of one-story houses that the film makers had found when they first descended on the city back in 1903. Now there was Culver City, Fox, and Universal City, as well as the earlier Edison, Biograph, and Vitagraph. The brand new Keystone Studio was under the direction of Mack Sennett, who had been an actor for Biograph when Griffith was first making movies there.

Six weeks after his first job as an extra Warren was given a bit part as a soldier in a movie called *The Massacre*, the story of Custer's Last Stand. With his mascara and his painted lips he was to look directly into the camera for a close-up, and when the great Mr. Griffith saw the daily rushes, he told the casting director, "Get that young man under contract. We need faces like that."

His spirits skyrocketed. He had a fixed income and independence at last. He moved out of Maria's apartment house and found a house to rent on Sunset Boulevard, near Biograph Studios. But months followed months, and no part came along of any greater length or importance than that of the soldier at Custer's Last Stand. He couldn't understand it. What were they paying him for?

Warren showed up at the studio each day, whether he was scheduled to or not. He followed Griffith around like a shadow, ready to light his cigarette, run an errand, find his megaphone. He was impossible to overlook. He was like a football player sitting on the bench, begging the coach to let him in the game.

If parts did not come along, invitations did. As a contract player he was invited to studio parties, where he made it his business to talk to stars and would-be stars and directors. He turned on his flashing smile, which got him into many a starlet's bed. The doors of bedrooms opened so easily to him that he came to consider it no more than his due.

Familiarity with the "in crowd" got him further invitations to private parties at the palatial Hispano-Mauresque villas of the Golden People. His hostesses felt that they could always use another handsome face. It wasn't hard for Warren to feel at home handing his hat to a butler or taking a drink from a maid. He had been raised to expect as much. It was his hosts and hostesses who were the *nouveau riche*. They were like children enjoying a new toy, spending their huge incomes on riotous living and wild parties. There were midnight revels and champagne baths in the fountains and starlets dancing topless for the entertainment of their friends. They drank to excess, they climbed in and out of each other's beds, and when that got boring, they turned to drugs. Cocaine was easy to come by and unbeatable for a pick-me-up. No one took it seriously; Triangle-Keystone had even made a light comedy, *The Mystery of the Leaping Fish*, with Douglas Fairbanks, about a detective who was stoned on coke.

If gossip was the food of the Golden People, scandal was their ambrosia. Traveling in the inner circles, Warren heard it all. Was it true about Mack Sennett's Bathing Beauty casting couch? And why did Griffith surround himself with young girls with that delicate, virginal look? Had Richard Barthelmess really posed for "French postcards" when he was trying to make it to the top? Some of the scandals made the newspapers, spelling disaster to the careers of the personalities involved: drug addictions, rape, even murders. As soon as the fans discovered that their stars had mortal failings, they abandoned them. Many a suicide told the final chapter in the story of a rejected movie idol.

Hollywood was Sodom and Gomorrah on the inside, but what the public saw was Dream City. While films were showing Bible stories and morality dramas, the virtues of home life and the sanctity of marriage, the public's Chosen Few were swapping bedmates and dancing on tabletops. Movies frowned on get-rich-quick schemes and on those who tried to rise above their station in life, while the Golden People got richer, built more swimming pools, and guzzled more champagne.

Hollywood was a boom town, loaded with rich, exotic citizens looking for thrills. It was made to order for the burglar and the swindler, the extortionist and blackmailer, the cultist, the sex freak, the healer, and the fortune-teller.

Almost a year after Warren came to Hollywood, he opened the paper one morning to see the pretty face of Mary May Manson. The newspapers called her Jeanie Sawyer. That was what the cross-eyed cook had called her. Her body had been found mutilated in a hotel room on Alvarado Street. The article hinted that she had been a gangster's moll and the autopsy revealed the presence of heroin in her bloodstream.

It made Warren stop and take stock of what was going on around him. Now that the initial hilarity of having free access to so many beds had begun to die down, he realized that if he hoped to make a lasting career in Hollywood, he would do well to exercise caution. If he had been with this girl just before she was killed, if some article of his had been found on her person, he would have been caught up in a scandal, and, guilty or not, his career would be finished, before it had even really begun.

He made a resolution. During the day he would be at the studio, the smiling bit player, the ubiquitous helper. But after hours he would keep to himself. From then on he declined most invitations.

By 1914, Warren had had many fine supporting roles, but his name was far from a household word; nor was his face as familiar as the little British comedian's, Charlie Chaplin, who had taken America by storm. D. W. Griffith, now with Reliance Majestic Company, made an announcement that he was about to create the greatest picture ever made. It was to be called *The*

Birth of a Nation, based on a novel of the Civil War entitled *The Clansman*. Into this endeavor he would channel all his talents and his energies. It was to be his masterpiece. Warren Eagan, then two years in Hollywood, was called to the director's office and offered one of the leading roles.

Chapter
THIRTY-SIX

From the very beginning Stephen had always let Katie manage the family money because she had far more experience stretching a dollar than he did. He admired the way she saw that they all had everything they needed and saved something out of every paycheck.

By 1913, Katie and Stephen were comfortably well-off. As head of the sales department at Edison Electric, Stephen was earning good wages. His second invention, the screw socket, found a market such as he could never have anticipated, and royalties were pouring in. For the first time in her life Katie had no need to scrimp. They were all well dressed and well shod, the house was warm in winter, there was always an abundance of food on the table, and they were able to buy a brand new Ford. In addition to all that, they were saving a great deal of money.

This was the source of the one recurring argument between them. Katie refused to put her savings in a bank. Every payday she put what she had left over from the last pay period in an empty coffee can, and when it was full, she recorded it in her notebook and hid it under an old paint canvas in the basement near the rear wall. When quarterly checks for royalties came, she cashed them and saved them the same way. Soon stacks of cans lined the basement wall, draped with canvases and old bedspreads. No one but Katie and Stephen knew where they were.

"That's foolish, Katie," Stephen said repeatedly.

"The banks pay you interest on your money. You're a smart girl. Can't you see that it's more sensible to deposit it than to stack it up against the basement wall?"

"I don't trust anybody with our money. Not even banks. It's safe where I put it. The basement is locked. And I don't have to worry about banks being robbed or closing up."

"Suppose we both get killed at the same time," Stephen said. "Who's going to know where the money is? Or even that there *is* any money?"

Katie's mouth fell open. "I never thought of that," she said. She sat down in a chair and frowned thoughtfully. "We'll have to write a letter and give it to a lawyer. We ought to write our wills, too, leaving everything to each other, or if we die together, to the children." She got up and paced the floor. "We'll give the lawyer the letter, sealed in an envelope," she said, turning toward Stephen and folding her arms. "It will tell the children where the money is."

"Sounds like *Treasure Island*," Stephen said.

Katie paid no attention. She was contemplating her plan. "Now who should we get? Mr. Schwab? Your father's lawyer?"

"To do what?"

"To make up the wills and to hold the letter, Stephen," she said curtly.

"Katie, wouldn't it be simpler just to put the money in the bank?"

"No. I won't do it. Get a lawyer, whoever you want, and bring him home to dinner."

At last one evening, he brought home a well-mannered, shy young lawyer named Daren O'Toole. Katie sighed with relief, assured that their money would be safe.

After the supper dishes were cleared, Katie insisted they get to the business at hand. The wills were written in their own handwriting and signed in the presence of Jenny and Lala. Katie had already written the letter about the location of the money and sealed it in an envelope. She gave it to Mr. O'Toole.

The transaction was complete. Katie went to the kitchen for a bottle of wine she had chilled in the icebox, and, for the first time in her life she drank spirits. The rest of the evening she was too tipsy to notice that young Mr. O'Toole was paying more than polite attention to her little sister Jenny.

In the next few weeks it became apparent that a match had been made. Daren came to call each weekend, and with Katie's permission took Jenny to meet his parents. One Sunday, Katie made a return invitation to Mr. and Mrs. O'Toole. In the fall of 1913 both Mrs. O'Toole and Katie were embroidering pillowcases for Jenny's hope chest.

Jenny was a senior at Esplanade High School the year she and Daren courted. Daren gave her a ring for Christmas, and they planned their wedding for June, immediately following her graduation. What fun she and Katie had, finding a house to rent just blocks from Katie's house and furnishing it bit by bit! Then, too, there was the trousseau to buy, sheets and towels and white muslin gowns with rows of lace.

Sometimes at night, as they embroidered by lamplight or dressed the boys for bed, Katie watched her sister chatting away about her wedding dress or her veil, her long black hair caught at the nape of the neck with a grosgrain bow, her smooth young face aglow with anticipation. She had grown into a beautiful young woman. When her eighteenth birthday came in February, Daren sent a cedar chest to the house, and Jenny pressed her hand to her lips, trying to hold back the tears. For a girl whose life had begun in a crowded tenement, who had slept in a bed with two sisters and worn the same dress to school for a year, she had come a long way for her happiness, and Katie wanted her to relish it. To Katie, Jenny was an angel, and she loved the girl with all her heart.

In the last few days before the wedding the house buzzed with girlish laughter and excitement. Katie, Jenny, and Lala went back and forth to the dressmaker's for fittings. Bouquets and floral decorations were ordered; a trio of violinists was engaged.

On the day of the wedding, when Jenny had put on her white-lace gown with the stock neckline and the leg-of-mutton sleeves and placed the delicate crown of orange blossoms on her dark hair, Katie thought she was the most beautiful bride she had ever seen. The wedding march began, and Stephen, handsome in his morning suit, came down the steps with his sister-in-law on his arm.

After the ceremony the party began. The house resounded with the strains of "I Love You Truly," and every time it was played, Jenny blushed and buried her face in her new husband's shoulder. At last the bride threw her bouquet from the gallery and left with Daren in a shower of rice.

Chapter
THIRTY-SEVEN

In the newspapers Katie read about someone called Archduke Francis Ferdinand being assassinated, and Austria-Hungary declaring war on Serbia, but it all seemed so far away and unrelated to their lives. In August, 1914, Germany declared war on Russia and France and then invaded Belgium. Soon after, Great Britain declared war on Germany, and suddenly it sounded as if all of Europe was embroiled in the conflict.

People at home were shouting "Neutrality! Neutrality!" and Katie wondered why. What did the war have to do with the United States, anyway?

Every evening, in their Model-T Ford, Stephen, Katie, Lala, and the babies motored around Spanish Fort and West End Amusement Park, where a band played nightly on an outdoor platform and a fountain shot jets of colored water into the night. First the jets would be ten feet tall, jade green. Then they would change to blue and yellow. Then, suddenly, from the center, a column of scarlet jets would shoot some thirty feet high. The spectacle was breathtaking.

The boys were much more interested in the "rides" at the Spanish Fort. They loved the bug and the whip best, but only Lala had the stomach to take them on the amusements.

The hobble skirt came into vogue that year, and Katie decided to buy one. It had been around New York and Hollywood for a year or more, but styles always took a little longer making their way to New Orleans. The skirt was so narrow at the ankles that Katie had to walk haltingly like an arthritic old lady. The newspapers said the streetcars had had to add an extra step to accommodate the "hobbling" ladies. Probably a made-up story, Katie thought. But she regretted having thrown her money away.

The skyline of the city changed dramatically. By night new buildings were outlined against the sky, their shapes geometric figures filled with squares of white light. Canal Street, too, was ablaze with streetlights. Electricity, once so hard to sell, had come into its own. Families had electric lights, electric irons were popular, and there was not a house in town without an electric fan. Edison Electric, now called New Orleans Railway and Light Company, was a thriving concern.

One morning in the spring of 1915, at the breakfast table, Katie turned a page of the newspaper and gasped in astonishment.

"Stephen! You're not going to believe this!" she said, scanning the article. She folded the paper so she could read it in detail. Johnny and Tommy, now five and three, got down from their chairs and ran to their mother's side.

"The headline reads, D. W. Griffith to make 'greatest movie ever,' and then there's a smaller headline, 'Local actor to have lead role.' And guess whose picture is in the paper?"

"Not Warren?" Stephen asked, half smiling, getting up from his chair to look over Katie's shoulder.

"What, Mama?" Johnny asked, tugging at her sleeve. "Who is it?"

"Look, honey," she said, drawing the child to her. "You see that man?"

"That's a lady," Johnny said.

Katie laughed. In the picture Warren was made up, and his hair was long for the part. To begin with, he was handsome to the point of being pretty. Only the

Confederate officer's hat and his somber expression made any kind of statement for his masculinity.

"That's no lady," Katie said, laughing. "That's your Uncle Warren."

"I don't want him," Johnny said, going back to his place at the table.

"Well, you've got him," Katie said, "whether you want him or not. Tell your friends you have an uncle who's a movie star. I bet they'll think it's swell."

"I don't want him either," Tommy echoed his brother's sentiments.

"Let me read you this, Stephen . . . Lala. It's so exciting." She put her napkin on the table and leaned back in her chair. " 'D. W. Griffith, undisputed master of the silver screen, held a press conference yesterday in which he stated that he is presently filming the "greatest moving picture ever made." The film is entitled *The Birth of a Nation*. It is based on a novel of the Civil War, by the Reverend Thomas Dixon, called *The Clansman*. Mr. Griffith is known for his last-minute rescues, his suspense, his crowd scenes, and his unusual camera angles. All of these skills will come into play in this great historical drama, where massive events will be measured by their effects on individual human beings.

" 'Of particular interest to New Orleanians is a young actor from our own city who will be starred in one of the leading roles. He is Warren Eagan, son of Mrs. John Eagan and the late Mr. Eagan.' "

"I'll bet my mother loves that," Stephen said.

" 'Mr. Eagan is a graduate of Jesuit High School and Tulane University,' " Katie read on.

"They're lying," Stephen said. "He didn't finish at Tulane."

"Shh . . . 'Mr. Eagan has been under contract with D. W. Griffith for the past two years and has acted in many supporting roles since his first part in the movie, *The Massacre*.' " Katie put the paper down. "I *thought* that was Warren in *The Massacre*. Remember, we went to see it, Lala? And I said I thought that actor looked like Warren?"

"I remember," Lala said.

"It was hard to tell under all that makeup, but didn't you think so, too?"

"I never saw him in real life."

"Oh, that's right. None of you has."

"How old is he, anyway?" Lala asked.

"Twenty-four. Just my age. Good Lord, do you realize I haven't seen that boy since he was seventeen? I bet I wouldn't even know him."

"Well, I've got to go to school now," Lala said. "I'll be home late. Spanish Club meeting after school."

"Okay, honey," Katie said. She waited till she heard the door slam. Then she poured herself another cup of coffee. The boys hopped down from their chairs and ran through the kitchen to the yard. "More coffee?" she asked Stephen.

Stephen nodded and she poured.

"When are you going to work?" she asked.

"In a few minutes," he said.

"Stephen, did I ever tell you what Warren did to me the first time he came to my room to give me a reading lesson?"

Stephen frowned. "When was that?" he asked.

"When we were both fifteen. You were living at the fraternity house. Your father had ordered Warren to give me an hour of reading instruction every night."

"In your room?" Stephen asked.

Katie nodded and sipped her coffee.

"I hate to ask what he did." Stephen eyed his wife over the rim of the coffee cup.

"Well, the lesson was over," Katie said, "so he slammed the book closed, and before I knew what was happening, he put one hand right here"—she put her right hand on her breast—"and the other hand here"—she put her left hand on her buttocks—"and he rolled on top of me on the bed."

Stephen laughed. "Why, that dirty little weasel!" he said.

"That's just what I called him."

"What did you do?"

"I picked up the slate, cracked him on the head, and knocked him unconscious."

"Oh, Jesus!" Stephen threw his head back and laughed. "You were too much for him, baby, even then."

"I came from a tough part of town, you know," Katie said. "He wasn't the first to try messing around. I remember the Macaluso boys."

"Hmm," Stephen said. "It's a wonder I didn't get a few cracks on the head. I did my share of messing around with Katie."

"Ah, yes," she said, "but the question is, Did Katie *want* to be messed around with?"

She held out her hand to him and he squeezed it.

Later, after Stephen had taken his coat from the hook in the vestibule, Katie put her arms around his waist to kiss him good-bye.

"Now, let's see how he did that again," Stephen said, backing up. "He put his right hand here . . . and his left hand like this . . ."

"Stephen!" Katie scolded. "Suppose the boys come back upstairs."

"Let them get their own girls," he answered. Then he fondled her in his own fashion and kissed her lovingly before leaving for the day.

Later in the spring, *The Birth of a Nation* played in New Orleans. The papers had not exaggerated, nor had Mr. Griffith; it *was* the greatest moving picture ever made. The crowd scenes were spectacular. The acting was superb. Especially, Katie thought, the acting of Warren Eagan as the brave young Confederate lieutenant. His death scene was a three-handkerchief performance, and in Katie's book that was good acting.

Katie had hoped Warren would come to New Orleans when the movie opened, if for no other reason than to be lauded by the citizens of his own hometown. But the studio had other plans: there was to be a premiere performance in Atlanta, and the stars were to make personal appearances. The papers gave Warren rave reviews and told of the many other offers he'd received since the movie's release. He had already been signed for another Griffith spectacular called *Intolerance*, which was scheduled to make its appearance in 1916.

Katie took Lala and the boys to see the movie, but Stephen declined. Katie's enthusiasm about his brother seemed to irritate him. When they had all returned, she waited till the children were in bed, and she and Stephen were alone on the porch.

"Stephen, why can't you be happy about Warren's success?" she asked. "Don't you find it exciting? Aren't you a little bit proud of him?"

"I can't be a hypocrite, Katie. I'm disappointed in Warren. He's never been here to see us since we're married. He doesn't even know I have two sons, for heaven's sake."

"Oh, yes, he knows," she said. "We had them before he left home. Your mother has friends on Esplanade who tell her everything. She told Mr. Gentry where to find us, didn't she?"

"And even knowing that, you can take it so lightly that he never came, even once, to see the boys?"

"You're a hard man, Stephen Eagan," Katie said. She pushed the swing and sighed. "Warren's your younger brother. He must have always looked up to you. He must have been waiting, hoping *you'*d call *him*. How did he know he was welcome? You could have made the first move. You were the oldest."

For a moment he didn't answer. Then he nodded. "I guess you're right," he said. He came to sit beside her on the swing. He kissed her cheek and drew her head to his shoulder. "How'd you get so smart, anyway?" he asked.

They sat quietly for a while, hugging and swinging.

"Stephen," she said, "do you think I could write a letter to Warren? Just to congratulate him? How would I send it to him?"

"I guess you could mail it in care of his studio. The name was in the paper. But you'd better write 'personal' on the outside or it will get lost in his fan mail, which he probably doesn't even open."

"Fan mail? Really, Stephen?"

"Sure. Write your letter, and I'll address it for you."

"Thank you, darling. I've been wanting to write him for months, but I didn't know where to send the letter. I want to give him some news and send him a picture of the boys. I know he leads a glamorous life, but I'll bet he's just dying for news of the family."

Katie knew it was an Italian trait to want to keep family close. She felt this strongly, and it applied as much to Stephen's family as to her own. She would never understand how Janet could let day after precious day go by without seeing her son and her grandsons. A time would come when the days would run out and she would have missed the only thing in life that really mattered: the love and warmth and closeness of her children. Now she was cut off from Warren, too. They must have had an argument, she thought, though she and Stephen had no firsthand information. What good was all the money in the world if she never saw her children?

Chapter
THIRTY-EIGHT

In the fall of 1916, Johnny started school. Katie buckled his knickers, tucked in his shirt, and tied his tie. She had managed to hold back the tears, but when she put the little cloth cap on the mass of black curls, she sobbed a little and kissed her son again and again. Johnny was used to a shower of kisses from his mother. In another year or two he would forbid her to make such a baby of him, or he would run away and hide if his friends were around to see it. But on the first day of school he put his arms around his mother and let her kiss away.

"Don't cry, Mama," he said. "I'm only going to school."

Katie was ashamed. It was she who should have been telling *him* not to cry. She blew her nose and, checking him over one more time, she took his hand and walked him to Holy Rosary.

Johnny loved school right away. In a week his teacher told Katie he was a bright student. She said he learned each lesson the very first time, and then helped the other students if they were having trouble. Katie blushed with pride and couldn't wait to get home so she could telephone Stephen at work. And Stephen was as pleased as she was that they had such a clever son.

One day, early in November, when Johnny had started walking to school alone, he came home for lunch and sat down to have his sandwich with his mother. Tommy had fallen asleep on the settee, and Katie had Johnny all to herself.

"Well, what did you do in school this morning, darling?" she asked.

"Mama," he said, "do I have a grandmother?"

Katie turned white. She folded her hands in her lap to keep them from shaking. "Why do you ask?"

"At little recess this morning, when I was playing in the schoolyard, an old lady came up to the iron fence."

"Go on."

"She called me over. She said, 'John, come here.' She called me 'John.' "

Katie nodded. "It's your name. What else?"

"Well, she just looked at me for a long time, and she looked like she was crying."

Katie pressed her napkin to her lips. "Dear God," she whispered quietly.

"She gave me a nickel," Johnny said. "I lost it. Are you mad, Mama?"

"No, dear. Of course not. Tell me more about the lady. Was she all alone?"

"No, she had another lady with her. A lady about like you."

Charlotte, Katie thought. Charlotte had never married. Katie still followed her activities in the society notes.

"What else happened, Johnny?" Katie asked, trying not to sound too eager.

"The other lady gave me a nickel, too," he said. "I lost it, too. Are you mad?"

"No. Johnny. Now tell me about the ladies. Did they talk to you?"

"Yeah. The old lady asked me how my daddy was."

Katie felt a constriction in her throat. It was so pathetic, to have to come to a school at recess to see your grandchild and ask about your son.

"So what did you say?" Katie asked.

"I said he was fine and so was my mama."

Katie smiled, tears in her eyes.

"How did the lady look?" Katie asked.

"Old," Johnny said. "She had white hair and a walking stick with ruffles."

"A parasol," Katie said. "Go on."

"That's all. She just said she was my grandmother, and she would come back to see me again. Oh, and she had a colored man with her, driving an ol' time buggy."

"Did she call him 'Mason'?" Katie asked.

"Yeah. That's what she called him. You know him, Mama?"

"Yes, I know Mason," Katie said. She rested her forehead on her fingertips. "I know them all."

"Whatsa matter, Mama?" the child asked. "You feel bad?"

"No, darling, I'm fine," Katie said, but she ate no more lunch that day.

It was not the last time Janet and Charlotte came to see Johnny. Katie spoke to Stephen about it and watched a frown deepen between his brows.

"I don't like them doing that, Katie," he said.

"Well, it can't do any harm," she said. "He *is* her grandchild, Stephen, and she's never been asked to come see him."

"Giving him a nickel!" He kicked the hassock, and it slid across the floor. "It's all so underhanded. Why doesn't she just call me on the phone and ask to see the boys?"

"She's afraid you'd refuse," Katie said. "So am I."

"Of course I wouldn't refuse," he said. He got up and stood at the window, looking out on the gallery. "As long as *I* don't have to see her."

Katie took this as tacit approval of a visit by his children to his mother. She gave the matter some thought. She knew that *she* would not bring them to St. Charles

Avenue. She decided to ask Della to come for them. She called in the early afternoon when Janet took her nap, and Della answered.

"Della!" Katie said.

"Oh, Katie," Della said, "Ah jus' cain't believe mah ears. Is it really you, li'l Kate?"

"It's me, Della. It's so good to hear your voice. How are you?"

"Gittin' ol', lak everybody. Mah laigs hurt wit de rheumatiz. But Ah still does a day's work. Heh-heh-heh."

"I sure do miss you, Della."

"Me, too, Katie. When you gonna come aroun' an' visit with those boys? We dyin' to see 'em."

"That's what I was calling about, Della. I know their grandmother would like to see them, and I'd like them to know her, too. But I just can't come back there, Della. I hope you understand."

There was silence on the line. Della had strong loyalties to her mistress. It was hard for her to know what to say.

"I wondered if *you* would be good enough to come for them and take them to their grandmother for a visit?"

"Would I! Oh, yes, Katie, Ah'd be the happiest gal in town if you let me do dat."

"Well, good! Come Saturday, then. Have Mason drive you. Say ten in the morning?"

"Ah sho' will, Katie. An' Ah'll be waitin' fo' Saddy lak it was de Second Comin'."

"Oh! Della, it'll be so good to see you. Come a little early, so you and I can catch up on the news."

She could feel the Negro woman's joy over the phone.

When they met on the steps, Katie ran to Della and wrapped her arms around her, just as they used to do in the Eagan kitchen. Della had welcomed her into her domain when Katie had no one else, and Katie would never forget it.

After tears and hugs and compliments Katie took Della on a tour of her house, proudly walking her into a well-scrubbed kitchen where every pot and pan sparkled. When the tour was over, the two women settled in rocking chairs on the gallery.

"Wheah *is* dose children?" Della asked. "Ah done waited an' waited to see 'em."

"Johnny!" Katie called out, cupping her hands to her mouth. "Tommy!" She stood at the edge of the porch and presently a curly black head came bobbing up the cement steps. Johnny stopped several steps below the porch. Then, seeing Della's white smile in her black face, he ran up the rest of the steps.

He was wearing a sailor suit of navy-blue cotton with a huge white collar embroidered with two red anchors. Following close behind him was a smaller version of the same outfit, worn by a strutting brown-haired imp with freckles. They both stood before Della with blank expressions. Katie was afraid of what they would say.

"Johnny, shake hands with Della," Katie said. Reluctantly Johnny extended a hand and Della took it in her own fat palm. "Tommy," Katie said, nodding for him to do the same.

"Are you a Negro lady?" Johnny asked.

"Yeah, das whut Ah is," Della said, grinning.

Katie realized that Johnny was in school now. There were probably Negroes there, cooking or cleaning. Johnny's world was no longer confined to the walls of his home.

Della opened her arms to the boys and took them to her breast in an energetic hug. They did not resist. They stretched their arms around her neck and hugged her back. Tears fell down Della's face.

"Dey lak mah own children, Katie. Ah watched Stephen grow up."

"I know," Katie said. She reached out and touched her friend's arm.

There was little time to visit, and Katie had much to ask. As soon as she could get the boys away from Della, she sent them inside to go to the bathroom and get a drink of water. Then she turned to Della with her questions.

"Della, why has she been visiting Johnny at school? Don't you find that strange? Has she got something up her sleeve? Or is she sick or something?" Katie touched her forehead meaningfully.

"No, Katie," Della said. "Ah tell you the truth, she jes' wants to see dem children so bad, an' she cain't think of no other way. Honey, she was so happy when Ah tol' her they wuz comin' t'day, she almos' cried."

Katie looked away. She felt selfish and guilty, enjoying her husband and children every day of her life, never thinking for a moment that Janet was yearning for them, too.

"Is it Charlotte who goes there with her?" she asked Della.

"Yeah. She dyin' to see dem, too. Dey jes' crazy 'bout li'l Johnny. Dey come home sayin' he wuz de smartest li'l boy dey done evah seed. De cutest, too. Course, dat's whut she useta say 'bout Stephen."

"Charlotte never married, Della? I wonder why. She was one of the prettiest girls I ever saw."

Della shrugged. "Too picky, Ah guess. At least, Miz Janet is. Dis one's too dumb, dat one's too po'. She never find one good enuff fo' Miz Charlotte. Fust thing you know, all de good ones is gone, an' de bad ones, too. All married. An' it's too late."

Katie shook her head sympathetically. "And what do you think about Warren?" Katie asked. "Did you ever think you'd have a movie star right in your own family?"

"Ump-ump," Della exclaimed, shaking her head.

"Did you see the movie, Della? *The Birth of a Nation*?"

"Ain' never seen *no* movies, Katie. Dey ain' no seats in dem movin'-pitcher places fo' coloreds."

Katie bit her lip. For the very first time she realized that she had never seen a Negro in a movie house. "I'm sorry, Della. Truly."

"Ain' your fault, Katie." She patted Katie's hand.

"Did Warren leave home on bad terms?" Katie asked.

"Sho' did. Dey had a big fight about him quittin' school. Been three years now. He never been back an' never made up."

"And she never sent him any money all this time?" Katie asked.

"Not a copper cent. Don' know how dat boy got along on his own all this time, spoiled lak he wuz."

"Well, it won't matter now. He'll be making gobs of money, just like Charlie Chaplin and Mary Pickford. He is already. I wrote him, you know, and he sent me a picture of his house in Bel-Air. It's a mansion."

"For true?" Della asked. Katie nodded.

"How's Treece, Della? She still workin' for them?"

"She daid."

"Della! What happened?"

" 'Member dat man she useta live wit? De one dat left her? De one she had de baby wit? De baby dat die with de crib death?"

"I remember."

"Well, he come back to git her, an' she don' wanta go. She scared to death o' dat man. Well, he drag her out de kitchen. I yell fo' help, but only Miz Janet be home, an' she be takin' a nap. So he drag her down de steps to his wagon, an' he go gallopin' off. Nex thing Ah hear from White Man, he done kilt her with a knife, not but a block away. Dat be 'bout a year now. We all felt real bad."

"Oh, Della, so do I," Katie said. "We were such good friends, Treece and I."

"Bettah come on, Della," a voice called from below. Katie walked down a few steps until Mason came into view. She ran to where he stood. She wanted to hug him, too, but she thought better of it. She held out her hand and he took it gingerly.

""How is ya, Katie?" he asked.

"Just fine, Mason. And you?"

"Okay, I guess. Lak an ol' man."

"I'll get them together so you can leave, Mason. It sure was good to see you again."

"Same heah, Katie," he said thickly.

Katie put sailor hats on her boys and gave them a final inspection. She wanted them to look just right when they went to their grandmother's house for the first time.

"Now be good boys," she said. "Give your grandmother a kiss, and don't forget your manners."

"What are they?" Tommy asked.

"You forgot already," Johnny said.

Della laughed aloud. "Ah see why she say he cute," Della said.

"Don't be in a hurry to get them home, Della. Let them have a nice long visit. I won't worry. Suppertime will be good enough. Tommy still takes a nap in the afternoon."

"No, I don't," he said, turning his head from side to side.

"If he skips it, it's okay, so don't worry. He'll fall out somewhere."

"You never did tell me 'bout mah Stephen," Della said with a catch in her voice.

Katie found it hard to speak. "When you bring them back, Della, he'll be here. You can visit with him then. He's a wonderful husband and father, and we're very happy."

"Ah sho' is glad to hear it, Katie."

Chapter
THIRTY-NINE

Lala stood behind the table, ladling punch into cups for soldiers between dances. One blush followed another so rapidly that her cheeks were constantly crimson. Lala was painfully shy. It had taken all her courage to agree to help at the Sunday-afternoon dances for servicemen in the Holy Rosary auditorium. The parish had been sponsoring the dances ever since the United States had entered the European war and had begun drafting men into the service.

It was the summer of 1917 and Lala was eighteen years old. She had never been on a date in her life, and she dreaded the time when she would be asked. She was certain she could never live through it.

Most of her shyness was due to a weight problem. At seventeen she had stopped growing vertically. She was short and plump, a perfect duplicate of her mother. Unlike Frances, however, she was fair and slightly freckled, with a fine nose and wide hazel eyes. What made her feel matronly was the generous bosom that was the trademark of the Raspanti girls, which even the new brassieres could not disguise.

With a silver dipper she filled a cup and extended it across the table, her eyes cast down. When the soldier hesitated to take it, she looked up into a pair of bright blue eyes. Her hand trembled, and she dropped the cup into the punch bowl. She felt herself blush again. The soldier was smiling shyly. He was red-haired with his own share of freckles.

"I'm sorry," Lala apologized. "I'll get you another cup."

"Never mind," he said. "Will you . . . can you . . . come out from behind there and dance?"

"I'm not supposed to," she said. "I'm helping."

"Let them all help themselves," he said, taking her hand as the cup sank to the bottom of the bowl.

"I don't know how to dance," Lala said, perishing of embarrassment.

"It doesn't matter. Let's go sit out on the steps. It's too hot in here anyway."

Lala surprised herself by going. The young man was tall and thin, the antithesis of Lala in appearance but every bit as shy and awkward. He spread his handkerchief for her to sit on.

"My name is Walter Garvey," he said. "What's yours?"

"Lala Raspanti."

Walter laughed shyly. "Lala?" he asked. "That's very musical. What's it short for?"

"My real name is Eulalie. My sister Jenny used to call me Lala when I was a baby and it stuck."

"It's nice, but I like your real name better. May I call you Eulalie?"

Lala nodded. She knew from the very start that Walter Garvey could have called her anything he wanted. All she had to do was look into those sky-blue eyes to know she was in love.

"I'm from Macon, Georgia," the boy said. "I was drafted in the army. I'm stationed at Camp Martin on the Loyola campus."

"I see," Lala said. "How long will you be in New Orleans?"

"At least six weeks of boot camp. Then . . . who knows?" He looked around at the building behind them. "Do you go to school here?" he asked.

"No." Lala laughed. "This is a grammar school. Our

parish church is next door. I've just graduated from Esplanade High, about a mile away."

"Oh, I see." Walter smiled. "You live near here?"

"About a block away. Along the bayou."

"Then I can walk you home. And we can . . . talk. I've had enough of this." He tilted his head toward the auditorium. "Have you?"

Lala nodded. She got up and took the arm Walter offered. When they reached the Eagan house, Jenny and Daren were sitting on the gallery, talking with Stephen and Davey and Katie. All conversation ceased when the family saw Lala with a young man in tow. No one could do enough to make him welcome.

Katie brought him a glass of lemonade and insisted he stay for supper. The subject of conversation reverted inevitably to the draft, which was uppermost in everyone's thoughts at the moment.

"I'm thinking of joining the navy," Daren said. "I'll be drafted sooner or later, and I might get stuck in the army. No offense intended."

"It's okay," Walter said. "I happen to like the army, myself."

"I keep telling him to wait," Jenny injected. "They're not going to take married men right away. Who knows? The war may be over soon, and he may never have to go."

"If Jenny had had a baby or two all this time, you'd have nothing to worry about," Katie said to Daren.

"Well, it wasn't for lack of trying," Daren said.

Everyone laughed.

Jenny's mouth fell open. She shot arrows at her husband with her eyes, and Lala blushed to the roots of her hair.

"What about you, Davey?" Walter asked. "Are you married?"

Davey was wearing a sport shirt, as he always did when he spent the day at Katie's. "No, Walter," he said.

"I'm a seminarian. I'm going to be ordained a priest next May."

"Oh, I'm sorry," the boy apologized. "I didn't know."

"No apologies. Please. As a matter of fact there *have* been some army chaplains talking to the deacons lately. Our teachers sort of halfheartedly encourage us to join." He tilted his hand this way and that. "They want to do their patriotic duty, but they hate to lose their parish priests."

"Davey, I didn't know you were giving any thought to that," Katie said.

"Not really," Davey said. He patted his sister's hand. "Don't worry."

"Well, the one person I don't have to worry about is Stephen. He's over the draft age, praise the Lord," Katie said.

"Over the hill at thirty-two," Stephen said, and Katie detected a note of regret in his voice.

Supper consisted of cold roast chicken left over from the noon meal, potato salad, and hot apple pie. The children came tumbling in around six o'clock with a friend from down the block who was staying for supper. The meal was noisy, but cheerful, and as Walter Garvey looked around the table and back again at Lala, he felt that he had found a home where he was comfortable.

After supper, when the table was cleared, poker chips and playing cards were taken from the sideboard, and the Michigan poker game began. It was the family favorite. Davey left to return to the seminary, and Katie begged off. She had darning to do, and things to think about. As she sat under the circle of light from the floor lamp, listening to the shouts when a "pay card" hit, she became very melancholy about the young men at the table.

It was hard for her to believe that the United States was really in the war and that they were training their strongest and smartest young men to go to Europe and fight in the trenches and maybe get killed. Any one of them here tonight might never come back. Daren or Walter or even Davey. Now *there* was something new for her to worry about. Warren would be drafted, too. She had forgotten about that.

What a tragedy that they had been drawn into the conflict! Even after the *Lusitania* business, President Wilson had promised to keep the United States out of it. But as the newspapers carried more and more accounts of the sinkings of American ships, people began to walk around with sober expressions, just waiting for the inevitable news that war had been declared. It made Katie sick to see billboards screaming out, "Uncle Sam Wants You," and soldiers marching in parade every time she went to Canal Street.

Everyone was putting forth his best to "beat the Jerries." Working men were buying liberty bonds. There were meatless days and gas rationing, and the country's industry had shifted to a wartime economy. Ladies were knitting socks and scarves for men in uniform.

"Mrs. Eagan." A voice shook Katie out of her reverie. She looked up into Walter Garvey's blue eyes. Lala was standing beside him.

"Call me Katie," she said.

"Katie, I've got to get back to camp now. I want you to know how much I enjoyed the evening. The supper and everything."

"I'm glad, Walter," she said.

"I'm the oldest of five boys, and I felt right at home here. It's just like this at our house on Sunday evenings."

"Then you must come back," Katie said. "Next Sunday. We'll count on it."

Walter grinned. "I'd like nothing better," he said.

Lala was beaming as she escorted her young man to the porch.

No one doubted for a minute that Walter would be Lala's "young man." The next Sunday, and the one after that, and every one that followed found Walter on the Eagan gallery, very much at home with Lala's family, and it was only a matter of time, they all knew, till the couple made an announcement.

As they got to know Walter better, they learned that his father owned a butcher shop in Macon, and that Walter and his brother built houses together, contracting out work to plumbers and roofers. His brother had been drafted, too, and was stationed in South Carolina.

Their courtship was brief. The war had made it so. There was no time for hope chests or showers or monogrammed linens. After soldiers were trained, it was not long before they got their orders to go overseas. Young couples in love were trying to grab a few months, perhaps a few weeks, of happiness before the orders came.

Walter and Lala were married quietly in a parlor at the rectory, with Stephen giving the bride away, and Jenny and Daren as witnesses. Walter's parents and his three youngest brothers drove to New Orleans for the wedding. When their car pulled up to the curb at the Eagan house, Katie could see nothing but red heads sticking out of the back windows.

There was no reception, at Lala's request. After the ceremony the newlyweds left for their honeymoon weekend at the Grunewald Hotel, after which Lala was to return to Katie's house and Walter would go back to camp. As long as he was stationed in New Orleans, Walter would spend the weekends with his bride at the Moss Street house.

Chapter
FORTY

One morning Katie skipped down the steps like a schoolgirl to meet the mailman. She enjoyed the freedom of the shorter, wider skirts. Some hemlines in the store windows downtown were a full twelve inches from the floor. Designers were going to the other extreme now, after the hobble skirt.

"Mornin', Sam," she greeted the mailman.

"Mawnin', Miz Katie," the black man said. His grin was like a yard of white ribbon. "Got a letter heah fo' Miz Lala. She be glad to see dat."

"She sure will, Sam."

Lala was the one who usually greeted the mailman. Her chief occupation these days was waiting for a letter from Walter. He had been sent overseas in September, one short month after they were married. She knew he was somewhere in France, fighting at the front, and she was worried sick about him. But this morning she was queasy again, so Katie had told her to stay in bed.

Sam continued down the walk to the next house, and Katie started up the steps, examining the mail as she went. There was a letter from Walter, all right. A few bills, an advertisement. Suddenly she stopped in her tracks. Then she was running up the steps to the gallery, waving the mail in the air.

"Stephen! Stephen!" she shouted. She was grinning from ear to ear. "Come and see what I've got. You won't believe it."

Stephen came out onto the porch, shielding his eyes from the sun. "What is it, Kate?" he asked.

She ran on past him, across the gallery and into the living room. Lala had seen the mailman from her upstairs window and started down the stairs to the living room. She sat on the steps now, weaving with pregnant malaise, and watched Katie and Stephen from between the balusters.

"Katie, give me that letter," Stephen said, trying to take it from her. She jumped up on the settee and held it high in the air.

"Not till you guess who it's from." She giggled and shrieked when he grabbed her by the waist.

"If you two children will stop playing," Lala said, "just tell me if *I* have a letter, so I can go back to bed and die."

"Wait, Lala, I want you to hear this." Then, putting her arms around her husband's neck, she said: "I promise to give you the letter, if you'll let me tell you who sent it."

"Okay. Okay. Go ahead."

"The return address shows it's from . . . the One . . . the Only . . ."

"Katie!" Lala shouted irascibly.

"Wizard of Menlo Park, the Great Man, the Inventor of all Inventors . . ."

"No. You're kidding," Stephen said.

"Thomas . . . Alva . . . Edison. Ta-dah!" And she handed the letter to Stephen.

"Are you sure it's for me?" he asked.

"If your name is Stephen Eagan."

Lala got up and came over to sit beside Katie on the settee, forgetting her misery for a moment. "Open it, Stephen," she said.

Stephen walked over to his desk and took out a letter opener. Ever so carefully, so as not to mar the envelope, he slit it open and sat in an easy chair to read. He read aloud:

Dear Stephen,

I know your father has told you that he and I were friends when we were young. He was also my strong right arm at Menlo Park. I visited him in his home in New Orleans soon after you were born, and I feel as if I've known you all along.

Word has come to me from many sources that you are a brilliant young engineer with imagination and drive. Sidney Gentry, who did such a fine job of putting Edison Electric back on its feet in New Orleans, reports that your education, your studies in Europe, and your natural creativity more than qualify you for a very special assignment I have in mind.

I have researched the five inventions on which you have obtained patents. They are excellent commercial improvements on existing inventions, and they tell me how your mind works. You look for practical, simple improvements on equipment already in use. You are the kind of man I need in my group.

Now let me get to the point. You may have read that I have been appointed president of the Naval Consulting Board in Washington, D.C. The board is presently doing research on torpedo mechanisms and other devices. I am picking up where I left off in 1898, when we experimented with torpedoes equipped with motors that furnished steering power and carried cables through which they could be controlled. Now, we are going further, with more sophisticated equipment and a better knowledge of what we can hope to accomplish.

I am trying to gather a few good men to work with me for the duration. I know it will mean some sacrifice on your part to leave your wife and children, but there would be no point in bringing them here. Washington is overcrowded. There are no apartments to rent, you would never see your family, and we sometimes work round the clock. The war doesn't wait for any of us.

I hope you will consider this a request to help your country, in a way that few men can. As a soldier, you could never do as much.

Let me hear from you soon. Your devoted servant,

Al Edison

Stephen let the letter drop to his lap. "Your devoted servant! Can you believe that?" he asked.

"He calls himself 'Al,'" Katie said. "Your father used to call him that."

"Why 'Al'?" Lala asked.

"Short for Alva," Katie said.

"He actually asked me to come and work with him," Stephen said, beaming. "Me! Why me?"

"He told you, darling. You're better known than you think," Katie said proudly.

Stephen got up from the easy chair and sat on the floor at Katie's feet. He took her hands. "Do you think you could get along without me, Katie?" he asked.

She threaded her fingers through his hair and put her arm around his neck. "Not easily," she said. "But I know I have about as much chance of keeping you here as flying to the moon."

"Then you'll understand if I go?"

She nodded. "Of course," she said.

"To have a chance to work with Edison himself! I never dreamed it would happen to me. And I'll be doing something for the war effort. I wouldn't have joined up and left you and Lala and the boys, and I'm too old to be drafted . . ."

"My old man of thirty-two," Katie said.

"I've been feeling pretty rotten sitting out the war while other men were going. The plant's almost shut down now, except for repair work. We'll have no new facilities for the duration. All the materials go to the war plants. So what good am I here?"

"You don't have to convince me, darling. I'm proud to see you go."

He took her in his arms and kissed her gratefully. Then he shot up from the settee and ran to call the boys in from the yard. He read them the letter.

"I'm going to have this letter framed," he told them. "One day it will be worth more to you than gold. Now listen to me well, both of you. I'm going to Washington, D.C., to work with Edison."

"Edison Electric?" Tommy asked.

"No," Stephen said, ruffling the boy's curls. "Edison, Thomas A."

The depot was a sea of khaki uniforms when the boys kissed their father good-bye. Soldiers were saying their last farewells to sweethearts and mothers. A band was playing "It's a Long Way to Tipperary." The boom! boom! of the big bass drum kept the rhythm of Katie's heart. She had promised herself not to cry. She was grateful to God that her husband would not be fighting in the trenches in France; she had that to be thankful for.

The children kissed him good-bye. Lala came next. Then Katie felt his arms close around her. She looked up into his eyes and he pressed his lips to hers. She had never loved him more in all her life.

In the months that followed, Stephen's letters were sporadic. Sometimes there were three in a week. Then two weeks would go by without a word. Katie understood that some project was underway, something that kept the research team going day and night, and Stephen had no time to do anything but work.

In his letters, he wrote:

* * *

This man [Edison] is remarkable. I remember
my father telling me about his endurance, but you
have to see it firsthand to believe it. He can sleep
an hour or two and awake completely refreshed.
And he's *seventy* years old! You can understand
that he expects no less from younger men. But I
can't keep up with him, Katie.

Our work is progressing well. I'm not allowed to
discuss what we're doing beyond what Mr. Edison
wrote in his first letter, but I think the things we've
done will save many lives. That means more to me
than you can imagine.

I hope the checks I'm sending are enough to keep
you going. It isn't as much as I made before, but I
know my Katie. At least, you'll always have a coffee can to turn to if you get desperate.

Katie had never stopped saving her money in coffee
cans. The children had watched their mother put
money in cans for as long as they could remember. To
them it was as routine as watching her fix their oatmeal. It never occurred to them to ask her why she did
it or where she put the cans. She always kept a can in
the pantry, and when it was full, she recorded the
amount and brought it down to the basement. She estimated that at this point she had already saved about
five thousand dollars. Yes, she knew where to turn if
she were desperate.

In October a letter came from Warren with a new
postal address.

Dear Katie,
    I'm in the army now! It was only a matter of
time till I would be drafted, and I was approached
by the Special Services Unit and asked to volunteer. Griffith encouraged me to enlist. You can't
make movies without actors, but you can improve

your public image, and the studios need that about now.

We've been traveling from camp to camp, entertaining servicemen. And what can Warren do? I hear you asking. Well, it's been discovered after all these years that Warren can sing. A Caruso I'm not, but I can carry a tune and lead the men in a rousing song, and my face is familiar to them. That seems to be the whole point of it, letting them meet some "celebrities." Unquote.

He had enclosed a picture of himself in his army uniform. Katie hardly recognized him with his shingled haircut. She put his picture in the frame of her mirror, alongside Daren's and Walter's. Daren had joined the navy in September, just as he had said he would, and was lucky enough to be stationed at the naval base in Algiers, right across the Mississippi River. He had been promised that after his basic training, he could come home each night to New Orleans. That was, of course, unless he got orders to go overseas. She looked at the three smiling faces of her young brothers-in-law, and she shook her head sadly.

She sat down at once and wrote Warren a letter about Stephen in Washington.

The second week in December Katie got a letter from Stephen with the news that he'd be home for Christmas. It would be only for two days, but Katie decided to make it the best Christmas he'd ever had. She got dressed one morning and went to Werlien's on Canal Street to buy him something she'd wanted to give him for a very long time, a player piano. She remembered how he had enjoyed the player piano at his mother's house. He was the only one in the family who had ever used it. Stephen loved music. Every evening on Moss Street, before supper was ready, he always played four or five of his favorite records on the Victrola. Now he'd be able to hear them on his piano.

Jenny and Daren would spend Christmas with them, as well as Davey, Lala, and the boys. Katie thought of Janet and Charlotte all alone on St. Charles Avenue. She wanted to invite them, but she knew that Stephen would be furious if she did, and she had no intention of ruining the day for him.

She planned her menu far ahead. She finished her Christmas shopping, saving the toys till last. She liked to take her time picking out baseball gloves and games and coloring books. Johnny would be getting a two-wheeled bike this year. Tommy had a little more growing to do to be able to reach the pedals. She knew she was spoiling her children, but she wanted them to have all the things she had never had as a child.

When Stephen's train pulled into the station, Katie was waiting as they dropped the step to let the passengers disembark. Stephen was the first man in the doorway. He rushed to his wife and picked her up and they held each other, sobbing and touching each other's faces to be sure they were not just dreaming. A wave of human bodies pushed against them, and still they did not let each other go. They kissed and they hugged, they laughed and they cried, all without words.

The boys had remained in the car with Lala, and when, at last, they saw their father coming, they ran to him and the kisses began all over again.

Back home, when they walked into the parlor, Stephen exclaimed happily when he saw the piano. He hugged Katie again and kissed her. Then he took a roll from on top of the piano and put it in at once.

"Now you're going to see how the piano works," Katie said to the boys. Then to Stephen, "I wouldn't let them touch it till you got here."

"Watch, Johnny," Stephen said. "First you put in the roll and hook it, like this. Then you turn on this key, and start pumping with your feet. Watch me."

Stephen pumped away. The keys began to rise and fall, as if by magic, and the two little boys stood, wide-eyed, as the bouncy notes of "Peg O' My Heart" came tumbling out of the upright.

They all sang along, reading the words on the roll over Stephen's shoulder. Everyone tried to sustain the carefree mood, just as if nothing at all had changed, just as if they were the same old happy family enjoying Christmas together.

No one could do enough for Stephen in the two days he was home. "A pillow for your back, Stephen?" Lala asked. "Here, rest your feet on the hassock," Jenny said. "Wait till you see what I cooked for you," Katie remarked. And when Katie lay in his arms at night, caressing him, kissing him tenderly, touching his dear, sweet face, she tried to forget that this was only a brief interlude, and that he would soon be gone again.

The holidays passed too quickly and Stephen left, like a shadow slipping in and out of their lives. During his stay he had not said a word about the work he was doing in Washington. Once in a while, as Katie stood beside him, her arm around his waist, she would catch him off guard, wearing a somber expression, looking around at his family and his home as if he were indeed fighting in the war and might never see them again. She shuddered when she saw that look. She held him close and pressed her head to his shoulder.

Chapter
FORTY-ONE

It was April, 1918, when the telegram came. Katie was sitting on the porch swing. She watched the Western Union boy drop the kickstand of his bicycle and start slowly up the steps. He kept his eyes down. Most telegrams he delivered these days were bad news, Katie thought. But she would like to have told him not to worry about this one. No, thank the dear Lord, Stephen was safe in Washington. But what about Walter? How selfish she was, thinking only of Stephen!

With trembling fingers she took the envelope from the boy. She had no change to give him, but he wanted none. He wanted only to get away. He rushed back down the stairs to his bike.

At last she looked at the envelope. It was addressed to her. Her hands shook as she tore it open. She read:

> The President of the United States regrets to inform you that your husband, Stephen Eagan, was killed in action March 23, 1918, when the submarine in which he was acting as technical advisor was sunk by a German destroyer off the coast of France.
>
> His mission was voluntary. He was a civilian. The submarine was carrying a new torpedo developed by the research group with which he had been working. He had accompanied it to supervise its operation.

The United States of America owes a great debt of gratitude to Stephen Eagan for action beyond the call of duty.

The War Department

Her eyes wide, her mouth open, she read it again. "The President of the United States regrets to inform you . . ." regrets to inform you? Oh, no . . . it was a mistake . . . terrible . . . horrible . . . unforgivable mistake. He wasn't on a submarine. Not Stephen. He was in Washington . . . here . . . in the United States. The wire was for someone else . . . some other wife . . . some other poor wife.

She read it again. Regrets to inform you that Stephen Eagan was killed in action . . . killed in action . . . killed . . . KILLED. Sunk off the coast of France. She crushed the telegram in her hand.

"NO!" she screamed, splitting the calm of the quiet morning. It echoed out over the water, that note of unbearable suffering, and sparrows flew from the trees. Clutching the telegram, Katie lowered herself tremulously to the rocking chair beside her. She opened the crumpled sheet with trembling fingers and read again, through a blur of tears that blinded her.

"No!" she cried out again and a devastating sorrow engulfed her. "Stephen!" she wailed with a mourning wail. "No! Not dead! He can't be dead!" She rocked now, frantically, wildly, as the tears fell down her face. Her hands gripped the arms of the rocker, and her body trembled violently. Her countenance was rigid with a look of pained surprise, for understanding had come at last, and with it the crushing weight of her own despair.

Blindly, in a frenzy of anguish and pain, she ran down the steps and across the street to the grassy banks of the bayou. She ran along the levee, like a woman gone mad, screaming, "Stephen!" and the wails broke in her throat. She tripped and fell on the soft, green grass, and she lay there, in the shade of an oak tree, and wept from the depths of her soul.

"I can't live!" she cried out. "I can't live! Oh, Jesus, help me."

The cry seemed to wrench itself from her heart. It was a cry filled with longing and loneliness, with mourning and desolation. She wept until there was no more strength to weep, no more breath in her body to cry out. And then she lay quiet, exhausted and motionless, and still the tears ran, as if they would run forever.

"Oh, Ste . . . !" she tried to cry out, but she had not the strength to finish his name. The mournful syllable was muffled in sobs and lost in incoherent images. Gone now . . . buried . . . under the water . . . the cold Atlantic water . . . a submarine for a coffin . . . sunk . . . exploded? . . . burst apart? . . . floating somewhere?

"No!" she screamed again, finding new strength, swinging her arm before her to wipe away the image. Was it quick? . . . like Papa? Please God! Not struggling . . . lungs bursting . . . like Little Joe. She groaned like a woman strangling for air, like a wounded animal waiting for death.

Her hair had fallen loose. The wind whipped it across her face and it was soaked with her tears. When she turned to lie on her back, dark skeins of hair lay wet across her face, and she did not move them. Her heart was inflamed with pain. Her body felt bloodless, drained, emptied of life. She could not think of getting up again . . . walking home . . . talking . . . cooking . . . dressing ever again. Life was over . . . finished . . . buried deep in the cold Atlantic.

Recollections came unsummoned: the smell of his skin, the crispness of his hair, the sound of his laughter, the feel of his lean, warm body molded against hers. Lying on her back, she raised her fists to the heavens.

"There . . . is . . . no life . . . without him," she sobbed, summoning God to hear her cry. "I . . .

can't . . . go on." Tears fell again. "Take me, God . . . take me, too."

For hours she lay on the grassy levee, oblivious to cars passing by and pedestrians glancing in her direction. Lala came home from Jenny's and went through the house calling Katie's name. She walked out onto the gallery and looked up and down the street and along the bayou's edge in search of her sister. At last she saw a figure sprawled on the grassy banks about a block away beneath an oak tree.

She ran down the front steps and across the street as fast as her heavy figure would allow. When she reached Katie, an icy fear swept over her. Her sister was as white as death, and as motionless. She lifted Katie's head onto her lap, and Katie's lids fluttered.

"Stephen!" Katie whispered.

Seeing the crumpled telegram clutched in her sister's fist, Lala opened it and read it. "Holy Mother of God!" Lala gasped. "Oh, Katie!" She enfolded her sister in her arms and they wept together. "Oh, God!" Lala cried out, "have mercy on us all!"

She rocked her sister in her arms, brushing her wet, disheveled hair from her face. How would Katie go on without Stephen? Lala asked herself. He was her strength, her hope, her love, her life. He was only thirty-three years old! He had so much yet to give Katie and the children, and he had been like a father and a very dear friend to Lala. Katie's strength was depleted from hours of weeping, but when Lala's tears flowed fresh, Katie found new springs to draw upon and she cried once again.

A policeman on horseback rode up and saw the sisters weeping beneath the tree. He stopped and dismounted. "Are you all right?" he asked with concern as he knelt on one knee beside Katie.

Lala handed him the telegram and the young man read. Then he looked up into Lala's tear-streaked face.

"My sister's husband," she explained.

"I'm sorry," he said. "May I take her home? Where does she live?"

"In the yellow house," Lala said, pointing across the street.

"I can carry her," he said, "if you can lead the horse by the reins."

Lala nodded. The officer held Katie in his arms, as limp and lifeless as a corpse herself, and Lala followed well advanced in her pregnancy, leading the police horse along the banks of the bayou.

Chapter
FORTY-TWO

"He's dead, Mother," Charlotte shouted. "Do you understand that? Stephen is dead." She walked over to where her mother sat in her boudoir chair and looked into the hard, unflinching eyes. "We never had a chance to tell him good-bye. We never got to say, 'Stephen, I love you. I miss you.' And now he's gone. Forever. It's all over. It's too late."

Janet stared ahead of her, dry-eyed, expressionless. In the days that had passed since they'd heard of Stephen's death, she had not shed a tear in Charlotte's presence, not a single tear for that wonderful son she had lost. Perhaps she cries when she's alone, Charlotte thought; I hope so, for her sake.

The day they heard the news, Janet had walked through every room in the house, shuttering every window and drawing every drape. It was her way of mourning without tears. Now, every room was stifling hot, and they lived in a perpetual twilight gloom. Janet never left her room; even her meals were brought up on a tray.

Janet drew in a deep breath and let out a little moan. She tried to adjust her stays to make herself more comfortable. Still the stays, Charlotte thought, keeping her aloof and erect, even in the daytime, even in the privacy of her own room. Her body is as rigidly confined as her heart.

Charlotte paced her mother's bedroom, sobbing, then

arms flailing, her face tear-streaked. Then she stopped and sat wearily on her mother's bed.

"I feel so ashamed for us both," Charlotte said.

"Ashamed?" Janet turned her wooden expression toward her daughter. "Of what?"

"Ashamed of you for putting him out of your life. And ashamed of myself for keeping silent all these years and letting him think I approved of what you had done. The longer I waited, the harder it was for me to speak out. I guess I'm just a coward." Charlotte met her mother's eyes unblinking. "Even *you* thought I approved, didn't you, Mother?"

"And you didn't approve?" Janet asked.

"What did I have to say? When it happened, I was a girl. I thought whatever you did was right. You always overpowered me."

"And now? In your more mature judgment?" Janet asked sardonically.

"I think you should have begged for his forgiveness long ago and made peace with his wife and his family." Then, seeing that her mother was about to snap back, she added: "But that was *your* loss, not his. Since the first time we saw little Johnny at the school fence, I've envied him. Oh, God, how I've envied him!"

"Envied him? He had nothing!"

"He had everything! He had a wife he loved, two beautiful sons, and a happy home. I'd have settled for ten years of that."

"So you say." Janet sounded weary. "I'd have to *see* Charlotte Eagan playing happy housewife without her monthly allowance. Why is it always the rich who can tell you how filthy and unimportant money is?"

Charlotte rested her elbows on the footboard of the bed. She lowered her head to her hands. She took no pleasure in this argument. She was heartsick for Stephen, and she had hoped to share her suffering with her mother. For almost a week she had been trying to break through that shell. But Janet Eagan did not break. She did not share.

One thing was becoming clearer to Charlotte every day: she had to get out of her mother's house. She looked at her mother now, in her long black mourning dress with its high neck and long sleeves. She wore no adornment of any kind, and her hair was now totally gray. In all she looked far older than her fifty-five years. Even her hands, now resting on the head of her cane, were a network of veins climbing over arthritic knuckles.

If I stay here, Charlotte thought, I'll grow old and mean like that. If I let this mausoleum close around me, I'll be buried here, in black, sitting in my boudoir chair all day, shuttered away from the world like my mother. We'll grow old together, she and I, two spiteful harridans tearing each other apart. Oh, no. I won't let it happen.

"How is Della?" Janet asked after awhile.

"No better," Charlotte answered. "I went to see her this morning. I think she's in a decline."

Della was confined to bed in the servants' quarters ever since she'd come home from the hospital. She had spent three weeks there after her stroke, but she had been sent home since there was nothing to do for her but feed her and make her comfortable. In Della's absence the house had not been touched. Dust had accumulated everywhere, and cobwebs were forming in the corners of the mantels.

Everything is dying or decaying around us, Charlotte thought. She had a vision of herself and her mother, sitting there in the shadows of her bedroom until they were covered with mold and cobwebs and racing spiders. She stood up suddenly, shaking herself free of the horror.

She stared into her mother's cheval mirror and saw the spinster that she was: tall, slightly bent now from years of hunching over to disguise her height, painfully thin, flat of chest, slight of hip. She touched her hands to her hair. It was puffed over the ears, giving her head a severe, bell-shaped look. Her eyes were still her best feature, wide-set and gray. And she still had her fine white teeth, but she rarely smiled to show them.

There were men who would be glad to marry her. She was still a young woman with a lot of life to live. She desperately wanted a husband and children. But for now, she wanted to get away. She wanted to talk to people who knew something else besides death and dying. She refused to grow old, a companion to her mother and a bitter, resentful recluse.

Chapter FORTY-THREE

For the first few days after the telegram came, Katie sat in her bedroom, gazing out across the bayou, her vacant stare fixed on the treetops in the park. Hours passed, and she did not move or speak. When weariness overtook her, she slept in a sitting position, face in hand, arm resting on the arm of the chair. Her sisters urged her to go to bed, where she could sleep more comfortably, but they could not tell if she had even heard them. No sound seemed to penetrate the wall of lethargy that she had built around her. They begged her to eat, but she waved food away with the same gesture Frances had used after losing her son. Something had died inside Katie the day she had read that telegram, and her sisters exchanged worried glances, wondering if she would ever be the same again. One thing was clear to both Jenny and Lala—if it had not been for Davey, she might have been a very sick woman.

Jenny moved over to Katie's house. She was glad to be useful in her own grief for Stephen, and glad to be busy so she would not dwell on Daren fighting somewhere on the other side of the world. She and Lala cooked and cleaned and did everything for Katie except look after the boys. Seeing to their needs brought Katie out of her apathy, at least periodically, and her sisters were wise enough not to take that from her.

Lala's baby was due any time. She had received word that Walter had been injured in a training accident and was recuperating in a hospital in Paris. She prayed that the injury would keep him there until the war was over.

Both girls went through their days with one eye on Katie, watching for a change in expression, listening for a word. At the least indication both would rush to her side to see if they might get her a cup of tea or help her up to her bedroom for a rest. They were willing to work from dawn till dusk and cater to her every whim, but they had no strength to offer when Katie's eyes welled with tears. They would sit beside her and embrace her, but then, they, too, would cry. They were both distraught over Stephen, and it would be many months before their own pain would lose its sharp edges.

It was Davey who was able to give solace to Katie without falling apart himself. He talked to her by the hour, sometimes offering spiritual comfort, more often helping her find her way out of her anguish in ways that the girls thought extraordinary. They would listen, sitting on the porch, knitting baby things for Lala, and they were amazed at his wisdom and his common sense.

"You'll have to give him up to Jesus, Katie, and learn to live without him," Davey said. Katie shook her head. The girls sobbed quietly. "You'll have to make up your mind to do it sooner or later. He's gone now, and he won't be back. You've got to face that."

"I can't, Davey," she cried, reaching out for his hand, the tears rolling down her face.

"You can, and you will. The question is when. You can go on like this, suffering agony, for two more years before you decide to give him up. Or you can do it in a week. I'll help you. God will help you. It's up to you, really, how long you tear down your health and make your life miserable."

"You ask too much of me, Davey," she said, shaking her head. "How can I forget what Stephen and I had together?"

"There's no need to forget. Those are cherished

memories. But that's all they are. Memories. They're finished. Stephen is gone. Give him to God."

She sobbed again, her face buried in her hands. "Do you think it's easy?"

"I didn't say it was easy. I said it was possible."

"You're a priest. You don't know what it is to fall asleep at night in the arms of the one you love. I think of his kisses, and his hand touching mine, and his look of love. If I don't have Stephen, I don't want to go on living. I wish God would have taken me, too. What on earth do I have to live for now?"

She cried aloud and pulled at her hair. Her voice was hoarse with anguish, just as her heart was raw with pain. Davey sat on the swing beside her and took her in his arms. He stroked her back gently and petted her. She relaxed slightly in his gentle embrace and her crying subsided. Jenny and Lala were sobbing, too, but softly, so as not to add to Katie's heartache. Davey took the corner of her apron and dried her face, as he had done years ago, before Johnny was born. He gave her his handkerchief to blow her nose.

Johnny came home from school and ran up the steps to the porch. He threw himself into his mother's arms, not even noticing that her eyes were puffed from crying. "I want an apple-butter sandwich, an' I need a nickel for Teacher 'Preciation Day."

He kissed her on the cheek and ran into the house, slamming the door behind him. Jenny and Lala shook their heads and smiled.

"You were asking me what you had to live for?" Davey asked.

Davey took a leave of absence from the seminary. Only two more months remained until his ordination. His examinations were over, and his grades were in. He would have a brief retreat before ordination. But in the meantime he was free to stay with Katie. He did not want to leave her for a minute, until he had set up a regimen for her recovery and he was sure she was following it. When she was alone, she cried until she collapsed. He saw how it depleted her, and he did not intend to permit it.

Together they took long walks every day, no matter how much she complained that she didn't have the strength. She had the strength, but not the will, and this is what he intended to give her.

They attended daily Mass together. Davey did not sermonize before or after the service. Katie knew how much she needed God's help. In the beginning she cried all through Mass every day. Davey knew how easy it was to cry when you were pleading with the Lord for peace of soul, so he didn't comment. After a time, with Davey's special type of therapy, the service seemed to lighten her burden and give her emotional fuel for the day.

Outings were part of the regimen, too. When Davey took Stephen's Model-T out of the garage, Katie cried and protested, but Davey ignored her. He drove Katie and the boys to the amusement parks, just as Stephen had done. Other evenings they packed picnic suppers and walked over to the park and played ball till it was dark.

When Lala's baby was born, they all had a wonderful new interest to absorb them, and Davey knew that the infant would do much to soothe Katie's pain. When almost two months had passed, and his retreat was coming up on the calendar, Davey took a good look at Katie and decided that she could make it now without him. He watched her pick up Lala's baby and sing to her as she rocked her on the porch. With peace of mind, he went into retreat.

On June 10, Davey became Father David Raspanti. He celebrated his first Mass at St. Patrick's Church, largely out of gratitude to Father Rafferty, who had arranged his scholarships all along the way. Katie, Jenny, and Lala sat in the first pew, and were the first to receive communion at his hands. Davey did not worry when he saw tears in Katie's eyes during the ceremony. He knew she was not lapsing back into depression; the ceremony was moving, and they were both thinking of their mother, who would have been so proud to see her son ordained.

Katie thanked God for the lightness of heart she felt at Davey's ordination, and for her priest brother who had shown her the way. That morning she decided to thank God in some special way for what she considered a miracle. First she would have a stained-glass window installed in Holy Rosary Church in Stephen's memory. And then she would do something much more personal, and much harder. Once she had promised God that if her mother lived, she would forgive her father. It was the hardest thing she could think of to do. Her mother had died, and Katie had felt no obligation to carry out her end of the bargain. In fact she had hated her father even more. What was worse, she had turned her back on the church and on God. She hoped, at long last, to make up for that.

She determined then and there to go to Janet Eagan and ask her to make peace. It had been over two months since Stephen's death, and it was barbaric to go on living the way they did. She would ask if they could not forgive and forget, if they could not be kind to each other, like mother and daughter. The thought of going to Janet scared her half to death, but she vowed to do it.

Chapter
FORTY-FOUR

The old man rang the doorbell and waited. He could hear the sound of a baby crying and a young woman making comforting noises. Feeling like an intruder, he shifted his weight and scratched his head, but then at last he rang the bell again.

Katie looked toward the front door. She had left the wooden door open to make the house cooler. Through the screened door she could see an old man with a large face and sparse white hair that fell tousled over his forehead. She picked up the baby in her arms and, holding it over her shoulder, patted the tiny bundle as she approached the door. She felt a strange mixture of weakness and elation, for she knew in an instant who it was.

"Good morning," she said softly. She found herself breathless in his presence.

"Good morning," the old man answered, bowing slightly. "Am I speaking to Mrs. Stephen Eagan?"

"Yes, sir."

"I'm delighted to meet you, Mrs. Eagan. I'm Thomas Edison."

"I know," she said. "Won't you come in, please?"

She opened the door with her free hand, and the old gentleman passed into the living room.

"Please have a seat, Mr. Edison," Katie said. It was a spectacular moment for her, being in his imposing presence, and one that she wanted to remember vividly, so she could tell her children and her grandchildren about it. She wished Johnny and Tommy were here, themselves, or Jenny and Lala. But in a split-second change of heart, she was glad she was alone. There was a kind of reverence in their shared memory of Stephen and in whatever message Thomas Edison had come to bring her. Edison lumbered over to an easy chair and lowered himself carefully.

"I can't tell you how happy I am to meet you, Mr. Edison," Katie said. "Let me put the baby down. I think she's sleeping now, and we can talk."

As if by a miracle the baby let Katie put her in the bassinet and promptly fell asleep. Katie returned to the settee facing the old man's chair.

"Is that your baby, Mrs. Eagan?" Edison asked.

"No, sir. She's my sister Lala's. She leaves her with me quite often. She knows it's the best medicine in the world for me."

Edison lowered his head and scrutinized his fingernails. "I was not sure you would welcome me," he said.

"I'm honored to have you in my home," Katie said.

"If I had never written your husband to come and work with me, he'd be alive today."

"You asked him to offer his talents to his country. You gave him a chance to work at your side. To Stephen, that was the most glorious privilege of his career. Of course Stephen would never have called it a 'career.' He was too modest for that."

"Yes. He was a rare man. Brilliant, really. Most of the improvements in the torpedo he accompanied on that mission were his. This is why he asked to go along. It was his brainchild. He had a strong sense of duty. He didn't consider his work complete unless he saw the torpedo fired. It was his sixth mission."

Katie's chin trembled, but she did not cry. "I thought so," she said. "When he came home for Christmas, he seemed so preoccupied. After he died, I realized why. He must have been out even before that."

"He was. He insisted on going. He was a man of great purpose and dedication. He was like a son to me."

"He would be happy to know that."

"I have brought you a medal, Mrs. Eagan. It is from the President of the United States, one which is rarely presented to anyone not in the military. Ordinarily you would be asked to come to Washington for the presentation, but I asked if I might have the privilege of presenting it to you personally, in the privacy of your own home, and President Wilson agreed. It is the Congressional Medal of Honor."

Katie's mouth opened. Edison reached awkwardly into his coat pocket and pulled out a velvet box and handed it to Katie. With trembling fingers she opened the box and glanced at the multicolored ribbon and the magnificent medallion.

"Thank you," she said at last. "And thank Mr. Wilson."

Edison smiled. "I'll be sure to do that."

She closed the box respectfully and placed it beside her on the lamp table. Her hand still resting on its cover, she said, "My sons will know what their father did for his country, and that Mr. Thomas Edison brought this medal to his house from the President of the United States. I'm very proud."

She took her handkerchief from her pocket and blew her nose. Edison waited. At last she smiled and asked: "Have you had any lunch yet, Mr. Edison? Won't you let me fix you something? A sandwich, maybe?"

"Mrs. Eagan," the old man smiled, "if I may be so bold, is that an apple pie I smell?"

"It most certainly is. I baked it this morning. Would you like a nice big slice?"

"With American cheese? And a glass of cold milk?" he asked.

"Yes, sir," she said. "Come on back to the kitchen, and we'll have some together."

Chapter
FORTY-FIVE

Arrangements for the stained-glass window were surprisingly easy to make. Father Coyle, pastor of Holy Rosary Church, told Katie that there were still four windows that had been inexpensively installed in the church in the hope that they would, in time, be replaced with commemorative windows. Holy Rosary was a young parish, and these things took time. The window commemorating Stephen could be turned over to an artist without delay if they agreed upon a design. He estimated the cost at five thousand dollars. Katie asked if the window might show a scene from the life of St. Stephen, the first Christian martyr. Father Coyle was to contact an artist and have him call on Katie.

That was the easy part of her promise; the visit to Janet would be her Armageddon. Katie was grateful that Davey had taught her how to drive, so that she could go to Janet's alone, without having to take the streetcar. One afternoon, within the week after the ordination, she left the boys with Jenny, explaining only that she would be out for a little while.

As the car drew near the St. Charles Avenue home, Katie wondered if she'd have the courage to go through with the visit. She felt faint with apprehension. Her arms shook on the steering wheel, and she circled the block twice before turning into the carriageway. At last she parked the car beside the house and pulled up the brake.

Standing in trepidation before the wrought-iron gate

of the vestibule, Katie looked through the glass door down the dark, empty corridor. She saw the rainbows through the leaded glass, thrown on the floor inside, just as she had seen them the first day she came to work here as a child. She drew in a deep breath and rang the doorbell. She could hear the chimes resounding throughout the house, but no one answered. Where was Della? she wondered. Or Janet? Or Charlotte? Surely someone must be home.

She turned the handle of the gate, and to her surprise it opened. She closed the gate behind her and gently touched the glass door. It swung open eerily, inviting her to enter. She started down the corridor, the floor creaking beneath her feet in the deadly silence. It was only four in the afternoon, but the house was as dark as night, with the draperies in the parlor drawn and the door to the library closed.

Back through the dining room she went, calling out names along the way.

"Della? Is anyone here? Mrs. Eagan?" The name almost stuck in her throat. "Charlotte? Are you there?" She continued on through the butler's pantry and into the kitchen. Nothing had been changed since she left, not a piece of furniture or a window shade.

In the quiet, motionless house her heart seemed to beat aloud. It hammered painfully in her chest, and her breathing was short. She took hold of herself. She went back through the first floor, opening every door. Then she climbed the circular staircase in the dining room. There was no glow in her rose-colored window to warm her now. She knew only a growing fear as she walked down the corridor and stood before Janet's bedroom door. She gathered her courage once again and knocked.

"Who's there?" Janet called out.

Katie did not answer. She was afraid that Janet would send her away. She turned the knob gently and pushed the door open. She entered and looked about her. It took a few minutes to adjust her vision to the shadows of the closed, shuttered room. And then she saw Janet sitting in her boudoir chair across the room, and she was shocked.

Janet's hair was now totally gray, swept back in waves to a roll at the back of her neck. Her face was thin and tight. She looked like a very old woman, but her posture was stiff and unbending. The loss of her loved ones was written in lines around her eyes and her mouth and on the hands that rested on the arms of her chair. Katie felt suddenly moved to compassion.

"So you came," Janet said. "At last."

Katie was jarred back to reality. This was the Janet she knew.

"I came to make peace with you, Mrs. Eagan," Katie said. "I hoped we could be some comfort to each other."

"It's a little late for that, now that Stephen is dead," Janet said.

"It's not too late to try for a new understanding."

"Why didn't you think of that, all the years you kept Stephen away from his family?"

"I didn't take him away, and I didn't keep him away," Katie answered. "When I left this house, I left with nothing but the clothes on my back. When Stephen came home from Europe, *he* came after *me*. I was little more than a child, Mrs. Eagan. But Stephen was a man. He knew what he wanted. He wanted me."

"And you didn't think it your duty to send him back to his family?"

"Why should I have? He was my life. I adored him. He wouldn't have gone anyway. We loved each other deeply. Why couldn't you just accept that all these years?"

The older woman's head seemed to be shaking involuntarily. It was difficult to see her from across the room. Katie walked a few steps closer.

"Are you ill?" she asked.

Janet did not answer.

"May I turn on a light?"

"No," Janet said loudly, extending a bony hand before her.

"I won't be staying long," Katie said. "Is there anything I can do for you?"

Janet looked up at Katie. Her eyes were hard, and her lips bore the same malevolence they always had. Katie felt the sting of the old woman's loathing, just as she had felt it the day Janet found her in the room with the ball gowns. All the blood seemed to drain from her body with the memory.

"I've managed ten years without your help," Janet said. "I think I would rather die than let you help me now."

Katie felt as if she had been struck. Even from Janet, this was unexpected.

"I had hoped you might be softened by your grief," Katie said.

"Did you think that I would welcome you with open arms?"

"I had hoped it was possible."

"How lightly one takes his own sins!"

Katie drew a breath to answer, but she held back. She pinched her lips. Janet had had ten years to think about the breach between them. If she hadn't forgiven her yet, she probably never would.

Janet spoke again. "I often wonder what cruel quirk of fate sent me into your path so long ago and made me pick you up and hire you, ragged little beggar that you were."

Katie sighed. The same old words, embroidered over the years, that Janet had hurled at her when she was seventeen and so much in love with Stephen and so vulnerable to pain. The words meant nothing to her any more. Stephen was dead. What else could matter? These were the ravings of a bitter old woman. Katie would let her have her say and then she'd leave. Clearly reconciliation was impossible. Stephen had known it. That was why he had never come back. At last she understood.

"I've never known a day of happiness since Stephen left this house," Janet went on. "John's heart attack was a direct result of finding out what was in that . . . that infamous letter . . . the news that you and Stephen were planning to be married."

Although she had decided not to answer, Katie spoke up now.

"You've made up that story over the years," Katie said. "You've chosen to delude yourself. Mr. John told you, in my presence, that Stephen would be lucky to have me for a wife. Mr. John loved me dearly. No, it wasn't *that* that killed him. You threatened to sue him for adultery and name me as corespondent. I think that had a lot to do with his heart attack. Stephen told me about it when we were first married."

"You lie!" Janet cried out. Her mouth twitched and her hands trembled violently. "And you used your wiles to make John give you that house."

"I didn't even know there *was* a house," Katie said wearily.

"God knows what you and John did here alone in this house . . . all those nights . . ."

"I'm leaving now, Mrs. Eagan," Katie said. "We've been over this too many times. I can see now that coming was a mistake. I had the foolish idea that we might share our grief for Stephen and our memories of him. But you never change. You don't forgive. It's hopeless."

She turned and left the room. In the corridor, light streamed through the glass door leading out onto the second-floor balcony. The sun was setting between the oak trees on the avenue. It seemed another world and another time that she and Stephen had walked together on that balcony and watched the Rex Parade.

Quickly she retraced her steps, eager now to leave the house for the last time. She would never come back, nor would she let her boys come visit here. It was no place for children, with its dark corridors and closed-off rooms and closed-off hearts.

She stopped suddenly at the end of the corridor, remembering the one thing she had left behind in her old bedroom that was dear to her. She ran up the staircase to the attic and opened the door to her room. There were cobwebs on the windowsills, and dust was everywhere. She winced at the musty odor. Quickly she leaned across the bed and pulled her Civil War book from the tiny shelf. Although she was eager to leave, she sat on the bed and opened the book to where she had pressed the night jasmine that Stephen had given her so long ago, when they were both so much in love. The flowers were brown and dry and stuck to the page, but she gently disengaged the sprig and brought it to her nose. The fragrance was gone, but the memory was fresh. She had put it in the book the day he had whisked her away so romantically in the carriage and kissed her until she was intoxicated. She wanted to cry again, but she knew she must leave. And she wanted to see Della.

With the book in her arm she raced down the staircase to the kitchen. To her surprise she found Charlotte sitting at the kitchen table, writing something, a list perhaps. The two women looked at each other for several seconds before either of them spoke.

"Charlotte," Katie said. "How are you?"

"I'm well, Katie. How are you getting along?"

Katie relaxed. She had not known what to expect. "I'm doing fine," Katie answered, venturing a small smile. "My brother Davey was my salvation. He's a priest, you know. He helped me get back on my feet again."

"I'm glad," Charlotte said. "You can't give up. The boys need you now."

The warmth of the sentiment was unexpected and welcome. Katie was grateful.

"I won't give up. Thank you for caring. I . . . I came to see your mother, to offer my condolences. I thought we might be friends."

"Have you seen her?"

"Yes." Katie shook her head. "There's no hope of making up."

"I could have told you that. My mother's the most vindictive woman in the world."

"Well, I'll be going now, Charlotte. I wanted to see Della. Is she here?"

"Della's dying, Katie. Didn't you know?" she asked. "No, I guess you didn't."

"Dying? I had no idea. Has she been ill long?"

"Two months. She had a stroke. She was in the hospital for a while, and then they sent her home. There's really nothing they can do for her there."

"Where is she now?"

"In her room in the servants' quarters."

"Who takes care of her?" Katie wondered why they hadn't taken that loyal servant into their home, why she wasn't under a doctor's care. She had given them a lifetime of service, so surely they owed her that much.

"Mason cares for her," Charlotte answered.

Katie frowned.

"They're common law, didn't you know?" Charlotte asked.

Katie shook her head no. She had never known. In all these years it had never occurred to her.

"I'll go see her before I leave," she said. "I'll go out by the back. And I just want to say, it's very good to talk to you."

"Yes, Katie," Charlotte said. "Very good."

Chapter
FORTY-SIX

Around the back of the carriage house a stairway led up the servants' quarters. As Katie walked upstairs, she felt a pang of guilt that she had never visited Della in her rooms before.

The back of the carriage house resembled the service wings on Julia Row, except that there were only two stories. There was a small balcony and a rough wooden railing enclosing it. Katie knocked at the first door at the top of the stairs.

There was a creaking sound within, and at last Mason opened the door.

"Katie!" he exclaimed. "Ah'm so glad to see you."

Katie put her hands inside the man's rough, knobby fingers. "And I'm glad to see you, Mason. How's my Della?"

"Come in, Katie. She rat heah. She doin' real good t'day. She be doin' even bettah now dat you're heah."

Once again Katie had to adjust her eyes to the semi-twilight of indoors.

"Heah, lemme light dat lamp," Mason said.

He struck a match on the sole of his shoe and lit a small kerosene lamp on the bedside table. The room came into view in the soft yellow light. It was a small room with the bare necessities of rough wooden furniture, but there were curtains on the windows and rag rugs on the floor. Everything was immaculately neat. Katie saw Mason's pipe on the windowsill, his slippers under the bed. How could she not have known?

Propped up against a moss pillow, Della rested, a shadow of the woman she had been. Her mouth was pulled to one side and it was obvious that her left side was paralyzed. She grunted and lifted her right hand for Katie to take it.

"She so glad to see ya," Mason said.

"Della," Katie said, and there was a catch in her voice. "I didn't know you were sick." She put her arms around the woman's neck and sobbed. "I would have come to see you before this. Mason, you should have told me."

"I didn' wanta bother you none, Katie. We been gittin' along."

Della nodded in agreement, but she could not speak.

"Charlotte told me she was in the hospital for a while, and they sent her home," Katie said. "Does a doctor come by to see her?"

"Ain' no use, Katie," Mason said. "Dey ain' nothin' to do but feed her an' wash her hands an' feets."

"I'd like to take care of her, Mason," Katie said. "Can you carry her to the wagon and take her to my house?"

"Oh, no, Katie. It ain' right. People would talk, a white lady, waitin' on a colored woman."

"Mason, you know I don't care about that. If people want to talk, let them. It won't be the first time."

For the next two weeks Katie cared for Della with the tenderness of a mother. She gave her bed baths and fed her slowly and patiently. She wheeled her bed out on the porch, where she could watch the boats go by and the cars coming around the bend of Moss Street.

After school the children sat at Della's feet and talked, and Katie could discern an attempted smile on the right side of her mouth. Sometimes her body shook with laughter, though there was no sound. The happiest times of all were the times Lala came with the baby.

Once Katie put the baby in Della's good arm, and tears fell from the black woman's eyes.

Mason came each evening to visit and to reiterate his thanks to Katie, which only embarrassed her. He stayed very briefly so as not to impose on her kindness. She had her own doctor visit Della regularly, a chore which he undertook with obvious distaste. She was certain he told others he was visiting a member of the Eagan family.

There was, indeed, nothing to do but wait on the woman, and time alone would tell if she would recover, remain an invalid, or have another stroke. On the fourteenth day of her stay at Katie's, Della died. Katie found her dead in bed in the morning. She was still warm. Katie crossed her hands on her breast and kissed her on the forehead. She called Mason to come and, together, they arranged for her funeral in a Negro cemetery on Claiborne Avenue. To Katie's surprise Mason had a paid-up funeral policy in Della's name, and he had made arrangements long ago for the Olympia Brass Band to follow the coffin to the grave, playing funeral dirges going and jazz music coming back, in commemoration of the soul's jubilation in heaven.

Davey and Katie marched in procession with the Negroes from the funeral parlor to the cemetery. Several of the musicians did a slow, shuffling kind of dance as they marched, keeping time to the rhythm with their swaying, ruffled umbrellas. It was a serious, sensuous, religious kind of performance, and many black faces were wet with tears, though they did not know the deceased. Negroes in the streets tagged along, dancing and singing, "second-linin'," as they called it. "Just a Closer Walk with Thee," in sweet, sad harmony brought gooseflesh to Katie's arms.

When the funeral was over, Mason drove Katie home, the tears rolling down his cheeks. Katie knew he would cry for many days. When he stopped at the curb, Katie asked him to come upstairs for a while.

"No, Katie, I thank you jes' the same. Ah wonts to be alone for a while."

"I understand. It was a beautiful funeral, Mason."

"You think so, Katie?" She could see how important this was to him, and she wished she had said it sooner. "Ah been thinkin', Katie, when Ah gits mah bearins, Ah sho' would like to come an' work fo' you. You wouldn't hafta pay me much. Mostly room an' boad."

"I'd love to have you, Mason, I really would, but I think you'd better stay on with the Eagans. Miss Janet needs you now, with Della gone. You're the only one who can help her. Charlotte can't do much around the house. But thank you for wanting to be with me, and I hope you'll call me if you ever need me. Will you do that?"

"Sho' will, Katie."

The old man cried and blew his nose. Then he was off in his buggy to the empty room behind the big house on St. Charles Avenue.

Chapter
FORTY-SEVEN

Katie watched Mason's buggy till it was out of sight. Then she turned her gaze up to her porch where a young soldier was sitting on her top step, cracking nuts in his palm. She smiled. He hadn't noticed her yet.

He had hung his hat on the back of a chair, and he sat bareheaded. As she watched, he picked slivers of nutmeat from a broken walnut shell. Then he disposed of the shell behind the bushes and put another pair of walnuts in his palm.

"So that's where all those walnut shells come from," Katie said, hands on her hips.

"Katie!" the soldier shouted, running down the steps.

"Warren!" she called back, and when they met, he picked her up and swung her around in a circle. "I didn't know you at first in your uniform! I guess I thought you'd look like the Confederate officer in *The Birth of a Nation*."

"Katie, you're dating me. That was three years ago."

"I know. But I've seen *all* your movies, and your hair was never this short."

"Army barbers are sadists. What can I tell you?"

"Oh, you're handsome just the same. It may be a good disguise to keep the fans from tearing you apart." She laughed. "There's something else different, too." She put her finger to her lips thoughtfully. "It's the mustache. That must be a late addition."

"It is," he said. "But you haven't changed a bit, Katie. You're as pretty and young as ever."

He reached out his hands and she placed her own in his. Katie was stunned by her brother-in-law's good looks. She could understand why women all over the country were mad about him. He was not only tall and well built, but his face was too perfect to believe. Dashing and dapper, the newspapers called him, but he was a whole lot more than that.

"Tell me, Katie. How are your boys?" he asked.

"Well, they're just the handsomest, most intelligent boys in the world. Johnny's eight and Tommy's six. Johnny's me all over, and Tommy looks like Stephen. They're at my sister's now. They'll be home soon and you can meet them."

She patted Warren's hand and they walked up the steps together. Katie sat on the swing and Warren took a rocking chair beside her.

"Katie, how long has it been?" Warren asked.

"Ten years, I think," Katie said.

"Incredible! Time stands still for you."

"Not so, but thank you just the same. I feel as if I've aged a hundred years since Stephen died."

"I know," he said. "It was a dreadful shock. Charlotte sent me a copy of the story in the *Picayune* right after the news broke. I just couldn't believe it, you know? I cried like a baby that night. I think I admired Stephen more than anyone on earth. I always wished I could have been more like him."

"Did you, Warren?" she asked.

"I thought about you, too, and my heart bled for you. I wished I could have come home right away, but I couldn't get leave."

"There were no services," she said. "They never recovered the body. So there was no need for anyone to come. I *did* get your note. I was grateful for that. There will be something in his honor later on, when the war is over, and the whole story can be told."

"I always enjoyed your letters, Katie," he said, "and the pictures of the boys. It was a touch of home, and it meant a lot to me."

"I enjoyed yours, too. They were witty and interesting, and say, that home of yours is a mansion!" She took Warren's hand again. "So, you're entertaining the troops," she said. "Well, what are you doing here? Are you on furlough?"

"No, we're putting on a show for Camp Martin tonight on the Loyola campus, and another for the naval station in Algiers tomorrow night."

"Really, Warren? One of my brothers-in-law was at Camp Martin, and the other one was stationed in Algiers."

"Where are they now?" Warren asked.

"Walter Garvey, that's Lala's husband, is recuperating in an army hospital in Paris, and Jenny's husband, Daren, is on a ship somewhere in Europe, probably right in the middle of all the fighting. We've been so worried about them both. Oh, Warren, do you think the war will be over soon?"

"The news is very encouraging. The Germans are wearing out. Everyone thinks they'll surrender soon. Maybe this fall."

"Wouldn't that be wonderful?" she asked. "What will you do then? Go back to Hollywood?"

"Oh, yes. I've got an agent lining up a picture or two."

"So you like it out there, Warren?"

"On a scale of one to ten?" he asked. "I'd say it's climate-ten, work-ten, people-zero."

"Then why do you stay? Aren't people the most important of all?"

"I stay because it's the only craft I know, and there's no place else I can make that much money."

"But what good is it all, if you're not happy?"

"Who's happy?" Warren asked, turning up his palms.

He stood up and unbuttoned the neck of his khaki jacket. The jodhpurs and puttees looked stunning on him. Katie could see now that he had been perspiring.

"Take off your coat," she said. "It's such a hot day. Let me get you something cool to drink. I think I have some lemonade in the icebox."

"Sounds good," Warren said, taking off his jacket. He draped it over a chair and rolled up his sleeves. "Let me come with you."

Warren followed her into the kitchen.

"First time I've been in your house," he said, looking around. "It's lovely. Really comfortable."

She stopped and looked into his eyes. She was remembering Stephen's remark that Warren had never come to his house.

"What is it?" he asked.

"Nothing," she said. What was to be gained by going into all that?

Katie poured two glasses of lemonade and they went back to sit on the porch.

"I stopped in to see my mother yesterday," he said. Katie listened raptly. He shook his head before speaking. "She's impossible. Completely impossible."

"What did she say?"

"Do you know that she still won't talk to me because I went to Hollywood to be in motion pictures? So all right, maybe it was a crazy kid's idea six years ago. But I've been successful. I've had good roles. I've made money." He shook his head again. "It wasn't what she wanted me to do, so I'm wiped out of her life. It doesn't matter that I've succeeded. Forget it. Sometimes I think it isn't just that Stephen and I didn't toe the mark. I think she just refuses to part with her precious money."

"I went to see her two weeks ago myself," Katie said. "I'd hoped we could be friends."

"You dreamer!" Warren said. "Don't tell me. She sent you away. She insulted you. Right?"

"Yes. Now I know why Stephen never went back all those years. But I did get to talk to Charlotte. I was glad of that."

"So did I. Poor Charlotte. She's nothing more than a prisoner there, in that dark, depressing house. If she ever left my mother to try to find some other kind of life, my mother would cut off her allowance. She's had proposals of marriage."

"Della said she had."

"Many. Even before I left home. But my mother always found something wrong with the men. It'll be just like Stephen. She'll have to give up her inheritance if she marries. Oh, the blessed family money!"

"I've been hearing about the family money for years. Just how rich *was* your father, Warren? Was he a millionaire?"

"Many times over."

"You're joking!"

"No, my dear," he said officiously. Katie wanted to laugh. For someone of twenty-seven, he had such an air of importance. And yet she really liked him. No, she admitted to herself, it was more than that. He excited her. There was an air of vitality about him. And she was bedazzled by his good looks.

"It was my grandfather, Franz Eagan, who really made the money," Warren explained. "There must have been more than twenty-four hours in his day, if you count the businesses he started. And everything he touched turned to gold. They've still got it all, my mother and Charlotte, in stocks and bonds."

"I had no idea there was so much," Katie said. "Stephen never talked about money . . . about the *Eagan* money. He cared nothing about it. The irony of the whole thing was that his mother thought she was hurting him by cutting him off." Katie shook her head. "All he ever wanted to do was to make a mark for himself in the field of electronics and be an inventor."

"Well, now that you know about the money, how do you feel? Disappointed?"

"Only for my sons, if it would have helped them in the future. Actually they may be better off without it."

"How do *you* get along, Katie? What income do you have? Tell me to mind my business, if you like. It's just that I care."

"We're really quite well off, but thank you for worrying. I have a great deal of money saved. And I get royalties from Stephen's five inventions. Did you know he had accomplished all that?"

"I didn't know he had even one."

"They're splendid inventions. Very commercial. They're all making lots of money."

"I'm flabbergasted! I hope you have a lawyer to advise you."

"I will have, if this war ever ends. My brother-in-law, Daren O'Toole, is my attorney."

"If I can make a suggestion, I'd like to see you invest some of your money in blue-chip stocks."

"Never!"

"What, then? Banks?"

"Not that, either."

"Well, Katie, what *do* you do with your savings?"

"I don't think I'll tell you. You'll laugh at me."

"I won't. Tell me. What are you putting your money in?"

She looked up at him from under lowered lids. "Coffee cans," she answered.

"Coffee cans. You're putting your money in coffee cans? What kind of dividend do you get?"

"Safety and security. No one can ever take my money away from me."

"You mean real coffee cans, now. The kind you get coffee out of?"

"Right. And I put real money in them, and I . . . hide them. If stocks decline, I don't give a hoot. If the banks close down, I don't care."

Warren threw back his head and laughed. Then he looked into her dark eyes.

"I told you you'd laugh," she said.

"Look, who am *I* to tell *you* what to do? You look like you've got it all figured out."

They smiled at each other and then they laughed. They laughed harder and harder until Katie had tears rolling down her cheeks. It was the first time she had laughed since Stephen died. She and Warren were both remembering the same episode.

"Remember the night you cracked my head with the slate?" he asked. "You really zeroed me, kiddo."

Katie laughed again. "You had it coming, Warren. You were a bad kid. I hope you don't grope like that anymore."

"In Hollywood, my dear Katie, it's required."

Katie blushed. She pulled at a strand of hair in front of her ear and twisted it around her finger. It was an old habit, something she did when she was embarrassed and trying not to show it, a habit Stephen had loved.

Warren felt something tug at his heart. It was not a new feeling when he was with Katie. He remembered the reading lessons years ago and the powerful physical urges she had innocently brought out in him even then. Innocent was still the word for Katie, and yet he sensed an earthiness about her that had never been tapped. After all the eroticism he had seen in Hollywood, he found himself more intrigued by the well-covered, adorable woman who sat beside him now than he had ever been by any other woman. He felt a momentary twinge of guilt, thinking of Katie that way, so soon after Stephen's death, but guilt never found a lasting home with Warren.

"You ought to come out to Hollywood some time, Katie," Warren said. "You should see a little more of the world. You have a little money and your boys are big enough to travel. You might even decide to live out there. The climate's fantastic."

"Oh, I don't know," she said. "I have no great desire to travel, and even less to relocate. New Orleans is my home. It's the place where I grew up. I'd be out of place anywhere else."

"What's so great about it?" he asked. "You grew up in poverty on Julia Row, and you hated it. I grew up with money on St. Charles Avenue and *I* hated it. Maybe there's something else, you know?"

She looked at him seriously. "I don't think life is much different anywhere else."

"Oh, my dear, you would be surprised."

Katie laughed at his affectation.

"Look, darling," he said theatrically, "I'm going to be in town about a week. I have permission from my C.O. to live at home while I'm here, but my mother's bounced me out, so how about letting me bunk here? I promise not to be a bother."

"A bother? The boys will be delighted. They'll have their friends lined up to see you for a nickel. Watch what I tell you."

Warren laughed. "Beats a lemonade stand," he said. "No overhead."

"And I'll be delighted, too," Katie said, looking into his blue-gray eyes.

"You're an angel. Can I take you and the boys to Galatoire's tonight?"

A shadow passed over her eyes. "Stephen asked me to go there once," she said.

"Did you?"

"No."

"Then there are no sad memories."

She shook her head no.

"Get the boys dressed when they come home," he said. "Tell them their Uncle Warren's taking them to dinner tonight."

Chapter
FORTY-EIGHT

Soon after his ordination, Davey was assigned as a novice priest to St. Rose de Lima parish, and given all the jobs no one else wanted—moderator of the Ladies' Altar Society, youth counselor, altar-boy instructor. But to Davey each was a sacred trust, and he charged into them all energetically.

Every Sunday he had dinner with Katie, Jenny, Lala, and the three children. Everyone had a hard time getting a word in edgewise. Davey wanted advice from his sisters on holding teen dances in his new parish. Jenny and Lala had news from their husbands in service. Walter was to receive a medical discharge and would be coming home in a few weeks. Lala couldn't wait for him to see the baby.

Warren's troupe was performing for wounded soldiers in hospitals in the South in the summer of 1918. When weekends came, if he wasn't too far from New Orleans, he hopped a train or thumbed a ride and wound up on Katie's doorstep, and she was always glad to see him. At the dinner table Johnny always begged him for stories about the movie stars he saw at the picture show.

"Uncle Warren, do you know Fatty Arbuckle?" the child asked one Sunday.

"Oh, yes. They call him the Prince of Whales." After a few seconds of total silence, the adults groaned at the pun, but the little boys frowned, not understanding. "I went to a big party they gave for him last year when he signed his new contract with Paramount."

"Tell us about the party, Uncle Warren," Johnny asked.

This was where the story ended. How could he tell this wholesome family about an all-night drunken frolic with a dozen girls stripping on the tabletops, and the corpulent Arbuckle joining them? Katie had said life was not much different anywhere else. How could she possibly know?

"Oh, it was just a real nice party, with lots of movie stars," Warren finished.

Katie eyed him quizzically. She knew Warren the man, the soldier, the brother-in-law, but she did not know Warren the actor. That was the hidden side of his life that he never talked about.

In August Warren got two weeks furlough, and he suggested to Katie that they open the camp at Milneburg and spend their vacation there. Nobody ever used the place. They'd take the boys, and Katie's sisters could come along if they liked. There was plenty of room. They'd just have to remember that it was very old-fashioned, with commodes and mosquito nets. They could have a good time, swimming and crabbing and have picnics on the beach.

To Katie it sounded wonderful. She was twenty-seven years old, and she'd never had a vacation in her life. The thought occurred to her that there'd be ghosts of Stephen there, running out on the pier, bronzed and beautiful. But weren't there ghosts of Stephen everywhere? Even deep down inside her? No, she wouldn't let that stop her. She decided to take her vacation and enjoy it.

Walter Garvey had come home at the end of July, and he and Lala were cooing like a pair of lovebirds, so they declined the invitation. But Jenny was eager for company and she accepted.

The camp was everything Katie had expected, with its four big bedrooms, its large family room and kitchen, and the gallery all around where, as Della used to say, "the breeze was strong enough to knock you down." It was built up on stilts out over the water and attached to the beach by a long pier with a hand railing. The railing was broken in places and some of the slats in the pier were missing, and Katie had to caution the boys to look down as they walked, or they might fall through.

"Is it deep?" Johnny asked.

"No, it's shallow," Warren said, "but you might fall against the pilings and hurt yourself."

Katie and Jenny spent the first day brushing away cobwebs, cleaning and dusting and mopping. Warren did the necessary repairs, replacing slats in the pier and covering the biggest gaps in the roof. Late in the afternoon of the first day, they were all ready for a swim.

The children had been in their bathing suits all day, but they had waited obediently for the adults to go in swimming with them. Warren had found two fishing poles for them at the camp and baited their hooks, and the boys had sat most of the day on the pier, hoping to get a bite.

Katie changed into her bathing suit in Janet's old room. Janet's bathing clothes, her rubber shoes, her ruffled caps were all in the closet. Katie felt like an interloper. This had been Janet's camp, and her father's before her. It wasn't so very long ago that she had enjoyed herself here with her children. How could a woman have wrapped herself up in bitterness and closed herself off so completely from the world?

Out on the pier that extended still further into the water beyond the camp, wooden steps led down into the water. Katie let her little boys down and looked about her. Other camps extended out into the water alongside them in both directions as far as the eye could see.

Many camps were connected to their neighbors' camps by piers. She remembered Treece telling her once that the whole thing looked like a "great big spider." And so it did.

The next two weeks were the laziest Katie could ever remember. She lounged for hours on the pier, watching her boys play in the water. Sometimes she read. Sometimes she just soaked up sun and had long talks with Jenny or Warren.

"Warren, do you know Theda Bara?" Jenny asked one day.

"Sure do. Great girl. Always good for a laugh."

"The vamp? I find that hard to believe."

"Now I'm going to shatter *all* your illusions. Her real name is Theodosia Goodman and she's the daughter of a Jewish tailor from Chilicothe, Ohio."

Jenny's jaw dropped and Katie laughed out loud, and they both vowed they'd never believe the movie columns again.

One afternoon Warren stretched out beside her on the pier. He had brought her a glass of lemonade from the icebox. She sat up, cross-legged, to talk to him.

"Warren, who owns this camp?" she asked.

"My mother," he said. "Doesn't my mother own everything?" He laughed cynically. "Well, actually, it was her father's, old Grandpa Charbonnet."

"What about her sisters? Do they have any claim to it?"

"One is dead; she had no children. The other one sold her share to my mother, so the camp is legally hers. Mother used to love this camp."

"But she never comes here anymore," Katie said.

"Oh, she'll never come here again," Warren said confidently.

"Well, what I'm getting at is . . . it will pass on to *you*, someday."

"And Charlotte. And you. Equal parts."

"Well then, isn't it a shame to let it go to waste in the meantime?" Katie asked. "I think we ought to fix it up. What do you think?"

"I say let's do it."

"No one can accuse us of anything if we're putting something *in* instead of taking something *out*, can they?" Katie asked.

"No one will even know." He smiled his handsome smile.

Katie clasped her hands together. "Oh, Warren, there are so many things I'd love to do. I'd love to paint the place and screen the porch, and have a brand new pier built, safe and strong . . ."

"And a new roof," Warren added. "And while we're at it, we ought to put in a first-class bathroom."

"Wonderful! Oh, we'll make it a little paradise! And you and I will split the costs, okay?"

"Terrific! Put 'er there, partner."

He held out his hand and Katie put her hand in his. He longed to reach out for her, but he let her hand go and tried to hide his feelings. He was surprised by the intensity of his emotions. He cleared his throat and tried to pick up the conversation.

"You can bring the boys out here on weekends even after I go back to California," he said.

"Oh, Warren, do you have to go?" she asked.

"Yes, I do," he said, brushing the hair from her forehead with his fingertips. "As soon as this war is over, there are three parts waiting for me. That's what Mr. Ten Percent tells me, and the money's too good to pass up."

He sat beside Katie and they dangled their brown legs over the side of the pier. "I'd like to line up some contractors to start doing these repairs," he said. "They can be doing the renovations while I'm in Hollywood."

"That's good, Warren," Katie said without enthusiasm. "But it just won't be as much fun without you here."

"I'm glad of that," he said. "I want you to miss me."

"Well, look, when you finish those movies, don't sign for any more. Save your money and sell your big house in Bel-Air and come back here."

"I can't do that, Katie. It's the only work I know, and I love it. My future looks very promising. If I came back here, I couldn't even pump gasoline in a filling station."

Katie didn't argue. Of course it made sense, but she was disappointed just the same.

"California is so darned far away," she said.

On November 11, the Armistice was signed, and the war in Europe ended. In the house on Moss Street they all laughed and cried and hugged each other. They drank two bottles of wine, and no one was sober when they went to bed.

Within weeks Daren O'Toole was home, and Jenny was delirious with happiness. Jenny and Lala both became pregnant right away. Jenny was euphoric. Before the war she had begun to think she would never have any children.

Warren was discharged and had to report without delay to his studio in Hollywood. He didn't even get to come home. Shooting was to begin on a movie at once. Katie missed him terribly and realized how much she had enjoyed his company and come to rely on his advice.

One evening, soon after Daren returned, Katie invited Jenny and Daren to dinner. She wanted to talk to Daren about her savings. Her conversation with Warren had unsettled her. It wasn't that she had changed her mind about banks, but the savings were now so large as to be unwieldy. There was over ten thousand dollars in small bills in the coffee cans. The basement was damp and the cans would in time corrode. She did not intend to let her life's savings deteriorate or become a banquet for a pack of roving mice.

"I'm still not interested in stocks, Daren," she said. "I'm afraid of them. I'm afraid of banks, too. I know that seems ridiculous, but it's a carry-over from my childhood. My mother never had an extra penny to her name. I'm not going to let that happen to me. I want to be custodian of my own money. But if there's something else you could suggest that would give me a return on my investment, maybe I should consider it."

"Yes, I have a very good suggestion, Katie," Daren said. "Real estate. Right now, with all the men coming back from Europe, there'll be a marriage boom and a baby boom. Every young family in America will be looking for a place to live. Rental property will be at a premium and rents will go sky-high. If I were you, I'd take whatever money I could spare and buy a bunch of doubles to rent."

"Doubles. To rent. Now that sounds like something I wouldn't mind putting my money into. It's something real, something I could always sell, if I had to, and get my money back."

"Right. And in the meantime, you'd be getting income from it."

"I'll do it. How do I go about it?"

"I have a friend who's in real estate. I'll have him call you and show you some property. And I'll tell you something else, Katie. Buy land. Raw land. This city's going to grow in all directions. Land along the lakefront, even as far as Milneburg, is going to sell for a fortune someday. And not too long from now."

Katie was elated with her new interest. For two weeks she and Ed Weisner, the real-estate agent, walked through every double for sale in the City Park area. In the end she bought five frame shotgun doubles on Grand Route St. John. Weisner couldn't do enough for her after that. He checked court records to see who owned huge tracts of lakefront property. Even though they were not listed with his company or *any* company, he helped her present her offers. Three of her offers were accepted, and Katie was now the owner of ten acres of land in the slowly developing area that would in time be called Lakeview.

With both her boys in school Katie had time to think about selling real estate herself. What Ed Weisner had done didn't look too hard. The prospect held tremendous appeal. What a thrill it must be to show property and sell it! she thought. And Daren had said there would be such a demand that it would be easy to sell.

She telephoned Ed Weisner one morning.

"Tell me something, will you?" she asked. "How difficult is it to get into real estate?"

"For whom?"

"For me."

"Oh, Mrs. Eagan, I don't know," he said. "There aren't many women in the field."

"Well, there's going to be one more," she said. "Tell me what I have to do."

Weisner gave her a book of real-estate terms and procedures. He taught her how to knock on doors in search of listings, which he would then advertise in the newspapers. He took her with him when he showed property and taught her how to prepare the forms. Sensing an alert and enthusiastic attitude in the young woman, he offered to let her answer the telephone in his office when he was out. If she made appointments that turned into sales, he would split the commission with her.

The first few months were slow, but at last, one day, she showed a client a fifteen-thousand-dollar house. The couple walked through once, inscrutable of expression, and then announced, "We'll take it." Katie felt weak in the knees. She wondered if she would still remember how to write up the purchase agreement. She drew her forms from her briefcase and wrote up the offer, full amount, in cash. In one transaction she had made a four-hundred-fifty-dollar commission.

She felt like kicking up her heels all the way home.

She couldn't wait to tell Ed Weisner. She couldn't wait to tell Warren. Warren! *This* was a business he could go into if he came back to live in New Orleans. Real estate. All he needed was an office and a telephone, and later on, a broker's license. That wouldn't be hard for Warren. He was smart as a whip. And the women would swoon over him.

They could go into business together, with Katie answering the phone and making appointments, and Warren showing the property and making the sales. They could both take listings and, once a week they could tour the new properties together. The best part of it was, they'd have first dibs on bargains before they advertised them to the public. They'd buy rental property together, renovate it and rent it, or sell it if they could make a good profit.

She decided to continue working hard for the next few months. Then she'd know if her sale had been beginner's luck or if she could really make a success of real estate. After that she'd suggest it to Warren and see if she could talk him into coming back home and going into business with her.

Chapter
FORTY-NINE

Charlotte paced the corridor outside her mother's door. Twice she approached the door and lifted her hand to knock but changed her mind. She *had* to talk to her mother, but she trembled inwardly, wondering if she could find the right words. Were there any right words? She was still intimidated by Janet, but she wouldn't take no for an answer this time. She had to get away from this house and from her mother, before it was too late.

At last she found the courage to knock.

"Come in," Janet said.

Janet watched her daughter walk obsequiously into the room, head bent, as if she were on her way to confession. As always Janet was in her chair, her hands resting on the head of her cane.

"Well," Janet said. "What is it, Charlotte?"

Charlotte sat down on the side of her mother's bed. She tried to hold her head up bravely, but her eyelids remained lowered.

"I have something to tell you, Mother," she said.

"Well?" Janet asked again.

"I'm going to be married."

"Just like that. You don't ask me. You tell me."

"This time, yes, I'm telling you, Mother, because I'm going to marry this man, whether you like it or not."

"Don't be too sure about that," Janet said. A frown creased her brow. "Well, where did you meet him?"

"At West End Park."

"And who introduced you?"

"Oh, Mother, you *are* ridiculous! What do you want me to tell you? That we sang together in the choir and we were formally introduced by the bishop? Well, I'm not going to say that, because I'm through with lying. I drove out there alone and he picked me up. He bought me a drink and he took me home. He kissed me, too, the very first night, and he's kissed me a lot more since. Do you want any more details?"

"There's no need to try to shock me, Charlotte. And I'm not interested in any lurid descriptions. I'm simply trying to protect you, you foolish girl. You are an heiress."

"Not as long as *you*'re alive, I'm not."

"You'll be a millionairess someday, Charlotte. Are you so naïve that you don't know there are opportunists lurking about who might know your every move? They could situate themselves for what would appear to be a 'chance' encounter . . ."

Charlotte rested her head on the foot of the bed. "I'm going to marry him, Mother," she said evenly.

"What is his name?"

"His name is George Hammond."

"Hammond? Hammond?" Janet said, frowning. "I don't know that name."

"I was waiting for that," Charlotte said, laughing cynically. "That's your famous line. 'I don't know that name.' Meaning, of course, that he isn't a Charbonnet or a De la Vergne or any of the other Creoles of the inner circle, and therefore he is unacceptable."

"If you know that, Charlotte, why do you put us both through this?"

"For ten years you've been cheating me out of happiness. I've had five proposals, Mother. In every case the man wasn't good enough. He wasn't rich enough, or else his great-grandfather didn't fight in the French and Indian War. And every time I let you do it to me. That's what's so hard to believe. But not this time."

"Don't be melodramatic, Charlotte. How old is this man?"

"He's forty-five. What difference does that make?"

"He's old enough to dupe you. You see him as a father figure."

"And if he were twenty-five, he'd be too young for me. He'd be flattering me, appealing to my vanity. Look, Mother, no age is the right age. And no man is the right man."

"Well, certainly not this one."

"Then you won't even see him?"

"Absolutely out of the question."

"I'm going to marry him, Mother. I'm thirty years old. This may be my very last chance, and I'm taking it."

"Then you'd better be prepared to live on love, my dear," Janet said. "That is, if this Hammond person is willing to marry you, after he finds out you won't come into a penny until after I die."

Charlotte got up from the bed. She stood in the middle of the floor, facing her mother. "So that's the way you have it figured out. He *has* to be a fortune hunter, right? Because, after all, who else could want poor Charlotte? What kind of an idiot could possibly love her for herself?"

"Has he seen this house?" Janet asked. "And your car? And your diamond rings?"

"Yes, of course, he has, but he loves *me*!" she said, touching her breast with her fingertips. "He doesn't need my money. He's a very wealthy man."

"He would like you to think so. You'd hardly fall in love with a pauper. What does he do?"

"I'm not exactly sure. He's inherited money and he's made some wise investments."

"That sounds general enough. Where does he live?"

"He lives at the St. Charles Hotel. He spends money like confetti. He buys lavish meals. He makes big bets at the track."

"Very impressive. He's putting on a good show." Janet got up and walked to the window. "First of all, nobody lives at the St. Charles Hotel. He's set himself up there to spring his trap. And you, my dear, are the pigeon. It's the oldest ruse of all. They're artists, these fortune hunters. They make huge loans, give themselves the proper backdrop, and dress like tycoons until they marry an heiress. It's worth a big investment when you're after stakes like these."

Charlotte trembled. She sat on the bed and lowered her head to her hand. "Why can't you believe me?" she asked. "He loves me for myself."

"You'd better be sure of that, Charlotte, before you leave this house, because if you go to him, your monthly income will be cut off. Not one penny will you get from me. You know I mean what I say. Be sure, for your own sake, that you tell him your financial situation before you marry him. Then see what he does. I will never agree to buy you a blackguard for a husband and let him put the family fortune in his pocket."

"The family fortune!" Charlotte shouted, pounding the bed with her fist. "You make me sick with that. You haven't found anyone in the family yet who wanted it. Both Stephen and Warren threw it in your face and walked out. And I can see it was a small price to pay to be rid of you."

She got up from the bed and strode over to the door. Her mother's voice stopped her.

"Stephen and Warren were men, Charlotte. You're a woman. If this man abandons you, you won't be welcome here, and there's no way in the world you can support yourself. You don't know a skill or a trade. You don't even know how to cook or keep house."

Charlotte smirked. "I hope you're proud of what you've made of me," she said. "The only thing I'm fit for is to keep you company. Is that what you had in mind all along?"

Janet retraced her steps to her chair. Charlotte

walked toward her and gripped the arms of the chair, her eyes narrowed with hatred.

"Why don't you die?" she asked. "And give us all a chance to live?"

Then she walked across the floor and into the corridor.

Chapter
FIFTY

Charlotte telephoned for a taxi and hurriedly packed a suitcase. She wasn't sure what to take. Night clothes? Toiletries? What was she planning to do? She decided on a few changes of underwear, hosiery, another dress or two. She'd go to George, of course, at the St. Charles, but what would she say to him? "My mother refuses her consent, but I've left home and here I am, bag and baggage." Would that be it? It was so awkward. They couldn't get married this evening; it was much too late already.

In the meantime what was she to do? One thing was certain. She could not spend another night with her mother. After what she had said to her, the break was clean and permanent. So where would she sleep, then? In George's bed? Is that what her arrival would announce to him? She felt her cheeks burning and she pressed her hands to them to cool them.

The taxi was prompt, and soon she was out in the January twilight, on the corner of St. Charles and Common streets, looking down the avenue at the row of awnings that slanted out over the sidewalks of the hotel. There had not been time to telephone George. She wouldn't have known what to tell him anyway. And she couldn't run the risk that her mother would hear the conversation. So here she was with her suitcase, ready to camp on her sweetheart's doorstep, a helpless spinster of thirty years old, with the door to the family home closed solidly behind her.

The lobby was warm and bright as the last rays of evening sun streamed in through the skylight. It was a mammoth lobby, two stories high, supported by colossal marble columns and surrounded by a mezzanine balcony. At the far end was a magnificent staircase that parted at a landing and continued in two directions to the mezzanine.

Guests were milling about in the lobby, clustering in little groups on velvet sofas. Ladies in flowing dresses of crepe-de-Chine and chiffon gathered in groups to set out for the evening. It was the dinner hour. Charlotte wished she had changed from the sweater and skirt she was wearing. Her casual attire made her conspicuous in the grand hotel. Now she prayed she would not run into anyone she knew. The St. Charles was all too familiar to Charlotte. Many of the debutante functions were held there, and she still attended the annual soirees, even though her own debut was more than ten years past.

Self-consciously she approached the registration desk. She knew that if she asked for the number of Mr. Hammond's room, she would certainly have to explain who she was. The clerk would see the luggage. What would he think?

"Charlotte?" a familiar voice said. She turned to see George Hammond standing behind her, smiling, wearing an amused and surprised expression.

She was so relieved to see him that she dropped the suitcase and threw her arms around his neck.

"Oh, George, I'm so glad to see you," she said. "I just . . . I can't . . ."

"Now, now, now, dear," he said, taking her hands in his. "You seem distraught. What is it? How can I help you?"

She reached for the suitcase.

"Here, let me take that," he said. Then, looking from the suitcase to Charlotte, he asked, "Are you going somewhere?"

"Just here," she said, lowering her eyes and blushing. "I really must explain." Crowds jostled them. "Do you think we could sit down somewhere?"

"Of course," he said, leading her toward a sofa. "Or better yet, why don't we leave your suitcase in my suite and go to dinner? Have you eaten yet?"

"No. I'd love to go. Thank you."

"I can't tell you how happy I am to see you," George said as he led her across the lobby to the bank of elevators. She drew in a deep breath. Everything was going to be all right. Why had she doubted him? He had told her that he loved her and she believed him. It was her mother's cruelty that had stirred up all her doubts and fears. George was here with her now, his arm linked with hers, and he had said he was glad to see her.

What a fine-looking, distinguished man he was! He was not much taller than Charlotte, but broad shouldered and narrow at the waist for his age. He wore his clothes splendidly. He had a full head of dark hair, and his silver sideburns were startling by contrast. His salt-and-pepper mustache was immaculately barbered. Even her mother would have been impressed with George Hammond. Well, Janet had given up her chance to know him. Charlotte and George would be married as soon as arrangements could be made, and Charlotte would go on living in the style to which she was accustomed, except that she'd never have to see her mother again.

George would take care of her from now on. As far as tonight's accommodations were concerned, she'd worry about that later. He was far too much of a gentleman to expect any privileges before marriage. Her heart was suddenly lighter than it had been in a long time.

"You're looking especially lovely tonight, my dear," he said. "Your complexion is radiant. Has something happened to give you such a glow?"

"I'm here. With you," she said boldly.

He took her hand and they stepped from the elevator. As they approached George's suite, Charlotte's breath quickened. Her thoughts flew in every direction. What if he thought the reason she had come was to go to bed with him, to make love to him? By the time he had turned the key in the lock, terror gripped her and her mouth went dry. He had released her hand, and she found herself backing away, almost preparing to run if she had to.

In one swift movement George Hammond swung the suitcase into the room and locked the door again. "Now, my dear," he said, looking back at Charlotte, "what would you say to a little aperitif to whet the appetite?" He took her arm and led her back to the elevator.

Oh, what a fool I am! she told herself. What a bloody, childish fool! This man has no improper designs on me. I suspect deception everywhere. My mind has been corrupted to think everyone is evil. Once again she turned a trusting smile to her fiancé.

"Thank you, George," she said, "for putting my suitcase in your room."

Hammond smiled. From the elevator they crossed the lobby and descended a short flight of steps to an arcaded walk on the ground level. The walkway, flanked by rose gardens, was paved with brick and spanned at intervals by arched portals. Beneath the arches were wicker chairs, to which George escorted Charlotte.

"I think the night is warm enough for us to enjoy our drinks out here," George said. "But tell me if you're cool, now, will you?"

"Yes, George," Charlotte said. "This is such a lovely garden. As often as I've been to the hotel, I've never been down this way." She fingered a frond of a potted palm that stood beside her chair.

"Yes. I'm very fond of this walk. It's private. We can talk here."

A waiter appeared from nowhere and George ordered white wine for them both.

He crossed his legs and laced his fingers together. On his little finger Charlotte caught the glitter of a huge diamond. She could tell that he was at ease in expensive clothes and fine surroundings. He was accustomed to giving orders and being waited on. This was the man who had asked her to marry him. A wave of love swept over her, and she knew that everything was going to be all right.

"Now, darling," George said. "Are you feeling better?"

"Oh, yes."

"Then tell me what this is all about. Why have you done me this honor tonight?"

"I know you'll think this is silly, George, but . . . I had an argument with my mother and I left the house. I had nowhere else to go and I . . ."

"You came to me. Just as you should. I want to take care of you always, whenever you need me."

Many times she had spoken to George of arguments with her mother. The night they had met, she had driven out to West End Park after just such an argument. He had driven her car home for her that night and had seen the house, so he *had* to know they were enormously wealthy. She had told him her father was dead, so he knew, too, that her mother controlled the money. Was he wondering, even now, if they had argued today about his proposal of marriage? Did he suspect that her mother had refused consent and threatened to cut off her income? His steady dark eyes hinted nothing.

The waiter brought the wine and George signed the check. They lifted their glasses and sipped the golden liquid. She decided not to give George the details just yet. Maybe she couldn't bear to know how he would react. She felt the wine burn its way down her throat and she waited for the glow that always followed. She wanted to enjoy that heady feeling a little longer. She wanted to have dinner with George and watch the tiny lines around his eyes as he called her his "dear girl." She loved him and she was grateful to him.

The dining room was familiar to Charlotte, with its exposed beams and tiled floors. The light fixtures were electrified gasoliers, and the tables were laid with snow-white linen and sparkling crystal and silver.

"Good evening, Mr. Hammond," the waiter said. He led them to a window table and handed George the menu. The man backed away to a respectful distance, awaiting George's pleasure. George scanned the menu. He motioned the waiter and questioned the availability of a certain wine not shown on the wine list. The waiter said he would check.

George took Charlotte's hand where it lay on the table. "My dear," he said, "what are you in the mood for tonight? Pompano? Trout meunière? Or would you rather a filet?"

"Trout, I think," she said.

When the waiter returned, George ordered in French for them both. His French was impeccable. Every word he said and every move he made fortified her faith in his integrity.

After dinner George suggested a walk around the lobby and the mezzanine. He spoke incessantly as they walked, explaining many things about the history of the hotel, which Charlotte already knew, but she loved the resonance of his voice and his superb articulation. The walk ended at the registration desk where George spoke softly with the clerk. The clerk nodded and reached for a key in the wall behind him. Then he turned the registration book around on its swivel.

"My dear," George said to Charlotte, "will you sign for your room, please?"

Charlotte smiled gratefully, assured once again of his honor.

"Are you tired," he asked, "or would you like to walk outdoors before you retire?"

"I'd like that very much," she said.

The night had gotten chilly, but the air felt good on her face. George spoke about his afternoon at the racetrack, relating how he had won "quite a bundle" on Little Lil, a long shot.

"Did you go alone?" Charlotte asked, holding on to his arm possessively.

"No, as a matter of fact I went with a friend. A gentleman." He stopped walking and looked into her eyes. "Why, Charlotte, I do believe you're jealous."

"I guess I am," she said shyly, "of anyone who shares your company."

"And why should you be? You're my sweetheart, aren't you?"

"Yes."

"Haven't I told you that I love you?"

"Yes."

"And that I want to marry you?"

"Oh, George, I had to hear you say it once again. Can we please be married right away?"

"Nothing would make me happier. Just as soon as we can get the license."

"And how soon is that?"

"Why, tomorrow morning, if you like."

"Oh, George, I *do* want to be your wife. Can we really be married tomorrow?"

"Of course we can, my darling." He took her face between his hands and kissed her softly. "Oh, Charlotte, you've made me a very happy man."

"Can we go back now, George, please?" she asked. "I think I *will* go to my room. I've had a difficult day, and I *do* want to be up early in the morning."

"Of course, my love." He consulted his watch. "I think I'll turn in, too."

He stopped at the front desk for his own key, and they got into the elevator together. When it stopped at the third floor, she looked at George.

"Is my room on your floor?" she asked.

"Oh, yes. I got you the room adjoining mine." Charlotte felt an icy fear sweep over her. "Please don't be offended, my love. I just wanted you to be near me if you needed me. You can lock your door from the inside, and I suggest you do," he said, smiling boyishly. "I have no intentions of forcing myself on you, with our wedding just a day away, but then, I *am* in love, and I'm only human."

Charlotte blushed crimson, but she nodded and tried to keep her composure. George had spoken frankly, but he had just wanted to set her mind at ease.

At Charlotte's door George turned the key and pushed the door open.

"Let me show you where the connecting door is, and make sure it's locked," he said. Embarrassed, Charlotte followed him and watched him try the knob.

"Satisfied?" he asked.

She nodded, turning her eyes away.

"Now, then," he said, "let me get your suitcase from my suite."

In seconds he was back. He placed the suitcase in her room, but this time he did not enter. He remained in the corridor and kissed her respectfully, barely brushing his lips to hers.

"Sleep well, my love," he said. "Tomorrow we will be man and wife. I'll see you in the morning. We'll have breakfast together downstairs."

Charlotte dimpled and nodded.

"I'll knock at your door at eight," he said.

Charlotte touched his face and reached up to kiss him again. "I love you, George," she said. "You're the most wonderful man I've ever known and I know we'll be happy together."

He squeezed her hands and walked down the hall to his room.

Inside her room Charlotte leaned against the door and sighed. A smile changed her features from those of a worried spinster to those of a girl in love.

She whirled around the room like a dancer, too excited to think about sleeping. She opened the suitcase and looked at what she had brought. There was a lovely nightgown she had never worn. It was white with pink-ribbon beading around a square-cut neckline, and gathers above the bosom, which flattered her boyish figure.

She pulled the gown from the valise, undressed herself, and put it on. Then she brushed her teeth and let her hair down, loosening the thick rolls of hair that covered her ears. She brushed her long hair vigorously until it fell in loose waves down her back. She pinched her cheeks to bring the blood to them and licked her lips. Then she walked barefoot in the carpet to a full-length mirror on the closet door. She could not believe the girl who stood before her. She was lovely! Not beautiful, but lovely!

More than anything on earth she wanted George to see her this way. She looked so young and fresh and vibrant. He had never seen her hair combed down or her eyes so full of love. But she dared not turn that lock! She could not risk it for fear that he would never respect her again. She turned down her bed and lay back on the pillow, gazing at the medallion on the ceiling. After a time she turned out her light, but she did not sleep.

An hour passed. There was no sleep in her at all. Too much had happened in one day, and too much lay before her for her mind to relax. Only a panel of wood stood between her and the man she was to marry! Surely he would be in bed. She could simply turn back his covers and get in beside him. She turned over and buried her face in her pillow at the thought of it. It was so bold! What would her mother say? The thought of her mother was the flame that set her afire. Suddenly she was out of bed and on her feet.

She brushed her hair again and walked over to the door. She drew in a deep breath and turned the key. On quiet, bare feet she walked to George's bed and stood there waiting. In seconds his eyes opened and he saw her.

He did not speak, and there was no need for her to speak. He turned back the linens and moved over to make room for her. Then he took her hand and drew her down into his arms.

"Oh, my darling," he said. "My dear girl."

He caressed her arms, and she felt small and thin and boyish in his embrace. He kissed her deeply, in a way she had never been kissed before. She felt aroused, but she could not relax and let it sweep over her. His hands were beneath her gown on her small, flat breasts. She was mortified to have so little to offer him, but George seemed not to be dismayed. He continued to caress her and he kissed her lips hungrily.

Suddenly Charlotte was aware that George was nude beneath the linens. Now she felt the warmth of his thighs against hers. She panicked. All the years of convent training and the taboos of a sexless mother had left their mark. She was sick with guilt and scared to death. She girded herself for pain, and let out a little cry when it came. She felt as if a knife were searing her body, splitting it in two. Perspiration broke out on her face. She sobbed like a child and clutched George's shoulder. And then she felt the hot blood running down her legs.

"I'm sorry," she whispered, trying to draw away.

"Wait just a minute," George said gently, holding her close.

She didn't move. Only her sobs broke the stillness. Then, suddenly, his body shuddered as passion overwhelmed him in an explosive climax. It seemed an eternity to Charlotte that she heard his moans of pleasure and she felt the weight of his body, smothering her.

At last he fell limp and rolled away and lay quietly beside her. He rested for a time, breathing evenly. Then he stroked her hair and touched her face gently.

"Charlotte," he said. "I love you very much."

Charlotte did not answer. She wanted to cry, from the unexpected pain and the emotional fatigue, but she restrained herself. He had hurt her badly. She was lying in a pool of blood, and she didn't know what to do next. Should she get up? She wasn't even sure she *could* get up. She had never felt less tenderness for George.

"Come, my dear," he said, helping her out of bed. "I'll get you towels and you can take a nice warm bath." He gave her his robe and brought her to the bathroom.

With the door closed behind her, Charlotte let her stained gown drop to the floor. She ran a tub of water and twisted her hair on top of her head. She lay in the water a few minutes, letting its warmth heal her. Then she washed and dried off briskly with a thick, soft towel and put on George's robe.

When she returned to the bedroom, George had removed the soiled sheets and he was putting on fresh ones. Then he held his arms out to her and she came to him. Together they lay on the clean bed, and he held her gently, tenderly, whispering words of love. She began to feel warm and content in his embrace.

"You were a virgin," he said.

"Of course," she answered brusquely. "I've never been married. We are conventional, religious people in my family."

"I know you are. I was simply stating a fact. That's why it hurt so much. I'm sorry, darling. It will be better the next time, and every time after."

She wondered why she had been so quick to take umbrage. After all, she had come to him like a slut in the night. Why shouldn't he think she had done this before? And why had she been so eager to defend the ways of her family? They had made her what she was, a pathetic old spinster who had nothing to offer a man. She couldn't even make love properly.

"Do you really love me, George?" she asked, needing constant reassurance.

"How can you ask me that? Of course I do. I love you with all my heart. Tomorrow you'll be my wife."

"Then you must let me tell you what happened today with my mother," she said. Did the arms that held her tighten just a bit? Or was she imagining it? "I told my mother you had asked me to marry you."

"I thought that was what had happened. Go ahead."

"I told her I had said yes. She was indignant that I had not *asked* her. My mother is a tyrannical woman. You have to understand that."

"So you've told me."

"She asked me every imaginable question about you. Where we met. How old you were. What you did for a living."

"And what did you answer her?"

"What you told me, that you had inherited money and made wise investments."

"Hmm. And what did she say to that?"

"I don't know how to tell you this, George. It's ridiculous, I know, but that is why I left home. My mother thinks you are a fortune hunter. Now, say whatever you like. I told you it was ridiculous."

"Of course, my dear, but we've got to make her see that it isn't so."

"No one on earth could convince her of that. I told her what a wonderful man you are, how well-bred and dignified. I told her how much you loved me. I told her you were a wealthy man in your own right, that you didn't need *my* money."

"And?"

"She said it was a ruse. She said you were an artist, baiting a trap for me. Absurd, isn't it?"

"Of course. Yes. Absurd. So then what happened?"

"I begged her to meet you. She refused. She said she would never give her consent."

"We can marry without it, my dear. You're of age."

"Of course, that's true," Charlotte said, "but what we have to face is the fact that I'll not receive a cent of the family money until the day Mother dies."

"Did she say that?"

"Most emphatically. And my mother doesn't make idle threats. I have both my brothers as proof of that."

"Well, can she do that, legally?"

"She has usufruct of my father's estate as long as she lives. She has been keeping me on an allowance. A generous one. But even that is gone now."

"Hmm." George was silent for a time. "Well, we'll simply have to go back and talk to her. I cannot allow you to make such a sacrifice for me."

"There's no going back," Charlotte said peremptorily. "The door has been closed. I cannot tell you how final that is with my mother." She touched the face of the man who lay beside her. "But it doesn't matter, George. We can be more than comfortable on your investments. That's obvious to me. You live well. Whatever I've lost, it was worth it to me to get away from her and spend the rest of my life with you."

"I love you for that," he said, kissing her forehead. "But would you tell me, just to satisfy my curiosity, how much of a fortune were you to inherit?" When Charlotte hesitated, he added teasingly, "Just so I'll know how much your love was tested."

She smiled and rested her hand on his chest.

"Each of my father's children would have been worth at least a million dollars."

George coughed. He coughed again. A spasm of coughing followed, and at last he got up out of bed. When it had passed, he took Charlotte's hands in his.

"I love you, darling," he said. "Please don't worry about anything. I'll take care of everything, from now on. Now I want you to go to your own room to sleep. You'll rest much better there by yourself."

"But George, I wanted to sleep with you."

"We'll have plenty of time for that. It would be more discreet, my love, if we were not together if anyone knocked at the door."

"Of course. You're right," Charlotte said.

She kissed her fiancé and bid him good night. Then back in her own room, she fell heavily into bed. Her body had stopped aching now, and her mind was at rest. George knew she was penniless, and still he wanted to marry her. By tomorrow she would be Mrs. George Hammond. She fell into a deep, untroubled sleep.

Charlotte slept until noon. She picked up the clock on the nightstand and put it to her ear. It was still ticking. The time was correct. She sat on the side of the bed, still groggy and fuzzy headed. She wondered why George had let her sleep so late. Perhaps he had overslept, too.

The events of the night before flashed through her mind and she smiled. Happily she got out of bed. She washed her face and brushed her teeth, and, still dressed in George's robe, she knocked at the adjoining door. There was no answer. She turned the lock and pushed the door open.

The bed was unmade, but George wasn't in it.

"George," she called out. "Where are you, darling?"

She looked in the bathroom and the sitting room. He was not there. He had probably gone down to make arrangements for the wedding. She dressed herself and coiffed her hair in her usual style with the poofs over her ears. She would find a new hairstyle, she promised herself, and change her whole image, now that she had someone to look pretty for. She put on her brooch and her pendulum earrings, took her handbag, and walked to the elevator.

In the lobby she asked the registration clerk, "Has Mr. George Hammond left a message here for me?"

"No, miss," he said. "No message."

"Well. Never mind. I'm sure he'll be back quite soon. I'll wait in the lobby. Did he say where he was going?"

"Mr. Hammond?" the clerk looked surprised. Charlotte nodded. "Mr. Hammond checked out last night."

"Checked out? *George* Hammond? But that's impossible. He *lives* here. There must be some mistake." Even as she said the words, Charlotte felt the water rising beneath her tongue. She felt as if she would be sick, right there in the lobby. Cold sweat broke out on her forehead and beaded her upper lip.

"No mistake, miss. He left about midnight last night. He gave us no forwarding address."

Chapter
FIFTY-ONE

One evening, in the beginning of 1920, Katie was in her kitchen, washing her supper dishes. She could hear Johnny and Tommy scuffling about upstairs, when they were supposed to be doing homework, but she chose to ignore it. Katie was glad her sisters had homes of their own now, and she could find these solitary moments to analyze her life. As she rinsed and dried dishes and washed her stove, she let her thoughts drift where they would.

It had been almost a year and a half since Katie, Warren, Jenny, and the boys had spent those two lazy, wonderful weeks at Milneburg Camp. Katie had not seen Warren since then. After his discharge he had not come home, since shooting was to begin at once in Hollywood on a movie in which he was to star. Since then every time he thought he'd get a chance to come home for a short stay, his agent would sign him up for another movie which would overlap, or he'd have to do retakes on the film he'd just made, leaving no time for the trip.

Warren was a prolific letter writer and a gifted story-teller. In his "waiting time" between scenes, he wrote page after page of light news and gossip. His anecdotes were witty and charming; Katie reread them a dozen times. She herself wrote once a week. After their first few months apart she began to sense that the feeling between them was deepening, that they needed each other and longed to be together. His salutations were no longer "Dear Katie," but "Dearest Katie," and his terms of endearment were more numerous. There was a sweetness, a tenderness about his messages that left little doubt that he was falling in love with her, although he had never said the words.

As far as Katie was concerned, she had felt that love was possible for them ever since they had sat together on the pier, discussing their plans for the camp. Even then she had had a prescience that their futures were inextricably woven together.

She could consider all this without guilt or remorse. She had worshipped Stephen, and if he had lived, she would have gone on loving him the rest of her life. But as Davey had told her almost two years ago, Stephen was gone now, and nothing could bring him back. She had loved him with her first fresh innocent love, and if he had not been snatched away from her, she would have grown to love him with a richer, more mature kind of love. But his life had ended as they were only beginning to know each other.

The stained glass window in Holy Rosary Church had only recently been completed and it had turned out even more beautiful than she had envisioned it. It depicted St. Stephen in the midst of the Assembly, just before his martyrdom, saying, "Behold, I see the heavens opened, and the Son of Man standing on the right hand of God." Below the window were the words, "In commemoration of Stephen Eagan, who gave his life for his country in April, 1918." It gave her such pleasure to see the window whenever she went to Mass, and to know that her children had it there to remind them of their father.

Katie finished her work in the kitchen and put out the light. She could hear the boys tumbling around and fighting upstairs. A lot of homework they're doing tonight, she thought to herself. She pulled the string on the floor lamp in the living room and threw herself across the settee. She was weary tonight and unusually pensive.

As if by a magnet her thoughts were drawn back to Warren. What were his goals at this time in his life? she wondered. More movies? More money? What good was fame if there was no one to enjoy it with, or fortune, if there was no one to spend it on? She remembered the many Sundays he had sat at her dinner table, answering questions about Hollywood actors and parties. There were details about his life he never talked about, but she used to watch his eyes as he spoke, and she knew he wasn't happy there. Not the way he was happy in New Orleans, at her dinner table, or out at the camp.

On Moss Street he could be himself, not a glamor god with painted eyebrows. He could laugh his boisterous laugh and play ball with the boys or enjoy a game of horseshoes with Davey and Daren. Ever since the day Katie had found him on her porch in his soldier's uniform, he had spent all his free time with her and her family, until the war ended. That was why she felt that *this* was where he wanted to be, and that maybe in the end he'd come back home for good.

In the past six months she had been enormously successful in the real-estate business. In the past month alone she had made three sales and gotten two listings. This so infused her with confidence and enthusiasm that she thought that this might be the time to try to convince Warren to join her. She had had her eye on a small house that Weisner had listed that would make an ideal real-estate office, with a little renovation. She could see the sign hanging out front: Eagan Realtors. She spent her free time dreaming up advertisements for their company and designs for business cards. If she could just get Warren established here in New Orleans in something he really enjoyed, well, the rest would take care of itself.

She tried not to let herself get too excited. She had

no reason to believe that Warren would even be interested. He might still think it absurd to give up a successful career in Hollywood to go into any business whatsoever. She kept trying to convince herself that Warren belonged in New Orleans, that Hollywood was just a phase in his life, a way of proving to his mother, and to himself, that he could make it on his own. There was ego gratification, too, and lots of money, and Warren needed both, where Stephen never had.

Rather than writing to him about her proposition, she decided to telephone him in Bel-Air. When the operator had put her call through, she was excited to hear Warren's voice.

"Warren? Can you hear me?" Katie asked.

"I can hear you just fine, darling. Is something wrong?"

"No. I didn't mean to frighten you. I just wanted to know when you think you'll be coming home. It's been so long since we've seen you."

"It's been a year and five months, to be exact," he said. "But it shouldn't be too much longer. We'll be shooting for at least another month, maybe six weeks. We had to start all over with a new leading lady, so that set everything back. But this time, nothing's going to stop me from coming home." He paused. "Katie, is there any trouble?"

"Oh, no trouble. I just have a very exciting idea I want to talk over with you. And I'm dying to see you."

"I'm dying to see you, too, Katie. But go ahead, tell me about your idea."

There was a crackling on the wire, and when Katie spoke again, her voice sounded muffled and far away.

"It's a business idea. I think I know the perfect business for you to go into here in New Orleans."

"What? I can hardly hear you, Katie. Can you hear me?"

"Not too well," she shouted. "Well, I'll never be able to explain it over this connection."

"I'm sorry, darling. I can't hear you. Write me about it."

"I will. And please come home as soon as you can."

"You can count on that. I miss you. Take care of yourself."

As Katie hung up the receiver, she pinched her lips and sighed in disappointment. She decided rather than write him about it, she would wait till he was in New Orleans to tell him about her proposal. She'd be able to explain it so much better in person. He had said he'd be home in only six more weeks. She smiled and her spirits began to rise. It would be the middle of March by then, so the weather would be warming up. They'd have to plan a weekend at the camp. He'd never even seen the renovations! Oh, God, it would be so wonderful to have him home! She hadn't realized quite how wonderful till now.

Chapter
FIFTY-TWO

Mason paced the floor of his small bedroom, his hands behind his back. He shook his grizzled head, wondering what he should do about Miss Charlotte. Ever since the day she had knocked at his door and told him she'd be staying in the room where Treece used to live, and made him promise not to tell her mother, Mason had been sick with worry.

It was one thing for Katie to come to his room when Della was alive. Katie was a friend. But for Miss Charlotte to *live* in the servants' quarters! He couldn't imagine what had gotten into her. She had said she would be there just a short time, but already, six weeks had gone by, and she showed no signs of leaving.

He knew she had had a bad fight with Miss Janet back in January. It had to be worse than their usual, because he had seen Miss Charlotte coming down the back stairs with a suitcase. At first he had thought she was coming for him, but instead she had walked out to the street and gotten into a taxi right in front of the house. Then, two days later, she had knocked at his door, looking sick and nervous.

It was a terrible burden for Mason. More than once he almost telephoned Katie to ask her what to do. She had told him to call if he needed her, and he surely needed her now; but that would make him a traitor to Miss Charlotte, since he had promised to keep her secret.

So he had let the days go by. He prepared her meals when he prepared Miss Janet's, and brought them to her on a tray. Each time she opened the door, she looked worse than the time before. Her hair was never combed and her clothes were never laundered. And now she had a wild look in her eyes that scared him. Mason was afraid she was losing her mind.

She ate hardly anything; the trays came back untouched. Only once had she gone out. Early one morning, a week ago, she had slipped by his door, darting glances in all directions to be sure no one was watching. Through his window Mason had seen her going down the stairs. By noon she was back. He heard her walking in her room, then crying aloud.

He had gone to her door to ask if he could help, begging her to go and tell her mother what was wrong. She had grabbed his arms like a crazy woman and made him promise again that he'd tell Miss Janet nothing. He had suggested going to Katie. He remembered how she looked, staring into space, as if considering the suggestion. But then she had begun to shake her head. No, no, no, she had cried out. He was not to tell *anyone* at all. She ate nothing that day, and he heard her sobbing late into the night.

Since then she seemed to have gone into a steady decline, just lying on the bed or rocking. He could hear the old rocking chair creaking late at night, and he wondered sometimes if Miss Charlotte was even aware that it had grown dark and it was time to be in bed.

He wondered why white folks gave him things like this to worry about. Hadn't he had grief enough of his own when Della died? It should be time for him to rest his head from worry. He stopped pacing and listened. He could hear nothing next door. No creaking of the rocker. No walking. No crying. Maybe she was asleep, but it wasn't even suppertime yet.

Mason decided it was time to talk to Miss Charlotte.

It was too much worry for him to have. If she didn't let him talk to Miss Janet, he'd go to Katie. Some white person in the family had to decide what to do.

The old Negro left his room and walked along the balcony to the next bedroom. He knocked at the door. He waited but there was no answer. He knocked again. Surely she would have heard. He turned the knob and looked inside.

The room was dark, but he could see the bed. She was not there. Her suitcase was open on the floor beside the bed, and her clothes were scattered about. The bed sheets were disheveled.

He closed the door and went back to his own room. He'd have to hurry now to start Miss Janet's supper. He was late already, with his pacing and his worrying. He decided to say nothing to her yet. When Miss Charlotte came back tonight, he'd talk to *her*. Something would have to be done. Something should have been done long ago.

Chapter
FIFTY-THREE

Janet got up from her chair and turned on the light on her nightstand when dusk had fallen. The supper hour had gone by, and Mason had not yet come with her tray. She wondered what was keeping him. The old man was getting slower every day.

She opened her bedroom door and walked out into the corridor, hoping to see him coming. She gave a start when, instead, she saw Charlotte standing just outside her door, unmoving, as if she had been there for some time. The sight of her daughter made her wince. Charlotte's eyes were glazed and she was as thin and frail as if she had been through a long spell of sickness. Seeing her mother, Charlotte gave a whimpering sound and fled. She opened the glass door out onto the upstairs gallery and Janet followed.

Janet had not been on the gallery in months. It was warm for March and fresh, with a hint of honeysuckle in the air. In the early darkness only the first few stars had appeared in the sky.

"Come inside, Charlotte," Janet said. "I don't like the night air."

Charlotte shook her head no, but she did not speak.

Janet frowned. She sat in a rocking chair, her cane propped before her, and looked at her daughter.

"You were never to come here again," Janet said.

Charlotte whimpered. She pressed her hand to her mouth. She turned away.

"So you've come back from your Mr. Hammond.

Much the worse for wear," Janet said. "What did he say to you when you told him you were penniless?"

Charlotte choked on a sob.

"Did he leave you?" Janet asked.

Charlotte sat in a chair near her mother and started to cry aloud. She let the tears fall freely down her face. At last she took a handkerchief from her pocket and blew her nose. Then she sat back in the chair, resting, her breathing punctuated with sobs.

"Perhaps you thought we might make amends," Janet said. "Speak to me, Charlotte. Tell me why you came here today."

Charlotte leaned toward her mother and found her eyes in the darkness.

"I must come back and live here, Mother," she said. "George is gone. I have no place to go. And . . . I . . . I'm pregnant."

Janet gasped, sounding as if she were choking. And then she was silent. She sat back in her chair, as rigid as stone, staring out into the night, saying nothing. Charlotte sobbed quietly, pulling at her handkerchief. She waited like a child who had been punished until her mother was ready to speak. If she had been frightened before, now she was petrified. The lengthening silence told her that there would be no forgiveness for her. Her fate lay in her mother's hands, and she must wait to hear her pronounce it.

After an interminable delay Janet spoke. "Of all the cruelties my children have done me in my life," she whispered hoarsely, "*this* is the worst one ever."

Five minutes passed without a word being said. The sound of chittering sparrows rushed in to fill the silence. A streetcar clanged by. Charlotte sobbed.

"You have shamed me," Janet said, "and you have shamed yourself to get even with me."

"No, Mother, no," Charlotte begged, and yet she knew there was truth in the words.

"You are nothing more than a slut," Janet spat out the word.

Charlotte was crying aloud again. All the pent-up fears and guilt of the past two months were finding release, and the tears seemed to come from a bottomless well.

"I have no idea where you'll go or who will take care of you, Charlotte, but it will not be me, and you will not live here. I have suffered enough at my children's hands without this unthinkable mortification. I will not harbor a woman giving birth to a bastard. Ask God to forgive you if He can. And do *not* bring that child here when it's born. As far as I am concerned, from this day forward, you are dead."

Janet got up shakily and walked back from the porch into the corridor and into her room. She turned out the lights and closed the door.

Chapter
FIFTY-FOUR

Katie stood on tiptoe, looking into every window as the train pulled into Central Station, but Warren was nowhere in sight. The locomotive puffed steam and the train eased to a stop. The redcap placed the stepladder at the door of the car, and Katie watched as passengers disembarked. At last she saw Warren waving with one hand, lugging his suitcase with the other. She was so glad to see him, she found herself laughing and crying at the same time. He put his suitcase down and they embraced.

"Katie! Oh, God, it's so good to see you," he said. "You look . . . beautiful!"

"So do you," she said.

He kissed her on the lips. It was not a passionate, lingering kiss, but it was sweet and personal and full of promises. Taking her arm, he charged through the crowd to the parking area. Then he drove the car out of the parking lot and into the tangle of traffic.

"Now tell me," Warren said, "what's this proposal you have to make to me? You get my curiosity aroused and then you clam up. You never *did* write me about it. That was a pretty rotten thing to do," he laughed. "I tried to call you several times, but you were never home. Where do you go at night, anyway?"

"I was probably out showing property," she said. "I'm selling real estate, Warren. Really *selling* it! I've had three sales in the last six weeks, and the commissions are fantastic. And I keep getting new listings. It's the most exciting thing I've ever done."

"But surely you don't show property at night," Warren said.

"I surely do. At night, on Sundays. Whenever the client wants to see it. But don't worry; I don't go alone. Sometimes Jenny goes with me. And sometimes I take the boys." She smiled. "Who's going to hurt a lady with two little boys?"

Warren laughed. He reached over and squeezed her hand. "Now, what are you planning for me?"

"Well, that's it," she said. "It's real estate. Now listen. I've been working for Weisner Realtors for over a year, using their office and their telephone. People call in, you see, when they read the newspaper ads. I make appointments and show the houses that Weisner has listed. Whatever I sell, I split the commission with Ed Weisner, because he's the broker. But if you and I had our own agency, *you* could be the broker and we wouldn't split with *any*body, except each other. Oh, Warren, there's a fortune to be made right now in real estate, with all the veterans getting married and having families."

"But, Katie," Warren interrupted, "I don't know anything about real estate."

"Well, neither did I until a year ago, but now I feel as if I've been doing it all my life. It's interesting. It's exciting. You meet people, you see beautiful houses, and best of all, you make lots of money.

"I've found the perfect little house where we could open our office," she said. "We could fix it up and hang out our sign. We could split expenses and profits right down the middle. All we need is a desk, a telephone, and a few listings, and we're in business.

"You'd have to sell for a while, and then, later on, you could study for your broker's license. You could do it in six months. You'd be perfect because you talk well and you're good looking. And who wouldn't buy a house from a motion picture actor?"

Warren laughed. She had his head spinning. "You give me too much credit," he said. "I'm no salesman." Katie had a déjà vu. Stephen had said that once. "Now, *you*'re the saleswoman," Warren continued. "If you give that kind of pitch to your clients, I'm not surprised you're doing well."

"All you have to do is like it, Warren," she said. "If you like it, you'll sell it."

He fell silent then, as though he was mulling over what she had said.

"What are you thinking?" she asked. "That I'm crazy, maybe?"

"No, darling," he said. The term of endearment pleased her. "I just don't know, that's all. It's all so uncertain. I don't know if I can make an instant success in a brand new business. And to do that, I'd have to give up a career that's really on its way. I have two more movies scheduled before the end of 1920, both with important directors and established stars. By that time, if all goes well, I'll really be on top."

Katie had known she would get objections, but these seemed so immovable. He was right, of course. The whole thing was a pipe dream. She sighed heavily.

"I hate to hear you sigh like that," he said. "I don't like to disappoint you."

"Well, everything you say is true. I know it seems ridiculous. But while you're in town, will you come with me on a few appointments? Just to get the feel of it?"

"I'll go anywhere with you, you know that," he said.

"And will you listen and try to pick up a little information, just to see if it's a line of work you could enjoy? You may *have* to know another business one of these days, whether you like it or not. You won't be young and handsome all your life."

He smiled at the compliment and reached out for her hand again. His head was whirling with the nearness of her. All of his senses were like open nerve endings. The fragrance of her hair and her skin intoxicated him. The warmth of her body beside him stirred a feeling that quickened and glowed. He envisioned himself touching her, making love to her, and his whole being came alive with desire. They rode along in silence for a time, his hand still holding hers.

The air around them was fresh with spring grass and blooming flowers. As they talked, he had been driving down the Old Shell Road which led to West End Park. The park was deserted except in the summer months, and the fountain of many colors was dark and silent. There was no activity at the yacht club that stood out over the water on its cement pilings like a dark, forbidding castle.

Katie hadn't noticed till now that they weren't following the most direct route to Moss Street. With the realization, her heart began to hammer in her bosom. Warren was now circling the long grassy oval that formed the approach to West End Park. The entire oval was hidden from sight, in the shadows of ancient oaks. He parked along the curb, and turned to look into Katie's eyes in the darkness. She was waiting, too, he could feel it. He could almost hear the beat of her heart as he moved closer to her and put his arms around her. Her lovely profile was silhouetted against the soft moonlight. Her lips were parted, and she was breathing in short, anxious breaths.

He drew her to him gently and kissed her. Instantly his mouth was hot and firm on hers. He held her tenderly, yet firmly, and mercifully so, Katie thought, or she would have fallen limp and breathless from his kiss. She was overwhelmed by the passion that swept over her like a terrible sweet song, full of brass and thunder, overpowering and demanding. She felt his hand on her breast, on her waist, on her hip and her thigh. His lips were warm on her neck and in the hollow of her throat. Slowly he began to unbutton her dress.

"Katie," he whispered huskily. "I love you! I want you!"

Katie looked about her. There was no one in sight. They were parked beneath the canopy of oaks, and the blackness was like ink. She opened the door of the car and walked around it and into the velvet darkness beneath the trees, and Warren followed.

She lay on the grass, a slim, voluptuous gray outline, her arms extended to him. He lowered himself beside her and took her in his arms. When he kissed her again, a delicious languor overcame her. She swept away thoughts of "shouldn't" and "mustn't." She knew only an unquenchable desire to surrender.

She was aware of his moving about, unbuttoning his clothes and hers. And then she felt the weight of his body on hers. In a swooning, overwhelming ecstasy he took her then, as though she was his to take, as though everything that had happened in the last two years was only time that had had to be marked off until now, until this.

She could smell the green life budding all around her. She heard the wind whispering through the trees about the lovers entangled on the ground in their velvet shade. Waves out in the lake broke against the cement pilings of the yacht club. An owl hooted and the cicadas sang. Her heart sang. There was a roaring, thundering passion in her ears, and she was one with all the lovers in the world. She ran her hands through his hair and drew his mouth to hers. He moaned with passion, and suddenly, fire engulfed them both, and Katie gave herself up to an almost intolerable joy. Her body shuddered, and she clung to her lover, helpless with delight. He moaned again. He covered her face with kisses. At last he fell away from her and rested on his back, cradling her in his arms, with her head on his chest.

"I love you, Katie," he said, after a long, full silence. "I think I've loved you all my life. I've never loved another woman, although I've had many women."

"I know," she whispered.

He held her face close to his chest. "My sweet darling. It's never been like this before. Do you believe me? You must believe me."

"I do."

"I kept wondering why I couldn't fall in love, why there was no one I ever wanted to marry. Now, I know. I know I was waiting for you, Katie."

He rolled up his coat and placed it beneath her head. Her eyes had grown accustomed to the darkness and she could see the whiteness of his teeth as he looked down on her. She took his face in both her hands.

"And I love you, Warren," she said. "I guess I've known it a long time, too. And I wanted you so much." She touched his face and ran her fingers through his hair.

He buried his face in her neck and kissed her throat and her shoulders.

"I can't believe this has happened," he said. "I can't believe I've had you at last. I've been a basket case from wanting you, since the day we met on your porch, almost two years ago."

"But you say you've always loved me, and it isn't true at all," she said, eager to play at love games with this gorgeous man she had so willingly surrendered to. "I have a very good memory. You were mean to me when we were children. You threatened to have me sent away."

"I wouldn't have done that if my life depended on it."

She laughed. "But I didn't know that. I was frightened and vulnerable."

"Poor darling," he said, kissing her lips. "Do you know when I first knew I loved you? It was the night you hit me on the head with the slate."

She laughed again.

"You'll never know what I went through, giving you

those reading lessons," he said. "I was a kid with the hots, I can tell you that."

"I think that was your permanent condition," she said, laughing.

"But only for you."

"And you let me think the worst of you, that you only wanted to *use* me. Why didn't you ever tell me how you felt?"

"I knew that you were already in love with my brother. What good would it have done?" He lay on his back, his hands beneath his head. "I remember the night you read for my father in the library. God, how beautiful you were!"

Katie rested up on one elbow, watching him.

"And I was so proud of you," he said.

"And you seemed so indifferent," Katie said. "So glad it was all over."

"I was, in a way. If it had gone on longer, I would have thrown you back on that bed again." They laughed together, and their voices rose like lyrics on the music of the night. Then they held each other close and kissed again.

"I want to be with you always, Warren," she said. "I can't bear for you to leave me again. That's why I've been trying so hard to find something we could do here together."

"I think we just found it, baby," he said, taking her in his arms again.

"Warren, listen," she said, laughing and pushing him away feebly. "We have to talk about this."

"First give me a chance to ask you if you'll marry me, Katie Eagan," he said.

"Oh, yes! Oh, yes I will," she said, circling his neck with her arms.

"You gorgeous, sexy, wonderful woman!" he shouted out into the night, and holding her in his arms, he rolled over and over with her in the soft green grass. "Don't talk to me about problems tonight, Katie darling. This is the happiest night of my life. All I want to do is go home . . . take a bath . . . eat . . . and get into a comfortable bed and make love to you again." He gasped. "What about the boys?" he asked.

"Don't worry," Katie said. "Jenny has them for the night."

Katie was quiet then. She lowered her head and blushed. She knew Warren couldn't see her face, but he was probably thinking she had planned all this, exactly as it had happened. As if reading her thoughts, Warren drew her to him and caressed her gently.

"Sweet Katie," he said. "Why are you upset? Do you think I've decided you're a designing woman?" He smoothed back her hair with his hands. "Don't you think I know how fine and pure you are? And that I'm the only one, other than Stephen, who's ever made love to you? I know you didn't plan this to happen. I'm the one who drove us out here, you know. And yet, you surrendered your sweet self to me because you loved me and you needed me." He kissed her warm cheeks and her lips. "What you gave me, you didn't give lightly. I know that. But what a package of surprises you are! For all your virtue, dear heart, you are some ardent lover!"

Katie buried her face in his shoulder and her eyes were moist with tears. He lifted her chin and kissed the tears away. Lazily they got to their feet and straightened their clothes. Then, holding each other around the waist, they lumbered clumsily to the car.

Chapter
FIFTY-FIVE

It was remarkable to Katie how the house on Moss Street came alive when Warren walked through the door. What a volatile, upsetting, delicious man he was! He unlocked the front door for her, and they came in together, laughing, their bodies still quivering with delight.

"Let me bathe and change first," she said, walking up the steps, "and then I can put dinner on the table while you're bathing."

He looked up at her roguishly, as though he had some other suggestion, but then he shook his head and sauntered into the living room, where he flopped on the settee to wait until she came down.

In the bathtub Katie scrubbed briskly and felt her skin glow, as much from the passion that still lingered as from the scrubbing. She dried off and powdered, stopping now and then to take deep breaths and to calm herself. At last she was dressed, having first discarded three outfits on the bed, trying to find the one that would look best. She selected a peach-colored dress that brought out the color in her cheeks.

She brushed her long black hair and, not wishing to take the time to dress it in any style, she tied it at the nape of the neck with a ribbon. Then, hurriedly, she skipped down the stairs.

Warren passed her on the steps, stopping for a wordless kiss and a quick embrace. Her heart raced again, and she drew in an audible breath. Flipping on lights as she went through the house, Katie staggered into the kitchen and took the dishes she had prepared from the icebox. She opened the cupboard, clumsily taking out pots in which to warm the food. She found herself tripping on things, dropping things, like a stranger in her own kitchen.

When the table had been set and the food was warming, she sat shakily at the table to think things through.

What a different person she was with Warren than she had ever been with Stephen! What she had done tonight gave testimony to that. Making love to him had opened her eyes to many things. Years had passed since she first met Stephen and fell in love and she had changed in many ways since then. It was not only that she had been younger, more innocent, more vulnerable then, though all of that was true. In the years between, life had dealt her many crushing blows: the loss of her mother, her humiliation at Janet's hands, and grief beyond all grief, the death of her beloved Stephen. She had toughened, hardened, learned how to give back in kind, and learned how to reach out for her own happiness. She knew tonight that she was a more physical woman than she had ever been before. She wanted something out of life to make up for all that she had suffered and all that she had lost. She wanted laughter and passion. She wanted love and companionship and excitement and fun. In a word, she wanted Warren.

With Stephen there had been stability and integrity; she had known what she could count on and she had gladly fallen into his mold, trying to live up to him. With Warren . . . she shook her head, smiling . . . she could discover her separate self. As beautiful as he was to look at, he was a compound of character flaws, and she loved every one of them. He was thoughtless and selfish and she knew that he would lie or cheat or do whatever he had to do to get what he wanted out of life. What had he told her years ago when she asked if he still "groped"? He had said, "In Hollywood, dear

Katie, it is required." She laughed out loud, all alone in the kitchen. How many beds had he slept in, if he thought it would help his career, to say nothing of those he had slept in just for fun? And yet, even without asking him, which she had no wish to do, she knew that when she married him, he would be hers forever, because he truly loved her.

She was well aware that life wouldn't be easy with Warren. First they would have to decide if they would live in Hollywood or New Orleans. And no matter how that was resolved, Warren would always be the man she had seen at her Sunday dinner table and lying out on the pier at camp: lazy, untidy, restless, and immature, a grown-up version of the pampered boy she had known so long ago. He would probably always be late for dinner, and he would never remember her birthday. But with that same impulsive boyishness, he would be full of frivolity and surprises. And he would love her. Of that she had no doubt.

She heard his footsteps on the stairs. She got up to turn off the fires, and suddenly he was behind her, holding her around the waist. He smelled of talcum and after-shave balm. She turned around to look at him. In slacks and a silk shirt, open at the neck, his hair falling in soft waves away from his forehead, he was so handsome he took her breath away.

She sniffed the air. "You smell delicious," she said.

"And you look delicious," he answered. He took her in his arms and kissed her passionately. All her strength drained away again. Recovering, she drew her hair back from her forehead.

"Do you think we can take time out for dinner?" she asked.

They laughed together and he sat at the table and spread his napkin on his lap. Katie smiled. Stephen had always helped her get dinner on the table, chipping ice for the glasses, pouring water. But this was her Warren. And she must not do this all the time, make these comparisons. But they did not worry her. Warren did not come out the worse for them. How could he? She was crazy about him.

Over dinner they talked about the boys, about her sisters, and about Davey's activities in his parish. She felt the slightest bit guilty, thinking about her priest brother and remembering what she had done just hours ago, but she brushed the guilt aside with little effort.

"Do you see what we've been doing?" she asked. "We always wind up talking about people and things here in New Orleans. Doesn't that tell you something about where you'd like to be, and where your heart really is?"

"Do we have to talk about this tonight?" he asked not unkindly. He reached over and covered her hand with his. "I know we still have many things to work out, Katie. But not tonight." He gave her a boyish, pleading look that melted her heart.

"Okay," she said. "Not tonight."

After dinner Warren sighed with contentment and pushed his chair back from the table. Katie started scraping plates and stacking them, when suddenly Warren came around the table, took the dishes from her hands, and put them on the counter.

"I know what we can do," he said, taking her hands in his. "Let's drive out to the camp."

"Now?" she asked. She glanced at the clock. It was nine o'clock.

"Right now. Leave those dishes alone. I've been dying to see how it looks, now that it's all fixed up."

"But, Warren, it's an hour's drive out there and an hour's drive back."

"What's the difference? We have all night. Come on. It'll be great. All the camps will be deserted in March so we'll have the whole lakefront to ourselves. We can sit out on the pier in the moonlight." He whispered in her ear. "We can spend the night there, Katie. Oh, God, I love you."

She felt herself dissolve in his embrace. She wrapped her arms around him and held him close, her breast heaving with desire against his body. Where wouldn't she go with him? To hell and back, if he'd ask her, or to the moon. She was his. This is how it would always be with Warren: breathless, sudden, unexpected joy. "Let's go," she said.

She grabbed her keys and a sweater at the mirrored hat rack in the corridor, and in minutes they were driving along Elysian Fields in the direction of the lake. As Warren drove, she talked to him about the renovations: the new bathroom with a shower, a wall heater, and a little dressing table; the screened gallery, the sturdy new pier. The roof had been entirely replaced. Now, with a fresh coat of paint, the camp was more comfortable and elaborate than many a city home.

"I hope we didn't get it *too* city-fied," Warren commented. "That was part of its charm, you know, its being in the country."

"Oh, no. It's just perfect, Warren," Katie assured him. "You'll see."

At last they were pulling the brake on the car and running across the beach and out along the brand-new pier to the camp.

"Look at the moon, Katie," he said, holding her arm and making her stop on the pier to look.

It was a huge yellow orb that looked down on them, and the night was thick with stars and bright as day.

"Oh, that's beautiful!" she said, putting her arm around his waist, sharing a long moment of blissful contentment. "Let's go in. It's a bit chilly out here on the water."

Passing through a patch of darkness under the eaves, they opened the door and stepped inside onto the gallery. No one ever locked the camp. The porch was screened now, since the renovation, and bright with patterned moonlight from the posts along its edge. They walked around to the back porch, and Katie stopped suddenly where she stood. She clutched at Warren, gasping, digging her fingers into his arm. Then she let out a piercing scream that echoed down the row of empty camps along the water.

Warren looked up. "Dear Christ!" he gasped.

Up above them a woman hung limp from the rafters, her legs dangling, casting shadows across them where they stood in the moonlight. She was hanging by her neck from a rope attached to a beam. The wind moved her body slightly and she swayed. Warren forced himself to walk closer.

"Oh, God Almighty, it's Charlotte!" he cried out. "Oh, Jesus, why?"

"Dear God!" Katie cried out. "Cut her down, Warren. Get a knife."

Horrified, Warren ran to the kitchen and came back with a butcher's knife. He looked about him and pulled a high stool to just beneath the hanging figure. This, no doubt, was what she had stood on to hang herself. Never in his life had he had such a chore to do. He was crying freely, like a child, as he reached up and cut the rope with one hand and held his sister's stiff slender body with the other.

He dropped the knife to the floor. Katie wanted to help him, but this was one time she could not. She was still standing where she had first seen the body, sobbing hysterically. Gently he lowered the body to the wooden table beside him. Then he let himself down from the stool.

"What could have happened?" he asked when he could speak again.

"I don't know," she answered. "I haven't seen her in almost two years. Not since I went to see your mother, right after Stephen died."

"We have to do *some*thing," Warren said. "Katie, darling, tell me what to do."

"We have to go to the police, Warren," she said. "Let's go down to the Lakefront station."

"But we have to tell my mother, too," Warren said. "Maybe we should do that first. Maybe we should bring . . . her body . . ." he sobbed, ". . . to my mother. Oh God, how could something like this happen?"

"We have to tell the police first, Warren. Come on," she said. "We'll go there now and bring the police back here."

Chapter
FIFTY-SIX

When the shock of Charlotte's violent death had diminished and the police had asked their questions, there was still one last traumatic revelation in store for the family: the dead woman had been pregnant. After the autopsy the coroner had given this information to the police and to Warren, who had acted in his mother's behalf. When the investigating officer questioned him, Warren said that he had no idea who the father was, as he had not been in contact with his sister for a very long time. The investigator then insisted that Warren ask his mother if she knew any men that his sister had been seeing. He had begged to be allowed to put this off until after the funeral, and the officer had agreed.

After making the funeral arrangements, Katie and Warren returned to Katie's house, where they sat on the settee together, emotionally depleted. The body was to stay at the funeral home until the following morning, when the hearse would bring it to St. Patrick's Cemetery. This had been another problem, for burials in Catholic cemeteries were unheard-of in cases of suicide. But Katie had asked Davey to intercede, and he had gone to see the archbishop this very morning. He had explained that the dead girl was his sister's sister-in-law, a practicing Catholic, and that the Eagan family was devout. He had pleaded with the archbishop to give Charlotte conditional absolution on the basis of probable temporary insanity. Thus it had been arranged, but the archbishop had been adamant that there be no Requiem Mass.

Katie made a move to get up from the sofa.

"I'll make a pot of coffee," she said.

"No. Don't go," Warren said, reaching for her hand. "I have something important to tell you. Sit down."

Katie did as she was told. A frown creased her forehead.

"Charlotte was pregnant," Warren said.

"Oh, my God!" Katie gasped. "So that was why . . ." She pressed her fingers to her lips and tears came to her eyes. "Poor Charlotte! Does anyone know who the father was?"

"No. Unless my mother does."

"He must have left her, Warren. Abandoned her. Poor girl! Oh, Warren, if only she'd told me!"

"How could you have helped her, darling?"

"I could have talked to her and told her not to throw her life away. I could've taken her in with me, and cared for her, the way I did Lala."

"With no husband on the scene? Do you know how people talk, Katie?"

"That never bothered me, Warren. I'm surprised it bothers you."

"I was thinking of your boys. Other children can be cruel when they carry back whispered gossip."

"They're much too young to have understood. Later on, if they had asked, I would have explained, and hoped they'd have enough compassion to understand."

"If they were Katie's boys, they would." Warren kissed her softly on the cheek.

Katie smiled wanly. "Well, anyway, it's too late now. After Stephen died, I often wished that Charlotte and I had been better friends. My sisters had husbands and lives of their own, but Charlotte and I would have needed each other. She would have had someone her own age to talk to. Who knows? This might never have happened. When she found out she was pregnant, if she had come to me, I would have taken care of her. She would have had Johnny and Tommy to love her and entertain her . . ."

Warren rested his head on the back of the sofa.

"And what would have happened to the baby?" he asked.

"She could have put it up for adoption. Lots of couples are looking for babies to adopt. I'm sure it must be a terrible thing to give up a baby, but nothing is worse than suicide. Life is too precious, Warren."

"I blame my mother for Charlotte's death," Warren said.

"Don't say that. She probably didn't even know Charlotte was pregnant."

"I blame her for how she raised us, to believe that it was such a shameful thing to have sex with a person you loved, whether or not there was a child."

"It wasn't just your mother. It's the society we live in. It's the church. It's convention."

"In Hollywood," Warren said, gazing at the ceiling, "when something like this happens to a young actress, she doesn't go out and kill herself. She has an abortion."

"Oh, no!"

"Oh, yes! An actress with a picture or two lined up, ready for her big chance . . . they don't risk all that for the sake of morality."

Katie frowned. "I hope you don't approve of that," she said.

"No, of course I don't. I was being facetious. I'm still Catholic, even if I've fallen away from the church."

"You can always go back, you know. I did that once." She rested her head on his shoulder. "I didn't mean to preach," she said. "I didn't want anyone preaching at me in those days."

"I can't believe you ever needed preaching."

"Why would you think that? You, of all people?"

Warren smiled tenderly. He kissed the hand he was

holding. "So you think you're really a sinner now, do you, Katie?"

"Of course, I am. We both are. You'll admit it, if you're honest with yourself."

He put his arm around her shoulder.

"I love you, Katie darling," he said. "I want to take care of you always. And when all this is over, I don't intend to let you ever be lonely or sorrowful again."

She tilted her face up to his and studied the large gray eyes.

"And where will we be," she asked, "when you're taking care of me, and not letting me ever be lonely or sorrowful again?" She looked down. "We've never decided *that*, you know."

"We'll be in Hollywood, Katie," Warren said decisively.

She sighed heavily and closed her eyes. "You're asking me to leave my family," she said, "and the only home I've ever known and uproot my sons and travel three thousand miles to a city where I'll be as out of place as a fish on dry land . . ."

"Yes, that's what I'm asking you to do," he said peremptorily. "I'm asking you to do it because that's where my work is, Katie, and that's where I *have* to live. You could start your own real-estate business in California, Katie. Try to understand."

"But you don't like movie people. You've never made close friends. You said so yourself, Warren. You know you're happier sitting here in my living room than you ever are in Hollywood."

"I'm happier here because *you're* here, darling. And I'll be happier there when *you're* there." He took her face between his hands and looked into her eyes. "Now, listen to me, and don't speak again until I've finished. Do you promise?"

She shrugged, but then she nodded.

"To me, the movie industry is the most fascinating

business in the world, and the only one I ever hope to work in. When I've finished with acting, I plan to direct or to write, but I've found the business I love, and I can't even conceive of leaving it. I can't explain to you the exhilaration I feel just before we shoot a scene. The actors take their places. The lights go on. The director shouts his orders. The adrenaline starts pumping. And then you're *on*, and the rest of the world disappears. Nothing else exists except the set, the camera, and a handful of people who, for that brief moment, are living out another life and another time. And what gratification you feel when a scene is well done! It's a rare kind of joy, Katie, and few people know it in their work."

He leaned back and stretched his arms along the back of the sofa.

"I hope you come to know what it all means to me. It's a craft. You learn to perfect it and you take pride in it. For nine years I've been working on that craft, and I've learned a great deal, I think. I'm no Douglas Fairbanks, but I haven't gone begging for roles, either."

"That's because you're so lovely to look at," she said, softening.

"For whatever reason," he said, smiling, "I'm in demand right now. I can make a fortune, and I *want* to make a fortune. I like being rich. I grew up rich, and I'm used to it." Katie smiled at his frankness. "So why should I give it all up to try my hand at a new business which I know nothing about?"

Warren waited. Katie rested her head against his shoulder.

"You never told me any of this before," she said. "I understand now how you feel about your work. I wouldn't stand in the way of that. And it's true, I could continue to work . . ."

"Does that mean you'll come?" he asked to reassure himself.

"Yes. I'll come."

"Katie! Katie!" he said, taking her in his arms. "You've made me so happy. Having you there will change my whole life. There'll be nothing missing from it now. I'll have the woman I love, and I'll have your boys . . . a whole ready-made family. I'll be a different person."

"Be careful, Warren. The studio may not like that much," she teased.

"Oh, I'm afraid they'll keep *you* a deep dark secret. I'll still have to be the working girl's heartthrob and the spinster's delight. It's ridiculous, but that's what I get paid for."

"I'll have an awful lot of competition out in Hollywood," Katie said.

"There's not a woman in the city as beautiful as you."

"Untrue!"

"You really don't know how beautiful you are, do you?" he asked. He got up and took her hand to lift her to her feet. He drew her to him and kissed her gently. "You've got *me* half crazy, I can tell you that." He kissed her again. "I'm leaving next week for California, Katie. I want you to come with me then."

She backed away in astonishment.

"That's impossible," she said. "I thought we'd be married some time in the summer. I can't expect Johnny and Tommy to adjust so quickly. Besides, they're in the middle of a school term. And I need time to get ready for this wagon train we're going to make. What about June?"

"June? You're asking me to wait another three months?"

"That's what I'm asking you to do," she said. "Go back to Hollywood alone, and come for me in June and we'll be married."

He regarded her earnestly. "You won't change your mind about going, though, will you?"

"I won't change my mind."

"Three months!" He groaned again. "How in the hell can I make it through three more months?"

"With hard work and resolution and lots of cold showers," Katie said.

This time he kissed her deeply, a lingering kiss that stirred them both.

"Come, Warren, I'll walk you to the door," she said, taking him by the hand. "I don't know where you're going to spend the night, but it won't be here. For one thing, the boys will be home, but even if they weren't, from now on we're going to start acting like a nice, decent engaged couple."

"I was afraid of that," he said. He pushed the screened door open, and they walked out on the porch. "Oh, Katie, I hate to stay in a hotel. I know you may find this hard to believe, but people *do* know my face."

"Why don't you spend the night with your mother?" she asked.

"Do you think she'll let me in?"

"Of course she will. Then you can take her to the funeral tomorrow. You're all she has left, Warren."

"I know."

Reluctant to leave, he sat on the top step and Katie sat beside him. He held her hand and fondled her fingers.

"I still have the hardest task ahead of me," he said. "I have to tell my mother that Charlotte was pregnant. I'm sure she knows nothing about it. But she may be able to give us the name of the man Charlotte was seeing."

"What difference does it make who the father was? Maybe it's better if we don't know."

"I agree, but the police insist it's important. They say I've got to ask Mother. In cases of sudden, violent death it's always possible it wasn't suicide."

"The way *we* found her?"

"I know. I feel the same. Well," he reached over and pecked Katie on the cheek. "I guess it has to be done."

"When will you talk to her?"

"Tomorrow. After the funeral."

Chapter
FIFTY-SEVEN

The limousine pulled up to the Eagan home on St. Charles Avenue and turned into the carriageway. The driver got out and opened the door for Janet. Slowly she got out of the car, cane in one hand, Warren holding the other. She was dressed in black and heavily veiled. She placed her cane on each step carefully, like a very old woman.

It had been a sad funeral, not measured in grief, but in the paucity of mourners. Janet and Warren and Katie were there, and Mason, drying his eyes and blowing his nose. Katie's sisters and Davey had come. They had never met Charlotte, but she was Katie's sister-in-law, and that was reason enough for them. No other mourners had dared to put in an appearance after the obituary in the morning paper that had clearly stated: FUNERAL WILL BE PRIVATE. FOR IMMEDIATE FAMILY ONLY.

After the brief rites Warren knew it was urgent that he talk to his mother. The police were waiting for his answers.

"Mother, please come into the library," he said. "There are things that must be said, and I'll be leaving town in a few days."

"The library hasn't been opened in two years, Warren," Janet said. "Come up to my room."

"No, Mother, please," he said. "I'll open all the draperies and the windows."

Warren couldn't bear the coffinlike atmosphere of his mother's room.

The sliding doors to the library were stuck in their tracks from dampness and lack of use, but he pushed them open and went around the room, opening shutters and pulling up windows. Soon a reluctant breeze began to circulate through the room and into the corridor.

Janet stopped at the hat rack to take off her hat and lay down her handbag. She walked to the library and sat in the armchair that had been hers when John was alive. Warren took the settee facing her.

"Mother," he said, "I know you're tired and deeply grieved, but there is a question I must ask you. If I don't, the police will. Do you understand?"

Janet nodded.

"Mother, did you know that Charlotte was pregnant?"

She looked up at Warren suddenly, and her eyes were wide, but her mouth remained expressionless. Immediately he sensed that his mother had known; she was simply surprised that he did, too.

"Yes," she said. "I knew."

"Then Charlotte must have told you herself."

"Yes. She told me ten days ago," Janet said. "I'll never forget it. It was the worst day of my life."

"The worst? Worse than today? Worse than the day you learned about her death?"

"Yes. Because there was no shame in her death. She took her life to vindicate her crime. There was really nothing else she could do."

"Nothing else? Are you mad? Do you really believe that?" Warren shouted incredulously. "What crime had she committed? She had made love to a man and she was carrying his child." He paused, and suddenly his expression changed from outrage to total comprehension. "Oh, now I understand," he said. "She came here to tell you she was pregnant, and you turned her away."

"There's no way to whitewash it, Warren. They may call it 'making love' in Hollywood, but here, where you were brought up, they still call it fornication."

"And what do they call it when a woman rejects her daughter, and that daughter takes her life? What do they call that, Mother?"

Warren's eyes had welled with tears, thinking of his sister's situation.

"She brought shame on me, Warren. And on herself. There was no place in my house for a slut."

"So instead you made place for her in the family tomb." His voice was trembling. "How can you call her by that name even the day you bury her?"

No words passed between them for a time. Warren lowered his head to his hands and cried. He thought of the young woman they had just put away, who should have had her whole life before her, and his heart ached for her. He remembered her the way she had looked when she made her debut, so young and fresh and pretty, with so many hopes and dreams. Other men had asked for her hand long ago. With any one of them she might have had a full and happy life. It was his mother who had always blocked the alliances. In more ways than one she had brought her daughter to that final scaffold at the camp. He felt nothing but loathing for the woman who sat facing him.

He looked up and was surprised to see her crying at last, daubing at her eyes with her handkerchief. When true love and understanding were needed, she had turned her back and refused to help. God only knew what she had told Charlotte the last time they met.

He wished he might walk away and never see his mother's face again. But there was business here to be finished.

"Who was the man?" he asked harshly.

"His name was George Hammond."

"Did you know him? Do you know where to find him?"

"No one will ever find him. He's gone. He was a fortune hunter. I told Charlotte so before she went to him."

"That must give you a great deal of satisfaction," he said icily. "Your daughter's dead, but once again you've saved the family money."

Janet sobbed aloud and raised her arm in supplication to her son. Warren got up from his chair and walked away from her.

"I'm leaving now, Mother, and I'll never be back. I don't want to look at you again. It would only remind me of what you did to Charlotte."

"Don't leave like this, Warren," Janet begged. She reached out toward him. "I need you. I need someone. You're all I have left."

"Whose fault is that? You deprived yourself of ten years you might have enjoyed with Stephen's family. And I hold you personally responsible for Charlotte's death."

"No! No!" she cried out, pressing her hands to her ears. "Don't say that to me." She sobbed aloud and tears streamed down her face. "Please come back, Warren, I beg you."

He turned his back and walked toward the door.

"I'll change my will," she cried out. "You can claim your share of the estate. You'll be a rich man."

"I *am* a rich man," he said dryly, turning to look at her.

"But what about Katie?" she asked, grasping at straws. "Katie can claim Stephen's share. Her boys will have every advantage."

"Katie doesn't want your money, Mother. Katie's made a mint on Stephen's inventions. You didn't even know about them, did you?"

Astonished, Janet shook her head.

"So you see, Mother, you can't even *give* your money away these days," Warren said, smiling cynically.

He walked over to the door. Janet got up to follow him, crying in little sobs.

"But Warren, I can't manage alone. I have no one but Mason to care for me."

"Hire someone. You can afford it."

He left his mother and stormed through the front door and down the steps. He got into the car feeling cleansed, vindicated. Then, suddenly, he rested his head on the steering wheel and wept.

"Rest quietly, sister," he said. "I think we got even at last."

Chapter
FIFTY-EIGHT

Johnny took a dry twig from the pecan tree in the yard and drew a circle in the soft mud under the tree. He traced a bull's-eye in the center of the circle. Then both boys took their bags of marbles from their pockets and picked through them, trying to decide which three to risk on the game. They reached a decision and lined up their marbles around the inner circle and each placed a special "aggie" in the center.

"I'm first," Tommy said, " 'cause you were first yesterday. An' if I win, I wanta play banana marbles."

"Just banana, not banana marbles, dummy."

Tommy ignored the insult. He knelt on the edge of the larger circle and bit into his bottom lip as he tucked his thumb behind the shooter. His thumb sent the shooter flying across the circle to the bull's-eye, knocking Johnny's aggie out of the ring.

"Yea," he shouted. "I won your aggie."

Johnny pinched the corner of his mouth. Determined, he knelt to take his shot.

"I remember Uncle Warren," Tommy said, "but I can't think of what his head looks like."

Johnny laughed. "Just remember how he looked in *The Drums of Fate*," he said.

"No. That's not the real Uncle Warren. That's Warren Eagan."

"Who do you think Uncle Warren is, dummy?" Johnny asked.

"The one in the picture had black stuff on his mouth and on his eyes."

"That's makeup. They hafta put that on in pictures."

"Why?"

"I don't know. Shoot. It's your turn."

Tommy knelt again and shot, and once more he hit his target, winning more of Johnny's marbles. Johnny heaved an exasperated sigh.

"Why did Mama get her hair cut?" Tommy asked.

"I guess 'cause she likes it that way," Johnny answered irritably.

"I don't like those sausage curls on her neck."

"I think she looks pretty. Come on, pay attention to the game."

"I paid attention," Tommy said. "I won."

"Katie," Jenny called out, knocking at her sister's bedroom door. "May I come in?"

"The door's open," Katie called back.

Jenny walked into the bedroom. Katie was putting the finishing touches to her new hairdo. Jenny circled her sister, giving little noises of approval and admiration.

"Do you look beautiful!" she said. "I *love* your hair!"

"Really, Jenny? You're not just saying that?"

"My God, no. You look like Olive Thomas in *The Flapper*."

"But I'm not trying to look like an actress. Maybe it's too much, with waves *and* curls. Maybe if I comb it out loose."

"Don't touch it. It's perfect. They're wearing it close to the head. Here. Let me see your dress."

Katie turned to face her sister. Her wedding dress was a cream chiffon, calf length, and she was wearing high-heeled pumps. Her eyes were like dark brown velvet, and today they were shining with excitement.

"I can't remember when I've seen you look like this," Jenny said. "You're positively radiant."

"Silly, isn't it?" Katie asked. "A woman twenty-nine years old, with two big boys. I'm acting like a teen-ager."

"You're acting like a bride," Jenny said, hugging her sister fondly.

Only Jenny, Lala, Davey, and the boys knew about the wedding plans, and they were overjoyed for Katie. Warren had written to ask Katie to keep the secret in the family. Warren's studio had been unhappy over the news of his forthcoming nuptials. This didn't bother Warren at all, but he had been given strict orders to keep his wedding out of the press.

"Does the old dragon know about the wedding?" Jenny asked, flopping down on Katie's bed.

"Not from *me*," Katie said. "I never speak to her. And I *know* she doesn't know it from Warren."

"He doesn't speak to her either?"

"He says he never will again. He blames her for Charlotte's death."

"You never told me why, Katie. Oh, I know she was pregnant. But I mean, why does he blame his mother?"

Katie sat on the bed beside her sister. "Charlotte fell in love with a fortune hunter, it seems. He got her pregnant and then he deserted her. I guess that's all we'll ever know about it. But when Charlotte told her mother she was in trouble, her mother put her out. I suppose Charlotte was so brokenhearted and humiliated, she saw no other way out."

"Poor girl!" Jenny said. "No wonder Warren will never forgive her!"

"He won't. He's like Stephen in that, but it's understandable. Oh, Jenny, she's so hardhearted."

Jenny leaned back against the headboard and crossed her legs.

"Wonder what she does all day in that great big house with nobody to talk to."

"Sometimes I wonder, too," Katie said.

"Say, why are we talking gloom?" Jenny asked. "On your wedding day, of all days. What time does Warren's train get in?"

"At eleven." Katie looked at her watch.

"And the wedding is at noon?"

"Yes. You'd better go get dressed yourself."

"Not giving him a chance to get out of it, are you?" Jenny teased.

"Well, what about *me* getting out of it," Katie asked playfully. "You don't have to be a movie star to do *that*."

"You know I'm kidding. He's a lucky man to get you, honey," she said, kissing her sister's cheek. "And . . . you didn't do so bad yourself," Jenny added. "A gorgeous actor and a beautiful home in California. It's so exciting, I don't know how you can stand it."

Katie laughed nervously. "I *am* excited, Jenny. I'm hysterical, if you want to know the truth. But I'll miss you, Jenny," she said.

"And we'll miss you so much, Katie," Jenny answered.

"Well, you'll have to come out and visit us," Katie said, her eyes brightening at the idea. "You could come this very summer. We'll have lots of room for you and Daren and the baby. And once you get there, it won't cost you a thing."

"Don't worry about that. We're due a good vacation."

"Just think how much you'll enjoy the Pullman car traveling to Los Angeles."

"Oh, Katie, I'll do it," Jenny said, borrowing her sister's enthusiasm. "I'll talk to Daren about it today."

"Lala and Walter should come out, too," Katie said. "I can't wait to tell the kids about the trip and the Pullman car. They've never been on a train. What am I saying? *I've* never been on a train." Katie laughed happily. "Warren wanted to get a compartment, but then

we would have had to get *them* one, and we wouldn't
have been able to keep tabs on them. So we're going to
let them take the upper berth and we'll take the lower."
Katie got up and walked away from Jenny so she
wouldn't see her blushing. "Just imagine, Jenny, speed-
ing through the night, lying down in a bed, looking out
of a window as you pass through little towns. Won't it
be like something out of a book?"

"It will be glorious, darling, and no one ever deserved it more."

They were both crying and laughing when they came
down the steps together to the living room. Jenny kissed
Katie and started for the door.

Arrangements had been made to have Davey perform the ceremony in Katie's living room with only her
sisters and their husbands in attendance. Warren was to
come directly to Katie's house from the railway station,
to try to steer clear of reporters.

It had been difficult to explain her forthcoming marriage to her small sons in the light of the secrecy involved. She had tried to downplay her excitement and
have them accept Warren as a natural addition to their
family. She tried to speak as little as possible about the
move to California and the changes that that would en-
tail.

How often she had almost slipped and told them
about it all: the beautiful Bel-Air home, the sandy
beaches and the California climate, and above all, their
entree into the studio where Warren would be making
movies! Warren's letters in the last three months had
excited her, so that she found herself looking forward to
living on the West Coast. What woman wouldn't be delighted over the prospect of a palatial home with magnificent furnishings? He had told her, too, how he had
been seeking out married couples with children, not
necessarily movie people, who led normal, happy lives
and got together for small dinner parties and conversa-

tion. They swam in each other's pools and had picnics, and their children went to school together. She'd have to be crazy not to look forward to all that.

Katie sat in the living room, waiting for Warren's taxi. Davey had arrived, and her sisters and brothers-in-law. It was after twelve already, and Warren was still not there. She tried to distract herself by going over all the arrangements she had made with Daren.

She and Warren were to keep the house on Moss Street, for visits to New Orleans. On Daren's advice, she had made arrangements to keep her rental doubles, too, by turning them over to a rental agency, which would handle collections and repairs. She was also to hold on to her lakefront property, since she obviously would not need the money. One day, Daren said, it would be like pure gold. Then there was the matter of cash savings. There was a great deal of money, and more coming in all the time from royalties and rent collections. This she had finally decided to put in large bills in a safety deposit box in the bank, with instructions to Daren, who had power of attorney, to continue to deposit her money in this way. She was not concerned about the interest. She wanted to know that her cash was safe there, if she or Warren or the children ever needed it. At last her business was settled; her mind was at peace.

A taxi pulled up to the curb. Katie's heart gave a thud. She ran to the porch, slamming the door in her hurry, and rushed down the steps and into Warren's arms. Eagerly he pressed his lips to hers, and she let that sweet familiar warmth flow over her.

"My precious love," he whispered.

Together they walked up the steps. Seeing them coming, Davey took his prayer book from the mantel and turned to the wedding ceremony.

Chapter
FIFTY-NINE

Sunlight streamed into Katie's bedroom window. Lethargically she shielded her eyes with her arm and disentangled her leg from the bedsheet. Trying to awaken, she raised up on one elbow and looked at the beautiful man lying beside her. What rapture they had had together! Every inch of her body glowed from it. She wanted to touch him, to rub her face against his, to run her fingers through his hair, and to kiss those firm lips beneath that mustache, but he was sleeping so peacefully.

First of all she had to get up and lower the shade before the sun blinded her. She didn't see her gown anywhere. If she wrapped herself in the sheet, she'd leave him uncovered and he'd awaken. The idea of sleeping nude was still new and risqué to Katie, but she had done it just the same. She was shattering a lot of conventions these days. She decided to make a run for it. Naked, she got out of bed, ran across the floor, and pulled down the shade, but before she got back, Warren's eyes were open and he was smiling.

With a squeal of surprise, she slithered back under the sheet, and he took her in his arms. "My gorgeous wood nymph!" he said. "What a sight to behold first thing in the morning!"

"I thought you were sleeping," she said, blushing.

He kissed her warm cheeks. "And you would have deprived me of that?" he asked.

She wrapped her arms around his body and kissed his smooth, muscular chest.

"I'll never get tired of looking at you," she said.

"Nor I you. I didn't tell you how much I like your short hair," he said, fingering a curl. "You look adorable, almost like a little girl."

"My dear heart," she said. "You're the treat that life has saved up for me."

They lay facing each other, bodies pressed together, flesh seeking flesh, mouth seeking mouth, and they made love easily and tenderly, moaning with delicious contentment and long-denied passion.

"I waited so long for this," he said. "I didn't think I'd make it."

"I knew you would," she said. "Continence is good for the soul."

"Yea, but it makes you mean," he said, laughing his boyish laugh. "I'll tell you what, sweetheart. Since we've been so deprived, why don't we indulge ourselves and stay in bed all day?"

"Not a chance," she said, getting up, this time taking the sheet with her. "The boys will be home by noon. My sisters don't mind keeping my kids, but there's a limit." As she talked, she picked up the clothes she and Warren had scattered around the room the night before. "A ten- and an eight-year-old are no picnic, you know. And what about the rest of the packing if we're supposed to get on that train this evening?"

For their wedding breakfast Katie prepared pancakes and sausages, with orange juice and hot coffee. Warren gorged himself and they laughed and talked gaily about the wedding and the way the boys had jumped for joy when they heard they would be leaving this very day for California. But when Katie made a move to clear the table, Warren frowned.

"I hate to see you doing that," he said. "Here, put that down, and come sit on my lap. When you get to Bel-Air, you're never going to clear a table again."

He pushed back his chair and Katie sat in his lap.

"Now, how're you going to manage that?" she asked.

"I have Carmen," he said. "She's my Mexican housemaid. I've had her for years. She cooks and cleans and she even massages my back if I'm tired."

"I'll just bet she does," Katie said. "Well, I'll take over that job now if you don't mind. And while we're on the subject, she doesn't have any bedroom chores, now does she?"

Warren threw his head back and laughed. "Carmen? Wait'll you see her." He puffed out his cheeks and held his arms out in front of him to simulate a belly.

"Okay," she said. "I'm convinced. But I'm warning you, I plan to be jealous. You'll have to send me flowers once in a while, just to let me know you still love me."

Warren smiled. But the smile quickly changed to a frown, and then back to a slow, uncertain smile again.

"Katie," he said, very much engrossed in his thoughts, "do you remember ever finding a flower in a water glass on your lamp table, when we were still on St. Charles Avenue? Oh, this was a very long time ago. Maybe fourteen years. I suppose you wouldn't remember."

"Jasmine? Night jasmine from your mother's garden?" A smile was spreading across her face. "Oh, Warren! Was that you?" Her eyes had brimmed with tears.

"Yes, Katie. I left it there. So you found it?"

Not answering, she got up from his lap and walked across the living room to her bookcase. Warren followed, lagging behind, not understanding. He watched as she stooped to remove an old book from the bottom shelf with the tip of her finger. She carried it to the settee, still smiling and misty-eyed, and motioned for him to sit beside her. She closed her eyes, spilling a tear, placing her hands on the cover of the book as if it were a ritual. The musty odor of the yellowing volume rose up in their nostrils as she opened the book to the page where the tiny flowers were pressed. The spray was dry now and brown, and once again, as she had done years ago, she detached it from the page.

"Here's your jasmine, my darling," she said. "May I offer you my most abject apology? All my life I thought it was from Stephen."

He took the fragile stalk from her, looked at it, and put it back in the book.

"Then you kept it for him, not for me," he said.

"That's true."

"But does this tell you, Katie, that I've loved you all my life?"

She threw her arms around his neck and hugged him. "Yes, Warren, more than any words could say."

Dell Bestsellers

- [ ] **COMES THE BLIND FURY** by John Saul $2.75 (11428-4)
- [ ] **CLASS REUNION** by Rona Jaffe $2.75 (11408-X)
- [ ] **THE EXILES** by William Stuart Long $2.75 (12369-0)
- [ ] **THE BRONX ZOO** by Sparky Lyle and Peter Golenbock $2.50 (10764-4)
- [ ] **THE PASSING BELLS** by Phillip Rock $2.75 (16837-6)
- [ ] **TO LOVE AGAIN** by Danielle Steel $2.50 (18631-5)
- [ ] **SECOND GENERATION** by Howard Fast $2.75 (17892-4)
- [ ] **EVERGREEN** by Belva Plain $2.75 (13294-0)
- [ ] **CALIFORNIA WOMAN** by Daniel Knapp $2.50 (11035-1)
- [ ] **DAWN WIND** by Christina Savage $2.50 (11792-5)
- [ ] **REGINA'S SONG** by Sharleen Cooper Cohen $2.50 (17414-7)
- [ ] **SABRINA** by Madeleine A. Polland $2.50 (17633-6)
- [ ] **THE ADMIRAL'S DAUGHTER** by Victoria Fyodorova and Haskel Frankel $2.50 (10366-5)
- [ ] **THE LAST DECATHLON** by John Redgate $2.50 (14643-7)
- [ ] **THE PETROGRAD CONSIGNMENT** by Owen Sela $2.50 (16885-6)
- [ ] **EXCALIBUR!** by Gil Kane and John Jakes $2.50 (12291-0)
- [ ] **SHOGUN** by James Clavell $2.95 (17800-2)
- [ ] **MY MOTHER, MY SELF** by Nancy Friday $2.50 (15663-7)
- [ ] **THE IMMIGRANTS** by Howard Fast $2.75 (14175-3)

At your local bookstore or use this handy coupon for ordering:

Dell **DELL BOOKS**
P.O. BOX 1000, PINEBROOK, N.J. 07058

Please send me the books I have checked above. I am enclosing $_____
(please add 75¢ per copy to cover postage and handling). Send check or money order—no cash or C.O.D.'s. Please allow up to 8 weeks for shipment.

Mr/Mrs/Miss_____

Address_____

City_____State/Zip_____